Praise for Julia Grice's previous novel, *TENDER PREY*

"The novel, set in a tiny ski town, begins fast, accelerates, and schusses to an unexpected conclusion."

—*New York Daily News*

"A tense page-turner, chilling [and] enthralling."

—Ken Eulo, author of *The House of Caine* and *The Brownstone*

From JAGGED LIGHT:

Kara wrote, *Dear Rob, I am angry because* . . . But it was hard to set it all down. I am angry because your daughter hates me. I am angry at myself because I don't think I can be the super-stepmother you obviously expect. I am angry because I had fantasized the perfect life for us, and it doesn't seem to be turning out perfect, does it?

Most of all, she thought, I am angry at Jerry Quick. She had seen a man who looked like Jerry this afternoon, had nearly fainted in referred terror, and Rob hadn't known why.

That was the real reason she was angry.

Because she was living a false life. She couldn't have a real life until she got rid of Jerry Quick, and she couldn't get rid of him because he was inside her.

Forever in her mind.

Also by Julia Grice

Tender Prey

JULIA GRICE

JAGGED LIGHT

TOR

A TOM DOHERTY ASSOCIATES BOOK
NEW YORK

This is a work of fiction. All the characters and events portrayed in this
book are fictitious, and any resemblance to real people or events is
purely coincidental.

JAGGED LIGHT

Copyright © 1991 by Julia Grice

All rights reserved, including the right to reproduce this book, or por-
tions thereof, in any form.

A Tor Book
Published by Tom Doherty Associates, Inc.
49 West 24th Street
New York, N.Y. 10010

ISBN: 0-812-51827-6

Printed in the United States of America

First edition: August 1991

0 9 8 7 6 5 4 3 2 1

*To all the warm people who illuminate my life,
but especially for my parents, Jean and Will Haughey,
and my sons, Michael and Andy Grice.*

I would like to thank Mary Lee Hicks, of the Valdosta, Georgia and Lowndes County Chamber of Commerce, as well as my literary agent, Al Zuckerman, of Writer's House, and most of all, my warmly cheerful and capable editor, Melissa Ann Singer.

Friends who gave generously of their love and encouragement include Richard Fitz, Bob Fenton, Margaret Duda, Katherine Neaton, Joyce Hagmaier, Dan Platz, Roni Tripodi, Erin Kelly, Elizabeth Buzzelli and Linda Bartell. I owe more than can ever be repaid to the Detroit Women Writers, a group of professional women writers that has just celebrated its 91st birthday. These women such as Vera Henry, Carolyn Vosburgh Hall and Bettie Cannon became my role models, mentors and friends. Lastly, a special thanks to the "Mainstream" group who gave more than they knew.

PROLOGUE

1980

Mick Jagger blasted from the car radio, his voice raw, silky, tough, sounding like a man who would do anything, anytime, to anyone.

Jerry Quick waited in line at the gas pump of the Shell Station on Lakeview Ave., watching while the attendant pumped gas into a Mercury Bobcat. He tapped out the rhythm of "Jumping Jack Flash" with his knuckles on the Buick's steering wheel and imagined himself kneeling between some girl's legs, pumping it into her in the exact, frenzied tempo of the music. The Stones. They knew how, all right.

It was 4:45 in the afternoon, and the sun overhead was molten orange, beating down on the streets of St. Petersburg, Florida. Rush-hour people sweltered in their hot cars, whizzing back and forth on the road, making Jerry glad he had the day off today. He took another swig from the paper bag he'd stuffed under the seat, and the whiskey

1

made everything seem brighter, hotter, the air full of yellow light.

The Stones pumped on, and Jerry diddy-bopped to the music, idly admiring the wedge-shaped section of his face that was visible in the rearview mirror. His skin was suntanned a cordovan shade of brown from hours of sunning himself at St. Petersburg Beach. Thoughtfully he pursed his lips, pressed them together, opened them, trying to decide whether, if he grew a mustache, the hairs would come in thick. He decided they probably would. He was twenty, and he'd been driving around for three hours, looking for the right sort of action.

So far he hadn't found anything right, and Jerry's lips pouted as he mimed in time to the music, waiting for his turn. He might as well go home, he decided. It wasn't going to work today. Maybe he would take a nap, eat some supper and go out and try again after dark. He had his regular route: Madeira Beach, Treasure Island, St. Pete Beach, a couple of high schools, the campus at U.S.F. in Temple Terrace. He guessed he'd try some bars he knew up near the college tonight.

Then the big silver New Yorker squealed into the station. It pulled up to the left of the pumps by the middle bay of the garage, long, shiny, chromed, and so clean that the sun mirrored off its paint. There were two girls inside it, a blonde and a brunette.

Giggling.

Jerry sucked in his breath. The blonde, who'd been driving, looked barely seventeen. She had hair the color of light ale, tousled and streaked with sun gold. She was his idea of a *Penthouse* girl, with her red mouth, haughty cheekbones, and perfect, beach-toasted skin.

From where he sat all he could see *was* skin, bare shoulders visible through the car window, no bra straps at all. Yeah, it seemed as if she sat there in that silver car stark naked. And laughing about it.

2

Of course, Jerry knew she wasn't naked; she was probably wearing a strapless bikini top or something. He let his eyes slide to the other one, the passenger. She wasn't as pretty. She had a narrow face with a chin that jutted and a mop of black hair half falling in her eyes. She wore a blue tank top; he could see the straps when she leaned forward to say something to the blonde. A mess of towels and suntan oil bottles stuffed in the back window said they'd been to the beach.

Jerry pulled in his breath, thinking *what if*.

Jesus, he'd been ready to go home and here they were, right in front of him; he couldn't have picked better himself. He believed in coincidences and omens, and he decided this had to be meant.

He tilted the mirror so he could study them without their knowing. Waiting for an attendant to notice them, they were having a good time, laughing, carrying on. The blonde let her naked arm dangle out of the opened car window, a birthstone ring catching the sun. A green stone, maybe an emerald, and not a little one.

Jerry stared. He had always hunted girls like her. He loved the way their skin was dark gold except for the bikini lines, and, down there, the tuft of gold-brown fuzz. He didn't like dark girls nearly as much, because they reminded him of his mother. In fact, dark ones somehow made him angry.

Apparently deciding no attendant was going to come, the blond one pushed open the door of the New Yorker and got out. Jerry's pulse surged in his throat.

Man.

She started toward the station, and now he could see why she'd looked naked. She wore nothing but a yellow strapless top and a pair of cutoff jeans cropped so high on the thigh that white pockets dangled below the hem line. Little threads caressed the insides of her perfect, tanned

3

thighs. And the cutoffs were so tight that he could actually see her cleft outlined, her female parts.

It decided him. He shifted in the front seat, feeling a tightening in his own crotch. The girl sauntered into the station, and the way she walked was another advertisement. Did she see him watching her? He couldn't tell. Girls like that flirted automatically, and knew all the time they weren't going to deliver.

The car ahead of him finished, and he pulled up to the pumps, taking his time because the girls hadn't even started to get their gas pumped yet. The 70-year-old gas jockey waddled over, four days' worth of white beard covering his standard-issue mahogany Florida suntan.

"Fill her up?"

"Five bucks worth."

"Right." The geezer's face revealed what he thought of guys who didn't fill up their tank.

While the gas was being pumped, Jerry watched the blonde who was now framed in the station door, talking to the kid inside. Pointing to her car, wanting something looked at. She had long, slim legs, baby legs, Jesus, so perfect he could crawl all the way up between them and eat her with a spoon.

When she walked back to her car and leaned in to say something to the other girl, the cutoffs tightened, pulling into the crease of her buttocks exactly like a picture in *Penthouse*.

Jerry couldn't believe it.

Did she *know* she looked like that? Hell, sure she did. She probably posed in front of a mirror when she was alone. Women loved to tease, holding it back like a guy didn't have a right.

His breathing tightened, and his erection pushed so hard against his jockey shorts that he had to squirm around, trying to relieve the pressure. They were two little rich-bitches, he decided. Probably lived down on the Bay in a

4

big house that overlooked blue water, with a big Chris Craft boat moored in a fancy boathouse. Even the boathouse cost more than Jerry made in the last two years as a parts clerk in an auto supply shop.

He paid for his gas with a five, then pulled around to the side to put air in his tires, timing it so that he finished just as the girls were paying, with a credit card the blonde fished out of a little pink leather purse. She was such sweet stuff. His heart hammered as he thought of the roll of duct tape, the knife, stuffed under the front seat along with the whiskey.

This was exactly what he'd been driving around looking for. It had ridden into the Shell station in a big Chrysler and he wasn't going to let it get away.

When the girls pulled out, heading east on Lakeview Ave., he followed.

Hell, when a girl wore shorts like that, she knew exactly what she was doing. She had no right to hold back when she wore clothes like that.

She had to expect what she got.

Whatever she got.

CHAPTER 1

In front of the cheval mirror in her bedroom, Kara Cleveland held up the spill of lace and sewn-on sequins that was her newly purchased wedding dress, and tried to decide whether or not to take it back.

The magnificent Italian-designed dress had caught her eye at the Boulevard Bridal Salon, with its fantasy scoop neckline, puffed long sleeves, and elaborate front panel. But now she wondered if it was too lace-encrusted, almost ridiculous for a 27-year-old woman who was 5'9" tall, and more the "tailored classic" type. Whatever had possessed her to spend a thousand dollars on it? She must have had a serious attack of romanticism.

She frowned, laying the dress on the bed again, struggling a little with its lengthy bulk. Did her sudden dislike of the dress signify that she was getting cold feet? She'd have a hell of a time getting it back in its plastic garment bag. It kept wanting to pouf out of the zipper.

The phone rang, and Kara let go of the dress, her hands

glinting with the two rings she wore. On her left ring finger was the marquise-cut two-carat engagement diamond from Rob. On her right hand gleamed the smaller emerald birthstone her mother, now dead, had given her for her sixteenth birthday.

She picked up the phone, cradling it on her shoulder, an expectant lilt coloring her voice. "Hello?"

She heard the long-distance, reedy hum of the wire, and a silence long enough to make her think it was one of the computer-dialed calls that now clogged up the phone lines. Then a female voice: "Karalynn . . . is that you?"

No one had called her Karalynn since high school. It was her old name, her baby name dropped when she went away to Michigan State.

Kara's hand tightened on the phone cord. "Yes?"

But she knew who it was, even before the other woman said, "It's me, Laurel. I've been calling and *calling*, you're never home any more, I thought maybe you'd moved away and changed your number."

Kara swallowed, her eyes focusing blindly on a ceramic-framed photograph of herself and Rob, taken last New Year's Eve, that stood on the dresser. Her fiancé, dark and handsome, was laughing into the camera while Kara, looking more serious, had her blonde hair turned fiery by the flash bulb.

Laurel. She was ashamed of herself, but she dreaded these calls, she always had, ever since the first one, when was it, six years ago? There had been probably five of them, and every one had made Kara's stomach clench, hot bile flooding her throat. It took her weeks to get over the depression they caused.

"Your Dad gave me your number, I talked to him last night," her former best friend said, a sharpness in her tone. Kara could hear her fast, shallow breathing. She wondered if Laurel was drunk. Several times the calls had come late at night, with Laurel's voice obviously slurred.

"Did you?"

"Yeah . . . The reason I called, I just wanted you to know. *I saw him*," Laurel whispered.

Kara's stomach gave a painful twist, as if the muscles of her abdominal wall had formed fists. "No," she said.

"Him. I saw *him*."

"Please—"

"Outside the hospital last Thursday night after I got off work, he was driving past. Remember that car he had, that old Buick? Well, he was in a car like that. Cruising. Looking. He looked right at me, Kara!" Laurel's voice rose, stitched with hysteria. "He looked right at me and I think he followed me home. I know a car followed me! I went right in the house but I still saw his lights! I tell you, I saw Jerry!"

Kara sat down on the bed beside the wedding dress, her throat closing. Why, why, did Laurel have to do this? It was so crazy, pathetic and vicious, all at once. She didn't have any sympathy for it. She was sorry, but she didn't. Laurel had never gotten rid of the past; she allowed her fears to become delusions. Phone calls to the prison in the past had always revealed the truth: Jerry Quick was behind bars, not out prowling.

But she tried to sound patient. "Laurel, you know you didn't see him. You couldn't."

"I did. He was there, Karalynn!"

"How could he be? He's in prison. He's been there for ten years. He was given fifteen to thirty years, he'll still be in prison when we're old women."

"I *know* when I see a face I recognize."

Kara's heart was pumping, her whole body had been jolted with adrenaline. She plucked at the blue T-shirt she wore, pulling it away from her chest. She could smell her own clammy sweat.

"How many times have you called me in the past five years saying you've seen him, Laurel? Four times? Six?

I've lost count. *You didn't see him.* There's no way you could have. It's a . . . a psychological thing, the way you think you see him—"

"It isn't! It's real! Are you saying I'm lying? That I'd make up something as awful as that?" Laurel altered her attack. "And if you'd call me once in a while, Kara-lynn . . . What kind of friend are you? A shitty one. You never call *me*, I always call you. And I know why. You want to forget about me, don't you? You can't stand thinking about me, can you?"

Of course it was the truth. That was the horrible part. It was true.

Guilt clogged Kara's voice. "Laurel—"

"You want to push me out of your mind—Oh, *I* know! That's why you didn't invite me to your wedding. Your Dad told me all about it. You're getting married to this architect guy. He designs houses. He's got a little girl, he's already been married."

"I have to go now," Kara said faintly. "I think I hear someone at the door."

"You're lying. You don't hear anyone. You just want to get off the phone. Well, all right!" Laurel shouted. "I saw him and you don't believe me, no one believes me, but that doesn't make it a lie. He hates us, Karalynn. He'd like to get us and do it again to us. *I know he does, I feel it, he's thinking about it, I feel it! He wants us—*"

Kara hung up, cutting off the hysterical voice in mid-shout. She sank against the headboard of her bed. Her stomach was actually cramping from stress. Laurel's cries still echoed vindictively in her brain, a witch's voice screeching a curse.

He wants us.

It was only a phone call, she told herself, unconsciously rubbing at the muscles of her stomach and midriff as she had done when she was a little girl. Her hands felt icy, her feet too, as if the defenses of her body had collected all of her blood into her center.

Calm down, she ordered herself. *Relax. Let it go. Laurel has problems, she takes them out on you. It all happened ten years ago, it's gone now, it's done.*

After the gruelling three-week trial, Kara had defied her parents, insisting that she had to get away and start over, where no one knew her. It was either that or collapse as Laurel had done, into crying spells, tranquilizers and alcohol. She had enrolled at Michigan State University, taken journalism courses, graduated *cum laude*. Then she got herself a job on a biweekly newspaper in Rochester, Michigan. Now she owned her own business, a shopper's newspaper called the *Bargain Hound*. It was published in four Detroit suburbs and beginning to make real money. In fact, she had a real future, even the possibility of becoming a millionaire someday, if she could expand to fifteen or more cities, the way she planned.

She was happy in spite of *him* and his violence. She'd lifted herself out of the victim mold and she was proud of herself for that, damn proud. And no phone call was going to shake her or ruin her day either.

She pushed the spill of her bangs away from her face and slid off the bed. Glancing at the dress, she decided to wrestle it into its bag later. She needed to de-stress herself before the tension created by Laurel's call blossomed into a full, temple-pounding headache.

Quickly she changed to a sports bra and tank top, and a pair of black nylon running shorts. If her past behavior held true, Laurel wouldn't call again for another year or two. She was safe until then. It was almost like going to the dentist, Kara assured herself, searching for some humor in the situation. It felt so good when he finally told you you didn't have to come back for six months.

* * *

The subdivision she lived in, Strawberry Grove, was in its Saturday afternoon mode. Barefoot children frolicked and yelled on intensely green lawns, dogs barked, and homeowners were running their usual motorized array of lawn mowers, edgers, trimmers and leaf blowers. At one home, teenaged girls in bikinis were hosing down a car, accompanied by a boom box playing loud rap music.

Jogging past, Kara grimaced. Whoever said suburbia was quiet and peaceful? As she ran, she wondered what to do about Laurel's call. Nothing, she decided. It was not worth the distress of actually telephoning the prison, a step which took several hours and glasses of wine for Kara to muster up the necessary courage.

She ran two and a half miles, returning home sweaty but in control again, looking forward to going over to Rob's in an hour to grill steaks on his deck.

She jogged up her front walk, zig-zagging onto the lawn to pick up a scrap of newspaper that had blown underneath one of the big blue spruce trees that loomed majestically on either side of the lot, forming a shade break. While she was gone, the mail carrier had delivered several packages, leaving them on her front porch, and she went up to retrieve them.

Panting, she examined the booty. Wedding gifts had been arriving almost daily since the invitations were sent out ten days previously. One box, from her former editor at the *Rochester Eccentric*, was quite large. She poked at it curiously, looking forward to seeing what was inside. The other two boxes were from Rob's relatives, smaller but equally intriguing. She would probably never receive so many expensive gifts at one time again in her life.

There were also several letters, including one from her father. She piled the packages on the hall table, to be opened later with Rob, and took the letter upstairs with her.

She stripped, tossing her damp clothes into a hamper

inside the linen closet, and stood there naked to read the letter. She was going to have to talk to her father about Laurel. He knew how she felt about Laurel's calls, but he encouraged them by talking to her, stirring her up. She had no doubt whatsoever that he and Laurel had hashed over the trial again, in exhaustive detail. Ken Cleveland believed Jerry should have been given the death penalty, and preferably made a eunuch first.

She unfolded the single sheet that carried the logo of a scuba and sailboard shop in Largo, which her father owned. A check for five thousand dollars fell out. Her father wrote that he planned to stop for some hiking in the Smokies before he attended the wedding. At sixty-six, Ken Cleveland prided himself on being in top physical shape and he had hiked most of the major mountain ranges in the United States.

His loopy scribbles rambled on. *Can't wait to see my baby girl finally make it to the altar. This time you will make it, won't you? If you don't, don't cash the check, ha ha.*

Just like you asked, I promise I will be good, honey. I won't talk to your Rob about what happened, but don't you think he has a right to know? After all it did happen. Now you are getting married and your husband has the right—

Kara didn't read the rest. She plopped the letter down on the vanity and stepped into the shower.

Damn him, she thought. He never gave up. She'd been raped ten years ago and it was still a central part of his life. It was more alive for him now than it was for her. He still fantasized punishments for Jerry, still talked about killing him with his bare hands.

She switched on the water and turned under the spray, fuming. It had been her father who had saved them that afternoon, arriving home early from his shop. Ken Cleveland had beaten Quick so savagely that the youth had been hospitalized for two weeks. He'd tried to attack Quick again at the trial, but had been held back by bailiffs.

It was as if her father was a victim too, Kara realized. He had lost twenty-five pounds, developed a duodenal ulcer. He became obsessed by the rape, questioning, blaming, ranting, raving, even writing letters to the Governor. Over the years he'd become less vociferous, but the tendency was still there. Now she just hoped he'd keep his solemn promise and not mention it at her wedding. She didn't really want him to attend, she admitted to herself. In fact, she had suggested that she and Rob elope, but Rob wanted the full, 150-guest wedding.

Her eyes began to sting with soap, and she tilted her face directly under the spray, feeling the strong rush of the water.

Kara loaded the wedding gifts into her white Mercury Cougar and made another trip for the food she was bringing; some A-1 steak sauce; a large piece of chocolate cake for Cindy, Rob's daughter; and a bottle of chablis. She and Rob spent most of their time shuttling articles between their two houses. Kara had two toothbrushes, one for his place, one for hers; and the supply of clothes she kept at Rob's took up about one-fourth of a closet. Marriage, they both said, would be a relief because they could stop commuting.

She turned on Walton toward town. Rochester, surrounded by modern subdivisions, was a drowsy little Victorian village that had been boutiqued and refurbished. Its main street was planted with trees and adorned with tubs of geraniums. It was the home of Leader Dogs for the Blind, and as she turned left on Rochester Road, Kara noticed one of the dog trainers, poking at a curb with his foot for the instruction of a young German Shepherd. The animal wagged its tail and looked cheerfully unconcerned.

She drove north, her route taking her within a half-block

of the *Bargain Hound* office. She resisted the urge to stop in for a few minutes to turn on her computer and start revisions for a feature she was doing called "Summer Collectibles Start With Beautiful Baskets." She didn't consider herself a workaholic, but the excitement of running her own business was sometimes addictive. She had a dream, and she knew herself capable of carrying it out.

Rochester Road petered out to insurance offices and big, 1920's-style homes with deep lawns, then a vacant plant that once made twist drills. Then some subdivisions, the Rochester Cider Mill, closed in June, and finally the blacktopped road that led to Rob's.

The upscale subdivision held only 15 executive homes, each one in the $250,000 to $550,000 range—expensive for Rochester. Rob's, which he designed himself, was the most striking of the group, constructed of cantilevered redwood and glass. Its thrust-forward effect reminded Kara of a jutting ship's prow. It had been written up in *Monthly Detroit*, and Rob often brought prospective clients to see it.

Kara had mixed feelings about Rob's house. It was three thousand square feet, far larger than hers, definitely more expensive, and with much more architectural merit. Its wooded lot was gorgeous, with rare, white trilliums that grew in spring only feet from the deck.

Still, another part of her knew she was going to miss her own home. She might not be an architect, but she had decorated her own place exactly as she wanted it. Now she'd be moving into an environment where her French country decor would really be out of place. Rob hadn't said anything, though. She was the one who worried that her things would be relegated to the basement or a garage sale.

As she pulled into her fiancé's driveway she saw a blue Datsun already parked there. Rob, his ex-wife Dee, and their 10-year-old daughter Cindy were standing beside it,

Cindy's weekend bag resting on the hood of the car. A typical post-divorce scene, as Dee dropped her daughter off for her scheduled visit.

Kara parked in the turn-around, and gathered up her purse and the grocery sack. The foil-wrapped cake was in danger of squashing, and she had to stop and rescue it from the wine bottle.

"Well, hi. Let me take that." Rob Devers greeted her, taking the sack and simultaneously planting a kiss on Kara's lips. They gave each other a token smooch, constrained by the presence of Dee and Cindy.

Kara pulled back and let her eyes meet his, feeling warmth arc between them like a friendly electrical connection.

"Good day?" Rob wanted to know.

"Oh, yeah, I worked all morning at the office, picked up my dress, and tried it on again. It still fits, thank God. And I ran my usual. You know."

Kara smiled at Rob's daughter and nodded to Dee, a thin, discontented-looking woman who had left Rob for an ophthalmologist who had since dumped her. Dee and her latest boyfriend were planning a trip to Mackinaw Island, in northern Michigan, so Cindy's visit this time would cover ten days, instead of the usual weekend.

"They just drove up, didn't you, Cin?" Rob turned to the child beside him. "Come on, Cindy, show Kara your new Barbie."

Cindy lowered her eyes to examine her scuffed, lavender-laced Reeboks. Then she loped over to the overnight bag resting on the hood of the Datsun. She fished inside the bag, bringing out three Barbie dolls. One of the dolls still boasted virgin yellow polyester curls, as yet unfrizzed by obsessive combing.

"This is Funtime Barbie." Cindy held the doll up by her feet. She herself looked like a raven-haired version of Barbie, with porcelain skin, winged eyebrows and a small, full mouth. "I earned the money for her washing cars. I washed two cars today, and I washed all the dead bugs and worms off the front part. Ugh, they're gross. I hate bugs!"

Kara grinned in sympathy. Dee lived in nearby Royal Oak near a large municipal park where outdoor lights attracted swarms of night insects.

"Well, at least you earned the money for your own Barbie," Kara said. "I think that's great."

She tried so hard for friendship with this child, and sometimes Cindy responded.

"Yes—" Cindy began.

"She *didn't* buy the whole doll herself," Dee Devers interrupted, her voice sour. "Just because she earned five dollars, this little girl thinks she can spend twelve dollars. I've tried and tried, but she has no sense of money. She thinks you can go to the 24-hour teller and get as much money as you want. She thinks a piece of plastic is all you need."

"Dad lets me push in his code," Cindy announced. "And I count the money afterward, too."

"See?" Dee shrugged, as if this proved her case. She took her leave, and got into the Toyota, backing up a few feet, then leaning out of the window to call to Cindy. "Bye, Cindy . . . You be a good girl, and don't you eat so much junk. You know your Dad gives you way too much chocolate. You're going to get fat if you don't stop pigging out so much."

"Yeah, okay." But Cindy was already making the reattachment to her father, swinging hands with him, her blue eyes, so like his, filled with adoration.

Kara followed the two of them into the house, seeing the way Rob leaned down to talk to Cindy, the way Cindy looked up at him, almost flirting. Had she been like that with her own father? Kara couldn't recall it clearly. Her

16

own childhood seemed lost behind a curtain of other experiences.

As they reached the side door, Rob stopped, holding the door open for his daughter.

"Scoot inside, Cindyella. Take the Barbies in the TV room and ask them if they've read the *TV Guide* this week. I've got to give Kara a real kiss, not one of those fake smoochies."

"Oh, Dad—"

"A *big* smoochy smoochy like this one," Rob said, lifting up Cindy and bussing her enormously, blowing in her ear until she squirmed ecstatically away, clapping both hands to her ears.

"Dad, you are freako," Cindy giggled. "I'm too big to do that. You give the wettest kisses. You'll blow germs in my ear and I'll get swimmer's itch, like you did last year at the swimming pool. Remember that? Your ears got so horribly itchy you couldn't stand it?"

"I remember, I scratched like a son of a gun. Inside with you, Cindy Sue, quick now, before I kiss you again."

"Daddeee," she squealed, running indoors. Almost immediately they could hear the sound of the TV clicking on.

"Crazy little kid," Rob said. "And I probably do feed her too much chocolate."

He pulled Kara to him and gave her a long, enfolding kiss. They held each other, Kara, tall though she was, on tip-toes to match Rob's 6'2" height. She breathed in the delicious male smell of him, shaving lotion and laundered T-shirt and clean hair. Finally Kara pulled away, conscious of her quickened heartbeat. "Cindy . . . She's a little bit jealous of me; you shouldn't flaunt us in front of her like that."

"I love you, she's got to know it. That's reality, and she'll have to accept it. Come on inside, I bought some

17

new potatoes at a stand on Orion Road. You can help me peel them.''

"You don't peel new potatoes."

"You don't?"

"No, all you do is scrub them."

"Great, because I haven't got a peeler anyway."

Kara followed him to the kitchen, feeling good again, relaxed and happy. Somehow when she was with Rob she always got swept up. She was laughing or being smooched or planting a garden or playing one of Rob's word games, or making love. The last when Cindy wasn't visiting, of course.

They walked into the huge, glass-enclosed kitchen in which a meal for twenty could easily have been prepared. There was a double freezer, an indoor grill, an oval island, walnut cupboards without doors, pots with plants, and a huge red and gold abstract painting. Rob had put a bag containing twenty pounds of potatoes on the counter.

"This many?" She couldn't help laughing.

"You mean I got too many?"

She said, "I'd say you bought generously."

He teased, "And what's this about you trying on the wedding dress again? I thought that was supposed to bring bad luck."

She suddenly remembered the call from Laurel. Flushing, she reached in the bag and began taking out some of the pale, clean, country-grown potatoes. "No, it's when the bridegroom sees you in it, that's when it's unlucky."

He ruffled her hair comfortably. "Well, keep it from my sight then, babe. The last thing we want is any bad luck."

CHAPTER 2

Rob's wooden deck, overlooking the woods, continued the ship feeling, its shape reminding Kara of a schooner prow thrust forward into waves of green trees. One double-trunked birch was almost as thick as Kara's waist. Fallen logs dotted the section of woods, covered with moss and fungi. Rob refused to clear them because he said they were part of the chain of nature.

They grilled steak, Cindy putting up a fuss and demanding that hot dogs be added to the grill.

"Dad, steak is ugly, I can't hardly cut it and it takes so much time to chew. I want two hot dogs. The cheese kind, the kind with cheese in their center."

"I haven't got cheese hot dogs, chicken."

"Mom gets 'em all the time. She makes 'em for me every day, and I have them in buns. You never buy hot dogs or buns, Dad. You never buy anything good."

Last week, Cindy had wolfed down half a Delmonico steak with apparent gusto, and had said not a word about

19

hot dogs. Kara waited for Rob to handle this. Charcoal smoke puffed in blue eddies across the deck, redolent of summer and leisure.

"Why don't you put cheese hot dogs on my shopping list, hon?" Rob asked casually, speaking to Cindy. "And buns. Right now, before we forget. Meanwhile, I guess you'll just have to tough it out with steak. We'll give you a small piece."

Full of self-importance, Cindy ran in the house to get a pad of paper and a pen. "Can I make your whole shopping list, Dad? What else do we need?"

Rob pretended to think. "Well . . . how about cauliflower and broccoli and Oh's cereal and peanut butter . . ."

Hunched over the writing pad, Cindy looked prettily earnest, a dimple flashing in her left cheek from the effort of cursive writing. She was the sort of little girl who in grade school was most popular, totally opposite from the skinny, awkward, bright loner that Kara had been.

"I can't spell cauliflower."

"Pretend you're in a spelling bee. Give it a good guess, and if you're even close, you get chocolate cake for dessert."

"We're having that anyway, I saw it in the kitchen, Kara brought it. Dad . . ."

"Sound it out," Rob said.

"Call. That's how it *sounds*. And then flower, it has that word in it, too."

Kara listened to them, stretched out in a chaise lounge with a glass of Paul Masson, letting the pleasant buzz of the wine reach into the parts of her that were still tense from Laurel's call. She watched Rob through eyes that smarted a little from charcoal smoke. She'd had other men before—she had broken two other engagements, one right after college, one shortly before she met Rob on a blind date. But other men had been unsatisfactory. Rob had heart and feeling. That counted for so much, she felt.

"Twenty minutes and the fire'll be ready," Rob announced, when the grocery list had been drawn up to Cindy's satisfaction, containing items such as Chipsies, microwave milkshakes, and grapes. "Did you say you'd brought some gifts over? What say we open them? We'll let Cindy do the honors."

Kara went out to her car and lugged the three boxes around to the patio, pushing back a tiny, rebellious twinge in her that wanted to open her own wedding gifts. But this was part of the bonding process with Cindy, she realized. Including the child in their plans.

"Oh, three packages!" Cindy exclaimed joyfully. She ran up to take the top box out of Kara's hands, putting it down on the lounge chair and starting to rip off the brown mailing wrap before Kara could even set the other two gifts down. The 10-year-old tore at the wrappings, flinging scraps of paper onto the decking.

"Careful, we need to save the card." Kara fished among the refuse for some kind of identification. The card said *From Aunt Tara and Uncle Bud*. These were Rob's relatives, people she had never met.

Cindy had already reached inside and was tearing at a Hudson's gift box. "This is . . . what is it, Dad? A sheet?" she said in disappointment, lifting up blue linen that fell in luxe folds.

"Looks like a tablecloth to me," Rob said. "And matching napkins."

"Oh . . ." As if it were Christmas, the child pounced on the next box. "Cuisinart," she spelled out, reading from the carton.

"Oh, great," Kara said. "Just what we need. I love to grate cabbage and do exotic things to carrots."

But Cindy was on the third package, which held an expensive crystal punch bowl etched in a floral pattern, with twelve cups. Cindy gazed down at the cups, her pretty face crestfallen.

21

"Is this all? Those are *dumb* gifts."

Rob wanted to know, "How so?"

"Because they are."

Kara was getting tired of this. "Well, the punch bowl is very nice. This is real crystal—hear how it rings when I tap it? We can have a party sometime and we'll serve punch with orange sherbet in it. You'd like that, Cindy, it's a good birthday party punch."

"I don't like sherbet," the child pouted. She got up and pushed past Rob, kicking at the wrappings as she went in the house.

Kara knelt to begin picking up the mess, her heart hammering with more anger than was warranted. Under other circumstances, she would have gotten out all the cups, arranged them, fingered the delicate crystal, marveled at its feel. Now the pleasure was spoiled.

She's only a little girl, she reminded herself.

"Here, I'll help," Rob said. He picked up the punch bowl and began to slide it back in its styrofoam support. His long, narrow hands were the hands of an artist, and he managed the chore deftly.

She asked, "Well? Aren't you going to go after her, talk to her, tell her how rude she's being?"

"And make her more defensive? Kara, she's having normal feelings. Every child of divorce fantasizes that her parents will get back together again and everything will go on happily ever after. You can't blame Cindy for that. She's just seeing the wedding gifts for what they are—solid evidence that her dream isn't going to come true."

"I know." Kara sank back on her haunches. "Oh, I know all that, Rob. And I'm being patient. She *is* so pretty and bright and she can be so loving. I just wish she would love me. That's the bottom line. And I'm not sure she's going to, and it makes me scared sometimes."

Rob put down the box and came over to hug her. "She will. I promise."

Kara snuggled into his arms, smelling charcoal lighter and smoke on him. She tried to laugh. "Well, I hope it happens before she's thirty."

Half an hour later, Rob forked three rib-eye steaks onto platters, and Cindy strolled out to join them, carrying her new Barbie and the miniature pink plastic comb that came with the doll, as if no conflict whatsoever had happened. She had changed her clothes, and now wore hot pink shorts and a minuscule white halter that revealed buds of newly forming breasts beneath the cloth.

During dinner, a chipmunk ran across the decking only feet from them, causing Cindy to drop her fork and point. The 10-year-old chattered about the day camp her mother was sending her to, and a TV special she had seen this week, eating all of her steak. Then she fidgeted at the table, swinging her legs back and forth.

"Can I be excused?" she asked Rob.

"In a minute, when Kara is through eating."

"But I want to go and play with my Barbies."

"Oh, it's all right," Kara began. "I know I'm a slow eater—"

"No," Rob said. "I don't want her to bolt up from the table. Anyway, I have an announcement to make."

"An 'nouncement?" Cindy immediately stopped swinging her feet and looked at him expectantly. "Does that mean we're going to Bob-Lo tomorrow?"

"We might go to Bob-Lo, yes, but that's not the announcement." Rob was looking at Kara, a smile playing about his mouth. "It has something to do with H."

Cindy bounced up and down in her chair. She loved word games and was an indefatigable Scrabble player. "H? Humongous? Hat? Harpoon? Hickey?"

Kara couldn't help laughing. "Do you know what a hickey is?"

"Oh, it's when a man sucks on a lady's neck and mooshes her all up and she gets a big red mark. Jennifer's sister got a bunch of them and her Dad was mad at her and grounded her for two weeks. I'm never going to let a man give me a hickey, I think it's grody."

"Well, that's a relief," Rob said, grinning. "Anyway, you didn't guess the right H. It has to do with honeymoon."

"Honeymoon?" Both Kara and Cindy said it simultaneously.

"That's right." Rob was looking self-important. "I've made a decision. We're going—"

"*You've* made a decision!" Kara didn't know whether to laugh or be indignant. "What about me? Aren't I half of the honeymoon couple? Anyway, I thought we were going to San Diego."

"We might and we might not. That's the surprise. I bought airline tickets today and I'm not going to tell you where they're for. What you have to do is pack for someplace warm, but you're not going to find out where until our wedding day."

"Oh, come on," Kara protested, laughing. "There's warm and there's warm. Florida's humid. Cancun is Gulf Stream. Phoenix, that's dry heat. Every one of them is different, and how will I know—"

Rob would not relent. "My sweet, you're driving to Metro airport blindfolded."

"Blindfolded?" Kara hooted. "You can't be serious. You *aren't* serious, are you?"

"I may very well be. We'll get you a nice lace blindfold knotted with white violets, and you'll be the fashionable bride on her way to—well, who knows where? You won't, until you're in the air."

Kara giggled at the thought of herself groping down a

boarding ramp with a lace blindfold over her eyes. "Oh, no," she moaned. "I can't believe this—would you really be that cruel not to tell me?"

Cindy made a noise, loud enough to stop Rob in mid-laugh.

"*I* want to go," she said.

Both Rob and Kara turned to look at the girl, whose expression had turned thunderous.

"Cin, oh, Cindyella, it's a honeymoon, baby," Rob said.

"I don't care."

"Children don't go on honeymoons, even when they're as pretty as you. A honeymoon is one time when a child is just a fifth wheel."

"I'd only be a third wheel," Cindy pointed out. She wore the grim expression of one who expects to have to bulldoze circumstances in order to get her way. "I want the surprise, too. I want to wear the blindfold."

Kara felt her light-hearted mood slip away. Here it was again—the jealousy. They had to watch themselves so carefully around Cindy. If they held hands, Cindy tried to wriggle between them. If they kissed, Cindy glowered. When they watched TV Cindy claimed Rob's lap. It was the behavior of a five-year-old, not a ten-year-old going into sixth grade, but Rob insisted that Cindy would grow out of it, that it was only a natural phase.

"I want to go, Dad, I want to go on the plane with you! I don't see why I can't. Jennifer went with her Mom and Dad to Fort Lauderdale and they let her sit in the seat between them and she got three cokes and three bags of smoked almonds."

"Cindy," Rob said warningly. "Jennifer's parents weren't on their honeymoon. You and I are taking some time this week to be together. We're going to Bob-Lo for sure, and we'll go on a trip later this summer, all three of us."

"I don't want a trip later, I want one now, I want to go

on the surprise, I want to *go*." Cindy's eyes had watered up, and moisture quivered on her long, feathery lashes.

"Sorry, pumpkin." Rob's voice was firm. "This trip is for Kara and me. We'll go to Lake Michigan later this summer, how would you like that? We'll go to Ludington State Park. Remember how much you liked the park last year? We'll climb the steps along the dune and—"

"I don't want Ludington!" Cindy screamed, jumping up from her chair and shoving it against the table, so that Kara's plate nearly crashed to the deck. "I don't want Ludington, I hate Ludington, I hate Lake Michigan, I hate it, hate it, hate it! I want to go on the plane and you won't let me because you're selfish and cheap!"

"Cindy!" Rob rose, his face angry.

"Cheap!" The ten-year-old screamed at her father. "A cheap old divorcy cheap spender who won't take me, and I hate it, I hate you, I hate everything!"

Cindy slammed into the house, banging the door behind her with as much angry force as an adult woman.

"Jesus," Rob said, staring after his daughter.

"I'll say." Kara sank down in her chair again, feeling her heart constrict. Her good mood of the day had slipped away like water down the garbage disposal.

"She's never said a word about the honeymoon before this," Rob said, shaking his head. "Damn. What did I do?"

"You made it sound like a wonderful surprise. You put it all on a child's level. And by the way, I detect some of Dee in those things she was screaming at you. 'Selfish,' 'cheap spender;' I don't think those phrases came from Cindy, do you?"

"Probably not." Rob spoke sharply. He harbored guilt over his ex-wife, whose two-year affair with a doctor had broken up their marriage. Later, Dee had begged to come back to him, but Rob refused, claiming the "basic trust" was gone.

Kara snapped back, "Well, you're the one whose child is agitating to accompany us on our honeymoon. I think you'd better go in there and soothe her feelings or she's probably going to hate me for the rest of her life."

Rob got to his feet, his brows beetled together, his mouth tight, the way it got when he was under stress. He looked at a loss, and if Kara hadn't been so angry herself, she would have felt sorrier for him.

"Go in there," she said. "Promise her a trip, just the two of you. She deserves at least that. I don't want her to think I'm going to steal you away from her. She wasn't screaming 'I hate Kara,' but the message came through loud and clear."

Rob stayed inside the house for forty-five minutes. Kara waited on the deck, her feet curled beneath her, staring at the late yellow sunlight flickering in the trees. Somewhere over Rochester Road she heard the unmistakable whoosh-whoosh of the gas jets underneath a hot air balloon. Soon the balloon itself drifted over the treetops, a blue and yellow striped adult toy in which three people rode, high above all worldly problems.

Kara watched it. Her eyes felt hot and dry. Was Cindy going to be a real problem to them? God, she hoped not. She hadn't really wanted to date a divorced man, she'd known that a man like Rob came with a few drawbacks.

But this. Cindy hadn't been so vociferous before, so open in her feelings. Looking at it from the child's perspective, Kara could see that she might be angry and fearful. After all, here was Kara, smiling and being kissed by her father, and now being taken on a surprise honeymoon from which Cindy herself was excluded.

Oh, shit, Kara thought. She slung her feet up on the chair that Rob had been sitting in, trying to relax. The worst of it was, she herself didn't know how she really felt about Cindy. The girl could be so bright and cute sometimes, so appealing that Kara wanted to hug her and comb her thick, glossy, black curls, and teach her how to apply nail polish so that it didn't chip all the time.

Then there were times like this. Kara found herself clenching her jawline, until she could feel her cheek muscles knotting. Cindy had looked so *mutinous*.

Rob came back out on the deck. There were circles of perspiration under the arms of his T-shirt.

"We talked," he said. "I told her I'd take her to Disney World. Damn, I felt like I was offering her a bribe. I was just trying to have a little fun, I was going to take you to Hawaii, that's where I got the tickets for."

"Oh," Kara said.

"We're staying at the Wailea Beach Hotel on Maui. Damn, Kara, I'm sorry. I hope you can be understanding. She's only ten and God only knows what crap my ex-wife fills her with. Dee is so embittered now and I'm sure it rubs off. I told Cindy to stay in her room until we're ready to leave for the movie."

Kara raised an eyebrow. "We're going to a movie after all that display?"

Rob looked uncomfortable. "Hey, this isn't easy for me, either. I already promised her a show. What am I supposed to do, punish her even more so that she feels more and more ill used and angry? It's a vicious circle."

"I don't know," Kara said.

"Well, I don't know either. I'm a divorced father, Kara, and I sure as hell don't have all the answers."

CHAPTER 3

The movie theater was in the Winchester Mall, and they stood for a few minutes out in the mall by the theater, where a kiosk featured posters of current pictures. Kara wanted to see either a new Steve Martin movie, or a Sally Fields romance that had been advertised in the *News*. Cindy begged to see *Alien Force*, a new *Alien* ripoff.

Even the poster, full of claws and dark shadows, bothered Kara.

She took Rob's arm. "Oh, please, I got dragged to see the original *Alien* and I'll never forget that awful thing that came bursting out of those people's stomachs. I thought I would have a heart attack. I had to leave before it was over."

"*I* saw *Alien* on Jennifer's VCR," Cindy put in. "We were on a sleep-over and we watched it four times. It was great. Oh, Dad, please, Dad, I want to see this *so* much . . ." She hung on Rob, begging, and Rob turned to Kara with eyes that, in turn, asked for her understanding.

"Oh, all right," Kara said with as good grace as she could muster.

"You sure? I'll hold your hand," Rob offered.

"Good, because I'm going to need it."

They were late, with no time to buy popcorn, and Cindy led them into theater # 4, heading down to the front row. Rob claimed he would get a crick in his neck if he sat down that far, so they compromised on the sixth row.

Kara sat glumly on one side of Rob, wondering just how 'understanding' she was expected to be. She could have been happily laughing at Steve Martin. Instead she'd have to sit through a darkened screen, tension and horror.

Twenty minutes after the movie had begun, a body was found in a futuristic city. It was mostly entrails, looking as if the producers had gone to a slaughterhouse for realism. Pictures segued into Kara's mind, fusing past with present. Gagging, she covered her mouth with her hand, then looked up to find the camera focussing close up on more grisly body parts. And children of Cindy's age attended movies like this with their parents?

Fighting nausea, she stood up, stumbling past Rob's knees, and headed up the aisle. The lobby was empty, except for a few teenaged employees of the theater who were standing around talking to each other. Kara found the ladies' room, and went into a stall and sat there until the attack of sweating and trembling went away.

Finally she repaired her makeup and went out to the lobby, where she stood staring at the movie posters, reluctant to go back in to the picture. *You're being a baby*, she scolded herself, but it didn't seem to help. Why was it that a ten-year-old could endure the movie and she could not?

Because she's never seen violence, Kara answered herself.

"Kara? Kar? Are you all right?" Rob was beside her, his expression anxious.

Kara tried to smile. "Don't mind me, blood and guts make my stomach turn. I guess I'm not much of a sci-fi fan."

"That's okay. Anyway, the bad part is over and they're on the asteroid now, looking for the creature."

"Goody. Then it's all right until next time the thing pops out and chops someone into hamburger?"

Rob looked troubled. "I know it wasn't your favorite, but Cindy saw the ad on TV and she's been dying all week to go." He pulled her to him, hugging her. "Thanks, Kar, for letting her see it. I do appreciate it, you're awfully good to her."

Kara wondered what she should say that wouldn't sound petulant or sugary. "Next time I get Steve Martin," she finally declared.

"A deal. Oh," Rob added, "Maybe while I'm out here I'll get some popcorn, and some coke. What do you want, buttered?"

She didn't really want anything. "I'll take buttered."

"Good, you can help me carry it," he said, assuming that she would be going back into the theater. Kara allowed him to make the assumption. She couldn't ruin the movie for the two of them, nor did she want to be forced to launch into long explanations of why violent movies churned her up so.

An hour later, they emerged into the mall parking lot. Dusk had fallen, and the sky was plum-purple, the air moist with leafy smells from a nearby stand of trees that had not yet been chopped down by developers. Teenagers who used the mall as a hangout were calling to each other, a girl shrieking with mirth.

"You have quite a grip," Rob said. He was shaking out his hand as if his fingers hurt from where she had clutched them during the movie.

"That's me, iron fist." Kara's back and neck muscles

ached from clenching her entire body. The last twenty minutes of the movie had consisted of a long chase scene that had left her shaking with tension. She hoped Rob hadn't noticed, but she had squeezed her eyes shut. She never should have gone back in the theater.

They shared a look. "I'll give you a back rub when we get home." Rob promised. "A nice, long one."

"My stomach hurts," Cindy interrupted.

Rob turned to his daughter, ruffling her hair. "No wonder, after you ate three-quarters of one of those big tubs of popcorn. I didn't think a ten-year-old girl could eat that much."

"Oh, Dad . . ."

They headed for Rob's Mercur at the back of the parking lot. Cindy dragged behind them, scuffing her feet and kicking at an old McDonald's cup someone had discarded on the pavement.

"My stomach *hurts*," she repeated as they got to the car.

"You shouldn't have had so much popcorn," Rob scolded.

"I didn't know . . ." Cindy responded pathetically.

They drove north through town, and then on Rochester Road through tunnels of dark trees and occasional subdivisions. Rob flicked on the radio, and Whitney Houston filled the car with pure, soaring self-confidence.

Kara stared out of the car window. For months, off and on, Cindy had complained of "stomachaches." The pediatrician had hinted at home problems, and Kara felt sure that the belly pains were caused by the oncoming wedding. It was no coincidence that the "ache" had begun just as Rob was offering to give Kara a back rub.

When they got to Rob's, Cindy balked at brushing her teeth, but finally did so. She curled up in front of the TV set, switched on a movie, and promptly fell asleep.

"She didn't say anything more about a stomachache,"

Rob whispered to Kara, as they both stared down at the sleeping child, her closed eyelashes feathered against the perfect, poreless complexion of a ten-year-old.

"That's because you haven't given me a back rub. Start doing that and she'll get it again."

"Kara—"

"Well, I'm worried," Kara insisted. "She doesn't want us to get married and she's showing it. I'm lucky she didn't yell 'I hate you,' at me this afternoon. I'm sure she was thinking it."

Rob uttered a rueful laugh. "Babe, if she was thinking it she would have yelled it. Our Cindy knows how to let it all hang out, I'll say that for her. She'll come around. You're good to her and she knows it."

Kara drew in her breath, letting it out slowly. "I hate the image of the wicked stepmother. It's so unfair."

"Well, you're not going to be one." Rob slid his arm around her. "Look, I'll carry her upstairs and then let's you and I go and do some serious hugging. I could use a hug, what about you?"

Rob's bedroom was enormous, carpeted in biscuit wool and hung with huge collages that had been done by a former classmate at the University of Michigan whose work now commanded six figures. Canvases of ocher, crimson, cobalt, made the room jump with color.

They lay down on the bedspread and began touching lightly. Rob was a patient lover, a necessity for Kara, who needed much holding and cuddling before she could begin to relax enough for the act of lovemaking to take place. She needed conditions just so: the room lit by one small lamp so that she could see Rob's face and feel safe; soft music playing; clean sheets on the bed.

They hugged, Rob stroking her and whispering love words to her as he knew she liked. Kara tried to let herself be swept away but she could not. There were too many things interfering, thoughts swirling and kaleidoscoping in her mind.

The call from Laurel, the letter from her father.

The violent movie with its bloody scenes.

Cindy.

She felt Rob's hand rubbing gently up and down her hip, dipping lower each time to the curve of her buttocks, cupping her flesh. Not too insistent, just tender. In the half-dark, her eyes watered. Was she being a fool to think that marriage was going to bring her happiness?

What if it didn't?

What if Cindy didn't get better, what if she threw more tantrums, got more stomachaches, became even more possessive of Rob? What if Kara wasn't happy living in Rob's ultra-modern house with its vibrant splashes of color that didn't fit with her country chintz? Or another scenario: Kara already knew that Rob could become totally absorbed in his work, forgetting about the existence of anything else. She herself had the same tendencies. She'd read about two-career couples who put their marriages on hold, sometimes for years. What if that happened to them? She didn't want a half-alive marriage.

Stop, she admonished herself, feeling a twinge of panic at where these thoughts might lead.

"Kar? Are you with me?" Rob's voice almost startled her.

"Mmmmm," she murmured.

"You seem distant."

She was flooded with contrition. "I'm not, oh, I'm not. Hold me, Rob, just hold me and tell me you love me."

"I do love you."

"Tell me . . ."

"Babe, I love you. Are you sure there's nothing wrong? You seem funny tonight. Too quiet or something."

"I'm fine. Hug me again. Please."

"Well, that I won't object to."

Afterwards, they lay close together, Kara curled on her side, her face resting on Rob's chest, his arm cradling her. She hadn't had an orgasm tonight, she seldom did, but she did have a warm feeling of love and completion. That was usually enough for her, and only occasionally did she feel cheated.

There was the sound of a car turning up the street, and headlights briefly splashed across the bedroom walls, rousing Kara from the half-doze into which she had fallen.

She pushed back the sheet and sat up, reaching for her clothes.

"Do you have to?" Rob asked sleepily. "Can't you stay here just this once and spend the night with me?"

"Not when Cindy's here. Rob, you know how I feel about that."

"But she's my daughter and I don't mind. Besides, we're getting married, Kara; it's not like you're some fast Saturday night pickup."

"I should hope not," she said, carrying her clothes into the master bathroom. "Anyway, in three weeks I'll be here all the time. I think I need a shower."

"Take one here."

"Oh, I think I'll wait till I get home. I don't want to have to put my clothes on again over clean skin."

"You," Rob murmured fondly, drifting toward sleep again.

Kara switched on the bathroom light and closed the door behind her. Rob's bathroom was like the rest of the house, full of windows, plants, paintings and light. Her naked reflection loomed at her in the vanity mirror, a slim woman with long thighs, and a stomach so flat that her hip bones jutted. Kara's eyes flicked toward the image.

Usually she didn't like looking at herself naked, but tonight something about the light, or maybe it was her

35

mood, drew her to move closer to the glass. Delicately she lifted her left breast.

Yes. There it was. Her silvery scar, just under the fullness, six inches long and jagged, as if it had been carved at random. Rob thought she got it falling off her bike when she was seven.

But no fall had cut that incision. *He* had.

And there was another mark on her buttock, too, that one faded to near invisibility. Even Rob had never noticed it.

Kara stared coldly at the breast scar, her eyes narrowed. There had been times when she had fantasized being given twenty minutes in a locked room, with Jerry Quick tied hand and foot, at her disposal. But she didn't know if she could really carry out her revenge fantasy. At seventeen, she had been numb, paralyzed, terrorized by what was happening to her. How did she know she would be any different now at twenty-seven, any braver?

She turned away from the glass and pulled on her brassiere, snapping its front closure over the scar.

Sunday morning she awoke at home in her own bed to the sound of rain rattling the downspout near the corner of her room. All night long a suffocating dream had plagued her. A handsome, dark-haired boy was drawing on her body with a felt pen, tracing out pictures of penises and testicles while Kara tried to beat him away with her fists.

She twisted under the sheets, flinging away the remnants of the dream as if they were scraps of thin paper. The rain. What was she supposed to do today? Oh, it was Cindy; she had volunteered to take Rob's daughter shopping for a dress to wear to the wedding.

She got up, showered, dressed, phoned Rob to arrange a pick-up time, and then sat down at her dinette table with the morning *Detroit News*. A 19-year-old woman had been set afire by unknown assailants and had managed to put the fire out by rolling in a ditch full of water. A man who had killed his wife and kept her body in a freezer for three years had been found guilty.

Dear Abby's column was on date rape, and Kara skimmed it, reading about a man who admitted he forced sex with his date after she wore a string bikini to the beach. "She wanted me to," he wrote Abigail Van Buren. "Or why else did she wear that suit?"

She put the paper down, feeling a light shiver go over her skin. Jerry Quick had testified in court about Kara's shorts, claiming before all the jury and courtroom audience that he had been able to see Kara's "front crack, her, you know, her female parts, right through the cloth."

She had been seventeen then. She hadn't known. How could she have known? All the girls had worn tight cut-offs like hers. She'd only been doing what they all did.

Feeling irritable, she drove over to Rob's and picked up Cindy, who was wearing her hair pulled on top of her head today with three lavender Care Bears plastic clips. The effect was odd: at once coquettish and childish. Cindy showed real promise of beauty when she grew up. She would be one of those girls with impossibly clear skin and huge eyes, wiles that would both captivate and annoy men.

"I want pink!" Cindy announced after they had waved good-bye to Rob and were strapped in their seat belts. "And shoes to match, with pink tights! I'm going to have everything pink."

"We'll buy the whole outfit," Kara promised. "And then we'll come home and model it for your Dad."

Cindy glowed. "I *love* pink. When I get married I'm going to have a pink wedding dress instead of old white."

" 'Old' white happens to be traditional," Kara said.

They took the M59 expressway to Lakeside Mall. It was still drizzling, and the sky looked cloud-washed, pearly, moist. Cindy chattered about a horror movie she wanted Rob to rent, *Halloween 4*.

"How can you watch stuff like that?" Kara wanted to know.

"Oh, I like it." Cindy grinned. "I like being scared."

In the girls' department of Hudson's, Cindy grew quiet as they leafed through racks of dressy little-girl frocks, most embellished with lace, ruffles, embroidery, or all three.

"I said I want *pink*," Cindy balked as Kara took out a pale yellow frock and held it up, marveling at the pleats and the price tag.

"Of course you can have pink, didn't we say you could? I was just looking at this one. Here are your sizes, Cindy, let's pull out all the pinks and see what we think of them."

"Oh, look," Cindy said, pulling out a pastel pink ruffled confection. "I want this one."

"But that's a size eight, and you wear a twelve."

"I want it. I want to try it on."

"We'll have to find it in your size, then."

Kara willed herself to patience, summoning a saleswoman who searched the racks for the pale-pink dress, then disappeared in the bowels of the store to report that they didn't have it in stock, but Hudson's Oakland Mall did. If they wanted, she would call over to the other store and have them hold back a dress in Cindy's size.

Kara hesitated. The trip to Oakland Mall in Troy would delay their meeting Rob.

"Oh, please, please," Cindy begged, pulling at Kara's arm.

"But you haven't tried on any of the other dresses. They have lots of other pink ones . . ."

"I don't want them, I want *this* dress, I love this dress, I don't want any other dress ever."

Well, that was being definite.

"Oakland Mall isn't that far away, ma'am," put in the middle-aged saleswoman, eyeing Kara with disapproval.

"All right," Kara said, outnumbered.

The trip, in weekend summer traffic, took twenty minutes, with a traffic snarl at the entrance to the crowded Troy mall, another snarl in the parking lot, and a near-accident when a fat woman driving a green van almost backed into them. But Hudson's had the pink dress ready, and Cindy went into the fitting room to try it on. She refused Kara's assistance.

"Are you sure? You might want some help with the zipper—"

"I can do zippers. I told you, I want a pink wedding dress."

"She knows what she wants, Mother," said the saleswoman.

Kara paced up and down the girls' department, waiting. Were ten-year-old girls always like this, so demanding? She felt at such a loss. She didn't know anything about children, had been an only child herself, hadn't done much babysitting. Maybe this type of behavior was normal. Maybe this was what any mother had to expect.

Ten minutes went by. Finally Cindy emerged, swathed in pink, her fresh prettiness almost touchingly evident. She had taken out the Care Bear clips and her lush black curls framed her face. She stroked the fabric of her skirt, petting it as if she were in love with the feel.

"Well, isn't that pretty, isn't she just a picture?" The saleswoman descended on them, obviously expecting a sale. "Isn't she going to look gorgeous at the wedding? Just as pretty as the bride."

While Kara cringed, Cindy's mood changed instantaneously.

"I don't want this dumb old dress."

"But honey, it looks beautiful on you," protested the sales clerk.

"It looks dumb and ruffly. Ugh." Cindy began plucking at the fabric, as if to rip it off herself. "And it's too long. I don't want a new dress, I don't want any dress. I *hate* this dress!"

Kara had had enough. "Go in the fitting room and take it off then. You'll wear your blue church dress to the wedding. And if you aren't careful taking it off, if there's one rip or tear in it, then no more movies for a month, and *I mean it*."

The girl eyed Kara as if to check the seriousness of the threat, then scurried off to the fitting room.

They left Hudson's and drove to Scallop's, where they were to meet Rob. In the car Kara was silent, afraid to say anything in the heat of temper that she might regret later. Cindy was spoiled and contrary. She had declined to try on other dresses, made them drive all the way across town, then pulled a pout and refused the very dress she had been mad for. This *wasn't* normal behavior for a ten-year-old girl, it couldn't be, and if it was, Kara was thoroughly sick of it.

Rob was waiting for them in a booth, a martini already in front of him. He looked fresh and cheerful. His architectural firm was trying to get a contract for a 12-story office building on Big Beaver Road, Troy's "golden mile" of offices, and Rob's forte was wooing clients.

"Hi, you two. We're still dickering but it's getting interesting. Find a beautiful dress for a beautiful girl?"

Kara was annoyed at his cheerfulness, his assumption that, of course, things had gone swimmingly. "It got away," she said. "I'll let Cindy tell you all about it."

Rob looked inquiringly at his daughter, who had the grace to look abashed, sliding into the booth and staring down at the heavily varnished wood surface. "It was *dumb*," the girl muttered. "I don't want a dress. I don't want *any* dress."

Rob and Kara's eyes met. Kara shrugged, sending him the message: *she had another tantrum.*

"Well, we'll talk about it later," Rob said. "Meanwhile, what kind of drink do you want to order, Cindy? Would you like some lemonade, or Sprite or root beer?"

Later, when Cindy got up to go to the rest room, Kara burst out, "I'm sorry! She led me on a wild goose chase. There was a dress she just *had* to have, but they didn't have it at Lakeside, so I had to drive all the way over to Oakland Mall. The minute she got it on and the saleswoman mentioned the wedding, all hell broke loose and suddenly the dress was 'dumb.' She doesn't want the wedding, Rob, and she's making a stink about it."

She knew she was saying too much, but her adrenaline was pounding and she couldn't stop. "Well, I'm tired of it. I'm not that patient. Frankly, I don't care whether she has a new dress for the wedding or not, and the mood I'm in, I almost don't even care whether she attends at all!"

Kara glared into Rob's eyes, embarrassed she had said it but damned if she was going to back down.

Rob looked startled, then anxious, then full of contrition. He rubbed one hand through his head of black, curly hair. "Honey, I'm the one who should be apologizing."

"What?"

"I shouldn't have sent you shopping with her. You have enough to worry about as it is, and I only piled more on top of you." He leaned forward to take both of Kara's hands in his. "Kara, this thing with Cindy, it's only temporary. It's just a phase she's going through and she'll get over it. And if she doesn't, it's not going to affect our relationship. I only see her two weekends of the month, do you understand me? I'll be living with you all the time."

Kara blinked, her emotions in a turmoil. Cindy's rejection of the dress had hurt her.

"It's not that easy," she began.

41

"Of course it isn't easy, but I love you, Kar, and you love me, and Cindy has to accept that."

"Then you're not mad?"

"Of course I'm not. I—" Rob stopped. Cindy was returning from the rest room, her stride jaunty, her temper spell of the morning apparently forgotten.

"What are you two talking about?" she asked. She slid into the booth next to Rob and gazed at them with beautiful, clear eyes. "You act like such love birds. Anyone can tell you're a bride and groom."

CHAPTER 4

Driving home from the Bikini Shoppe in St. Petersburg, Florida, where she worked, Jerry Quick's 50-year-old mother clenched the steering wheel so tightly that her muscles ached. She could smell the sour, acrid odor of her own nervous sweat.

Sally Quick Porris slowed her one-year-old blue Cutlass Ciera, taking the turn into Magnolia Point subdivision, or, as her husband, Ed, was fond of calling it, "Magnolia Rest Home." Mostly retirees lived here, in two bedroom cinder block homes with fanatically tended lawns. Steam drifted upward from the puddles left by a late-afternoon cloudburst.

Rape.

Sally repeated the word to herself, as she drove down the street. Her son, Jerry, had been charged with the two girls, but the prosecutor had tried to get him for some other cases, too, only there hadn't been enough evidence.

Sally didn't believe any of it. Those two little bitches—

she still felt certain they lied. She knew it couldn't have been like they said because a child couldn't have come out of her body who could have done that . . . that monstrous thing.

She had his room all ready for him, the second bedroom. Ed was giving him a job at one of the muffler shops he owned, and Sally had even bought her son a membership at Vic Tanny because he had written he was lifting weights in prison.

She pulled into their driveway and parked under the carport, her eyes searching the house for some sign of her son's arrival. However, the mint green cinder block house looked just as it always did, half buried in an overgrowth of tropical bushes.

Then Sally heard the rumble of the central air conditioning unit, which had been turned off when she left the house in the morning. Her breath clogged in her throat. He was here. He had used the key under the yucca plant, just like she told him.

She went inside, automatically putting her purse on the kitchen counter. A beer can sat in the sink, a few flecks of foam still clinging to its top. She ran through the house, gladness and fear scorching through her.

"Jerry? Jer—Oh, Jerry—!"

He was not in the living room. She hurried down the hall that led toward the two bedrooms. She was breathless by the time she reached the back bedroom where she and Ed slept.

She stopped, shocked.

A muscular man lay sprawled asleep across their queen-sized bed, bare-chested, wearing only tight, out-of-fashion suit pants.

"Jerry?" Cautiously she approached him. Her visits to Raiford had been sporadic, only once or twice a year, mostly because Ed, her husband, objected to her going.

She had not seen Jerry except behind a glass window, and certainly not without a shirt.

She stared down at her son. Ten years ago Jerry had been a thin, wiry and handsome boy, with a shock of dark hair that kept falling in his eyes. Girls had adored him, but he only wanted the blonde ones. Now here he was, lying across her bed as if he owned it, looking more like a battered street fighter than the Jerry she remembered.

He must have been lifting weights six hours a day from the look of him. His chest was deeply muscular, his arms beefy, too. There were jagged scars puckered along his rib cage, as if someone had carved them with a broken bottle. A crude tattoo on his left forearm looked as if he had done it himself with a ballpoint pen. Scratched out on his skin were the numbers 13½.

Even his face was different, with knotted muscles clenched along his jawline and a nose bumpy on the bridge from being broken.

She wondered if he had lost any teeth. Prison must have been terrible, she thought, shivering. It must have been brutal.

"Jerry?" she whispered. Remembering he was a sound sleeper, she raised her voice a little. "Jerry. Wake up."

Jerry Quick aroused instantly, his eyes flicking open as if he hadn't been sleeping at all but had merely been lying there to fool her. Suddenly he was Sally's own Jerry again. His eyes were blue, bright, glistening; that hadn't changed. And his hair was soft and glossy, a little long but clean.

"Hey, Ma. Hi. My parole officer dropped me off."

The two of them clung together, Sally patting her son's back over and over. He was her boy.

"Jerry, oh, Jerry," she kept saying as they hugged. She wondered at the unfamiliar hardness of his biceps as he gripped her. He was a 30-year-old man now, she reminded herself, feeling estranged from him again.

45

Jerry pulled away. "These clothes, hey, they're something. These the new styles? They gave me the same old fucking clothes I wore in there. Hey, I think the suit got eaten by moths. And I could hardly get the pants zippered."

"What?" She felt bewildered, disoriented, as if he'd suddenly started talking Chinese.

"I need clothes," her son said impatiently.

For the first time, Sally looked at the mess Jerry had made of their bedroom. Slacks and pullovers, shirts and sports jackets, were spread all over the bed and dresser, as if Jerry were packing up Ed's stuff for him to move. Belts and ties lay in a tangle, and Jerry had even gone into the back of the closet to get out several pairs of running shoes and dress shoes.

"Jerry?" She said it nervously. Her third husband had an erratic temper, and once had slapped Sally so hard her entire face had swollen. She would never get this stuff back in the same order as Ed had left it.

Jerry grabbed up a pair of white Levi's Dockers and a blue and white pullover, holding them up for her admiration. "What do you think of these? Just my luck, you'd pick up a guy with a 34 waist like me."

He posed like a shopper in a fine men's store, the shirt held up in front of him. A muscle flickered tensely near his mouth.

"Jerry, please . . . put them back."

"Even the shirt, large, that's gotta be a sign, huh? Some kind of sign. Except I've got more muscles than he does; the sleeves are all too tight." Ignoring her protests, Jerry turned and began rummaging in the pile on the bed again. "*Green* pants? These look like they belong to the Jolly Green Giant."

Sally drew a breath. "Those are golf pants, Jerry. Ed's a golfer. Those are Ed's, they are his clothes. He'll be

46

home in an hour, he wants to meet you. He wants to tell you all about your new job . . .''

Jerry wasn't putting the clothes away.

"Jerry," she repeated. *"Those are Ed's."*

"I know they're fucking Ed's. I'm borrowing them." Jerry's glistening blue eyes held a look that made her heart sink. He wasn't going to stay here; the knowledge filled her like a dose of bitter medicine. If he was going to stay, he'd never dare rummage through Ed's closet like this because he'd be afraid of the consequences. He was only going to be here a few minutes.

That's why he dared. Before Ed got home, Jerry would be gone.

Her hands closed on the ugly golf pants, gripping the twill fabric between clammy fingers. "You just got here," she pleaded. "I haven't seen you—"

"You'll see me. In a while. Meanwhile, I got to have me some clothes, Ma; I can't go around in that old shit they gave me at Raiford. I got things to do. Something to take care of."

"What, Jerry? What do you have to take care of?" He gave her a hard look. "Okay," she added hastily. "I know you need clothes. Then I'll get them for you. We'll go to Maas Brothers in the morning, we'll shop—"

"Why should I shop when I can have this stuff, just like brand new, and I don't have to wait? He's got so damn much, he can spare some of it, can't he? And a car," Jerry added. "I got to have that, too. You got the keys?"

He held out his hand.

"No." She shook her head. She loved her Ciera, and it only had 8500 miles on it. She was making payments of $368 a month.

"The Ciera, isn't that what you drive? I saw the spare keys. You keep them on a hook in the cupboard." His eyes locked on hers, not gleaming any more but searingly hard.

"I can't give you my car," she protested weakly. "I have to drive to work. Ed leaves at six, and he has to—"

"Oh, let your old man drive you. He'll love it. Get more time for lovey dovey. Fucky fucky."

At the obscenity, Sally felt a flash of bitter disappointment. She couldn't believe this was happening. She'd wanted to celebrate—she had been going to take Jerry out to Red Lobster tonight.

"Hey," Jerry harried her. "If you don't hand it over I've already got the spare keys and I'll just drive off in it. You better give it to me, I want it as a gift, okay? A getting out of stir gift. I deserve that. Shit, I deserve a lot."

Taking her assent for granted, he slipped Ed's knit shirt over his head. It fit him tightly across the chest, making him look far different than Ed did in the same clothes. Casually her son unzipped his pants and changed into the Dockers. She noticed that he was wearing threadbare cotton shorts, prison issue.

"Hey, how do I look? Pretty fine, huh? You sure this is the latest fashion? Good old Ed does know how to pick out his clothes, right?" Jerry was making love to the mirror, turning and posing, almost strutting, as if a bevy of invisible girls was admiring him.

Sally felt sick. Jerry looked thirty but he was still acting like the 20-year-old he'd been when he went into Raiford. Did he really think he could walk in here, "borrow" Ed's clothes and take her car, and leave her with the payments and Ed to deal with?

"I'm *not* giving you my car as a gift," she began. But before she could finish the sentence he whirled on her.

"Shut up, rat-cunt!"

She gasped, drawing back. His mouth had drawn thin, and a little tic twitched his upper lip. He hadn't had that tic either when he'd gone in. It was new.

She tried to breathe evenly, afraid of him as she'd never been before. Her life with him seemed to pass in front of her eyes like some horrible TV movie. Her first husband, Carl, raping her with a coke bottle, while 5-year-old Jerry watched. That day she'd discovered Jerry trying to put a perfume bottle in a 6-year-old playmate's vagina. The phone call from Mrs. Farinno, Jerry's ninth grade teacher. Jerry had tried to grab her after class. He had pulled a knife on her and tried to cut off her blouse with it.

And more. More things she refused to think about.

She turned away from her son, sagging and trembling. "Okay, Jerry. Okay. Take the car then. Bring it back when you can."

She waited as he went about stripping the room of the clothing he wanted, packing it in a soft-side suitcase he found at the back of the closet. He made his selections quickly, adding several pairs of shoes including the Reeboks, which he examined curiously, touching the contoured soles as if he had never seen such things before. He probably had not. Reeboks hadn't been popular in 1977.

"These'll fit," he said to no one in particular. He added some belts, socks, jockey shorts and a light jacket.

At last Jerry was finished. He hadn't been able to stuff everything into the suitcase, but carried some of the pants draped over his arm. He pushed past her, so that Sally had to step aside to give him room to exit into the hallway. Now she could smell a sour odor on him. It was the smell of a man who had not worn deodorant in years.

"You got any money?" he asked as they reached the small, cramped living room.

"Nothing but $40. You know I don't."

"I know you hide it, Ma, you always did. Where'd you put it, huh? And I want what's in your purse. You can get some more from good old fucking Ed, he'll give you some

49

when he comes home. Unless you want me to wait for him, get what he's got. You want that?''

Sally felt nausea well up in her throat, imagining Ed dealing with this. My God, Ed would explode and Jerry would explode back. What would Jerry do if he exploded? After ten years in prison, what had he learned?

"No, I don't want that," she heard herself say. She went to the kitchen and took down the picture framed in seashells, reaching into the cardboard backing. Reluctantly she pulled out $500 in new, automatic-teller twenties, money she had been hiding from Ed.

"All of it," Jerry ordered.

Sally went to the matching picture, and stripped $350 more from its backing. She put the bills in Jerry's hand, avoiding his eyes. There was still one more cache but it was under the living room carpet in the corner by the TV, and she hoped he'd think this was all.

"Your purse," her son ordered.

Sally got her purse and pulled out her worn Buxton wallet. She had $42.88 in the billfold, and another $40 tucked into her checkbook. Jerry snatched the bills from her hand and stuffed the money loose into the pocket of the white pants.

"You'll need a money clip for those bills," Sally said, feeling unutterably sad and old. "Here, I've got one I was saving for Ed's birthday. You can have it, Jerry."

She pulled the clip, still in its Zales Jewelry Store sack, from the drawer in the bottom of the coffee table, and handed it to Jerry. He gave her a crooked smile as he accepted it. Her heartbeat was awfully fluttery now. The muscles of her esophagus were clenched around a huge burning knot.

"Got to go," he said.

"Jerry . . . where are you going?"

"Oh, places. I'll know when I find out."

"Are you going right now? This soon? Jerry, I . . ." But she stopped, her anger warring with her fear and grief.

Carrying the bag and the clothes, he went in her utility room, rummaged for a few minutes, and emerged carrying something hidden in the shirt. He sauntered toward the front door, his walk rolling, cocky.

What else has he done, that I don't know about? The thought hit Sally like a slam in the chest. *What did he do in prison? What will he do now?*

Jerry was already halfway down the steps to the carport. He stopped to look at the Ciera for a few seconds, assessing it, then pulled open its door, tossed the suitcase and clothes in the back seat, and got in.

Sally watched him.

He started the car, revving up the motor with too much gas, so that it didn't even sound like the familiar vehicle Sally knew. Squealing the tires, he backed out.

She didn't wave good-bye, but just stared numbly. Without glancing at her again, he backed onto the street, squealed the tires, and sped away.

He did do the rapes, she finally acknowledged to herself as she went back into the air conditioning.

He did all of it.

CHAPTER 5

Cindy had planned a sleepover with her best friend, Jennifer, whose father worked at the headquarters of K-Mart Corporation, in Troy. He owned a large library of videos, and Cindy and Jennifer would make microwave popcorn and overdose on *Supergirl*, *Grease II* and *Predator*.

Cindy rushed around the house, packing her Barbie dolls and begging one of Rob's T-shirts to wear as a nightie. "And we're going to wash our hair! And Jennifer's mother is going to use her curling iron on us! Have you got any ribbons, Dad? I need a pink ribbon to put in my hair when it's curled."

Rob produced a length of Christmas ribbon, and Cindy stuffed it in her bag and darted for the front door, where Jennifer's father was already tooting his horn for her.

"Bye, Dad, bye!"

"Say goodbye to Kara," Rob ordered.

Blue eyes looked melting, innocent. "I was going to. Bye, Kara."

She was gone, taking her energy with her like a force field that surrounded her. Suddenly they could hear the refrigerator motor and the hum of the air conditioning. The rain had stopped, and sunlight streamed through the wall of windows in the living room, bringing out the raised texture of the paintings. Outdoors, a dog barked. Rob was smiling at her.

"Let's make love."

"Now?" Kara hedged. "It's afternoon. We have company coming tonight, remember? I invited Angie and Russ."

"That's hours away," he murmured. He caressed a hand down her hip. She smelled the faint odor of martini on his breath, mixed with his own special smell, clean shirt, clean skin, fresh-washed hair.

She countered, "But we don't even know what we're going to serve them."

"Steak?"

"Rob—more steak? They must think we have a whole cow down in the basement."

He raised an eyebrow. "I thought we did. Chicken then? I bought four breasts. Right now let's go upstairs. The house is so quiet, we can't waste it."

Kara nodded, wondering why she didn't feel in the mood for lovemaking. Maybe it was the incident with Cindy, the extra stress, the small distance she felt had been put between Rob and herself. Cindy forced her to confront her doubts, and that was scary because she wanted no doubts. As her father had mentioned in his letter, she had already broken off two engagements. That didn't give her a wonderful history of commitment.

Rob had never shouted at her as Chuck had done, or slept with other women like Ken. He was a sweetly reasonable man. But they would not be starting fresh, there was all the baggage of his previous life. She didn't know if she could be a Florence Henderson mother, and the

Brady Bunch brood sounded frightening and complicated to her.

They walked upstairs, Rob behind Kara still caressing her backside. She could hear his quickened breathing and even smell a slightly different odor coming from him, gamy, salty, male. The smell of sex. Some trick of the afternoon light streaming in the upstairs windows created diamond twists on the stair risers, fraying out like broken glass. Kara avoided looking at it. There had been a similar reflection when—

She let the thought go no further, instantly slicing it off.

Sex was a careful thing, a delicate thing. She always had to be on guard or there would be a third person in bed with them—an enemy.

At the top of the stairs Rob pulled her to him and began kissing her open mouthed, his tongue flicking out to tantalize her own. She tried to relax, leaning into him, responding to his kiss. They had just made love last night, she hadn't thought he would want to again so soon.

Why couldn't her life with this lovable man be the way things were in books? Kara had never experienced the type of love scene described in Silhouette Ecstasy romances and she wondered if the authors themselves had. Could a woman really surrender her whole self and identity to some man's heavy breathing? What about the problems and thoughts of every day? These were always present for Kara, some times more faintly than others but always there.

In the big, painting-hung bedroom she saw that Rob had changed the sheets. He hadn't bothered to pull up the comforter but had left the sheets folded over invitingly. Plainly he'd planned this.

"Let's hug, babe, I was thinking about you all morning, I was thinking about this . . ."

"With clients there?" she teased. "Lawyers and whoever."

54

"Mostly whoever. And they weren't half as pretty as you."

Rob pulled her down on top of the sheets with him, wrapping his arms tightly around her and rolling with her, pinning her underneath him. He lavished her with more kisses.

"Rob—" She began to struggle a little. He was so turned on. Usually he was quieter than this, gentler, but he'd had two martinis at lunch and some wine after they got home.

"Mmmm, you smell so good, Kar, I can smell your perfume. What're you wearing? That *Samba* stuff I got you? That's a classy scent, it makes you smell like a flamenco dancer." His kisses nibbled, urged. "God, you're so damn sexy."

This was her fiancé, the man she had known for two years. His soft lips nuzzled at her neck, pushed at the neck of the shirt she wore, licked warmly along her collarbone. Shivers ran up and down her skin, her stomach clenching.

"Rob . . ."

"You're so pretty."

He unbuttoned her blouse gently, unfastening each button with a kiss. He tongued the smooth skin of her chest, trailing the wet warmth down to her breasts. Kara stiffened, growing more uncomfortable by the second, although she couldn't say why.

His breathing, maybe. Ragged, heavy with desire. Or the faint whiskey flavor of his breath, or the way Rob's body seemed to cover all of hers, leaving no room for her to move. It was amazing how heavy a male body could be when it was on top of you.

It was the way he—

He

Panic stabbed her chest like a butcher's knife.

She rolled away from Rob, violently pushing at him with both her hands and feet, frantic to get away. Escaping, she twisted to the far side of the bed, her breath heaving in her throat. Tears of humiliation sprang to her eyes. She didn't want to be like this. God, she didn't.

Rob flopped over and lay on his back, staring up at the ceiling. His breathing slowed.

"I don't *like* you coming on like that!" Kara blurted. "I'm sorry. I've told you, Rob, I can't stand it when you come on so strong."

He said nothing. He loomed beside her, lying there too still, as if she had quenched some vital force in him.

She began to tremble. "I'm sorry. I suppose I—I'm not like other women, other women you've had."

"You're fine," he said.

"No." She had to turn so that the pillow would soak up the sudden moisture that appeared in her eyes. "I'm not fine, I'm practically frigid. That's the word for it, let's be honest. I'm just not . . . not free the way I should be."

"It's okay." But his tone said that it wasn't, his tone said that he was hurt, that he interpreted this as rejection, that he was trying to understand but coming up short.

Damn, she thought.

They lay still, an abyss stretching between them. Her fault, she thought bleakly. Outdoors, blue jays squawked around Rob's bird feeder, and the teenagers next door revved up a car motor, laughing. A woodpecker drilled into a tree trunk, the sound absurdly like a cartoon. These were all sounds she would be hearing regularly, Kara told herself, after they were married, because she would be living here. But right now they only pointed up the silence between herself and Rob.

She steadied her breathing. She wasn't quite sure what had begun this. Daylight. That jagged reflection on the steps, maybe. Or the smell, the feel of Rob's body. *Something.*

In the years after, she had read every book about rape

she could get her hands on. Some of them had spoken about this phenomenon in victims. Later sex with husband or boyfriend was sometimes marred by triggers. The partner would do something that the rapist had done and the victim would recoil in horror, everything flooding back on her.

"I don't suppose you want to talk about it," Rob said after a long time.

The idea repelled her. She couldn't have him knowing. He would always look at her differently. He would mention it, make her think about it, rail against Jerry, make macho threats, maybe even use it against her, accuse her of seducing the rapist, as her father had once done.

She moistened her lips. "I told you I'm sorry."

"Sorry has nothing to do with it. You rolled away from me like I was an ax murderer, Kara. And it isn't the first time."

She lay there. Her stomach was clenched into an impossible knot.

"Is it something about me? Something I'm doing?"

"No."

"You told me I was too turned on. So maybe it was that. I know you like things slow, I know you need lots and lots of time. I hurried you. I shouldn't have. But Kara—"

Here it came. The question. Was it something palpable, judgeable, something that Rob could understand that would let him off the hook?

But Rob didn't ask the question after all. "Let's try again," he said softly. "We'll just hug. No sex, okay? We'll just hold each other. I'll rub your back."

So they lay on Rob's bed on the clean sheets underneath a splash of June sunlight, while Rob rubbed her neck and back, easing out the kinks with his strong, lean hands. He massaged her impersonally, gently, smoothing away her fear until she was drained and sleepy.

How she loved him.

But could she keep the rape from him forever? was the question that came to her as she drifted away at last into sleep.

At six-thirty Kara started dinner for four. Guilt feelings nudged at her from the afternoon. She hadn't seen Dr. Hay, her old therapist, in two years, but maybe it was time to go back. She still had some things to work on, she guessed. She had come so far in ten years and she wanted to go the rest of the way; she wanted her happiness to be perfect.

She busied herself in Rob's kitchen, preparing spinach-stuffed chicken breasts from a recipe she had clipped from an advertising page in her own paper. It would be colorful, garnished with tomatoes, and the only difficult part would be cutting the cooked chicken into one-inch slices. But Rob owned a collection of Norwegian knives that would do a surgeon proud, and she could probably find one that would do.

"Mmmm," Rob said, coming into the kitchen. "Smells like chicken."

She felt relaxed from the nap. "That means good, I hope. You eat so much steak I'm afraid that's all your nose will register."

"You can reform me. Anyway, the Beef Council loves me."

"Oh, I'm sure they do."

Angie and Russ arrived at eight-thirty in a cloud of motorcycle exhaust. Angie Bianca was Kara's current best friend, their friendship dating back to freshman year at Michigan State. Now Angie worked for Kara as sales manager at *Bargain Hound*. She was an aggressive, skilled sales person who could earn $60,000 somewhere else, but chose to stick with Kara because she believed in Kara's dream and wanted to head the sales force for fifteen or twenty shoppers.

Angie's boyfriend, Russ DeFlores, was a power train engineer at Ford Motor Company, in Dearborn, and had just bought a new Gold Wing Honda.

Rob went out to admire the cycle with Russ, while Angie, still carrying her metallic gold helmet, followed Kara into the house.

"Wedding gifts?" Angie said, pointing to the stack of boxes they had left on Rob's hall table.

"Mmmm."

"Well, what are they? What kind of loot did you get?" Angie had a figure like Bette Midler, and was dressed tonight in a Midler-esque jumpsuit unzipped to her considerable cleavage. There was an ambient sexuality about Angie that attracted men. She never had less than two men interested in her, and Kara remembered when there had been five.

"Oh, a tablecloth, another food processor, and a crystal punch bowl. Cindy ripped them open like it was Christmas morning, but then she decided we got rocks in our stocking. I believe the phrase was 'dumb gifts.' "

"Great kid." Angie made a face.

"Well—She's having trouble adjusting, that's all."

"Hah," Angie snorted. "I bet that's the understatement of the year. You're just lucky Rob only gets her on weekends. If you had to live with her full-time, I bet she'd drive you crazy. Daddy's little girl takes it hard when another woman comes along and steals Daddy away."

They walked into the kitchen, where Angie automatically began helping Kara chop carrots and slice celery for a tossed salad. Kara frowned, for some reason not wanting Angie to think the worst of Cindy.

"But it isn't like that, at least not a hundred percent. Cindy is warm and loving and bright. She's never said she hates me, she's never come right out and said anything bad against me. I do things with her—I'm teaching her how to sew . . ."

"Smart. She'll make herself a nice little ruffled apron so she can be 'Dad's' cook and hostess."

Kara put down the carrot she was peeling and laughed to hide her annoyance. "Hey, if she wants to cook I'll let her sew all the aprons she wants. Maybe I can teach her to make Chicken Kiev and Shrimp Marinara. We'll eat like kings. I'll get fat."

"She probably wouldn't mind that."

"Oh, shut up."

They peeled and chopped, grinning at each other, their momentary irritation rapidly fading. They saw each other every day at *Bargain Hound*, sometimes putting in 10, 12 hour days, but they still liked each other and they gave each other emotional support. Their friendship had survived being college roommates, boyfriends, lovers, fiancés, a spat or two, a messy divorce for Angie, and Angie being Kara's employee.

"Seriously, kid," Angie said. "You really ready for this wedding? It's scary, how close it's getting. Is it only three weeks away? Two showers down, one to go."

Kara tipped a chopping block full of carrot slices into a stainless steel salad bowl. Outdoors there was a roar as Rob and Russ started up the Gold Wing. "If you're scared, think how I must feel."

"You don't have to do it, you know. You could put it off indefinitely. Wear the ring, talk about getting married in the abstract, keep your house, give yourself some time to get to know him better."

"Better?" Kara smiled. "I've known him two years, Ang."

"That's not long enough. I knew Kenyon four years and look what happened to us. I wish I'd put *him* off for about thirty-two years."

Kara mimicked the stooped-over posture of a senior citizen. "Hey, Paw, think it's about time I moved in with you to the Rest Home? We know each other well enough now—let's see, ain't you eighty-nine this year?"

"I'm serious. You and Rob don't see each other every day the way some couples do. You only see him two or three times a week. You're on your best behavior with each other. You haven't seen him at his worst. You haven't seen him trimming the hairs in his ears yet. Or sitting down on the john to pee, the way Kenyon used to do."

"Hey. What is this? I thought you were going to be my matron of honor, not my voice of doom."

Angie laughed, flipping slices of tomato into the salad bowl. "Think that'll be enough tomato? Oh, don't mind me. One bloody divorce and I think everyone else is headed down the same path." Her smile faded. "All the same, Kara, I keep getting this funny feeling about you. It's pretty weird and psychic."

"You and your psychic feelings. What's this one about?"

"I don't know. I dreamed about you last night, I dreamed that you were dead."

"What?" Kara stood holding a shaker of parmesan cheese, a shiver rippling through her.

"You were on some stairs and a man was pushing you up them. The carpet had this diamond pattern on it. Like light. Yeah, like that. You were crying and there was a mirror . . . Then somehow you were lying on the floor dead. I woke up all shaky; I couldn't get back to sleep for the longest time."

Kara managed some reply.

Her tongue felt stiff, her throat suddenly dry. It was eerie—more than eerie!—what Angie had dreamed. Angie didn't know anything about the rape. It had happened before they met and was the one huge secret that separated them. In fact, she had told no one about it. Even Dr. Hay did not know all the details.

61

Angie went on, "I suppose, since you're getting married, and part of our friendship will change, maybe my unconscious mind interpreted that as dying."

"Who's talking about dying?" Rob's voice filled the kitchen. The two men stamped in, hearty, cheerful. "You should take a look at that Gold Wing, Kara, it's enough to make me want to go down and buy one. Get Russ to take you for a ride. It's superlative. The gentleman's cycle. What a toy."

She felt cold. "Maybe after dinner."

"Oh, come on out now and take a look," Rob urged. "See if you'd like being a biker's moll."

"I already am one," boasted Angie. "Russ is getting me a leather jacket and pants, and a rain outfit. One of those sexy slicker two-pieces."

Kara obediently followed the others out to the front door, feeling separated from their merriment. Always, always, she seemed at a distance from the people she cared about. What would she have been like if, ten years ago, Jerry Quick hadn't seen her and Laurel that day in the gas station? Would she have grown up free, confident, sexually assertive? At ease with herself, like Angie? Sometimes she envied Angie very deeply.

Life was a constant series of paths, and some of those paths you were pushed onto. Then you had to go forward whether you liked it or not. You couldn't ever go back and retrace your steps.

If she could go back, she would scream and kick and claw. She would poke her fingers into Jerry's eyes and rake her nails across his face.

"Come on," Rob urged. "Let Russ take you for a ride."

"All right," Kara said, managing a smile. She went to the door.

CHAPTER 6

Jerry switched the license plate first, doing it behind a Shoney's Big Boy by the trash dumpster, where the employees' cars were parked. The plate he selected was on a dented Thunderbird with a red finish that had been bleached orangy by the Florida sun. It had probably been brand new about the time he was taken to Raiford.

He had been inside long enough for a new car to turn into a pile of junk. The idea was scary somehow, and he felt his hands shake as he used the screwdriver he'd found in his mother's glove box.

In less than three minutes he had the job done. He wondered who the Thunderbird belonged to. Some busboy or line cook? Whoever it was, they hadn't been in prison, they'd been out doing whatever they wanted to, going to rock concerts, swimming at the beach, watching TV.

Suddenly he jammed the point of the screwdriver across what remained of the car's finish. *Fuck you*, he wrote with the screwdriver, digging it in.

Across Busch Boulevard there was a pancake house. He gorged himself on hash browns and blueberry pancakes, scowling at the middleaged waitress and making her so nervous she nearly dropped the syrup jug.

He didn't like them brunette or over thirty-five. Why'd they let women like that work in a restaurant anyway, with their pinched, disappointed mouths and their eyes that looked you over and decided you were nothing but a punk. Women like that were too much like his mother. They acted so holy, but they picked their noses just like everyone else and made ugly noises when they had sex.

He knew all about ugly noises. How many times had he watched his father doing stuff to his mother, back when he was six, seven? The thing he remembered most was the ragged, sawing sound of her voice, the gasps and begging. She thought he didn't remember that any more, but he did. He still thought of it sometimes. His father had shown power over his mother, bent her to his will, made her do what he wanted.

His meal finished, he went to a hardware store and bought a couple of extra rolls of duct tape, a small hammer, a better knife. He was angry at the high prices but paid. Then he stopped at a liquor store to buy some Jack Daniels. Another thing he hadn't enjoyed in ten years; hell, four swallows and he'd probably be crocked but he hungered for the high it would give him. He opened the bottle in the car, tilting it up to drink still in its long bag, the way winos did.

The whiskey burned his gullet, enflaming his nerves.

God, he'd been afraid he would never get drunk again, and now here he was with a whole bottle and money to buy fifty more if he wanted. He could hole up in some motel room and drink them all and when the maid came knocking, he'd throw one of the bottles against the door. Listen to the glass break. He could almost hear the sound now.

He drank some more of the whiskey and then drove out on Busch again, past Winn Dixie and Fatty's Ribs, muffler shops and putt-putt golf. It was 6:00 and yellow light glared off car windshields. Traffic surged around him, old men with white hair trying to cut him out.

This world, he thought with a rush of anger. It had gone on like this, the cars, the people, the rib places selling their half and whole slabs, all of it functioning without him, as if he didn't exist, as if he meant nothing.

Now that he was back, he still didn't make any difference. He didn't exist. It was eerily like being invisible.

Angrily he jammed his foot on the brake and turned around in a parking lot of SunWorld Realty, pealing the car out the way he had come, toward I-75 and the Frankland Bridge. His next stop was St. Petersburg.

If you don't finish things, they come back and wrecks you, was what this con, this old black guy named Whitetop, had told Jerry in Raiford. Whitetop was seventy-six, seventy-seven years old, stevedore strong, doing life for murdering a white man.

Boy, you listen to me. Old shit like a poison, it fester and blacken and grow lessen you do something about it. You got to go back and find it, know what I mean? Then you goes free, then you sits under a shade tree and smiles. Even that AIDS stuff, man. It come because people don't get their shit right.

Jerry thought of that as he drove across the little bridge that led to Coquina Key. The blue of Tampa Bay was visible between houses, flat, hazed, its color washed out by humidity. And hot, the sun almost yellow overhead, cooking everything in glare. It was beginning to bring back pictures in him, another day like this, the same sort of heat.

He drove slowly, getting the feel of it again. Rich bastards lived in places like these. They all owned boats, all thought they were hot shit. He wondered what some of these guys would do, what *Cleveland* would do, if he had to spend a week in Raiford, let alone ten years.

Jerry's laugh growled low in his throat.

Rapists got the butt end of everything in prison, reviled by cons and guards alike, punished over and over in ways the courts had never thought of. How would Cleveland like to be forced to swallow a big plug of prison soap, gagging it up and having it pushed back down again and again? Or be attacked in the machine shop with an electric drill? Blood running down him and two weeks in the prison hospital with infection.

Or, worst of all, to be shoved face down over a work-bench and have somebody's cock jammed up his rectum. Jerry shuddered, remembering the pain, the fear that he'd be split apart, his bowels spilling their contents to the inside of his body. After his second rape, he'd found Whitetop and it hadn't been as bad.

But the worst thing was the fear. The AIDS fear.

Addicts who'd used dirty needles, guys who used prostitutes, homos, shit, a prison was full of guys like that.

He felt his stomach twist, and unconsciously touched the glands in his neck, as streets flicked past him with names like Porpoise, Wahoo, Searobin. He bore left, searching for Mullet. Yeah, that was the name of the street, he still remembered it after all that time.

The house sat on an impossibly green lawn, salmon-colored bougainvillea massed to the side of the lot, giving it privacy from neighbors. It was a two-story Colonial with pillars, its windows shaded by green awnings to protect it from the sun. A circular window upstairs was etched with small, pie-shaped panes. From that window, he remembered, there was a panoramic view of Tampa Bay. It hadn't changed; even the carved wooden sign nailed to the front porch remained as Jerry remembered it.

The Clevelands.

He drove past the house twice more, disappointed that he didn't see any sign of women living there. Where was she? The tall blonde who'd stared at him in the mirror, eyes streaming with tears? Crying, recoiling, lips wobbly with her fear. She had hated him so much she burned with it. Even when he fucked her she had held back, refusing to give in, to offer one damn thing.

He reached over the seat for the bag with the Jack Daniels and took another swig before driving on down Mullet Drive. He parked along the street where he saw three or four cars already. He'd learned how to do this in Raiford. Whitetop told him, people never watched their own neighborhood. As long as you looked like you belonged, you could do anything.

Getting out of the car, he strolled back the way he had come. He wasn't nervous. In Ed's pants and shirt he looked the part, and he even began to enjoy himself as he observed the life of the neighborhood. Two men were getting into a *Barefoot Lawn* truck, their uniforms a yellow and green that exactly matched the truck. A pool boy lugged a big box of chemicals, sweating in the humidity.

People really lived like this, Jerry thought.

Taking his time, he walked back to the Cleveland house. As he drew near he glimpsed a man behind a picture window, bent over something. Yeah, it was a duffel bag. He must be packing.

Ken Cleveland zipped the duffel bag shut, pinching it together to hold the jeans, sweaters and hiking gear he'd stuffed inside. He was frowning, thinking more about Karalynn, and the conversation he'd had a few days ago with Laurel Fearn, than he was the prospective hiking trip.

"I think about him all the time," Laurel kept saying. "Don't you, Mr. Cleveland? Don't you think about him?

67

I keep hoping I'll read in the paper that he died in there—died in prison.''

"Guys like that never die in prison," Ken had responded bitterly. "They live to be a hundred years old, laughing at all of us."

"If I had the money," Laurel said in a drained voice. "If I had the money . . ." But she let her voice trail off and did not say what she would do.

Ken didn't have to work very hard to guess, though. He'd had the same sort of fantasies himself, constantly, not only right after the rape, but every day since then. In some of the fantasies, he had Jerry Quick tied up, and was bloodily slicing off the man's balls. In others, he was beating him with a baseball bat, pounding and pounding, a dozen home runs on the man's skull. Pounding until Jerry's mouth was shapeless and his eyes were smashed.

There was no punishment too severe for what a man like Jerry Quick had done, Ken believed. Sometimes his thoughts scared him with their violence. Sometimes he even wondered if there wasn't a small part of him that was like Jerry . . . and somehow that was the most frightening thought of all.

He went upstairs to his study, turned on his answering machine, and returned downstairs to switch off the air conditioning and turn on a small radio. His assistant manager at the shop would take his mail.

When his hiking trip was finished, Ken planned on driving up to Michigan, assuming there was still a wedding for him to go to. He had his doubts about that. Karalynn's history of engagement longevity was definitely poor. One of the engagements—to Chuck, was it?—had only lasted three weeks. She always got scared and ran. At this rate she'd be forty before she found something that lasted.

Oh, well. He would let her keep the check he'd sent. What was he going to do with it, get married again himself? No way.

He hefted up the heavy duffel, and proceeded through the living room to the garage.

Jerry took another turn around the block, and was just thinking about coming back later when Cleveland's garage door opened and a dark-colored Cadillac backed out. Cleveland himself was inside. Man, he was leaving already; this was incredible. And there appeared to be no dog.

Wary, yet fascinated, Jerry darted another look in the direction of the departing car. He felt his gut tighten, his balls draw up close to his body. He still carried the scars from this motherfucker. An old man and he'd come at Jerry like a screaming freight train. Jerry had never breathed right in his nose since.

Jerry kept on walking past, and as soon as he was sure the Cadillac was gone, he retraced his steps. In the blousy part of his shirt, tucked in his waistband, were the tools he would need: the tape, the hammer, and the duct tape.

Within three minutes, he had broken in. Cleveland had glued a fake security service label on his sliding glass door, and there was a radio playing, but Jerry shook his head at the man's stupidity. Hell, did he think thieves didn't know about stuff like that? In Raiford they traded information, it was like a goddamn business seminar, only the business was ripping people off.

He stepped inside the house, breathing in its smells. Cigarette smoke and dust and stale pizzas, the odors of a man who lives alone in a house. Junk was everywhere, stacks of laundry, books, magazines, beer cans, popcorn kernels, shoes, travel folders, a T-shirt flung across a chair. The shirt said *Bay Sail 'n Scuba*.

Jerry narrowed his eyes at that shirt. He thought of himself stabbing at a soft belly through cloth, feeling the tough resistance of skin and then non-resistance. When you stabbed someone you could smell the hot, foul stink of blood and intestines. Most people didn't know that. A man's insides stunk, Jerry had learned.

But a man would fight back, he knew. Women were much better, they gasped and cowered and cried, they let you take power.

He walked around the house, half remembering it. When he was here before, he'd been concentrating on the girls, he hadn't seen anything much. But the stairs. He remembered those. He walked upstairs, stepping on reflections of light created by that round window at the top, angling the sun.

The upstairs smelled unused. The girl's bedroom from ten years ago had been turned into another junk room, sports equipment and swim fins and scuba diving masks piled on the bed and on the floor. There were some golf clubs and an exercise bike, too.

Jerry glanced at the floor; he noticed that the carpeting had been replaced. It had been gold before, spattered and soaked with blood. Now it was light blue.

The mirror, however, was still there. Jerry stepped forward, turning a little so he could see the way the heavy muscles of his chest and forearms bulged out the shirt that had been Ed's. He had made the two girls stare at themselves, made them watch themselves, watch everything that was being done to them in the mirror.

It had been an incredible moment.

An incredible high, even better than sex, such a rush of power and energy and electricity that, for an instant, he'd been too shaken to do what needed to be done. He'd recovered quickly, of course. He'd never imagined. Never dreamed. The feel, their eyes, their terror, the way that girl Laurel had screamed and begged.

God.

The best twenty minutes of his life.

And then that fuck Cleveland had burst in and wrecked things, and suddenly Jerry was angry and afraid and alone at Raiford with guys who had the power to butt-fuck him any time they pleased, and give him AIDS, too. He could have AIDS right now. He didn't even know. They didn't give blood tests in prison because guys would go half crazy if they found out they were carriers.

Suddenly he could smell blood, and he was tired of the room, leaving it quickly to explore further down the hall. There was a bathroom, a blue terry robe hanging on the corner of the door, saggy looking and comfortable. A towel on the floor. A man's bathroom, with no frills, and a dirty sink.

He strode to the next room and discovered what he was looking for, a desk where Cleveland probably made out bills and made telephone calls. Like the rest of the house it was untidy, piled high with papers and catalogs and three or four *Penthouses*.

Jerry lifted up one of the magazines, flipping it open to a page where two naked girls, twins, were licking each other's nipples. Both had identical brown nipples and sparse blond muffs. He'd seen the issue before at Raiford. He'd lived for pictures like this . . . and now he was going to get the real thing again.

A small black machine like a baby tape recorder sat on the desk with a little label on it that said Code-a-Phone. It must be a phone answering machine, but he had never used one and didn't know whether this one was set to *on* or *off*. Unless that little red light . . . ?

Yeah, the machine was on. The answering machine made him feel angry, excluded. *He* had never owned one, nor had his mother.

His eyes were drawn to a photograph on the wall over the desk. It showed a young woman of about twenty-six, with glossy wings of blonde hair combed away from her face. She had high cheekbones, full lips, and cool, private eyes, far prettier than any women who had ever appeared in *Penthouse*.

Jerry stared, feeling his mouth hang open. A light shiver passed all the way over his body, from shoulders to groin. Jesus, was this Karalynn? The blonde girl grown up? It had to be.

Looking at the picture made him sweat. She looked too perfect, like someone he could never have. A girl who would gaze straight through him and think he was a punk, an ex-con. If she stood in an elevator with him she would pull herself away, not wanting to touch him. She would pretend he was not even there. He could be the handsomest guy in six states, and she would be repelled by him, because he wasn't her class.

Savagely he swiped at the photograph with the flat of his hand, knocking it off its nail. It crashed to the desk top. Through smashed glass Karalynn Cleveland gazed up at him, cool and remote, the lines of her nose and cheekbones beautiful.

Jerry knocked the picture onto the floor and kicked it under the desk, where it hit the baseboard. Then he bent and picked it up and held it like a weapon, smashing it against the desk until the glass was powdery and the photograph inside was crumpled and torn.

He was shaking.

Finally he remembered why he was here. He threw the picture against the wall and began going through the desk. Angrily he jerked open the top desk drawer and rummaged through papers, envelopes, rubber bands, business cards, until he found what he was looking for.

A little black address book.

CHAPTER 7

"You're looking very good, Kara," said Dr. Hay, her old therapist, ushering Kara into her office. "You've put on four or five pounds but you were too thin before."

They smiled at each other, assessing the changes two years had made in them. Dr. Berniece Hay appeared tireder, the creases at the corners of her mouth and at her eyes scored deeper than they had been. She was sixty-six and looked it, with a cap of silver hair that was fine-spun, like dandelion fluff.

Kara wanted to get the preliminaries over with. "I guess I just needed a shot of 'Dr. Hay,' something to make me feel better. Not that I don't feel great," she added hastily. "Because I do, really. Everything's going just great. More than great! It's only that . . . maybe I need . . . just some talking," she finished lamely.

She looked around the small office, which seemed just the same as the last time she was here, a womb-like haven from the world of ugly emotions and problems. There was mauve carpet, a muted gray and mauve striped wallpaper, soothing floral paintings. A reproduction grandfather clock ticked peacefully, a counterpoint to the traffic noises from Walton Boulevard, on which the clinic fronted, not far from Crittenton Hospital.

Kara took her old seat on the rose-colored loveseat, shifting nervously. She'd stopped the sessions before because they had become too uncomfortable. She didn't want the same thing to happen again. This visit would be more in the line of a check-up, not a major commitment to months of therapy.

"Tell me where you are in your life right now, Kara," Dr. Hay began. "What's been happening with you."

"Well . . . my business is taking off, and I'm really dreaming big. I'm applying for another bank loan to expand to two more suburbs, and I really think they're going to give it to me this time. Also, I'm getting married in three weeks."

"Congratulations."

"Yes, to Rob Devers, remember? I'd just started dating him when—the last time I saw you. He's an architect, he's very nice, he's divorced with a ten-year-old daughter, he lives here in town . . ."

Kara embarked on an enthusiastic and upbeat version of the past twenty-four months, covering Rob, the wedding plans, the business, Cindy. She felt the therapist's eyes focused intently on her as she described Rob and even Cindy in glowing terms. Once or twice Dr. Hay wrote something on a small pad of paper she kept near her chair. Glancing at her watch, Kara realized she had used up forty of her allotted fifty minutes.

Suddenly the whine of an ambulance siren cut into the peace of the small, mauve-carpeted office. The sound, emanating from the hospital only a half mile away, cut across Kara's words like a surgical knife. She tensed, recrossing her legs and suppressing a shudder. That wail, screeching along her nerve ends—*God*.

"Does the sound bother you?" Dr. Hay asked.

Kara felt a flash of irritation at the typical therapist-type question. Of course Dr. Hay knew it bothered her.

"Yes," she replied shortly.

"Can you tell me what you are feeling right now, Kara?"

"I'm feeling—okay, I'm angry," she burst out. "I got another phone call from Laurel this week. I hate them! I hate those calls! Why can't she leave me alone, Dr. Hay, why does she have to do that to me?"

She repeated the conversation, conscious of the clock ticking away, their session drawing to a close. "She was just like always, hysterical. She said *he's* thinking about us. He wants to find us and—and do it again—" She steadied her voice. "Laurel just upsets me so. I know I let her get to me. I shouldn't, but I do. And I feel so guilty afterward."

"And now you've been thinking about everything she said," Dr. Hay prompted.

"Yes, it was the way she believed," Kara said slowly. "I mean, she really *believed* everything. She really thought she saw him, and that's so creepy. Because sometimes I think I see him, too. And I dream about him sometimes, that he's down there in that prison in Florida, thinking about us, having terrible fantasies about us, remembering what he did. Getting off on it, or maybe blaming us, wanting to hurt us. I mean, why wouldn't he? We testified against him."

"But he's in prison now. He doesn't know where you live."

An image suddenly popped into Kara's mind.

Blood everywhere, gushing like red paint, shiny in the light. And the piece of Laurel he'd cut off, the nipple still visible on it, the hunk of meat he had carved off her friend

75

and just tossed to the floor, while Laurel screamed blood-curdlingly . . .

Blackness flowed in over her eyes. Dr. Hay's office seemed suddenly to consist of white dots on black, a photographer's negative image. Strange, thready sensations clashed in her brain.

"Lean over," she heard Dr. Hay say. "Lean over, Kara, put your head between your knees. That's it . . . that's it . . . Now just stay there for a minute until the blood goes back to your head again."

Kara did as she was told, and in a minute the blackness receded and she could sit up. Clammy perspiration covered her face, and her hands and feet had gone cold.

"I nearly fainted, didn't I?"

"You came close. Do you feel better now? You'd better just sit still for a couple minutes while we talk. I'll give you a few extra minutes in the session."

Kara nodded. "I can't believe I almost passed out."

"That's why Laurel calls, Kara. She knows very well that you get these feelings. She wants to upset you, to work on your guilt, to make you pay. She's never gotten any professional help, and she blames you because you were rescued by your father in time to avoid being cut the way she was, you didn't have to suffer the way she did."

"*I* suffered, too."

"But to her you got off easy."

"She blamed me for not inviting her to my wedding, Dr. Hay." Kara heard herself steer the subject away. "I didn't want to invite her, I couldn't. It would have been disaster to ask her. Even my father—you know how he is. He'll come up here, he'll have a few drinks too many, he'll start talking about rape. Oh, not Jerry, I made him swear he wouldn't mention him, so he'll talk in general about it. He'll start lecturing everyone, ranting and raving.

I just wish Rob and I could run off and elope!'' she finished angrily.

"Oh? Weren't you planning a celebration?"

"Yes, at Abiding Presence—we were. Are. But I've been having so many doubts. I'm not *sure* the way I was when Rob gave me the ring. I . . . I get these little jiggles of worry. Is it right, am I taking on too much, will I be able to handle it?"

"Will you be able to handle what, Kara?"

"Why, the—'' Kara stopped. She dropped her glance to her lap, where her hands were now twisted together, perspiring against the fabric of her cotton skirt. Her rings caught the sun, the diamond sending out a crystalline flash of light. She'd forgotten how perceptive Dr. Hay was. The woman was almost psychic in her ability to see beneath the surface.

"Kara, the last time we saw each other, you had just met Rob Devers and you were wondering how much of your past to reveal. You were very anxious about that."

Kara began fiddling with the diamond, turning the two carat stone around and around, so that its facets alternately glittered and were opaque.

"I didn't tell him," she finally blurted.

"I had a feeling that was the case."

"And now it's getting bad, Dr. Hay, because he knows me well enough to know there's something I'm holding back. In bed, that's where I can't hide it. The other day . . ." Kara moistened her lips nervously. "He said I rolled away from him like he was an axe murderer. Normal women don't act like that. I'm afraid I'm going to lose him!"

The therapist nodded. "You've held back an important part of yourself, haven't you?"

"That's it, in a nutshell," Kara said bitterly. "But why should I tell him? He'll ask all kinds of questions. He'll make me relive it detail by detail. He—I'll have to tell him when, where and how. I can't," she whispered. "I *can't* go through it all over again. I worked too hard to forget it, to get past it."

Dr. Hay gazed out of the window toward the shopping center across the street, its anchor store a Great Scott supermarket. The parking lot had been carved out of a natural bluff, and an erosion-protection fence had been erected at its edge, consisting of huge blocks of cement piled behind wire-mesh fencing.

"Look out there, look at that wall," Dr. Hay remarked. "You've built a wall, too, Kara, around the rape, a containment wall. You built the blocks high and you built them thick. But when you least expect it, a piece of mortar shakes loose and falls out. Your wall gets a hole and things seep through."

Kara's laugh was ragged. "Yes. Yes."

The therapist leaned forward, something in her expression making Kara think fleetingly of Eleanor Roosevelt. "Kara, you've never faced that rape. Not really, not head on. Oh, we've discussed it here, and you've learned that it wasn't your fault, that you were a victim, you didn't cause that violence to happen to yourself or Laurel. You've learned that rape isn't about sex at all, it's about violence. And that's good, you've made a lot of progress. But you've tried to handle the rape by walling it off, sealing it away. And that device doesn't work so well any more, does it? Walls don't really work, not forever."

Walls. Involuntarily Kara shook her head. Every muscle in her body felt clenched. She was living a false life, a life built around a terrible secret she couldn't share with anyone, not her fiancé and not her best friend.

She jerked her eyes upward to meet Dr. Hay's again. "But how?" she cried. "How can I deal with it when it happened *ten years ago*? I can't get on a time machine and go back to 1980 and make it happen differently. And will telling Rob make things different or better? Will it soothe and heal me? No! How can it?'' she burst out. ''It'll only make me feel worse. Because he'll pity and blame me. He'll ask questions! He'll say that I—that I was the one— that *I*—''

''He'll act like your father?'' the therapist inquired gently.

Kara reached for one of the tissues that Dr. Hay kept in a hand-painted box on a small coffee table. She wiped her eyes, scrubbing at the tears that stabbed like tiny knives. The clenched feeling in her stomach was growing stronger.

''My father made me relive the rape every day,'' she said. ''I suppose I hate him for that. Yes, I guess I do. I really don't want him coming to my wedding. I wish I'd told him not to come, but I didn't want to hurt his feelings. Can you believe it?''

Dr. Hay's voice was calm. ''Kara, you're feeling the effects of the wall you've built, aren't you? It's affected all your relationships. But especially the one with your fiancé.''

''Yes, it has,'' she said dully.

Dr. Hay glanced at the grandfather clock, and then at a case folder on her desk. ''I'm going to have to break now, but I want to say that I think we should arrange for some more visits if it's all right with you. This is something that will need working on.''

Kara got to her feet. ''You want me to tear down walls, don't you? Get out an axe and just chop them down.''

''Are you happy with the walls, Kara? Is this the way you really want it to be?''

She felt a rush of anger. ''It doesn't matter to you if it hurts, if I have to go back and rake up hell, because all you have to do is sit there and listen and give me your brilliant metaphors for what is wrong with me! It's so easy, so easy for you—*you weren't raped*!''

Dr. Hay rose too, giving Kara a sad, Mona Lisa smile, as if such outbursts occurred in this office eight times a day. "No, I wasn't raped. But I've received special training in working with women who have been, and I've attended seminars that focus on rape. I think we have much to talk about, Kara, and next time—"

"There won't be a next time!" Kara screamed.

She couldn't believe the waves of anger that surged through her, like electricity gone amok. She had gone completely whacko, she decided. She backed out of the office, shutting Dr. Hay's door with a bang, and hurried through to the clinic waiting room. There, she stopped to write a check, and thrust it through the glass window at the receptionist. She half-ran out of the building to her car.

She got in and sat there, shaking with release of tension and shame. My God, she had *screamed* in there. She had shouted at the woman who had helped her so much before, who had given her hours of kindness. Her head had begun to throb, and she rubbed at her temple with the heel of her hand.

Dr. Hay lived in a therapist's never-never land, where people could talk out anything, no matter how ugly or traumatic, and "come to terms with it," one of her favorite expressions. But some things, Kara believed, you could not come to terms with. They seared you, they scarred you, even mutilated a part of you, just as a mastectomy mutilated a woman's chest. Just as Jerry Quick had mutilated Laurel.

As Kara sat there, she felt the anger recede, but she knew it would still remain underneath, like a small bad spot in an otherwise perfect apple.

She had walled off her rape.

So what?

It had protected her, hadn't it? It had enabled her to lead a normal life, finish college, start her own business, meet a man like Rob. Most people would say she was doing pretty well.

She *was* doing pretty well.

She started the car with a roar of the motor that caused a teenaged boy, slouching toward the clinic with his mother, to stop and stare. She pulled out of the clinic and turned right into the traffic, heading toward the village of Rochester.

She was supposed to meet Rob at the Cooper's Arms, a restaurant on Main Street that had been designed to resemble an English pub. She and Rob had their first date here, in one of the high-backed wooden booths that featured a romantically dark atmosphere. To her the restaurant would always symbolize the excitement of having Rob suddenly reach across the table and take her hand in his for the first time.

She pulled around to the back, where a small parking lot, used by local residents, opened up off an alley. There was one empty space. Pulling in, she leaned her head against the seat back and breathed deeply.

It was ridiculous to upset herself as she had. She herself had chosen to go back to Dr. Hay—what had she expected the woman would tell her, that everything was fine and good? Therapists always saw a need for their services, especially when they were getting paid seventy-five dollars an hour. Besides, if she didn't calm down, Rob was sure to notice something. He was very quick at sensing her moods.

She pulled down the lighted makeup mirror on the visor and began to reapply her makeup, using pressed powder to get rid of the faint tear tracks still visible on her skin.

As she was getting out of the car, she saw Rob's silver-metallic Mercur pull into the alley.

"Kar! Hi, there!" He pressed the button that lowered his window and leaned out, grinning at her. He looked rakishly handsome today, a glossy thatch of dark hair falling over his forehead. "Hungry?" he called out. "Just a minute, I'll park. Is there another space in that lot? Or am I going to have to go on the street? Damn.''

She waited while he backed out of the alley and found a place on the street. In a minute he loped toward her, wearing light blue pleated pants and an open-collared, striped shirt. A pair of women crossing the street paused to look in his direction, their eyes lingering.

Kara swallowed, feeling a surge of pride and fear. Other women envied her this man, she'd have to be a fool not to recognize that. He was what her mother used to call ''a catch.'' She couldn't mess this up. She couldn't lose him.

To hell with Dr. Hay. She was never going to go back there. She was going to marry Rob and bend all of her efforts to being happy with him, to putting the rape permanently behind her.

The restaurant's back room was filled with the usual businessmen's lunch crowd, five men to every woman. Kara knew many of them. She greeted several downtown store owners who had taken ads in *Bargain Hound*, and a photographer with whom she had worked at the *Rochester Eccentric*.

''When's the day you get your ball and chain welded on?'' Wally wanted to know.

''Ball and chain? Give me a break,'' Kara said, grinning. ''Anyway, it's the first week in July.''

''Hey, how's the business going? I hear real good things about you, I hear you're going to give a lot of people a run for their money.''

''I plan to,'' she said proudly.

She and Rob were shown to a booth set in a long row of other booths, each illuminated by a red-gold, flickering candle. The glow illuminated the interesting lines and hollows of Rob's face. When the waitress came, Rob ordered her a strawberry daiquiri and himself a martini with a twist.

"Hey, babe," he said when the girl had left. He put his hand over hers on the glass. "You look kinda frazzled today. A hard time at work?"

Work. It seemed hours since she had left her office for Dr. Hay's. "Oh, the usual," she told him. "Phone calls all over the place, and my receptionist called in again with that bladder infection. I swear she gets one every two months. Angie and I took turns answering the phone until I could get a Kelly Girl. And Angie keeps telling me we need another salesman, so I've got to start interviewing for that. I don't know where I'm going to find anyone half as good as she is. Or half as crazy. Maybe I'm weird, but I like crazy people, it adds a little life to the place."

She was chattering too much, but she couldn't seem to stop. That was her reaction to stress—talk. She told Rob some of her plans for distributing *Bargain Hound* in Waterford, west of Pontiac, and Drayton Plains. She repeated a weird story Angie had told her about a cactus.

"Angie's cousin took it home from the store and she said to her husband, 'This cactus looks like it's breathing.' So they called up the plant store and the man told them, 'Go and get a garbage bag and put the cactus in it and tie it up tightly. Then put the bag in a closet, and we'll be right over to pick it up.' So a man drove right over and picked up the bag, and as soon as they got it in the yard, the cactus exploded. And do you know what was inside?"

"I can't possibly guess," Rob said.

"About 250 baby tarantulas! If they hadn't called the plant store they would have had the house full of tarantulas! They must have been breeding right inside the cactus!"

"You mean, that wasn't a joke? I thought you were telling a joke."

"No, it was real. It really happened. Angie's cousin swears it's true."

Rob laughed at her story, and then his face changed,

and she realized he was looking at her with almost the same expression as Dr. Hay.

"Kara. You're talking a blue streak, and if you fiddle any more with that straw, the waitress is going to come and take it away from you."

Kara looked down at the table top where somehow she had created a pink puddle of strawberry. "Sorry."

"Is anything wrong?"

"Wrong? What would there be wrong?"

"I don't know," he said. "Sometimes I think there's something you're not telling me, something major."

She flushed. "A tough day at work, that's all."

"Maybe. I just get the feeling there's more to it than that."

"What would I not tell you? All I'm hiding is a maaaad passion for you," she parried, giving him a flirty smile that showed her pretty teeth on which her father had spent several thousand dollars for braces. She had only had the braces off a year when—

God. Stop.

Rob opened up the menu. "What are you having? I'm not that hungry today, maybe I'll just get a salad."

"What? You, salad?" she teased.

He looked aggrieved. "You know I only eat steak on weekends. I almost never eat meat for lunch, I really prefer something light."

"Okay."

"Well . . ." He restudied the menu. "There is a nice ground round."

The waitress returned, order pad in hand. Kara ordered the salad, Rob the ground round. Kara allowed herself to relax, leaning back in the booth and starting to enjoy the ambiance of being here. She decided that she *would* tell Rob about the rape, maybe in a year or so when they were more comfortable with each other. When they were safely married, two old married shoes.

At the thought a wave of feeling flooded her, so intense that her eyes moistened.

"Hey. Handsome guy. I love you," she said, touching his hand, sliding her fingers through his.

His eyes gleamed as he joined in the little love-game they sometimes played. "Even if you become a millionaire? Will you still love me when you're filthy rich?"

"When *we're* filthy rich," she said.

"Use me, abuse me, keep me as your love object," Rob said. "I want to be a rich woman's toy." He smiled at her. "Hey, babe. Thanks for putting up with me and everything that comes with me. Don't ever change."

"I won't," she promised.

CHAPTER 8

Jerry was almost ready now to do what he had to. He got on I–275 and headed north over the Frankland Bridge again, the blue of Tampa Bay making his eyes smart. To take his mind off things, he tested the feel of Sally's car, trying to get used to the new dashboard. He hated driving a car he wasn't familiar with. Ten years he hadn't driven. It made him feel not a man. Exiting the bridge he screeched the tires just to show who he still was.

Jerry Quick and fuck them all.

Bitch, he thought, meaning his mother.

Not wanting to give him her car. Then hiding her money from him as if she thought he might steal it. Hell, he damn well knew she had more of it stashed away, she'd always done that, kept it in little piles through the house. Her insurance policies, she said. He bet she still hadn't given him all of it.

At Hillsborough Avenue he suddenly pulled off the freeway and found a Sambo's. He squealed into the lot, peeling rubber. He laughed bitterly to himself as he stood in the small, tiled lobby waiting to be seated. He might have been away for ten years, but not much had changed with Sally. Only the man. Ed or Ted or whatever the fucker's name was. She bowed and scraped to him, giving everything to him, while her son had to wait.

The restaurant smelled of grits and hash browns, the smell going directly to the salivary glands in Jerry's mouth, although the pancakes he'd eaten were still not digested.

He'd fantasized about hash browns at Raiford, lying on his bunk, picturing their crisp brown-latticed top greasy with butter and salt, meaty white on the inside. And beside them a bottle of Heinz, so thick you would have to pound it with the heel of your hand to get it to pour. And being able to order plate after plate if he wanted, sitting there and shoveling it in until his belly was a drum and his lips burned from too much salt.

"One?" inquired the hostess, an 18-year-old blonde whose uniform was too tight and too short, clinging to perky breasts and a high, little waistline.

He answered her. "Yeah. One."

"Smoking okay?"

Did they always ask that in restaurants now?

"Yeah, if you got a match." He gave her a Jerry smile, crooked and just slightly mocking, and a long, heavy-lidded look that had worked excellently before, and apparently still did. The girl giggled and flashed a look at him.

"At the cashier they have book matches. Would you want a booth, sir?"

"Hey. What's this sir stuff?" He kept the smile, kept the contact with her eyes. "Come to a good restaurant and they call you sir."

"Sorry." She giggled. "It's what they tell us. We have to call customers sir."

He read her name tag. "Well, I'm going to call you

Juli. You're too pretty to work here, know that? You oughta be, I don't know, in a fancier place, wearing a silk dress maybe. Or at the beach in a bikini. A *string* bikini.''

"This way." She flushed pink, leading him to his table with a self-conscious hip sway. Two old ladies in a booth eating spaghetti looked up and stared at him. Jerry strutted a little. He still had the effect, still could work the women.

He seated himself in a booth for four, and she handed him the menu. "Coffee?"

"Yeah. Coffee, black."

She gave him a shy smile and left for the kitchen, her hips twitching under her brown nylon uniform, faint rims of panty lines visible. Jerry watched her, imagining her kneeling down in front of him, her naked buttocks thrust up to him, her dark soft nest visible beneath the crease. Maybe she'd be whimpering a little, her voice breathy. Whimpering meant they were eager but trying to hide it. Jerry enjoyed it when they held back like that, because it made the final triumph so much better when he pushed into them and mastered them.

Even the thought was getting him hard.

Oh, Jesus, it had been a long time. If thoughts counted, he must have fucked a hundred thousand girls at Raiford, listening to them squeal.

He examined the menu, deciding on two breakfast specials with extra hash browns. It was a good ploy. She'd giggle when he ordered so much food, she wouldn't think he really wanted two meals. He'd grin at her and invite her to sit down in the booth with him and eat one of the breakfasts. She'd laugh and blush, intrigued. But of course she couldn't do it because her manager would kill her. So he'd ask her who the manager was, because he was going to go up and request special permission.

By then she'd be laughing and blushing and flirting, entranced with Jerry, interested in him. So he'd ask her to go on her dinner break across the street to another restaurant with him. Once in the car, in the parking lot . . . Jerry knew how to go from there.

Girls had always been easy for him and he knew by the way this one acted that they still were. The knowledge buoyed him, made him feel high. He might be older but he was *Jerry*. He wasn't going to die of AIDS, he was going to go back digging into his previous life and he was going to *make it all right*.

She was back with the coffee. "Here's your coffee, all nice and fresh."

She was nice and fresh. He watched as she set down three of those little containers of cream.

"I think I'll have two of the #2 breakfasts," he said, cocking his head to one side.

"Oh," she said. "I'm not your waitress."

"You're not?"

"Inez is your waitress, she'll be over in a minute to take your order."

She pointed to a dark, squat girl who looked Cuban. He felt rejected, put down to size. "Hey, I don't want another waitress, I want you. I thought maybe you could sit down with me, have a little breakfast. They do let you taste this stuff they serve, don't they?"

She smiled nervously. Maybe one of the other waitresses had said something, spooked her. Maybe it was the "13½" engraved on his left forearm, with the white, ridged scar where the homemade prison tattoo had become infected. It meant *twelve jurors, one judge, and a half-assed chance*.

"Oh," she said. "I've tried most of the food here and it's good, see, but I have a boyfriend and he doesn't like me flirting around."

"And you do everything your boyfriend says?"

"Yeah, just about. See, we're getting married next

Christmas.'' And she flashed a tiny engagement ring at him, a puny band crusted with a few diamond chips.

Jerry felt a hollow blackness yawn inside him, a blackness that was edged with flashing silver razors. Shit. He couldn't even pick up an 18-year-old waitress.

"Okay," he said, feeling his mouth go hard.

She backed away, frightened at the change in him. "I'll get your waitress."

"Don't bother. I'm leaving. This place sucks."

"But sir—"

He wanted to kill her. He wanted to make her kneel and jam a knife right up her tight young ass until she howled. She shouldn't have called him sir again. Why had she done that, why was it women did things like that? Women knew how to cut off a man's balls, to lay them out on a platter for him, steaming and hot.

He pushed past her, stalking past the booths full of people, hating them for their complacent, overweight faces shining with hamburger grease. He was full of the black feeling. That bitch was lucky he had other plans, because otherwise he would have waited for her outside the restaurant. Taken it from her, because that's what a man did when a girl would not give it. A man had a right to take what he wanted. Her fault if she would not give it over when he wanted it.

The fucking slut bitch.

CHAPTER 9

The small office building that Kara rented had started life as a Cape Cod bungalow. It sat back from the street in a row of boutiques, sandwiched between Needle Nook and Wild Wings, the area flanked by a large ACO hardware on the south corner. The front door still bore the original etched glass panels. In tune with the boutiquey neighborhood, Kara had had a wooden sign carved that depicted her logo, a floppy-eared dachshund.

She pulled into the eight-space parking lot, taking the space near the door that was tacitly reserved for her. On the porch, three tubs of geraniums added to the boutique effect. She paused to pluck a dead blossom from one of them, tossing it over the porch into the welter of lilac bushes at the side.

She had a love/hate relationship with this building.

She loved its cozy hominess, the beautiful dark doors and baseboards that were right out of the 1930s, the original cut-glass chandelier. But the bathrooms had perpetual plumbing problems, the insulation dated from the thirties, and ice dams over the upstairs windows had ruined the plaster.

Also, the place was far too small. She didn't know how she was going to stuff another sales person into the rooms that already seemed cramped with her staff of four. With her plans for expansion, she would soon have to move. That meant one more thing to do, shopping around for office space. She pictured herself occupying two or three more offices before she finally reached the size she hoped for.

She walked in, pausing to greet the 22-year-old college student that Kelly Services had sent her. The girl was simultaneously trying to type invoices and answer the phone.

"Six messages for you," the girl, Lynette, told her. "Petruzzello's called about your reception, and Meadowbrook Florist called about your flowers, they said to call them right back. A lady wants to know if you ever use stringers. A woman says you spelled her name wrong. And a Dr. Hay—"

"All right, thanks." Kara took the sheaf of pink messages and carried them through to her office, which once had been a dining room and still possessed a massive, red-burnished mahogany breakfront. The walls were hung with framed front pages of *Bargain Hound*, including the first issue ever published. She had also hung photographs of herself with Isiah Thomas, the basketball star, who had once given her an interview, and Cheryl Tiegs, who came through town last fall to promote her line of clothes.

At her desk was a Zenith computer, and beside it Kara's new HP LaserJet Series II printer, with two cartridge slots. She and the receptionist shared the printer.

"Hey, how was lunch?" Angie poked her head around the door. Her bleached hair was tousled, the way it always got after she'd been on the phone for a while. She had the habit of running her fingers through it.

"I blew my diet," Kara admitted, putting the stack of messages by the phone. She decided she would not return Dr. Hay's call—what was the use? She would write her a note of apology and tell her she would not be back.

"Strawberry cheesecake for dessert," she added, sinking into the expensive executive chair that Rob had bought her this year for her birthday. It was very luxe, with controls that tilted the seat forward and back, and also moved it up and down. It reminded her of a bucket seat in a car. She twirled despondently around in it.

"Yeah, well, not to worry," Angie said dryly. "You still wear a size eight, so I don't think you need to hate yourself too much. Want some coffee?"

"God, I'd love some."

"Oh, and I got a call this morning from Sterling Furs. She's finally buying a half page and I think I can convince her to get twelve insertions . . . is that a *coup* or is that a *coup*?"

While Angie went to the Mr. Coffee Kara kept on the breakfront, Kara leaned back in her chair, feeling the firm pressure in the middle of her spine. She felt depleted, as if Dr. Hay and Rob had taken all of her energy.

"What's that sigh?" Angie said, pouring coffee. "Did you and Rob have a spat?"

"No . . ."

"What do you mean, *no* . . ." Her friend mimicked her tone.

"I mean, I guess I just have the jitters, that's all."

"I knew it. I knew you did."

"But it's okay," Kara said hastily. "Lots of people get cold feet before they get married. I'm not going to let that stop me from marrying Rob. I'll just tough it out. In about six months, I'll laugh at all of this."

Angie handed Kara a mug that said *I'm 80% Sweetheart, 20% Bitch, Don't Test Me*. She had given it to Kara for her birthday, filled with chocolates. "Can I write that down? In six months you're going to laugh."

"Ang—"

"Well, you know what I think."

Kara reached under her desk to the power strip for her computer, and touched the switch with her toe. The machine activated itself with a burble. The screen blinked and produced a full color menu.

"Oh, shit," Kara said.

"Now, is that any language for a bride-to-be. You're supposed to be all sweetness and sunshine."

"Well, I'm not."

"Hey, I told you, maybe you ought to postpone it for a while. Rob won't mind that much, he's devoted, and maybe it'll give Cindy a chance to calm down, too. She needs some time to get used to you. Divorce isn't easy for kids either."

"It isn't Cindy," Kara sighed. She pushed the F1 key to call up WordPerfect. There was a flash of black, then the screen became a deep, electric blue, with the program's status line in the lower right corner.

"I mean, it *is* Cindy, and it's just everything all at once. The wedding. Umpteen phone messages, the flowers, the cake, the reception. Do I want chocolate or spice cake? Do I want to serve ham and chicken, or chicken and fish, or chicken and beef? I'm even vacillating on my wedding dress. It's home hanging in my closet and I'm wondering if I'm going to look like a frilly fool weighted down with thirty pounds of sequins and lace. I mean, all that lace isn't me. Sometimes I wish we'd just elope."

She surprised herself with the passion in her voice, with an edge of desperation.

Angie shrugged. "Elope? That's what I did when I got married to Kenyon. We were married on vacation in Maui. In the courthouse in a town named Wailuki, I couldn't even pronounce it. But when you do it that way, it doesn't feel permanent. Nobody's there to witness it, nobody who counts in your life. It's not sanctified or something, it just makes it that much easier to break up later.''

Flutters swam in Kara's stomach, like tiny, aggressive goldfish. "I'm not going to break up. Once I marry Rob, that's it.''

"That's what I said, too.''

"Dammit, Angie—''

"Look, just wait six months," Angie urged. "It won't hurt to postpone the festivities. You'll just lose a couple of deposits. Why do you have to do it now?''

"Because he wants it.''

"Maybe, but do you want it? I don't think you do, Kara, not a hundred percent. I think you're very ambivalent about this.''

They sipped their coffee in silence, while Kara moodily played with the keys on her computer, typing lines of Z's, then erasing them. It wasn't the wedding she really wanted to talk about, she thought.

No, it was Jerry, and the phone call from Laurel. But she and Angie might as well be in different counties. She didn't have anyone to talk to about this, no one in whom she could confide her full feelings. She'd even dumped Dr. Hay, the one person in Michigan who knew most about her. Ironically, it was only Laurel who she might have talked to—but even then, she and Laurel did not live the same nightmare.

He had carved on both of their bodies—but the difference was huge. With Laurel it had amounted to an amateur mastectomy, a literal hacking-off of most of her right breast. An act so hideous that it surpassed viciousness and became totally monstrous. Yet the injury he had inflicted on Kara had been mild by comparison, just a line carved under her breast and some almost invisible scars on her buttocks.

Kara could not even imagine the type of mind that could

have conceived such an act. She truly believed that Jerry Quick was not human, not as she thought of it.

He possessed the body of a man, yes, and the brain of a man, but somehow it had all gone cancerous with violence. Jerry was terrifying because he had no soul or spirit, no goodness or caring. He was totally selfish. Terrifying because he would *do anything*.

"Kara?" She heard Angie say. "Jeez, what's wrong with you? You've been staring at that computer for the past five minutes. And there's nothing on the damn screen."

"I'm fine."

"Well, I'll be very glad when you finally make up your mind about this damn wedding," Angie snapped. "In case you don't know it, you're getting hard to live with."

Later, after she had returned her phone calls, with the exception of Dr. Hay, Kara keyed up the basket story and forced herself to finish it. Suddenly the writing seemed wooden and crude. She began cutting sentences, adding some more quotes from Dolly Beaton, the owner of a basket boutique on 4th Street, one of her advertisers.

"Baskets are folk art," she typed, then sat staring blankly at the screen, remembering the hoarseness of Laurel's voice, the absolute certainty.

She felt sure that Laurel was right.

Jerry Quick *was* thinking about them. Suddenly she could sense his thoughts, the dank, hot savagery of his fantasies about them.

She had not called the prison, she thought uneasily. Maybe she should, just to assure herself that he was still there safely behind bars serving out the thirty-year sentence he had been given by the judge. If she knew he was still there, she'd relax, wouldn't she? She'd push him to the back of her mind, off into the haze of the past.

She reached for the telephone to dial information, then stopped in the middle of dialing the 904 Florida area code.

She put the receiver back on the cradle, her hands shaking. The very thought of talking to some warden or warden's assistant made her tremble.

Talking to a real human voice, to someone who was literally only a thousand yards or so away from Jerry, would bring him entirely too close for comfort. It was the same feeling that had always paralyzed her before when she attempted to call the prison.

Talking to the prison would bring Jerry back into her life.

And God help her, she was terrified of that.

At home that night, Kara prepared herself a chicken and shrimp Lean Cuisine. While it cooked, she busied herself cleaning out the refrigerator, discovering several foil-wrapped packages that were growing penicillin, and a moldy leftover salad that dated from the shower Angie gave her in May.

Finally she played back her telephone messages.

Her first caller was male, his voice stiff and self-conscious on the tape. "This is Rog Runyan . . . Is August first okay for move-in? Ah, we had to move the date back because my wife has to visit her Dad in San Diego . . . Okay, um, I'll get in touch later."

This was from the professor at Oakland University who was going to rent her house. Some hesitation in Kara hadn't allowed her to take the final step of putting her house up for sale. Instead she'd put that off until interest rates were better. Rob hadn't said anything. But she still felt guilty about it, as if she weren't fully committing herself to him.

Then another male voice. "Hey, prettiest woman in Rochester. How about having lunch with me next week? Wine, cheese, candlelight, and me. Oh, yeah, this is Drew, at Dalrymple Wallcovering."

She grimaced to herself, not knowing whether to be flattered or annoyed. Most of the local merchants knew she and Rob were getting married and she felt sure Dalrymple, a notorious flirt, was among them. Still, in a business like hers, contacts were everything if you expected to take business away from established papers like the *Oakland Press* and the *Eccentric* chain. She made a note to call Drew. She'd think of a way to defuse him.

Her last message was from Rob. "Hi, Kar, I'm going to be out wining and dining the Taubman people again tonight, over at the Fox and Hounds. Call you when I get back. Love ya . . ."

She erased all the messages, reset her machine, and sat down to eat her TV dinner, finishing off the meal with a wedge of melon. She had brought home printouts of her ad revenues and expenses, and planned to go over them, preparing figures for her loan application.

But her attention kept wandering, and finally she put the papers aside and went to stand at her patio door. A fragrant, indigo dusk had fallen, alive with june bugs that buzzed and batted at the screen. Next door her neighbors were entertaining, and party voices penetrated through the spruces.

A wave of melancholy swept over her as she closed and locked the patio door, sliding the wooden broom handle into the groove so that no intruder could force the door open. She flicked the lock, then tested it, prodding at the cut-off broom handle again, making doubly sure it was in place. She proceeded around the rest of the house, locking and checking all the doors and windows on the first floor.

Rob teased her about this, calling it her "nightly ritual," but Kara stubbornly persisted. She could not sleep until she was sure the house was intruder-proof, and sometimes she felt compelled to get up again after she was in bed, and repeat the check. She knew she wasn't alone in this. One rape victim she met, a woman lawyer, was so paranoid about rape that she carried a loaded pistol with her wherever she went, even leaving it on the vanity within grabbing distance when she showered.

Rob phoned an hour later as Kara was soaking in a warm bath, her private release for stress. She leaned out of the tub to reach for the cordless phone, which she had brought with her and set on the bath rug.

"Hello?"

"Hi, babe. Feeling any better?"

"Better? I feel okay. I'm just taking a bath . . ." Kara moved in the tub, creating a ripple of water against the porcelain.

"I can hear you splashing. God, I love naked women in bathtubs. Can I come over and scrub your back?"

"Mmmmm," she said invitingly.

"I'm a very good scrubber, very thorough."

"Are you?" She undulated her hips under the water, wondering what it would be like if Rob was in the tub with her. If they soaped their bodies their skin would be slick and slippery, sliding against one another.

"Want me to come over and show you? Stay in the tub, Kara, don't get out. It'll take me five minutes to change and ten minutes to get over there. I've already got the sitter here."

"Mmmm," she said again, touching herself.

"Jesus, Kara . . ." Rob's laugh was excited.

"Come on over," she murmured. "Come on over."

"I will. Fifteen minutes."

He clicked off, and Kara stretched out in the water, moving her hips again, observing the way the water moved and peaked in the damp strands of her pubic mound. Then reluctantly she got out of the tub, drying herself with a thick-piled mauve towel she had bought at Hudson's. If she stayed in the hot water for fifteen more minutes, she'd be enervated, and the skin on her fingers would wrinkle. She would go in her bedroom and wait, she decided, and then climb back in the water again as soon as she heard Rob's car pull in.

She awoke to the sound of Rob's voice calling her name.

"Kara . . . Kara! Wake up, you fell asleep on me. So much for making love in the bathtub, huh? Sorry I was delayed, I had to get gas, I was running on fumes."

She sat up groggily, realizing that she was wearing only a little cotton camisole she'd pulled on before going to lie down on her bed.

"Oh, God," she groaned.

"You were dead to the world."

She went to pull on a robe, angry at herself for falling asleep. What must Rob think of her? That she'd deliberately called him over here, implying they were going to make erotic love, then fallen asleep on the bed? Now she wasn't in the mood any more. Naps always did that to her, making her grumpy.

Rob had changed to jeans and a short-sleeved pullover. He walked past her to peer into the bathroom. "I see you left the bath water. I bet it's stone cold." She heard the sound of him testing the water. "Yeah," he said. "It's cold all right."

Like her, was the implication Kara picked up.

"I'm sorry," she began.

"It's okay, Kara."

"No, it's not okay. I . . . I teased you, I led you on."

He came out of the bathroom and sat on the bed beside her.

"No, you didn't lead me on," he told her. "You were genuinely turned on, you came in the bedroom to wait for me, and you fell asleep, that's all. We both work long, hard hours, Kara. Besides, it took me about twenty-five minutes to get here, that's enough to put most anyone to sleep who's lying on the bed anyway."

She smiled at him, grateful for his understanding. Most

men would be pissed at her. She knew she should suggest that they still make love, but the words died on her lips. Sexually, she was so fragile, and both of them knew it.

"Well," she said. "Now that I'm awake, do you want to go downstairs and watch a movie? I taped *Mystic Pizza* and we could watch that. Or I've got *Fatal Attraction*, Angie loaned me that one. Wouldn't you like to see Glenn Close rise up out of that bathtub again? Speaking of bathtubs."

"No, thank you, that's not my idea of a fun scene," Rob said. He looked at her. "Kara . . . babe . . . I know something is on your mind. Do you want to talk about it? And whatever it is, it's not a bad day at work."

She flushed, looking first at him, then down at her lap, where she had shielded her body from the eyes of her fiance with white terrycloth.

"Hey. We're going to be married, remember? I'm going to be your husband, Kara. Doesn't that mean that we should communicate a little? That we share whatever is going on with us?"

She felt herself turn pinker. "I'm not a very good communicator, am I?"

"No, you're not. It's something to do with sex, isn't it?" he persisted.

"Do we have to talk about it?" She got to her feet and walked across to the bedroom window, gazing out at the branches of the spruces, dark now and tangled with shadows in which even now someone could be hiding.

"No, we don't *have* to talk. I thought you'd want to."

"I do want to. I do want to share. It's just that—this happened a long time ago, and it's—it's hard—I'm just not good at sharing!" she burst out. "Don't make me, Rob, don't make me right now."

There was a long silence, and she knew if she turned she would see Rob sitting on the bed, frowning.

"Is this about a man?" he finally asked.

101

"A man?"

"Yes, is it about a man? Some guy you dated, someone you maybe had sex with? Is that what you're hung up on?"

Jerry. She felt her heart pound in her chest. She was going to have to tell Rob soon, wasn't she? Because if she didn't, he would keep asking her questions, and it was going to stand between them.

"It was just a kid thing," she lied.

"Like what? Some guy pushing you or maybe forcing you?"

He was entirely too close for comfort. "No, not like that. My folks were—conservative, that's all. Uptight about certain things. Uptight about sex."

Did he believe her? She heard his steps on the carpet, and turned, praying her emotions were not written all over her face.

"Kar. You'll share things with me, won't you? I mean, you won't keep things from me, even if they're sensitive. Because we're friends. I want us to be friends, too."

"We're friends."

"Best friends," he said, sliding his arms around her waist and pulling her close. He buried his face in her hair, and she felt the warm plumes of his breath against her ear. "I need you, Kar. I get uneasy when you distance yourself like that."

CHAPTER 10

Jerry was on I-75, trucking out of the scrubby middle flats of Florida and into Georgia. Little towns flashed past him: Ellisville, Providence, then Lake City and White Springs. Over the state border would be Valdosta, Georgia, and that was where he would stop for a while, relax, stretch his muscles, start getting the feeling back again.

He thought about Whitetop. An old, barrel-chested black man with grizzled white hair, and scars on his face. He had chocolate eyes that were deep, sad and angry, like a junk yard dog's. Whitetop had survived it all—beatings, floggings, riots, weeks in the "hole," shower room fights, killings and attempted killings, mixed with a despairing boredom.

"I done *hard* time, man," Whitetop would say, opening his purplish lips to reveal black gaps of missing teeth. "I did time in New York State, man, in Joliet. That's a hard joint. They done buried guys in there."

Whitetop would point to his own kinky, cotton-wool

skull. "*Inside*, that where it at. You don't get out of no prison by becomin' a con. You got a spirit in here, you let it out at night, it go flyin' all over the fuckin' world, it go where you want it to."

That wasn't the first time Jerry heard about spirits leaving the prison and going flying in the night. Doing time, there were two choices. You could do "hard time." That was where you went half wild and crazy thinking about things still happening on the outside, your wife or girl-friend, your buddies, your mother. You let go into your emotions and your depression. The first year Jerry was at Raiford he met this writer guy doing 3–5 for possession of LSD. The guy got crazier and crazier, writing out poems on pieces of paper all day. One day his wife didn't show up for visiting, and the guy freaked out, flooding his toilet, yelling, breaking up his cell, slamming his forehead against the wire mesh until it bled.

Visits were hell, because you built up your emotions for weeks for a half-hour visit and sometimes your visitors never showed.

Whitetop said it was easier if you didn't have *any* visitors. Jerry's Ma, Sally, she'd come a couple of times a year, when Ed let her. Jerry even looked forward to that. He had this fear, when people stopped thinking about him, he'd drop away and become invisible, he wouldn't *be* any more.

"Easy time" was what Jerry had tried to do. That was when you pushed the outside world out of your head and lived day to day. You let it all slide over you, got involved in the rivalries and gossip and bitching and plans, just let it happen, man.

There were ways you survived. You had to join a "fam-ily," a group of cons bound together in a way that was part sexual, part street gang, part brothers. You needed the family, not just for sex but for protection. If you didn't have one, you were fucked, you were out in the cold, your ass hanging in the wind.

Whitetop was Jerry's family.

Nobody messed with Whitetop. The old man might look like an Uncle Tom but he carried a shiv made of a stolen spoon and those old, gnarled, black fingers could flash and weave a blade like a coral snake.

Another way you did time was body building. Almost all of them, including Jerry, pumped iron. They all had pecs and lats that rippled, and thick, muscular glutes. It was a way you could see progress, see something *happening*, and it was also a way you could feel better about yourself, feel like a man instead of a penned-up animal.

Losers, Jerry thought. Some of these jerk-off artists couldn't make it on the outside, but they all talked tough. Every day you were surrounded by con men, bank robbers, murderers, insurance defrauders, even a guy who had put Drano up his wife's pussy. Blacks—lots of those. White crackers. Skinny kids and Hell's Angels types. Guys who could not read and some who could barely talk. Guys on hunger strikes, and guys who thought their cell was bugged by the FBI. Cons who would tell you everything you ever wanted to know about heisting a truck full of stereos, but would kill you if you stared at them too long.

In the early years Jerry found a way to stand out at Raiford, and earn a little money. He became a tattoo artist. After Whitetop had messed up with the tattoo on his hand and he'd had to have the infection lanced in the prison hospital, Jerry decided *he'd* give it a try. Shit, all you needed was a knife tip or needle and a ballpoint pen. His specialty was naked women. He did this big tattoo on this guy's back, a girl bending down with her legs apart. A big pussy showing, bigger than life, with the hole right there to see. After that, they lined up. Harley Davidsons, he could do those too, and he was much in demand.

Jerry didn't mark on himself though. He only had one

tattoo, the 13½. He wanted to stay good-looking and clean for when he got out.

Clean. He snorted bitterly as he accelerated around a truck. He got raped twice in those first months before he found Whitetop. Then it happened again last year. Whitetop had been in the infirmary then with flu, leaving Jerry uncomfortable and loose. The guy, Capper they called him, was this big black motherfucker with needle tracks all over his arms and legs, and big, ugly, junkie hands swollen from so many veins gone bad.

Capper had been a pimp in Tampa, had run seven or eight girls, and one of them died of AIDS. Now, Jerry didn't have to be very smart to know what that meant. Pimps screwed their whores regularly to keep them in line. So that meant Capper screwed a hooker with AIDS, and Capper screwed him.

Just thinking about it made Jerry ball his hands into fists, clench his fingers until the knuckles popped. That shit coulda given him AIDS . . . a long drawn out, horrible death. They said your brain got fried, you became demented and didn't even know what you were doing.

AIDS took you whether you were clean or not. It took you when it wasn't your fault, when you had not done one goddamned thing to bring it on, when you were totally innocent.

These thoughts consumed him as he passed over the state line into Georgia, pine trees and red dirt out the window, nothing to look at but freeway signs and cars filled with old folks, "snowbirds" going north again to escape the Florida humidity. If he wanted to place blame for any AIDS virus he might be carrying, he, Jerry, did not have to look to the asshole con who had raped him, or even to Whitetop, who he suspected might have it.

No, the real blame went to those two girls. Laurel and Karalynn.

They sent him to prison, didn't they? Little bitches testified in court against him, told all the world how he had cut them and fucked them with blood all over them, getting off on seeing himself in a mirror. How he had dipped his hand in their blood and smeared it in his mouth and laughed at them.

They lied, the bitches. He didn't remember doing that. He had just been trying to take what they would not give, and had punished them a little, and had got carried away by his passion for them and his need.

He drove up behind an old guy in a Lincoln Continental, and rode up real close, practically on the guy's bumper. But when the blue-haired wife turned around to glare at him, Jerry dropped back.

Shit, what was he doing? If those two old farts stopped at a rest stop and called the State Police, he would be fucked. Or he read they had car phones now. That would be even worse, they could have the cops on him in minutes.

He drove along soberly, obeying the speed limit, forcing himself to be in control, to put his thoughts into a narrow track, focus them on a goal.

Those two bitches.

They were his goal.

CHAPTER 11

It was another June day of humid, blue brightness. Only nineteen days to go now until the wedding.

"Kara? Kara Cleveland?" Sitting in Dr. Ruth Kenneally's office, nervously leafing through a copy of *Glamour*, Kara looked up at the sound of her name. The office nurse was waiting, crisp, expectant.

"What are you in for today, Kara?"

"The—the premarital blood test and physical."

"All right, please step over here to the scales."

She weighed in at 122 pounds, three pounds under her usual 125. The nurse led her to a small, painfully clean examining room and told her to strip and don a flimsy paper gown with a stretchy paper waist tie. As she put on the gown, Kara's nervousness increased geometrically.

After the rape, she'd worn a gown like this. A harassed doctor had stitched up her cuts, asked questions, examined her internally, and smeared her vaginal fluids on a glass slide for others to see. She had cried and asked for her mother, but a brusque nurse told her she had to wait until the doctor was finished.

At one point she'd actually been left to lie with her legs in stirrups, and a young, male resident had barged in to see her lying there with her legs spread. He had not even apologized, just begun asking more questions.

Even now, Kara could feel cold waves of anger at the unfeeling treatment. The exposure had been degrading, the feeling transmitted to her that because of the mode of attack she and Laurel were sexual oddities.

Now Dr. Ruth Kenneally entered the examining room, a short, plain, pleasant-looking woman in her early thirties whose scrubbed face bore no makeup whatsoever.

"Hi, Kara, how've you been? I read *Bargain Hound* all the time; in fact, I tried one of your recipes the other week. The oatmeal apricot muffins. They were pretty good."

Ruth Kenneally had no idea of Kara's past history, and Kara had told her usual lie about the scar under her breast, that it was caused by a bicycle injury. Still, Dr. Kenneally did know of Kara's exam "nerves," which were impossible to hide.

Now the physician smiled reassuringly and stood by the table, engaging Kara in a long conversation that covered oatmeal cookies, the Belle Isle Fun Run both had raced in this year, and the advantages and disadvantages of several types of running shoes. As she did so, she prepared Kara for examination. Tensely Kara lay down, slid her rump down on the table, and inserted her feet in the stirrups.

"I hate this," she muttered.

"Most of us do. Something about that cold speculum . . . Have you been feeling all right, Kara? Normal periods?"

"Oh, yes . . ."

"No pain on intercourse?"

"No . . ."

109

"And you're on birth control pills, right? No problems there?"

"No."

"I understand we're doing pre-marital blood tests. Congratulations. Later in my office, I'll show you a video."

"Video?"

"We're required to do AIDS counseling now. Okay, relax . . . I can't examine you when your muscles are tense."

The physician began pressing down on Kara's abdomen, probing her ovaries and in the process pressing on her bladder. Kara lay breathing shallowly, tears brimming to her eyes. She hated the fact that a woman's body subjected her to this humiliation. Thank God her doctor was not a man. But even having a woman do this to her was unpleasant. The rape had ruined her in so many ways, Kara knew with the anger that always filled her on the examining table. She could live to be eighty-eight years old and she would always hate having her legs in stirrups.

Getting the blood drawn was almost a relief, and signalled that the ordeal was nearly over. As soon as the doctor left, Kara slid off the table, tossed away the now wrinkled paper wrappings, and hurried into her clothes. After this the video, even on AIDS, would be a picnic.

Giddy with the aftermath of completing a difficult chore, she was on her way again. She completed her other errands—a stop at the photographer's studio, another stop to pick up her bridal veil—and drove to Rob's. She had agreed to take Cindy to lunch so Rob could go in to the office.

"Hi, sweets." Rob came to the door and kissed her. He had on the slacks and casual shirt he wore when visiting building sites. "Thought while you had Cindyella out, I'd just pop by that building down on Kirts, check out the foundation. She's really looked forward to lunch; I think she's decided on pizza."

"Pizza?" she said in dismay. Bready crust and

cholesterol-laden cheese sounded heavy and dreadful for lunch on a summer day. Kara had been thinking more in terms of Friday's, where the menu offered everything from fajitas to steamed vegetable platters and fresh fish. Friday's also had a selection of summery fruit drinks that Cindy would adore.

"Get a big side of salad and just pick at the pizza, that's what I do sometimes. You know kids. Cindy's upstairs, she's doing something with her Barbie dolls. I went out this morning and bought her this Hawaiian Barbie named Miko, with hair down to her knee caps."

"Rob." She felt her eyes moisten. "Rob? I need a hug."

"Need a hug? You've got one."

They stood holding each other, and then Kara said into the clean, fragrant cotton of his shirt, "I finally got my blood test. I can go pick up the results on Tuesday."

"Yes?" He moved her back to gaze into her eyes. "That means next week we can drive over to Pontiac and get our license." He grinned, a dimple flashing in his left cheek. "I'm getting my hooks into you and that's going to be that."

She hugged him, feeling as if she'd stepped into a canoe on a river with a very strong current. "Guess I can't get away."

"You're going to be stuck with me, babe. But I'll make it up to you. Every year on your birthday I'll get you a new vacuum cleaner."

She laughed.

Rob patted her rump. "Go on now, go upstairs and admire her Barbies. I told her you'd take her and get her some more doll clothes. Meijer's is having a big sale on Barbie items."

"Thanks," she said dryly.

"I'll give you the money."

"No, that's not necessary."

She went upstairs to find Cindy perched on the bed in her room, surrounded by an army of Barbie dolls, My Little Ponys, and Pound Puppies of varying sizes, shapes and colors. This was all post-divorce bounty that she kept specifically at Rob's house, with another, even larger collection that resided in Royal Oak at her mother's.

"Hi, Cindy. I hear you got another Barbie."

"Yes, she's Hawaiian." Cindy held up the doll, whose mop of black hair was grotesquely full. The doll wore a scrap of clothing in a Hawaiian pattern, and a lei made of plastic flowers.

"Pretty hair," Kara ventured.

"I have a big collection now, I've got thirteen Barbies at home and they all have dresses and costumes. And I have five Ken dolls."

"Sounds to me like Ken is kinda outnumbered."

"Oh, he doesn't mind," Cindy said, getting off the bed. "Dad said you'd get me some more clothes. But I really need a suitcase for her to put her clothes in. Do you think they might have that at Meijers?"

Unlike the day they had gone shopping for the dress, Cindy appeared in a good mood, and happily chattered in the car as they drove to Pizza Hut. The restaurant was filled with a lunch crowd that included a busload of giggly teenaged girls apparently bound for a cheerleading camp.

Cindy was agog with interest, and kept eyeing the tables jammed with girls as she munched her cheese pizza.

"*I'll* be a cheerleader sometime," she told Kara.

"That's good . . . or maybe you'll be on a team yourself," Kara felt obligated to add a feminist comment. "You could be on the basketball team, or hockey, or tennis. Then you wouldn't have to cheer, you could play."

"Cheering is better," the girl pronounced.

Silence fell between them, and Kara contemplated what she ought to say next. She was disappointed to feel that Cindy was really a little Barbie Doll-in-training. Was she going to grow up to be a plastic woman, all lip gloss and stewardess smiles?

"Cindy . . ."

The child looked up.

"I know it's been hard, having your Mommy and Daddy get a divorce. I know you must feel kinda . . . well, kinda left out sometimes."

Cindy stared at her, blue eyes going suddenly opaque. The blankness was a little unnerving, causing Kara to talk faster.

"Maybe you're even afraid that you're not going to see as much of your Dad as you'd like. After the wedding, I mean."

Cindy dropped her glance to her plate, where her nibbled-at pizza crusts could provide a day's portion of food for a hungry Ethiopian.

Kara struggled through her prepared speech. "Cindy? Just because your Dad loves me, doesn't mean he doesn't love you. He loves you very much, very much. He wants you to visit us all the time . . . *We* want you to visit. Our getting married isn't going to change the love that your father has for you, Cindy. He'll always—"

"I know that," Cindy interrupted coolly. "Can we go now? You said we could go to Meijers."

"Why, yes we can go. But Cindy . . ."

"I said I want to *go*."

Kara was annoyed that her careful talk had fallen apart. "Okay, but we have to wait for the check."

"Can I go to the car?"

"I said, when the check comes."

They glared at each other, and once more Kara felt the wave of hurt, helplessness and anger that overtook her when she tried to deal with Rob's daughter. It was really hopeless, wasn't it? Cindy was never going to love her or care about her, or see her as anything other than a rival for Rob's love. Every other weekend they would go through this sort of routine. She would knock herself out for this child, and Cindy would spurn her efforts.

Did she really want to spend the next eight years trying to please someone who disliked her?

She managed to catch the attention of the waitress, and within minutes they were headed out to the parking lot again.

"I want to get the suitcase at Meijer's," Cindy had the gall to say as they were getting in the car.

Kara stopped in her tracks and stared at the ten-year-old. "Cindy, you were rude to me in there, and I'm not going to accept rudeness. I would like for you to like me, but if you don't, then you are still going to treat me with *politeness* and *good manners*."

"Okay," the child mumbled.

"I mean that," Kara finished. "Are you listening to me, Cindy?"

"I *am*," said the girl, eyes filling with tears.

Cindy seemed chastened as they trudged up and down the aisles of Meijer's, a huge store that was a combination of supermarket and K-Mart. When they arrived at Rob's, shopping bag in hand, his car was not in the drive, so Kara let them in with her key.

Cindy turned on the TV to *Days of Our Lives*, and, to the sound of panting love scenes and lovers' spats, Kara spent an hour showing Cindy how to make doll dresses out of circles cut from magazine illustrations.

Cindy forgot her huff and giggled when Kara made a slinky black gown for Hawaiian Miko, then made the doll move in a disco step.

"You're funny," Cindy giggled. "Dolls can't dance."

"This doll can. See? Watch her boogie down."

"She wants to dance with Ken," Cindy said, finding one of the Ken dolls.

For a few minutes they "danced" Barbie and Ken.

Cindy sprawled on the floor, black curls falling on either side of her face, moving her doll with abandon. Her eyes sparkled, her expression alight with fun. It was as if the incident at Pizza Hut had never occurred.

What turned this little girl's buttons on and off? Kara wondered. When she tried to make Cindy like her, she didn't. When she gave up, the child started responding. Being a ''step,'' she suspected, was going to be a herculean job. Probably Cindy would never come to completely accept her. She could picture Cindy at twenty-two, refusing to have Kara at her wedding. Yes, that was a scenario definitely possible for their Cindy.

She let her eyes focus past Cindy, into the distance. In less than three weeks, this difficult ten-year-old was going to be her stepdaughter.

It seemed overwhelming.

How *did* a stepmother become loved? Or was that something she should not even expect?

CHAPTER 12

It was nearly eight o'clock, and the sky overhead was tinted sickly white. Heavy, yellowish clouds lay sullenly at the horizon and promised rain maybe sometime in the night. Even with the Ciera's air conditioning running Jerry could almost taste the heavy summer humidity of the air.

He pulled off at Valdosta at U.S. 84, where numbers of motels were lined along the roadway. Signs advertised someplace called the Mill Store Plaza, with "46 Factory Stores," and "Trolley Car Rides."

He drove along, wondering if he should stay in one of the motels or just drive straight through. The rows of motels seemed to mock him with indecision. Should he stay at King of the Road Motor Inn, Holiday Inn, or Quality Inn? American Inn, Howard Johnson's, or even Jolly Inn? Most seemed to be fairly filled up with cars. He glimpsed old couples lugging suitcases or strolling toward restaurants, the women with blue-white hair, and bald old guys with paunches.

116

Snow birds, this whole town existed for them, right beside I-75 so they would not have to drive even a mile out of their way.

Those rich old farts. They didn't have anything better to do with their lives than drive back and forth to Florida. While he'd been behind lousy fucking bars, sandwiched in a bunk in a former recreation room, crammed in with eighteen other guys.

He bypassed the motels and kept going on U.S. 84 into town, turning left on a street called Patterson. The town seemed old, many of the buildings shabby. There were dusty azalea bushes, and black people everywhere. He could picture this place about 150 years ago, with plantation overseers leading gangs of slaves through town. Shit, maybe Whitetop's family had lived right here, slaves to some rich fart.

He drove through town, passing some houses with white pillars. Then an old Methodist church with towers, spires and buttresses, to him looking about a hundred years old. And more blacks, and some old white ladies in pants suits. One old woman carried a covered dish, probably a pie. She walked carefully, as if afraid she might stumble and drop her pecan pie all over the cracked and dusty pavement.

Shit, he thought, was that all there was in this town? Old folks and blacks? What about the young cooze, where was that? Weren't there any *girls* around here? Anything young and sweet? Jesus!

The sight of another old lady emerging from a 7-Eleven, dressed in bermuda shorts and a loose sleeveless top that showed her billowy, jiggly, wrinkled upper arms, decided him. Hell, he refused to believe that Valdosta, Georgia didn't have anything young to offer. Hadn't any of these people ever heard of "Georgia Peaches?"

A sign for the Valdosta Mall attracted him. He made a U-turn and headed east on Brookwood to Oak, and then

Bay Tree Road. A shopping mall, where was his head, what was wrong with him? He might have been away from it for ten years but he wasn't dumb.

Shopping malls, that's where the pussy hung out.

How could he have forgotten? Jeez, he had spent hundreds of hours in Tampa and St. Petersburg following girls in his car, and the mall had been one of his prime pickup places, after the beach. He couldn't remember how many girls he'd followed out of Maas Brothers, the big department store.

He pulled into the huge parking area and parked, staring at the long, low mall that had a big Belk-Hudson store at one end and a Sears on the other. It was prime hunting time, because girls would be leaving the mall right about now, heading home.

He parked and went in the center entrance. He stepped inside and was struck—like an explosion in front of his eyes—with the bigness and richness and marble-floored shininess of it. To his right were Piece of Pie Pizza and Stonewall's Deli. To his left, Lighthouse Christian Books. He could see more stores, dozens of them, stretching before him, like Christmas windows through which hungry kids could peer. Shoppers walked back and forth. Mothers pushing kids in strollers. Teenaged guys. Young girls.

But the girls.

Wearing these tight, blue spotted jeans that looked like they'd been dipped in bleach about a thousand times, then glued to their skin. With blond hair in masses of curls, streaked with yellow and wild-looking.

And makeup! Red lips that pouted, and eyes elaborately painted with blues and purples, the lids outlined in black.

A girl with a frizzy nest of yellow hair sauntered past him. Jerry could not take his eyes away from her fingernails. So long they curved like claws, and a little jewel had been glued to one of the nails, with a tiny chain that dangled as the girl walked.

Jerry eyed her incredulously. Could such nails be fashionable? They looked like claws to him. And she looked like a whore. Hard. Shit, she was only sixteen, and looked like she would rob you and kick you in the balls.

Girls like her . . . they were dirt. Like his mother must have been when she was young, ready to roll over for anybody. Tough, the kind that coldly held it back from a man. But this girl disappeared into a store called Casual Corner before she could sense the virulence of his look.

He told himself to be more careful. You couldn't let them sense your presence, or the thoughts you were thinking about them. Otherwise, they'd spook. He'd had it happen before—when they realized what he wanted and tried to get away from him. One girl in Pinellas Park, when he was nineteen, had actually tried to run him down with her car. If he had not jumped up onto the fender, he would have had his legs crushed.

He wandered on. The mall was shaped like a big cross, with side corridors opening onto more stores. He walked around, both interested and repelled by the bigness of it, the strangeness.

Stores he'd never heard of. A store named Triphengers that had clothes he couldn't tell if they belonged on men or women. A place called Starship Records and Tapes. He walked in and fingered racks full of compact discs. He didn't even know what they were or how to play them.

He left again, almost stumbling into a couple of kids in his haste to get out of there. Jeez, this place was freaking him out. He felt like a man dumped in a foreign country. Tapes he didn't recognize. Clothes that seemed strange. Gadgets in the window of Radio Shack that he'd never seen before. And the prices of things were so high. $79.95 for a shitty men's cotton sweater.

He hurried down the main concourse again, passing Chick-Fil-A and Corn Dog 7, Eckerd Drugs and World

Bazaar, The Station and Round One. Then a cafeteria called Morrison's.

He calmed down a little. He'd been in Morrison's plenty of times down in St. Pete, it was a chain he knew and felt familiar with. Hell, maybe he should even go in and get himself a cup of coffee and some cherry pie. Maybe some stew or lasagna—real food, not prison shit.

He went into the cafeteria line, took himself a tray and went by the food choices, again overwhelmed by the sheer variety of choices. Did he want stir-fried chicken, roast chicken or fried? Veal parmesan or roast beef? The shrimp special? And the desserts, more varieties than the prison served in ten years, all available to him instantaneously.

"Help you, sir?" A black woman behind the counter smiled at him. She was about twenty, with dark, liquid eyes and yellowish quadroon skin.

He realized he'd been standing there gawking at all the choices like a real hayseed. "The special," he blurted.

"Which one? The shrimp or the chicken?"

"Shrimp," he said at random. He reached out and began loading his tray with desserts. A high, fluffy-looking chocolate pie that looked good, a lemon meringue, some cheesecake that was decorated with huge, almost artificial-looking strawberries. Then he put that one back and substituted a large piece of very dark chocolate cake with about an inch of chocolate frosting. Chocolate was one of his favorites. He stuck his finger in the frosting and licked some of it off while he was waiting for the girl to dish him up his shrimp.

"Give me an extra big portion," he cajoled her. She did so.

He paid for his meal with the money from his mother's private stash, again angered at the price, $17.99. How could prices be that high? Then he found a table and sat down with his meal which took up most of the table top once he got all the dishes off the tray. An old guy sitting at the table next to his was staring at his prison tattoo.

Jerry angrily turned so that his left arm did not show. Old bastard! Old fart!

He wolfed down most of the shrimp, and then started tasting the desserts, taking a bite from one, then from another, mingling the flavors in his mouth. Hog heaven, he thought, beginning to enjoy himself. He'd heard of this before, guys getting out of stir and acting like they'd never seen food before, going into stores and going crazy buying stuff. Now he was doing it. Yeah, and he liked it. He decided he was going to eat everything he wanted for a while, indulge himself a little. He had ten years to make up for—thanks to those two coozes, Laurel Fearn and blond princess Karalynn Cleveland.

When he got to them, he was going to make them regret what they had done to him, all right.

Meanwhile, here he was in Georgia and he had almost forgotten why he came to the mall—girls.

Slaking the first demands of his appetite, Jerry glanced around the cafeteria, assessing the other customers. A couple of young airmen sat near the wall. There must be an Air Force Base near here.

Yeah . . . over there, by the side wall, two little blondes who looked about sixteen, seventeen years old. Jerry turned his chair slightly so that he could eye them over his pie.

These two were more to his liking. (Funny, how pairs of girls always appealed to him more than singles. He couldn't remember how many pairs of girlfriends he had followed from the beach. Something about two . . . it always excited him much more. One to fuck, one to watch, and then reverse it. Yeah, that was the way to go.)

He assessed his prey. These girls weren't as whorish as the one he'd seen in the concourse with the jewel hanging from her fingernails. They wore white knit tops, V-dipped in front to show perky little breasts. One had on a cotton skirt and sandals, the other tight jeans. They were just finishing milk shakes, sucking up the last of the fluid through straws, their little pink mouths pursed sexily.

Pretty enough to be homecoming queens.

Jerry was amazed at how fast he got into it again, the speed-up thrill of his heart as he focused on the girls. He timed the finishing of his meal to match theirs, so that he'd be ready to leave at the exact time they did.

He followed them out of the mall with no trouble to a battered Mustang. While he was inside, the sky had turned dusky, swept with long ribbons of lavender clouds. Birds swooped overhead, fighting for the night insects, and he saw a jet trail, splitting the sky in half like a stiletto blade.

He followed the Mustang through town, through the older streets and finally to a raw, new little subdivision consisting of small pre-fab houses. To Jerry's disappointment—this happened so often—one girl dropped the other one off, and continued on alone.

He kept following her, past the city limits, along a road lined with shacky houses, fleabag machine ships, and dirt trails. A sign for a trailer park announced "Dogwood Park, New Models and Pre-Owned." She went past that, too, turning down a reddish dirt road. The setting was oppressively rural. There were pine trees everywhere. Insects chirred and rustled, and he could smell stagnant water. He wondered where the hell she lived, in the middle of a swamp?

There was no other traffic on the road; he couldn't believe his luck. He speeded up, and when she slowed to negotiated a hairpin turn, Jerry got closer and rear ended her car. Not hard enough to cause his own car much damage, naturally. That wasn't what he had in mind at all.

It was just enough of a nudge to cause her to stop, and sit there crying and blubbering 'cause she'd bumped up her Daddy's car. Girls were notorious for doing that—Jerry didn't think he'd ever driven past a fender-bender where some girl wasn't crying.

He reached under the seat, got his roll of duct tape and his knife, slipping them into his shirt.

Being good-looking helped. Smiling, waving to her, looking as harmless as possible, he got out of the Ciera.

Kimberley Sissons sat sobbing in the front seat of her brother's car, thinking how Bob was going to yell at her when he found out she'd taken his car and then bumped it up. Bob, two years older than she, was incredibly selfish about the car and seldom let her drive it, even when she asked him real nice.

Maybe Bob would even make her pay for the damage, which would be a real disaster, since her only income came from babysitting.

"You ain't hurt, are you?" said a voice through the opened window of the Mustang. She looked up, blinking away the film of tears that obscured her vision.

He was good looking . . . in an exciting, older-man way, and his bare forearms were thickly corded with muscle. He looked like a construction worker, except that his clothes were better. Kimberley was immediately intrigued. Her falling-asleep-at-night fantasies always had her meeting a boy exactly like this . . . crossing her path, meeting by accident.

She gave him one of her prettiest, flirty smiles. "No, I ain't hurt, but it's my brother Bob's car, he's goin' to k-kill me, just kill me. I wasn't supposed to take it out . . . is it wrecked awful? I'm ascared to look . . ."

"No, it's hardly touched, just a little bump. Want to get out and see? C'mon, get out and look," he encouraged.

Hesitantly she did so. She felt him looking at her, and she couldn't help preening a little, thrusting out her breasts. She was petite, which she'd learned that boys really liked. She'd splurged with her babysitting money and bought a hair-painting kit, to streak her hair blond. Boys liked *that*, too. In fact, boys usually liked Kimberley quite a lot.

She walked with him around her car to stare at the back bumper, where a definite new crumple marked the point of impact. Dismay filled her. Her brother watched over the Mustang like a hawk. She'd never be able to hide this from Bob. He'd probably tell their father. Who still believed in using the belt . . .

She started to cry again.

"Aw, it ain't that bad," the nice looking man told her. "Just a little old bung, hardly nothing. A good bump shop fix that up for you in no time. Come on over to my car, I'll get out my insurance papers and stuff."

He led her to his car, to the passenger side, and while she was standing there expectantly he suddenly pulled a knife out of his shirt.

The blade flashed molten silver in the moonlight. Kimberley stared at it, transfixed, for a brief second too terrified even to scream.

He shoved her off balance against the car, pain slamming through her right hip. He clamped one hand over her mouth, while, with the other, he jammed the knife tip into her side. His palm tasted bitter and salty, and Kimberley began struggling, twisting wildly away from him, trying to break away.

"Bitch!" he panted. "Rat-cunt!"

She felt a jabbing pain in her side, like a stitch. He had actually cut her.

"Oh, please," she begged, terror loosening her muscles so that urine began to stream down her leg, puddling on her shoe. "Oh, God, please, please!"

He pulled away from her a little, and she saw something in his hand that terrified her even more—a big roll of what her father called "duck tape." She reared backwards, sobbing as a horrible panic washed over her.

"P-please, hey, please!" she cried.

He smiled at her, moonlight reflecting off the whiteness of his teeth. There was something in the front of his pants, something that pushed out the cloth. She realized with horror what it was.

He was going to do something terrible to her, Kimberley realized. He was going to hurt her awful.

She twisted wildly, kicking out at him.

But he caught her and dragged her into the car, shoving her backward onto the seat so hard that her head hit the center column. Then he took the knife and yanked her skirt up. With the sharp tip, he speared the bikini panties down, creating a long line of red that ran from her waistline to mid thigh. She cried out, sobbing.

"You're mine now," he told her thickly. "Yeah, you're mine, and I'm gonna be the King of the World for you. How about that, bitch-girl? Rat girl? *Cunt* girl?"

CHAPTER 13

Kara awoke, sweating. In her dream, her hands had been tied behind her. Jerry was forcing her to climb a set of stairs on which was splayed a jagged, diamond-like reflection of sunlight. He harried her with the tip of his knife, jabbing it at her naked buttocks.

"Go on, rat-cunt! Hurry, before I stab you! Go! Hurry!"

The dream faded, leaving behind the sour taste of bile. Kara lay in bed, caught up in the familiar panic attack. She had tried to describe this panic to Dr. Hay, but her words had seemed inadequate to describe a terror as violent as a heart attack, as having your leg sawed off without anesthesia. No one, she reflected, could ever know what it was really like unless it had happened to them.

Breathe, she instructed herself. *Breathe slowly. Deeply. Get control. Stop thinking about it. Push it away.*

After a few minutes the trembling abated, and she realized that she was lying in bed still clutching a section of the sheet, almost twisting it in sweaty hands. She could hear the morning birds outside her window, quarreling like a gang of children. She had fed the baby jays this spring and now they were all obstreperous adolescents, whose presence at the feeder drove away the quieter sparrows and finches.

What time was it? She struggled up to look at her digital alarm clock.

6:46 a.m.

Shit. She lay back down again. She didn't usually rise until 7:15—it was the nice thing about living in Rochester, the drive to work took only eight minutes, fifteen in winter if the hill into town was icy.

She closed her eyes, pulling the sheet up so that it covered most of her face. It was going to be a typically long day. She had four candidates for salesperson to interview, her "Bargain Hunter" column to write, a meeting with a rep from a news syndicate, and the usual plethora of phone calls from various advertisers and readers that always overloaded her time.

Also, a local cartoonist, Jim Bird, had submitted a batch of cartoons featuring their mascot, "Bargain." She was meeting with him at 2:30 p.m. to discuss a contract. Jim was only twenty, a student at nearby Oakland University, definitely talented, and would probably soon get snapped up by some advertising firm. Meanwhile she hoped to sign him for at least two years if she could manage it.

Her mind drifted, and half an hour later she was startled to hear the alarm clock. Within seconds of its harsh buzzer, the telephone rang. She batted her arm toward her bedside stand, nearly knocking the phone to the floor.

"H'lo?" Her voice was always scratchy in the morning.

"Sorry, did I wake you up?" Rob sounded amused. Kara's morning bleariness was one of their jokes.

"No," she croaked, trying to talk and clear her throat

at the same time. "I always knock the phone over when I try to answer it."

His low laugh was sexy. "I wanted to remind you we have tickets to the Birmingham Theater tonight. I'm going to be in and out of the office all day and I was afraid I might not catch you."

"Okay."

"I'll pick you up at six and we'll have dinner at the Midtown Cafe." The Midtown Cafe, unlike its name which suggested a diner, was an elegant Birmingham watering hole and restaurant within paces of the theater. It was frequented by everyone from affluent ad execs to celebrities like Lorna Luft, in town to do a play.

"Well, I'll let you go," Rob said. "I've got more meetings with those Taubman people, and we're working like hell to get some kind of idea of what they really want. 'Avant garde,' they said, whatever the hell that means. Trying to figure out what people really mean is a bitch, Kara, especially when a couple mil in commission depends on it. I've got Cindy over at Jennifer's today. Thank God for Jennifer."

They hung up, and Kara lay for a few minutes longer in bed, her thoughts seguing back to her dream, and Jerry Quick. She really should call the prison. She castigated herself for being a coward, for not wanting to face it. Shamed, she knew that in her own way she was just as neurotic as Laurel.

But maybe she could have someone else do it. Her father's attorney, Harry Fendon, had an office in St. Petersburg, and would probably still remember her.

The more she thought about it the more sense it made.

"Harry? Harry Fendon? This is Kara Cleveland— Karalynn Cleveland. My father is Ken Cleveland." Kara was in her office, about to begin her column, which was a compendium of the best local sales, and tips on bargain hunting techniques.

"Oh, yes, Kara," the attorney said warmly. Over seventy now, he had been the executor for Kara's mother's estate.

They exchanged pleasantries and then Kara explained to him what she wanted.

"Of course I'll call the prison, Kara; I'll do it this morning. There shouldn't be any problem—I have to leave for court, but I'll try to get back to you within the hour."

She thanked him and hung up, feeling relieved. She could hardly wait for the word that would put her rapist where he belonged, and where he still was, in Raiford State Prison. Then the disturbing call from Laurel could be laid to rest, and she could go on with her life.

She buried herself in finishing the remainder of the copy. She then saw two appointments and returned three calls. However, the attorney still had not called back.

Nervously, she wondered why. Prison red tape, surely. Still, an uneasy premonition—a sense that something was not right—seemed to drift across the edges of her mind, like cigarette smoke. She cleaned out the Mr. Coffee machine, made a second batch of coffee, then poured herself her fourth cup of the day.

Bringing the cup to her desk, she sank into the chair Rob gave her, suddenly not liking the way it felt.

She reached underneath her and began manipulating the controls of the chair to tilt the seat so it wouldn't press into her legs so much. The chair tipped forward too far. She readjusted, and it was too far back. Annoyed, Kara got up and rolled the chair against the wall. She really wanted her old chair back. With its nice, soft cushion, and seat back that only did one thing, but did it superbly well.

"Ang?" She went in the back and poked her head in Angie's office. "Do you remember what we did with my old chair?"

Angie was poring over ad copy, playing with one long blond hank of hair. "I think we put it upstairs—we were going to give it to the new sales person. Why?"

"I want it back."

"You want it *back*?" Angie looked up. "Kara, it's never been away. It's your chair. The only reason it's upstairs is because you and I carried it up there. Do you want some help bringing it downstairs?"

"That would be nice," Kara said shamefacedly.

Angie went upstairs with her, and they raided the former bedroom set aside as an office for the new salesperson, switching chairs, and lugging Kara's old chair down the narrow staircase. Its casters bumped along the wall and created little scrape marks.

"Well," Angie said, hands on hips, when the chore had been accomplished. "I hope the new person appreciates sitting in the lap of luxury. That new chair is definitely a high-roller item."

Kara was instantly crestfallen. "Oh, God. You didn't want it, did you? I'm sorry, I just didn't think, Angie. You can have the chair if you want."

"Oh, no, I like my own chair fine. What's Rob going to say when he sees that you switched?" Angie questioned.

Kara flushed, feeling like an ungrateful jerkette who was throwing her fiancé's gift in his face. "I don't know. I'll pay him back the money for it, I guess, if he fusses about it. I shouldn't have let him give it to me. It has so many gadgety buttons. I'd really like my office life and my home life separate," she burst out, going into her office again and closing the door.

Her mood hadn't improved as she sat down in her old chair, testing its familiarity; she'd forgotten how the slightly listing seat used to annoy her. It was the phone call to the prison that had made her edgy, she knew. Why didn't Fendon call back? Had he forgotten? Had something gone wrong?

She twirled the chair, wondering what Rob would say when he learned she'd switched chairs. She felt sure he already guessed her ambivalence that she'd expressed by taking the new chair upstairs.

Why, she wondered, couldn't life be simple? Why couldn't she be an ordinary, starry-eyed bride, untroubled by doubt, convinced that "her man" was wonderful and that there would be no problems? A bride who didn't have to worry about telephone calls to prisons?

The phone rang, causing her to jump. She snatched it up. "Yes?"

"Harry Fendon on two," said Lynette.

"Yes, Harry?" Kara said, picking up. Her stomach had begun to tighten, and her throat felt suddenly dry.

"Sorry it took me so long to get back to you," Fendon said. "But I had some trouble getting through to the Warden's office. They're busier than an anthill at picnic time, and then they switched me around and I ended up talking to his parole officer. A Mr. Rudolf, also a very overworked gentleman, and at the moment more than a little annoyed."

Her heart skipped a horrid beat; the air she breathed suddenly thinned. "His parole officer?"

"I have some bad news, Kara. Jerry Quick was released yesterday—"

"Yesterday?" Kara repeated, feeling herself go white.

"Yeah, under a special program for inmates who were under good behavior. The prisons are so damn crowded now they have to make room for new offenders somehow. The parole officer drove Quick to his mother's home in Tampa. He had a job lined up at his stepfather's muffler shop in Temple Terrace, and was supposed to stay at his mother's home. I say supposed."

Yesterday? "Oh, my God," Kara said, white-lipped.

"He was at his mother's house less than an hour. He went in there and raided the place for clothes and money and a car. She called Rudolf the next day when he hadn't shown up with the car. It's a blue Cutlass Ciera, last year's model, and she was very unhappy at losing it. She said he took money, too, around $940."

"Oh, *God.*" Kara felt herself turn to jelly, her body flattening itself against her old chair as if she had no bones. A wad of sour nausea rose to the back of her throat, and her heartbeat seemed to be fibrillating in her chest.

"The date," she whispered. "The date you said he got out. Are you *sure* it was yesterday?"

"Yep, the twelfth."

"That's a definite date? There isn't any mistake?"

"I got it straight from the parole officer."

And yet, Laurel swore she had seen him. Oh, God, oh, God. But the dates weren't the same, she finally realized with a swoop of her heart. So Laurel had lied. Or believed her own lies. Or been totally delusional . . .

The phone was ringing in the outer office, and Kara heard an odd buzz in her head. Black and white dots were dancing in front of her eyes, blending and swirling. She braced her hands on the edge of her desk, steadying herself out of the fainting spell.

"Kara, are you still there?" The attorney had become concerned at her long silence. "I'm sorry. They've put out an APB, of course. He's in violation of parole and they'll pick him up as soon as they find him, and take him back to prison."

"What . . ." She spoke through dry lips. "What are the chances of that?"

She could almost see the man shrugging. "Pretty good if he goes back to any of his old haunts or tries to visit his mother again, maybe to get more money. They know the car he's in and they have its license number, Kara."

"But . . . license plates can be changed."

"I'm sure he'll be picked up in a few days. Anyway, I don't think you have real reason to be concerned. From what you've told me, you've moved five or six times since the trial, and you've had an unlisted phone number for years. There's no reason for him to know that you moved to Michigan. Just keep a low profile and don't go back to Florida for a while; stay out of Florida is my advice."

"All right," she whispered, from somewhere finding the manners to thank the man. She hung up, staring at the telephone.

Jerry was loose.

Another wave of dizziness and nausea struck her, and she had to brace herself against desk and chair, holding on until it receded. Dammit! She couldn't collapse into a ball of fear now. She was a grown woman of twenty-seven, not a silly seventeen-year-old. She was a respected businesswoman who was going places, and who already was earning more money than ninety-five percent of women her age. She had prospects, plans! She was worth something!

She calmed herself down. The attorney, after all, was right. She *had* moved many times, and she'd had several phone numbers, all unlisted. There was no reason for Jerry to find her now, and in a few more weeks, her last name would be Devers, making her even more difficult to trace.

However, she should call Laurel and warn her right away.

But when Kara went to the Rolodex she kept on her desk, she realized that she had not kept Laurel's number, either here or in her address book at home. She didn't even remember for sure what town Laurel lived in. Some small town in Ohio, but which one? Her father might have the number, but he was hiking in the Smokies.

Still, remembering her father had remote on his answering machine, she dialed Ken Cleveland's phone.

133

"At the beep, leave a message. I might call you back," was his laconic tape.

"Dad," she said as soon as the beep played. "Dad, please, Daddy, if you phone back to get your messages, would you give me Laurel's number if you still have it. I really need it."

She wavered, wondering whether to say more, and then finally hung up.

She sat staring at the phone. Surely she had done what she could. But guiltily she realized that she had failed her former best friend. It was her biggest sin, Kara knew with deep shame, one for which she would surely be judged. But she hadn't wanted to be dragged into Laurel's constellation of fears and neurotic sightings of Jerry.

She wasn't a superwoman, she could not give help and sympathy when she felt so vulnerable herself.

Maybe in a few months she would call Laurel, she promised herself. Another year or so, when she felt stronger, when she'd had the chance to enjoy the safety of being married to Rob. She'd make her peace somehow with Laurel and maybe even persuade her to get professional help.

CHAPTER 14

Jennifer's bedroom was the most beautiful room that Cindy had ever seen. It had pink flowered wallpaper, a bed canopied in the same pattern, and even pink shelves built into the walls that held a fabulous array of dolls. There were dolls of every kind, from wonderful little newborn babies, dressed in long lacy gowns, to princess dolls and even Raggedy Anns, in addition to Jennifer's collection of Barbies, which far outnumbered Cindy's.

The only thing that was spoiling the day was Jennifer's mood. She and her mother had yelled at each other for about twenty minutes because Jennifer had left her wet bathing suit on a wooden table. Now both girls were banished to Jennifer's room, with orders not to come out until dinner.

"I *hate* mothers," Jennifer said, pouting. Her cheeks were still red from the quarrel. "I hate this grody room. I hate staying here all afternoon. We're going to be so bored, and there isn't even any TV."

Cindy loved the room. There were cardboard boxes stored in Jennifer's closet that contained old costumes from the days when Jennifer's mother had been in a church drama group. These were stuffed with long dresses, rhinestone necklaces, shawls, shoes, purses, even some old girdles and bras and men's suits.

"Let's play with the costumes," she suggested.

Jennifer was still mad, and not about to be nice. "Oh, those crappy old things. Who wants to play with those?"

"Let's. It'd be fun. I love old dresses, don't you? And there might be some high heels in the box. We could put them on. And all the necklaces."

"You can't wear those shoes. I've got big feet so I can get into them, but your feet are too little, Cindy."

"No, my feet are as big as yours," Cindy protested.

But when the girls held both their feet out, Jennifer's, long and slender, were definitely bigger.

Pretending that she didn't care, Cindy busied herself rummaging through the three cardboard boxes of folded-up costumes.

"Look—look at all these," she said to Jennifer. "Is this an evening gown? Look at all the sparkly things."

"Don't you know anything? Those are sequins."

"Sure, my mom wears them all the time."

"She can't wear them all the time, silly," Jennifer said. "You wear them to dress up fancy, to go out to a party where all the men are in these black tuxedos with the black ties. My Mom and Dad go to parties like that all the time. Does your Mom?"

Cindy flushed. Jennifer sometimes made her feel funny. Like she wasn't as good, because her Mom and Dad were divorced and she came from a broken home.

"Come on," Jennifer urged, suddenly changing her mood as she leaned over the box and began to paw through it, restlessly tossing dresses aside. "Look, a white dress and a tuxedo jacket. You can be the groom, Cindy, and I'll be the bride.''

Bride. A word that had so many feelings with it. Cindy blinked, feeling a tiny rush of hurt that began telescoping into a much larger one.

"No," she said.

"You have to, because I want to, and it's my house. My Mom is babysitting you, Cindy, and these are my Mom's costumes.'' Jennifer shook out the crumpled white garment, which was so long it dragged on the floor despite her efforts to hold it up. There was a lace hem and yards of stiff netting.

Cindy backed away. "I suppose you're going to be the bride,'' she said.

"Yeah . . . You can wear this, you can be the groom.'' Jennifer thrust the jacket into Cindy's hands.

Holding the jacket, Cindy said, "I don't want to be the groom, I want to be the bride.''

"Well, we can't have *two* brides, silly,'' Jennifer pointed out reasonably. She lifted up the white dress and began trying to get it over her shoulders. "Help me with this. Help me get it on. There's too much cloth.''

Cindy started to help, then stopped. "This game sucks, Jennifer, because you always tell me what to do. You're too bossy.''

"I am not.''

"Are so.''

"Are not!'' Jennifer's head emerged from the neck hole, her reddish hair touseled. "Anyway, Cindy, your Dad is getting married and you're getting a step. And everyone knows about wicked stepmothers.''

"They do not,'' Cindy said, staring at her friend. Her mother had said much the same thing. Her mother had had a step, and her stepmother had cut her hair short like a boy's and her mother cried. Would Kara ever do that? Kara was the prettiest lady Cindy had ever met, and she desperately longed to have blond hair like hers, instead of her own black. Kara always brought her chocolate, and helped her make doll dresses.

But a wedding . . . she didn't want her Dad to be in a wedding.

"All steps are bad, Carey Wallisberg said so," Jennifer went on. "*Her* step made her sit at the table for two hours until she ate her green peas. And they wouldn't let her go to Cedar Point. Now, come on, put on that tuxedo so we can play."

Cindy loathed peas, and her Dad and Kara had not let her go on the plane. The anger and hurt of that day came flooding back, stronger than ever.

"No," she said, backing toward the door, where she could hear the sounds of Cindy's mother vacuuming downstairs.

"Baby," taunted Jennifer.

"You're the baby!" screamed Cindy. "You! Not me, you! You don't know anything, do you? You are such a grody person, Jennifer, *you don't know anything at all*!"

She turned and picked up the small plastic purse her grandmother had given her and ran out of the room, running down the stairs two steps at a time, and out of the front door into the summer afternoon.

Kara spent the day giving herself reassurances. She was hundreds of miles away from Jerry Quick, shielded from him by a string of address and phone number changes. In East Lansing she'd had a dormitory address, and had also lived in two apartments. She'd lived in two more apartments in Rochester before she bought her house. She felt she would be very hard to trace, especially by someone who had been incarcerated for ten years.

And Florida was a three day drive away.

She forced herself to put it out of her mind while she interviewed the two candidates for salesperson. One was a woman who said she had sold ad space for the *Oakland Press*. She was about thirty, blonde, and wore a ring on almost every finger, plus a tennis bracelet, and a diamond pendant. To Kara she seemed edgy and too nervous, constantly fiddling with a cigarette she had asked if she could smoke. She would project that same unsettledness with customers, Kara felt sure. Besides, she preferred to keep a non-smoking office.

She ended the twenty-minute interview, thinking that people had no idea how they really projected themselves.

The other candidate, male and early sixties, said he was early-retired from Chrysler Corporation. He was a twinkly-eyed Dick Van Dyke type, very outgoing, and Kara knew her accounts would be favorably impressed. But Chrysler Corporation? He'd probably pulled down $80K before, plus a car and bonuses. What did he want with her?

She asked him the question. "Well," he responded, "I live in Rochester over in Grosse Pines, and you're so close I could even ride my bike. Your set-up is so nice and small. I thought you might need some help on a consulting basis."

She felt both offended and disappointed at his assumption that she was small potatoes, a retirement hobby. She promised to keep his resume on file, and rose, dismissing him with a hand shake.

When he had left she sank back in her chair, her thoughts about Jerry returning. She knew she wasn't going to feel easy until she had heard from Fendon that Jerry Quick had been picked up and was in custody. Anger filled her. Why had they let him go like that? Why couldn't victims be given a voice in sentencing and parole? Victims were usually allotted short shrift in the law enforcement process, she had learned. People didn't want to think about victims' rights or indeed victims at all. They wanted to push it all aside, just as she herself had pushed Laurel Fearn aside.

Violent rape was too ugly to admit into your thoughts and most people didn't.

Next she interviewed the young cartoonist. Jim Bird was a scrawny young man with wire-rimmed glasses who looked exactly like the media stereotype of a computer hacker. He read over the agreement Kara had asked her lawyer to draft up, and to her relief, signed it with only minimal haggling over details.

After Bird left, she closed her office door, a sign to her staff that she did not wish to be disturbed. She found herself standing at the window looking out. Pairs of women shoppers strolled past as they visited Wild Wings and the other neighboring boutiques.

Kara eyed them with a stab of envy. *They* didn't have anything scary or frightening or guilt-inducing to bother them. *They* hadn't boxed themselves into the impossible position of needing someone to talk to, and not getting it because they hadn't been honest with one single person in their life.

She gave herself up to a few stinging tears. Even Rob, much as he loved her, was the last person she could confide in. It was too late. How could she spring it on him that she was a rape victim . . . then ask him for emotional support because her rapist had violated his parole, all at once? She couldn't. It was impossible. Rob would not know what to think, would be angry and hurt that she had not trusted him. Trust was an important issue for Rob and was one of the reasons he had divorced Dee.

Angie's voice outside her door rescued her from her attack of self pity. "Kara? Kar? You okay?"

"What? Oh, yes . . ." Kara quickly scrubbed at the wetness around her eyes, and went over to open the door and let Angie in.

"Jesus, kid, you look awful. You *have* got the wedding blues. Holing yourself up in here." Angie had the knack of sounding tough-cheerful. Kara could have kissed her for her normality, her blond hair tousled as usual from the hours she spent daily on the phone drumming up business. The wedding blues. Of course, that was what Angie thought.

A tiny beat of a second passed in which Kara actually considered telling Angie everything. She desperately needed some kind of support. Angie's life hadn't exactly been roses either. After her messy divorce in 1984, her friend had undergone an abortion and nearly died of pelvic infection—a fact few knew. Since then she had lived with daily guilt. Surely Kara's story wouldn't shock her friend. Maybe she'd be hurt, yes. But not enough to not understand.

But then the second passed and Angie had her by the arm and was steering her out of the room. "Look, girl, you need a drink and you need one bad. I've got a bottle of Bailey's back in my office and a couple of glasses. Let's go have some."

"In the middle of the day, Ang?"

"Don't be such a priss. Come on, I'll tell what's-her-face to hold our calls. You need something, Kar. You look positively choked. You and Rob didn't have a fight, did you?"

"No fight," Kara said, allowing herself to be led.

"Hold all the phone calls for us, please," Angie threw out to the girl from Kelly Services as they went past the front desk. "We're going to be in a meeting."

Angie's office was a cluttered space created in what had once been the house's kitchen. Cupboards had been removed and replaced with paneling, and there was a desk, and a comfortable, nubby-weave couch on which Angie had piled stacks of the four-color P.R. and rate folder they gave to prospective advertisers. Every table top held heaps of papers, issues of *Bargain Hound*, proofs of ads, and Angie's cryptic phone notations, which only she could read.

141

Angie rummaged in what once was the pantry, until she had located a package of plastic cups dating from their last Christmas party, and the bottle of chocolate cream liqueur, still in its gold foil gift box.

"Here it is, Bailey's, the thinking woman's anesthetic. Sorry, no ice. How much do you want? A lot, I hope."

They sat talking and drinking Irish Cream, getting deeply engrossed in one of their sessions that covered men in exhaustive detail. Angie enlarged on her often-expressed theory that men of today were actually aliens who, 80,000 years ago, had been marooned on the planet earth and forced to mate with the female natives. The original males, much weaker, were killed off by viruses imported by the more virile visitors.

"Another reason the original men died out," Angie elaborated, sipping Bailey's. "They were only two-inchers, physically speaking. They couldn't put the pedal to the metal. Now, if we ever get any more visitors from outer space, of the male persuasion, I wonder what they'll be like compared to the males we've got now . . ."

By 5:30 p.m., Kara was on the way to being drunk, and had nearly allowed herself to forget that she and Rob had a theater date tonight. For the first time since the call from Fendon, the rape and Jerry Quick receded from her mind and gave her some relief. She could have sat there all day laughing with Angie, who could be very outrageous, and was the only person she knew who had actually once attended a Halloween party dressed as "Foxy Grandma Flasher."

What would she do without Angie? And yet all these years she had kept a secret from her, and might easily go on doing so. Why? Because she was a coward. She'd been so proud of herself for not being a victim any longer, for being a survivor—and yet she was still a victim, she realized. As long as you had to hide things you were a victim.

They had finished half of the bottle when there was a timid tapping at the door.

"Mrs. Cleveland? Mrs. Cleveland?" It was Lynette, the Kelly Girl.

Angie answered through the door, "We're still in a high-level meeting. Highest level."

"It's Mr. Devers. He said Miss Cleveland should be sure and call back right away. It's very important."

"Let him wait," Angie told Kara grandly. "Let all men wait."

"No . . ." Kara got up and opened the door. "Lynette? When did he call?"

"Just now. I just hung up."

"Did he say where he was calling from?"

"Home."

"Okay, thanks." Kara excused herself and went to her own office, where she quickly dialed Rob's number. She felt woozy from the unaccustomed Bailey's, and the cloyingly sweet taste of the chocolate lingered on her palate. But she didn't think she was drunk. She just felt very relaxed.

Rob picked up the phone on the first ring. "Kar? It's Cindy," he told her. "I can't find her."

"What?"

"She went over to Jennifer's this noon to play and I had to visit a couple of building sites. Mrs. King said she would keep Cindy for the afternoon. But something happened—I don't know what. I got back to the office and Mrs. King had been trying to reach me. She said the girls were playing 'Bride,' and suddenly Cindy just stalked off. She ran outside the house and was gone. That was two hours ago."

"Oh, no," Kara said, not disguising her dismay.

"Mrs. King gave me a list of little girls that Cindy might

know, and I've called most of them. They haven't seen her." Rob sounded discouraged and angry. "Some of them barely know her, Kara. She only visits here on weekends, she doesn't have lots of friends in Rochester the way she does at home. The scamp, I'd like to wring her little prima donna neck."

"I'm coming over," Kara said. "I'll help you look."

The northbound traffic on Rochester Road was heavy, clogged with commuters on their way home from office centers in Troy, Warren, Southfield or Detroit. Kara had gulped down a cup of coffee before she left, annoyed with herself for the Bailey's, which had been a foolish attempt at escape. She drove just at the speed limit, chafing when a fender bender temporarily slowed progress at Dutton Road.

Recklessly she followed the example of a carload of teenagers, and pulled out on the right shoulder, driving around the gridlock.

She finally pulled into Rob's driveway and parked, hurrying inside the house. Her fiance was just hanging up the phone, his face set, lips drawn together in a thin line. "I called the emergency room at Crittenton," he told her grimly. "I was afraid—but she hasn't been admitted, thank God."

"Crittenton!" Kara thought it highly unlikely that Cindy was a hospital case. "Don't you think that's a little premature?"

"Probably, but I just wanted to eliminate that particular worry." Bob leaned toward her, sniffing. "What's that I smell? Chocolate?"

"Bailey's. Angie wanted me to have some, it's her birthday," Kara lied, disgusted with herself for the ease with which the untruth dropped from her lips. But how could she say, I was drinking because I'm getting cold feet about our marriage and because my former rapist has just jumped his parole.

"I think we should look for her in the car," Rob said.

"Right."

"The little devil . . . why did she do it, Kara? Running off like that without a thought. Dee poisons her mind, Kara. I don't know what she says to her, but she sure as hell says something. Dee is so bitter. She hates me because I wouldn't take her back after she had that affair. It's probably Dee who doesn't want us to marry, not Cindy."

A thought which might have some merit, Kara realized.

They got into Rob's car and drove to Jennifer's house, which was situated in the village itself. Cindy had met Jennifer at day camp last year.

They circled up and down the adjoining streets, working their way out onto Rochester Road again. The Dairy Queen was doing a big business, knots of children and teenagers crowding its center enclosure where the windows were.

"You don't suppose she stopped to get a Dairy Queen?" Kara wondered, trying to hide her renewed anger at Cindy.

"She'd better not."

Rob pulled into the lot behind the building, inching his car into the narrow drive that was an obstacle course of protruding car bumpers and kids with Dilly Bars and Blizzards. They found a space and went inside. The space was full of children wearing bathing suits, shorts, "Y" and swim club T-shirts. Fresh-faced Rochester children, of course, many of the little girls extremely pretty. No Cindy.

While Rob asked the middle-aged woman behind the window if she had seen a girl of Cindy's description, Kara stepped back along the wall. She guessed she just wasn't in tune with Rob's anxiety about this. Somehow she didn't have the feeling that Cindy was in any danger. In fact, if she wasn't at the Dairy Queen, they should probably try the other ice cream shops in town. When Rob returned, shaking his head, Kara suggested that they drive to the Baskin Robbins in the center of town.

Rob looked disgusted. "If she's just stuffing herself with ice cream—"

Kara heard her voice rise. "Anything to torment us. Don't you see, Rob? She ran off when Jennifer wanted to play 'bride.' It's no accident that she keeps getting upset every time the word bride or wedding is mentioned."

"We'll talk about it later," Rob said sharply. "After I've found her and paddled her butt."

They drove down the hill into town, a walk that would be more than a mile and a half for Cindy from Jennifer's. Five minutes later they had found a parking space in front of the local 31 Flavors, and two minutes after that they had located Cindy herself, who was seated at one of the small, school-desk chairs inside Baskin Robbins, finishing the last of a hot fudge sundae.

Cindy looked up, startled, as they entered. She looked adorable, Kara noted, with her snub nose, big eyes, and chocolate-smeared upper lip. There were dried tear streaks on her cheeks, and she carried a small shopping bag from The Little Green Apple gift shop.

"I had five dollars, Dad," Cindy announced. "I had enough to get a little, little kitten on a key chain. And then I looked in the windows and there was a balloon man and I was hungry."

"Hungry!" Rob glared at his daughter, for once unmoved by her Barbie doll charms. "Jennifer's mother told me she gave you pizza for lunch. And she gave you cookies. How could you be hungry? You just ran off, that's what you did, and Mrs. King was worried sick." Kara could see the anger in the tenseness of Rob's face, the way his neck muscles corded tight. He walked over and took his daughter by the elbow, pulling her out of the chair. "Have you paid for this?"

"They *always* make you pay first, Dad," Cindy said, pouting as more tears sprang to her eyes. "I didn't like her old games, that's why I ran away. Jennifer plays grody games. Jennifer sucks!"

"Don't you talk like that! Where did you learn to talk like that? You're coming out to the car with us, and there's going to be no dinner for you, young lady."

"I didn't *do* anything," Cindy whined as they walked to the car. Her face looked crumpled with surprise as if she had not thought Rob capable of such wrath.

On the sidewalk Rob stopped to stare at his daughter. "Cynthia Darlene Devers, you did plenty. You took off and left without telling Mrs. King where you were going and I won't stand for it, not while you're visiting me. You might pull that trick with your mother but you're not going to pull it with me."

"I want Mom," Cindy cried as Rob pulled open the car door.

"Why?" Rob demanded furiously. "So you can go to her and tell her you only got three pieces of pizza and about eight cookies and a big sundae at Baskin Robbins? You've behaved like a pig today, in more than one department, and I'm not very proud of you. And when we get home you are going to call up Mrs. King and apologize for your behavior."

"Dad . . . please. . . . " Cindy sat huddled in the back seat, her bravado fading.

"Don't say another word," Rob warned.

"But Dad . . ."

"You are in the doghouse with me, Cynthia, and I don't want to hear one more word."

Cindy stared to cry, and Kara turned her head, unable to bear the sound of the child's high-pitched sobs.

"I hate you, Daddy!" Cindy yelled through her tears.

"You don't hate me."

"I do hate you, I do, I do, I do! And I hate Kara, too. She's not my mother—she's nothing but a step!"

"Cindy!" Rob said sharply.

"She is, she is, she's nothing but a step. Steps are horrible, Jennifer said so!"

"Jennifer doesn't know anything about it."

"She does, she does so," the child wept.

In the front seat Kara sat silently beside Rob, waiting while he switched on the ignition. Tears brimmed to her own eyes in spite of her efforts to keep them back. This was totally hopeless, she thought dully. Cindy did hate her. She'd finally said it aloud—and the child meant it, too.

How was it possible to fight against that? And did she even want to?

At least Kara gave Rob credit—after her obligatory phone call he sent his daughter to her room without dinner and without TV. A stack of Nancy Drew books on her bedside table would be her only amusements, aside from the half-dozen or so Barbie dolls perched on her dresser, and the rows of other dolls and toys Cindy seldom touched.

"You are not coming out of this room again tonight except to go the bathroom," Rob said sternly.

"Dad!" Cindy cried. "There's a movie on cable tonight—"

"I don't care if there's a movie on cable," Kara heard her fiancé tell his ten-year-old daughter, and then his voice lowered and she could not hear the rest of it, something about "Kara," and "Kara's feelings," and "you don't hate." She didn't even want to hear the rest of it as Rob ordered his daughter to love Kara, or at least to give it a chance.

What kind of love was that, when you *had* to feel it? She didn't want anyone loving her merely because they had to. Even a child of ten. And she supposed Cindy felt the same way as well.

Restlessly, she paced Rob's living room, stopping to touch one of the bright paintings with her fingertip. The swirled paint had been mixed with some kind of plastic, so that it could be worked for texture. There were cross-hatchings and lines that looked as if they'd been done with a comb. It was "very good art," as Rob had told her once. But totally opposite in conception, mood and style from her own favorite painting, a romantic pastel of flowers in a basket, guarded by a snoozing tabby cat.

Where would the tabby hang here, in this starkly modern "show" home? Somehow she and Rob had not settled a lot of those crucial details. The omission suddenly struck Kara with sharp foreboding. Rob was sweet, he was warm and wonderful and caring, but they were so different. There were problems . . . if she were to be totally honest, Cindy was only one of the problems.

She sighed, turning away from the picture, depression seeping through her.

"Well, I've laid down the law," Rob said as he descended the minimalist stairs, with spaces for risers.

"Good," Kara said automatically.

"Her mother has spoiled her," Rob added.

Kara said nothing. And then, to her surprise, she did open her mouth. "I'm sure you're very right, Dee has influenced her in a negative way. But I'm sure it's more than just her mother."

"What?"

"Sorry, but I think it takes both parents to spoil a child. You've created an unreal world, Rob. A world where everything happens just for her. You've filled her weekends with treats and gifts, making every Saturday and Sunday into a—a mini-Disney World."

"I beg your pardon," Rob said coldly.

"I know I'm right. Every weekend when she gets here

the first thing she wants to know is, 'what are we going to do today, Dad?' And then she pouts if you haven't got something special planned. She doesn't care about seeing you . . . us . . . all she wants is the fun, the treats, the trips to the zoo and to the movies."

Rob swiveled his head to stare at her, and she could see by the ruddiness of his complexion how angry he was. "Sure," he burst out. "Sure, it's all that simple, isn't it? You forget, Kara, that Cindy is a child of divorce, shuttled back and forth between her parents. How am I going to share any time with her if we don't have something to do? We can't just sit and look at each other. So what if I take her to the zoo or to the movies? I can afford it. I want to take her." He narrowed his eyes at her. "My divorced father lifestyle isn't the real issue here, is it?"

Kara felt a little wave of fear. She had never seen him look exactly like this, lips thinned with anger.

"What do you mean?"

"I mean just what I said. You're angry because Cindy said she hated you. You're angry at *her*. She's just a child, Kara, a little ten-year-old girl."

"Some ten-year-old girls get their periods," Kara snapped. "And Cindy's already getting breasts. So don't tell me she's that young. And, yes, I am angry at her. She has done nothing but be rude and hateful to me for the past year, but it's just about quadrupled since we announced our engagement. She hates me, she hates the idea of the wedding, and she wants to break us up."

"No!" Rob exclaimed involuntarily.

"Sure she does. What else is this all about? All the pouting and crying and manipulating—it's meant to divide us, Rob. She'd like nothing better than if I were to hand your ring back to you right now and tell you to forget it."

The words popped out of her mouth before she could stop them. They hung in the air, swollen with meaning.

Rob's face darkened, his eyes growing suddenly moist. He looked exactly as if she *had* given him the ring.

''Is that what you want?'' he asked quietly.

''No,'' she whispered.

He turned away, not touching her, the set of his shoulders rigid with hurt. ''Then don't talk like that.''

''I . . . I'm sorry,'' she said, swallowing. ''I think I'd better go home until we cool down.'' His back was to her, and she wondered what was going on in his head, how badly her words had stabbed him. ''I guess this was our first real fight,'' she added, hesitantly.

He did not respond.

''Please. I'm sorry. Can't we kiss and make up? I can't go home like this, Rob, with you so angry.''

''Okay,'' he said, turning. He held her perfunctorily. She tried to slide herself into his warmth, into the circle of caring that had always surrounded them before, but found the feeling missing.

''Please,'' she begged.

Obediently he tightened his grip on her, but the feeling still did not connect. ''We'd better sleep on it,'' he told her heavily. ''I need a little time to get back to normal, Kara. I'll call you in the morning.''

''Okay,'' she said, getting her purse. He did not walk her to the door, and she let herself out, feeling another surge of the anger and fear, a feeling that terrified her by its familiarity. This was the kind of scene that had happened before she had dumped her other two fiancés, Chuck and Ken.

Was it going to happen again? Was she going to break it off with Rob? She felt all of the symptoms gathering within her, waiting only for the right trigger to set them in motion.

''Oh, Jesus,'' she said aloud to herself as she trudged across the driveway to her car.

CHAPTER 15

It was noon again—on what day, Jerry didn't know.

He had been driving so long that his eyes burned from the constant effort of watching the road. Waves of tiredness swept through him, so that several times he caught himself nodding off at the wheel for dangerous seconds of blankness. He had driven all night since Valdosta. Blending with the traffic, afraid he would see some State Police car on his tail.

But he felt he did not have that much to worry about. As far as the girl went, she never did see his license plate. He would bet she couldn't describe the car he drove either. If she described anything at all. She had been naked, sodden and bloody when he left her, tossing her into a swampy area along the deserted Georgia road. At the time it had seemed an enormous, super-charged, explosive high, but now he realized it was only preparation, and the high had not been that intense after all. Not the way it could be.

Unconsciously he lifted his right hand off the wheel and examined his fingernails. A bit of dried rust-red decorated the half-moons of his nails. He picked at it without thinking.

He hummed to himself, flicking the radio from station to station, trying to keep awake. At least the new music wasn't strange to him—they'd had little to do at Raiford but listen to the radio, fighting over the stations. The big blacks usually won out. So he'd listened to a lot of rap.

He flicked the dial now, trying to find anything but rap. He was never going to listen to that shit again if he could help it—he was a free man. He was flying now, and things were going to be great from here on.

He pulled off into a rest area near Atlanta and snoozed for about four hours. His sleep was restless, though, because of the fact that he couldn't really stretch his legs out. He tossed and turned, dreaming that Capper was raping him again. The huge, distended cock rammed into his anus, splitting him apart as a butcher splits a chicken. Splitting apart his rectum and tearing his intestines!

He cried and sobbed and screamed as his intestines started rolling out of him, all blue-white and shiny. They tumbled down onto the floor. Then they became link sausages, endlessly clipped together. Only these were purplish, and rotted-looking with growths on them. AIDS growths . . .

He awoke with sourness at the back of his throat. To his horror it was vomit, and he was forced to open the car door and throw up onto the dirty asphalt of the rest area parking lot. He listened to the raw sounds of his retching. A truck driver on his way in to the men's room stared at him.

Shit. This was *their* fault, all of it. Those two bitch girls who had begun everything.

He went into the men's room, rinsed out his mouth, shaved, used the facilities and changed his clothes. He put on some khaki twill pants this time, Levi's, and a light blue shirt that said Land's End on the label. It was a little tight around the biceps, but would do. That shithead Ed, his mother's husband, sure did have a lot of good clothes. When he got settled, Jerry was going to buy some of his own.

He drove on, the road blurring in front of his eyes. He reached Cincinnati and spent a night at a Day's Inn. For a joke he registered as Jerry Cleveland, but the desk clerk was only interested in getting the money up front, since Jerry had no credit card.

He bought some whiskey at a party store and used it to drink himself into enough oblivion so he could sleep without the nightmare. The next afternoon he was on the road again.

Ohio. The green and rolling Ohio farm country seemed almost unreal to him, too flat, with farm houses visible from miles away, dotted on the horizon.

He didn't like that sensation of too much space. Did people really live that kind of life, out in the fields riding farm tractors all day in the boiling sun? He had no idea what crop the guys on tractors were planting. It was as alien to him as a slum in Rangoon.

He pulled into the little college town of Oxford, Ohio, about five o'clock. He drove into town, passing one or two dingy Mom and Pop motels. Then some big dormitories to his right that were surrounded by an oasis of big, umbrella-like shade trees.

He didn't want to stop to ask directions, so he just winged it, taking a random turn to the left, then a right. The streets had pleasant, middle-America names: Church Street, Walnut, Beech, Elm, Campus Avenue. But something about the place hit him wrong. Maybe it was the dozens of old-looking brick campus buildings, all alike with their cream-colored trim. The big trees arching ahead, creating caverns of shade. Or maybe it was the two coeds who cut across the street in front of him, blond and clean-looking. One carried a couple of books so thick they must have weighed five pounds each. He felt diminished at the sight. Summer classes, he thought.

The downtown was amazingly small, dominated by a big water tower that stuck up over everything about ninety feet high, with graffiti painted on it. *Mod Lives, Class of ?*, it said in dripping blue paint. There were a couple of restaurants, one with a big glass window front filled with plants. One little movie house, and a bookstore called the Miami Co-Op. People strolled around with ice cream cones or lounged on a long row of wooden benches, like the place was a damned park.

A *collegiate* world, he thought scornfully, where even girls were studying to be engineers and professors. Girls smarter than he was.

He drove up and down, searching for the College Street address he'd found in Cleveland's book. The street was comfortably shabby, lined with big, old houses that had sagging front porches and front yards beaten down to dirt. A handpainted sign was nailed to a porch pillar: *Party Is Here*. Another house was labeled *Animal House Annex*.

At one house, three girls sunbathed on a roof, playing a big portable radio. He didn't wave to them, though. He didn't want anyone to remember his passage through here.

Finally he found the house. It was gray, its paint peeling, but large and rambling, with an addition built on at the back, half buried in overgrown forsythias and lilacs. Two pots of petunias set on the front steps needed watering. He touched his foot to the brakes, slowing slightly so he could take the house in.

And then he saw her, seated on a side porch in an old-fashioned rocking swing hung from chains, dressed in a white hospital uniform. Puffing on a cigarette, she stared straight ahead of her almost blankly, lost in some angry thoughts.

Laurel Fearn.

His heart skipped little beats, as the impact of it beat into him. Laurel. The damn address book had been accurate one hundred percent. Here she was, by God, just as the father had written down. It was a sign. If God hadn't wanted him to come here he would not have laid out the trail for him so beautifully.

He drove past, sneaking sidelong looks. In court, Laurel had been white-faced, but still pretty. Now she looked like one of the female prison guards, her eyes dark holes of bitterness. Her complexion had gone sallower, and her black hair was lanky and oily, as if she seldom bothered with it. She handled the cigarette with abrupt, stabbing motions.

Bitch, he thought, as his car rolled on to the corner.

Later tonight, he would come back.

He spent a couple of hours in the little movie theater, watching a Dolph Lundgren picture which turned him on with all the shooting. Then a pizza, and he drove around for a while, out by a place called Hueston Woods.

It got dark. Hatches of insects began to twirl around in the hot air, filling it with their dancing bodies. Jerry changed his clothes in the car, putting on jeans with a long-sleeved navy blue pullover. Dark clothes would help him blend into the darkness. He changed out of the Reeboks to black shoes. The last thing he needed was someone to see the white shoes twinkling back and forth as he walked. He'd bought a flashlight and made sure he had it with him.

He drove back to College Street and found a new spot to park. Then, batting his hand in front of him against a sudden swarm of the summer bugs, he walked back to Laurel's.

It was a simple matter to break into the house. The alley behind the street was used for parking by residents, so his heading back there would not attract undue attention. Once in the yard the tangle of forsythia bushes would hide his activities.

The house was old fashioned, with high ceilings, and smelled poor. The kitchen had a linoleum floor so old that the pattern was worn off in some places. The counters were cluttered with washed dishes that had been spread out on towels to air dry, while a plastic can held a load of coffee grounds going rancid. It reminded Jerry so much of the home he'd grown up in that he got the creeps.

Silence, though. Was she in here sleeping in a bedroom, maybe sleeping naked to catch the night breeze? He felt great to be in her house, controlling it, in power here. His cock began to harden, the sensation urgent. *Man.* Breaking in was better than he thought. He would put one hand over her mouth, the knife first at her throat.

She'd be so terrified she'd shit. Legs open, wide to him, her black hair gaping.

He explored around, searching for Laurel's bedroom, getting harder by the second as he flashed the light ahead of him. But the sounds of the house disappointed him. He heard no breathing, no light, female snoring.

Shit . . . he began to think. Was she going to cheat him?

Then he smelled talcum powder and saw a door standing half open. He froze, listening. Not one fucking sound of a person, nothing but traffic out on the street and the yappy bark of a neighborhood dog.

He shoved at the door, slamming it open viciously. The noise echoed his rage at being thwarted. The rat-cunt wasn't here.

He burst in. The room was hardly big enough to turn around in. There was an unmade twin bed. Nurses' uniforms hung from a hook on the inside of the door. Ashtrays brimmed with butts and ashes, and a tiny closet was packed with clothes and boxes.

He kicked at one of the boxes, smashing the cheap cardboard until a mess of photos fell out. He picked one up.

Laurel holding some green bird. He threw it on the floor again and stepped on it.

He poked through her dresser drawers, discovering worn cotton underwear with holes, some Miami University sweatshirts, rows of pill bottles containing Tylenol 3 and Darvocet, probably stolen from a hospital, several penny and nickel rolls, and an envelope containing $135. Grinning, he pocketed the money and the pills. His erection had gone soft, but his balls ached.

There was also a broken china figurine hidden in one of the drawers. It had been shattered into four or five pieces, as if she'd gotten angry and hurled it at the wall, and now was hiding the evidence of her rage.

He glanced at his watch: midnight.

He took a leak on her bed, getting a strangely euphoric feeling as his yellow piss steamed out onto the faded patchwork quilt.

It was midnight when Kara pulled into her driveway, feeling anxious and edgy, uncertain of what she should do next. The seriousness of their disagreement had shocked her. Again she felt as if their relationship was perilously close to the tipping edge, a sensation she did not like.

As she pressed the garage door opener, for some reason Laurel came into her mind again, but not the angry, victim Laurel. Instead she remembered an occasion a month or so before the rape. She had gone to pick up her friend to attend a movie together. Laurel had been in the Fearns' Florida room, playing with a new cockateel.

"Sweetie, sweetie, sweetie," Laurel had cooed to the bird holding it up, close to her face. "Who do you love, sweetie? Do you love me? Do you?"

A gentle moment, one of the last she had ever shared with Laurel. Odd, that she should remember such a small thing now, after ten years. Did Laurel still own a bird? Was there any love in her life now, a boyfriend perhaps?

She had never asked her those things, never wanted to know them.

As the garage door came up, she pulled in, seeing the stack of boxes she had packed, preparatory to moving in with Rob. There was a garbage bag full of old tennis balls she used for practicing her serve, stacks of old issues of *Bargain Hound*, even scuba gear: a tank, dive belt with weights, B.C. vest, flippers and mask. The last time she had dived was four years ago with her father. Her life, she thought glumly, boxed and packed and waiting for . . . what?

She carried out her trash and left it by the curb for pickup the next day by Oakland Disposal. In the house, she went through her locking-up ritual, and then dialed Rob's number. She couldn't wait until morning to settle this; she knew she would never sleep. She waited impatiently while the phone rang. Finally, on the fifth ring, just before his machine kicked in, he picked up.

"Hello?" He sounded as tired and depressed as she felt.

"It's me. I love you. I really do."

A heartbeat of time while he reacted. "I love you, too," he finally said.

His tone sounded soft and loving again, a little husky, as if this had been emotionally tough on him, too.

Kara gripped the phone, her entire body sagging with the intensity of the relief she felt. God, she couldn't lose Rob. She couldn't let anything trigger her again, the way it had before. She would just fight against the urges, not give in to them.

"I really, really, really do love you," she whispered. "Hey, I don't know what got into me tonight. I was shrewish. And I guess you were right, I did have hurt feelings. Forgive?"

"Forgive," he said.

A little silence fell between them, as they each wondered if they should say more, communicate it out. Kara thought of a dozen things to say and discarded them all. She was so afraid that if she started talking she'd say something else to offend him. They both needed a couple of days to get back to normality. And even then, she'd have to be very careful what she said.

"Want me to come over?" Rob inquired after a minute. Then he added, "Oops, no, I can't, I've got Cindyella. Damn, I'll be glad when we're married and we don't have to go through this constant back-and-forth."

It was a safe topic. "We're the suitcase couple," she tried a lame joke.

"Staying at home in one house, sleeping in one bed, watching one TV set, that's the way I want it to be," Rob said. "Oh," he added. "I'm buying a camcorder, did I tell you? Cindy's growing up so fast. Before we can turn around, it'll be the senior prom. I want to be able to get some really good pictures of her growing up."

Their conversation drifted to innocuous matters, as if the quarrel between them had never occurred.

"I wish I was with you right now," Rob finally murmured.

"Oh, I do, too—" She stiffened. She had heard a sound in the driveway, a chillingly ominous clatter.

"Kara?"

"Just a minute," she said. Putting the phone down, she hurried to draw aside her living room curtains and peer outside. On the apron of her driveway was her neighbor's black labrador retriever, ransacking the garbage bags she had left out. Scraps of paper and tin cans were already scattered all over the cement.

"It's just Marshall," she said, picking up the phone again. "The dog next door. He's on a food run. I'll have to buy some spray to put on the garbage cans. Rob . . ."

"Yes?"

"I do love you so much. I hate it when we fight. Never let us quarrel for long, will you?"

"Kara—" Then Rob cut off whatever he had been going to say. "Well, I won't," he finally promised.

CHAPTER 16

A few minutes after midnight, Jerry saw car headlights flash in the narrow driveway. He got up off the living room couch where he'd been lying, and moved, cat-like, into Laurel's bedroom again. The opened closet door, laden with clothes, made a natural hiding spot.

He waited, listening as she used her key on the back door (with that shitty little lock she had, why'd she imagine it was safe?) There was the squeak of rubbery shoe soles on the kitchen linoleum. Then a click as she switched the kitchen light on. This instantaneously created new shadows in the room where he was, new streaks of light and dark.

He waited, listening to her open the refrigerator, pop open a can of beer. He was getting hard again, his breathing quick. She sighed, muttering something under her breath. Then there was a heavier, clunky sound and he figured she was taking her nurses' shoes off, tossing them in a corner of the kitchen.

He thought about the nurse's uniform. White, slick, nylon, a little tight and short, hugging her ass. The sheer fabric would give a good, clear view of the lacy bra underneath, and bikini panties, French cut, high on the hip.

Yeah. What kind of nurse was she? Did she give back rubs? Enemas? Did a guy lie there naked, stripped down, while she did things to him? He imagined himself turning the tables on her, making *her* strip and kneel down, presenting herself to him. He was getting an enormous hard-on, almost painful in its rock-hard intensity. Even better than with the girl in Valdosta.

He got the knife ready. Took assurance from the feel of it in his hand, the way it fit like an extension of his fingers. With it he felt powerful, invincible, in total control. Nothing could touch him or hurt him when he had that blade in his palm, and no one would ignore him.

He heard cupboard doors open and shut. Then, to his dismay, there was the sudden blare of a TV set, which wasn't what he had in mind at all. Was he going to have to leave the bedroom, go out and scoop her up from in front of the late movie? Fight with it for attention? That didn't feel right to him. Angry, he shifted his position, hating her for not doing what he wanted her to do.

But then, during a commercial, without any warning, she suddenly walked into the bedroom.

She walked straight to the closet. Jerry jumped with the suddenness of it, setting him off balance. *She* was the one who was supposed to be surprised, not him.

She saw him.

For a half-second, they stared at each other.

Laurel stood frozen, her eyes so wide with shock and horror that they looked absolutely round. She had already begun unbuttoning her uniform and it hung open, revealing a white cotton bra and a thin rib cage that showed her bones. She was smaller than he remembered, far more fragile, and he could smell her fear.

"Hey," he drawled. "Recognize me?"

Laurel's indrawn breath, a half-scream, told him she did.

"Oh, God!" she cried out, clutching at air. *"Oh, Jesus!"*

"We're going to have us some fun, rat-cunt," he said, showing her the knife blade, weaving it in front of her. Her eyes followed it, mesmerized. He already had the duct tape out, in his left hand.

"No," she screamed. "God . . . no. . . . please. . . . "

He blocked her way out of the room. "Lots of fun, just like before."

"Please," she screamed. *"Oh, my God!"*

She cowered in front of him, seemingly frozen, paralyzed by the sight of the weaving blade and by the grin on Jerry's face, the huge bulge in his pants. He was getting higher and higher on her fear. Jesus, he loved this. It was such a kingly feeling, better than drugs or sex or *anything*. He was into it now, flying. Invincible.

But she had taken a wild step backward, edging toward the first floor window. Maybe she planned to jump out of it. Yeah, that was exactly what she was going to do.

Jerry knew he had to make his move now. He lunged forward, choking his left arm around her throat, while, with his right hand, he jammed the knife against her jugular.

"Don't scream," he ordered her savagely. "Or I'll cut your goddamned vein. I'll bleed you."

She fought a little more, so he stabbed again, not enough to kill her. He dragged her toward an old bureau mirror, speckled with motes of dust. Mirrors always made it better, he liked watching everything and he wanted her to watch, too. He taped her hands and cut off her uniform, sawing the cloth with the knife when it wouldn't come down off her hips.

He cut off her panties, added them to the pile. He felt

so good. Blood ran down her neck, and down her bare hip. She was sobbing now, sinking to her knees, mucous running from her eyes and nose.

Now all she wore was the bra. He pulled her upright again, and hit her with his hand to quiet her. Feverishly he yanked at the front clasp of the bra.

The cloth fell away, revealing her narrow chest. The sight hit him like a blow. Laurel had one normal breast, a soft, saggy little tit with a dark nipple. But it was the other side that appalled Jerry. God. He'd never seen anything like it. He wanted to gag.

There was nothing but a monstrous scar.

Just this sunken area, stitched across, puckery in places and uneven, with *no tit*. He couldn't believe it. Jesus, it was what he had done to her, he hadn't ever thought about what it would look like after. No plastic surgery. She had just left it all like garbage for him to see.

He stepped backward, sickened, fighting the reflex to vomit. He'd expected . . . somehow he'd expected her to be normal again and she wasn't. He felt things crashing in his head, a terror as awesome as a tornado. Years and beliefs and fantasies, all imploding.

She had done this on purpose. She made herself ugly just to mock him. To show him . . .

He let out a horrible howl of rage.

Then he leaped on her with the knife.

Another June day, brilliant in its intensity of sunshine.

"Park here, Daddy," Cindy ordered. "Park here, here, here, otherwise we're going to have to walk too far to the front gate, Dad! I don't want to walk a mile before we even get inside the zoo."

"Hold your horses, Cindyella," Rob said, half-laughing. "There's a back entrance right there by the fence, can't you see it? That's where we're going to go in."

"Where?" The girl leaned forward in the back seat so that her head was between Rob's and Kara's. "Where? I don't see."

"Right there, kiddo." Rob pointed. "Now will you just relax, huh, and quit back-seat driving? Listen. Can you hear the giraffes roaring? I can."

"Giraffes don't roar," Cindy giggled.

"These giraffes do. They're mutant giraffes, they've got enormous vocal cords and they can sing, too. If you'd just listen for a minute, and not talk so much, you could hear them."

"Oh, Dad," Cindy said, giggling.

The temperature was 83 already and climbing. Pungent animal smells drifted over the zoo fence, almost sickening in the heat. They got out of the car and joined the family groups straggling toward the back entrance. Nineteen-year-old mothers pushed strollers that contained babies wearing only Pampers. Arab women in saris pulled along brown six-year-olds in jeans. There were teenaged girls in incredibly tight shorts, a young black couple holding hands, a troop of Cub Scouts. The visitors to the zoo were as polyglot as the animals that would be inside.

Going down the cement ramp, the odor of straw, manure and exotic feed grew even stronger, and a clatter of iron wheels on tracks marked the passage of the zoo train.

Cindy squealed with excitement. "Dad! Dad! I want to ride on the train! I want to do that first!"

"Okay, Cindyella, but let's look at these exhibits now, as long as we're right here," Rob began. "I think the penguin house is somewhere near here. It's refrigerated, and you can see all these cute little penguins on an ice floe, and then swimming under water—"

"Oh, later, Dad, I want the train first. I rode on it when I came here with my class, there was this tunnel, and it got all dark when we went through it, and we all screamed, even our teacher screamed . . ."

Kara sighed, and resigned herself to an entire day of catering to Cindy. She had taken another day off work, just to please Rob and smooth things over between them, as well as show her devotion to his child. She resisted the urge to find a phone and call Angie to make sure things were all right at *Bargain Hound*. Today was for Rob—her gift to him.

They visited the reptile house, the penguins, and then found a refreshment stand and stood in line so that Cindy could buy a large coke with almost no ice in it, and a hot dog.

"I thought you weren't hungry, Cindy," Rob said in annoyance when the girl ordered a package of chips as well.

"Well, I am! The zoo makes me hungry. It makes me crave hot dogs and cotton candy, too," the child added, swiveling her head to stare at a four-year-old boy carrying an enormous cloud of sticky pink, half of it on his face.

"I draw the limit at that," Rob said. "And no more snacks, either. You pigged out yesterday at Baskin Robbins . . . do you want to get chubby?"

"I'm not chubby!"

"No, but you will be if you keep stuffing yourself."

They walked from exhibit to exhibit, stopping to stare at somnolent polar bears, drowsy lions, and scraggly buffalo with ratty-looking, shedding coats. Children shouted at the animals, trying to stir them to some sort of action. Cindy told Rob that he should buy them a camcorder so they could take pictures of the animals.

At the elephant enclosure, while Rob and Cindy went up close to the fence, Kara sank down on one of the benches. She'd rather people-watch anyway. The people here were incredible. Everyone from four-hundred-pound women to groups of tourists chattering away in Japanese, Norwegian and other languages.

A man with a swaggering walk on the far side of the

exhibit caught her attention. He was young, maybe around twenty-one, and he wore jeans that fit tightly around his narrow, arrogant rump.

Yes, she thought, with an odd tremble that began in the center of her stomach. That was exactly the way it was. Arrogant.

Unaware she was staring at him, the man walked closer to the fence to get a look at the four huge, gray elephants that were lumbering about or lying in the shade. Kara watched him with a kind of concentrated, distilled horror.

Jerry Quick. That was who he looked like. The arrogance, the young, strutting maleness. Even his walk was like Jerry's, with exaggerated swing of hips and thrusting downward of his heels, so cocky even in the courtroom when he was exposed for what he was, a monster.

Jerry.

She tore her eyes away, feeling a wave of fear wash over her so violent in its intensity that the elephant exhibit actually wavered in front of her, turning black. It was one of her panic attacks coming on, so swiftly that she had no way to protect herself against it. She sat rigidly on the bench, trying not to gasp.

"Kara!" Suddenly Rob was beside her on the bench, pulling her up. "My God, are you okay?" She felt him shake her. "I was just turning around to tell you something and I saw you start to faint . . . are you okay?"

"I'm fine," she mumbled.

"You look awful, your face is white as a sheet."

"I said I'm fine."

Rob motioned to Cindy, indicating she should continue to look at the elephants. He slid his arm around Kara, hugging her up close. "It's too hot today, it's the heat," he told her. He fanned her with a zoo directory he'd been carrying. "I shouldn't have dragged you with us today. I know you took time off from work, and it was very generous of you. But maybe you'd rather be at the office."

"No, I—I wanted to be here."

He thought it was the heat and she let him think it. She sat up, feeling perspiration dampen her face and soak into the sleeveless top she wore. Glancing to her left, she saw that the man who looked like Jerry Quick had gone. She realized he had been an illusion, not much different from the sightings that Laurel had claimed she saw.

"I'm okay," she added, taking deep breaths.

"You sure? We can go back to the car. We don't have to stay here. Cindy won't mind."

Cindy would probably mind very much. "No, we promised Cindy and I don't want to disappoint her."

"Okay," Rob said doubtfully. "But I don't want you keeling over."

Three hours later they were finally trudging back to Rob's car, exhausted from the long trek through the zoo, and an even longer wait for the zoo train, which had been packed with children. Kara still felt shaky from the "Jerry" sighting, angry at herself for her weakness. There was no way that Jerry could have been at the zoo.

They got to their car to find that someone had discarded a dirty Pampers on the hood of Rob's car. He threw it into a trash barrel with a sound of disgust. "Urine!" He exclaimed. "It's acid, it'll eat my car finish."

"Oh, *gross*, Dad," Cindy groaned. "Ugh! People can be such pigs!"

"I heartily agree."

"When I have my babies, I'm never going to do such a grody thing, ever. I'm going to have five children," Cindy announced.

Rob raised an eyebrow.

"Five little girl babies," she insisted. "My Mom said I could have them if I want. She said I could have all the babies I want."

Nobody was in a mood to argue with that.

169

When they got to Rob's, Cindy rushed in and headed straight for the den, her sneakers skidding and making a mark on Rob's beautiful bleached oak flooring.

"You'd better go and lie down," Rob said to Kara. "You were terrific, walking all around the zoo like that, but I know you didn't feel good. You still look pale."

"I'm just pale because I've been working every day, pale is my natural color," Kara said, smiling. "I'm okay."

He hugged her. "Well, I want you to rest a little, anyway. You were so patient today with Cindy . . . and I want to thank you."

Tears suddenly sprang to Kara's eyes—tears that he would be so grateful for something she should be doing anyway. "She *is* a beautiful little girl," she told him. "So full of life, Rob, you can't deny that. She has such enthusiasm when she's happy."

He nodded. "I love her, Kar."

"I know. I'll love her, too. I promise."

They stood holding each other, Kara's head bent into the warm, sweetly male-smelling hollow of Rob's neck. And that was when they heard Cindy's voice from the den as she talked on the telephone.

"The zoo . . . yeah, the zoo," she was saying. "We went there today and Dad bought me two cokes and a hot dog and an ice cream and some potato chips. But, Mom? . . ."

The child had obviously telephoned her mother to talk, and to share every moment of her day with Dee. It was a habit Rob frowned upon, as it took away from his time, and, he believed, gave his ex-wife too many views into his privacy. He felt Dee had no right to know every detail of his life.

"Damn," Rob said now. "She's on the horn to Dee again. I've told her to keep those calls down. She spills every goddamned thing we do to her mother."

The child's voice rose again, clearly penetrating into the

room where the adults were. "Yeah, Dad has lots of money," Cindy remarked in a boasting tone. "Yeah . . . he affords a camcorder, and I'm going to take pictures of the zoo animals . . . yeah, I bet it costs a lot of money."

Dee apparently responded. Then, as Rob started toward the den, Cindy's voice rose. "Why don't you come and live with Dad? . . . Yeah, he's got a real big house here, with so many rooms. You could live right here with us. Then you wouldn't have to go to your job, Mom."

Chapter 17

Their fight went into the night, long after Rob ordered a pizza and Cindy was tucked into her bed, exhausted from the day at the zoo. Their views were diametrically opposite. Rob believed that Cindy, with her fantasy that her parents would get back together, was only behaving naturally. He claimed that her feelings would shift in time to include Kara in her life.

Kara believed the reverse—that Cindy, on the contrary, was growing *more* hateful with each day, and that she was doing everything she humanly could to break up their relationship.

"Dammit, children are the cause of most second marriages breaking up!" she told Rob at midnight, as they sat outdoors on his deck, no yard lights on because of the mosquitos. A diaphanous moonlight sifted down on the woods, turning leaves and branches silvery.

"How do you know that? Who said that?"

"Angie told me—and Angie ought to know, she's been

divorced, and she has a lot of friends who've remarried and then got divorced for the second time. Children can really do a couple in, Rob. They play one against the other.''

"I'm not saying they don't, Kara.''

"Well? My God, Rob, we both stood right there and heard her tell her mother that she wanted *her* to come over here and move in with you!''

"She's only a child,'' Rob sighed. "Kara, we've been over it and over it. Why can't you try to be a little more understanding? It's the fantasy all kids of divorce have—that their parents are somehow going to be reunited and get back together again. You can't blame Cindy for that. She's being normal, for God's sake. Even a child psychologist would tell you that.''

"We ought to take her to one,'' Kara said defiantly.

The woodsy sounds of night were suddenly interrupted by one of the teenagers next door, revving up his car motor as he backed out of the neighboring driveway. The sound grew thinner with distance and finally disappeared before Rob spoke again in a cold tone. "You really mean that, don't you?''

"Of course I do. Rob, she *knew* both of us were standing right there. She *knew* we'd overhear her! She did it on purpose. That's what you refuse to admit, that your child does these things on purpose, she does them because she wants to cause trouble between us. And she's causing it, all right,'' Kara added bitterly. "I bet she's lying up there in her bed right now as happy as a flea.''

"She's asleep, Kar,'' Rob said wearily.

"You know what I mean. Rob, you just won't listen, you won't admit to yourself that we have a real problem in Cindy. You think she's normal! Well, maybe she is and maybe she isn't . . . I'm so confused I don't know any more. But I do know this—I don't want to live with a child who hates me.''

"Oh?"

"She's going to make both of us miserable," Kara went on, knowing she had stepped onto shaky ground, from which there could be no possible safe retreat. "She's going to keep right on, playing you against me, and me against you, and you against Dee, and me against Dee, and every other possible combination she can work out. I can't stand that kind of manipulation. I dread the thought of it."

He was staring at her, the whites of his eyes visible in the ambient glow that came from moonlight and a neighbor's lawn light. "My God, Kara," he said.

She gazed at him stubbornly, too proud to back down, hurt coursing through her. "I'm sorry, but that's how I feel."

Rob's voice trembled with anger. "Well, at least we know your real feelings, don't we? Tell me something, Kara—did you get these kind of feelings before your other two engagements, too?"

She spun, shocked. "What?"

"You heard me. Gossip travels. I heard all about them . . . what were their names? Ken? Chuck something? You dumped both of them, didn't you? One only a couple of hours before the wedding. Are you going to do that to me, too, Kara? Is that what this big fight is really all about? To give you a good excuse? That's what you really want, isn't it? An excuse."

Kara stared at him. "That's not it. I'm not looking for an excuse to dump you," she whispered.

"You sure could have fooled me." Rob's voice rose. "You're hiding something from me, Kara. Do you think I'm some kind of a fool that I wouldn't guess?"

"Please—"

"Dammit! And at the zoo, when you felt faint. It wasn't the heat. I'm not that stupid. Something's got you, and it's worrying you like a dog with a bone."

She drew herself up. "I've told you. My upbringing was—"

"Upbringing, bullshit," Rob snapped. "And this thing with Cindy . . . you can't be willing to drop me over a child that I see two weekends a month! You act and talk as if she's going to be living with us all the time—as if she's going to be with us twenty-four hours a day. Well, she isn't! You knew I had her when we met. If you didn't like it, you should have bailed out two years ago, not now. You had plenty of chances, dammit!"

Even in the darkness she could tell that his face was red. He seemed larger, his face and body puffed up, and his stance, leaning toward her, was aggressive. Kara felt a moment of doubt and disbelief. Rob was usually so easygoing. Now she felt as if she didn't even know him.

"Do you want me to bail out?" she cried.

His silence went on a fraction of a second too long. "It's not that. Kara—"

"Well, if you do, I will. Here." Furiously she grabbed at her ring finger, yanking at the engagement diamond, which did not want to slide off her knuckle. She started to cry as she jerked at the ring, hurting her finger. Finally it came off and she shoved it at him, tears streaming down her face.

"You don't mean this," he said, staring downward at the ring, where the diamond caught a stray beam of light and winked like a tiny star.

"I'm sorry," she sobbed, and rushed past him into the house. She ran to the hall table where she had left her purse and slung it over her shoulder, digging into it for her car keys. Rob had followed her into the house.

"Kara—" he called. "Kara—"

"I mean it!" she screamed at him. "I'm leaving. I have to go home."

"Okay." His voice was hard, cold and quiet.

She left, crying.

* * *

She started home, sobbing so hard that she could not see to drive, and had to pull aside onto a dark, subdivision street. She sat behind the steering wheel, rubbing her finger where the skin still hurt from where she had ripped her engagement ring off.

She had actually broken her engagement—for the third time. She had really done it. She had never been so furious at Rob—not in their two years, not like this. She had actually raised her voice and screamed at him.

She bent her head over the steering wheel and cried. How, how could it have happened like this, so damned swiftly? One remark from a child, hours of fighting and . . . finish.

It was all her own fault. The realization was like a freight train running through her head. Cindy had triggered it, yes, there was no doubt about that. But she, Kara, had flung the ring.

Why? Why had she done it?

Was she that scared of marriage? Of commitment? What was wrong with her, that she could not carry an engagement through to the ceremony? She knew she had been uneasy for weeks, ever since she had bought the lace-encrusted dress and sent out invitations to 150 people.

God, she thought, pounding her head. What were they going to do about that? They'd have to call all the guests, cancel reservations, cancel the cake, the photographer, send back wedding gifts. Rob would cancel their wedding trip to Maui, her blindfold "surprise" . . .

At the thought of the innocent fun he had planned, she sobbed and sobbed, clenching the steering wheel as if it were a bulwark, holding her down to the earth. Finally, when a man walking a dog on the sidewalk paused to stare at her in the car, she managed to stop. She fumbled in her purse for a tissue, and blew her nose. Her eyes already felt swollen. Crying usually turned her into a red-eyed fright.

Slowly she drove home.

Her house was waiting for her as she pulled into the driveway, familiar and comfortable, the lights on from the timers so that the windows glowed yellow. She pulled into the garage, seeing the ugly stack of boxes and plastic garbage bags.

Another problem . . . the professor from Oakland University who was waiting to move in. What was she going to do about him? Was she going to have to move to an apartment because she'd signed her house away? Thank God she had not actually sold it. She had at least saved herself from that disaster.

She started to cry again and was still crying as she closed the overhead door and let herself into the house.

There was no possibility of sleep, of course. She was far too strung-out, too grief-stricken for that. She couldn't even sit still for long, but kept pacing the house, checking the window locks, re-checking them, compulsively straightening up her kitchen, which looked woebegone as she had hardly prepared a meal here in days. Well, she'd be cooking here again. Lots. She was back on her own again by her own choice, and how did it feel? she asked herself bitterly.

It didn't feel good at all.

She flung herself down on the couch, and sat staring dry-eyed at the late movie, something with Mel Gibson, she didn't know what it was titled. She could not have recalled any scene that she watched. Midway through a scene with motorcycles, she reached for the phone and dialed Angie.

Her friend's voice was muffled and sleepy. "Shit, Kar, it's 2 a.m."

"Ang? Oh, God, Ang . . . I broke up with him." Kara started to cry.

"Jesus, not really."

"Really. I really did it. It was over Cindy . . . I'm such a goddamn fool."

"You're not a fool, Kara, I saw this coming. This has been brewing for a long time. Tell me what happened."

Kara went over it, losing control a couple of times as she came to the part where she and Rob were on the deck yelling at each other. "He—he knew all about my other engagements," she stammered. "He must have been talking to someone . . . I didn't mean for him to find out like that. I was going to discuss it with him but I didn't."

"You can't just marry someone and not talk to him about your past," Angie said. "Not when your past is a matter of public record, so to speak. I mean, there are any number of people here in Rochester who knew about your other engagements. It's natural to expect them to gossip a little."

If only Angie knew, Kara thought sickly, feeling as if she lived in a convoluted garden of lies. "I know."

"You and Rob didn't really talk all that much, did you? I mean, not about important things."

"I don't know . . ."

"You both just sort of went along with the fantasy. You never got real, Kara."

At that statement, far more truthful than Angie realized, Kara started to cry again. She stood holding the telephone while tears ran down her face and dampened the receiver. Oh, Angie was right, so right! But what was she going to do now? The milk had been spilled. She could hardly go back to Rob now and start confessing all the painful things in her past. After two years, she'd look like a fool.

"Do you want me to come over?" she heard Angie ask.

"What? Oh, no . . . I'll be okay."

"Are you sure? You sound rocky, Kara."

178

She couldn't trust herself with Angie tonight. She was too raw, her feelings too near the surface. She might talk about things she would regret later. She put Angie off. "I—I'll see you tomorrow morning. Maybe we can sneak out for breakfast or something. I . . . I feel too crappy tonight. I think I'm just going to go to bed."

"Okay, then," Angie said doubtfully. "If you're sure."

"I'll be fine. I just need some sleep."

"You know damn well you're not going to sleep. Why don't you sit down and write a letter to Rob? Put all your feelings down on paper. Maybe that might help."

"Write him a letter?"

"Yeah, I read this book, you're supposed to start by putting down all the reasons why you're angry. Then you go into all the reasons you feel regretful, then why you're sorry, then all the things you fear. Then finally you end up with all the reasons you love the person. It's supposed to be very purging."

"Okay," Kara said dully. "I'll try."

In her study Kara sat at her pigeon-hole desk, staring at a legal pad, waiting for the first words to come to her. Nothing came.

Angie and her self-help books, she thought, rubbing her burning eyes. The whole philosophy behind self-help books was that you could create your own miracles, and right now Kara didn't feel capable of creating anything.

She wrote, *Dear Rob*, then sat for long minutes staring at the lined pad. *I am angry because* . . . But it was hard to just categorize it all in a cold, hard list. I am angry because your daughter hates me. I am angry at myself because I don't think I can be the superstepmother you obviously expect. I am angry because I had fantasized the perfect life for us, and it doesn't seem to be turning out perfect, does it?

She scowled at the sheet of paper. But most of all, she

found herself thinking, wasn't she angry at Jerry Quick? She had seen a man who looked like Jerry this afternoon, had nearly fainted in referred terror, and Rob hadn't known anything about Jerry at all. She'd let him think it was the heat. But all along he'd guessed she was lying.

That was the real reason she was angry.

Because she was living a false life.

Because she was living with a terror she didn't know how to get rid of or deal with or talk about.

Because she couldn't have a real life unless she got rid of Jerry Quick, and she couldn't get rid of him because he was inside her. Forever in her head.

She managed to fall asleep sometime around 4:30 a.m., and tossed and turned restlessly, her slumber disturbed by the dawn light that began streaming in her window only an hour later. In her dream, she was in the bedroom again with Laurel, watching as Jerry cut away Laurel's panties with a knife. Blood dribbled down Laurel's thigh as he cut away the nylon cloth.

The blood ran down her leg in a current, that collected in a puddle at her feet, that became a red stream and a torrent and a flood . . .

Kara woke gasping. She sat up, realizing that her hand was clenched at her chest, exactly at the spot where, ten years ago, Jerry had cut her breast with his knife tip. During the night the temperature had gone down, and she sat shivering, clutching herself.

Work. She had to go to work today. Thank God, her day had some kind of structure. She didn't have to stay home by herself and wallow in the morass of unpleasant thoughts that had attacked her last night. She remembered talking about breakfast to Angie, and decided that was exactly what she'd do. They would go to Denny's and indulge in a Grand Slam Breakfast, and she would get her head on straight again.

Dully she dressed, putting on a beige linen skirt and peach blouse, a loose, unstructured peach jacket, a string of beads Rob had given her once. She took off the beads and exchanged them for a silver pendant, then remembered Rob had given her that, too. Finally she stood there with her jewelry box open and cried some more, and decided to wear no jewelry.

She gave Angie a quick call and arranged to meet her at Denny's, on Main Street. Ned Banki, the other salesman, had a key and would open up.

Angie was waiting for her in the lobby, a *Detroit News* and a *U.S.A. Today* under her arm, purchased from the machines in front. "Did you read that Eddie Murphy is getting sued again?"

"What?"

"I said did you read that—oh, never mind. You look terrible, kid. Your eyes look like cherry tomatoes. Jeez, Kara—"

They hugged each other, and Kara felt a wave of feeling for her friend who didn't know half the things that were wrong with her.

"How many? Two?" the hostess wanted to know.

"Yes, two." Angie took charge.

"Smoking?"

"Non."

They were seated in a booth that overlooked the parking lot. A waitress brought them black coffee and took their orders, scrambled eggs for Kara, over easy for Angie.

"I feel so awful," Kara said.

"Maybe it's not over, huh?" Angie sipped her coffee.

"I think it is. Oh, Ang . . ." Kara's voice broke again.

"Well, maybe after you both calm down you can talk and get some things straightened out. Lots of people have fights just before the wedding, it's pretty common. Remember Kathy Frieze? She and her fiancé had a big spat over the wedding vows, and they canceled everything—the

181

church, the minister, the flowers, the whole bit. Five days later they were back together again. It happens.''

Their breakfast came and Kara poked at the eggs on her plate and tried to eat some whole wheat toast, wondering if what Angie said was true. The problem was she'd fantasized some Danielle Steel romance, and life was more like Erma Bombeck.

They rehashed the entire quarrel, including Cindy's contribution, and Angie gave her opinion, which was that all three of them needed to see a counselor.

''What?''

''It's a family problem, kid—something wrong, I don't know what. Cindy's not relating right, Rob needs some help in managing the divorced daddy bit, and you . . . Kara, I get this funny feeling, I've been getting it more and more lately.''

''What kind of feeling?'' Kara said uneasily.

''Oh . . . I can't put my finger on it. It's just that you're not *there* sometimes, you seem distant, like you're holding back, like there's something you're not telling, something awful.''

Kara could only stare, her coffee cup halfway to her lips.

''Well?'' Angie gazed at her with sharp blue eyes. ''I've known you for how long, Kar? Since State, so that makes it, what, ten years? I've always had that feeling. But I thought, well, maybe it was your upbringing, or your mother dying sophomore year, I always felt so sorry for you when she died. Yeah, I thought it was that. But now I don't know. Say something, Kar. Don't just stare at me, say something.''

Kara set her cup down and felt a wild surge of hesitation and desire. She remembered the dream Angie had earlier, about the jagged piece of light. Angie was sensitive, she picked up things, she sensed vibes.

Now . . . now was the time to tell . . .

But she couldn't. She was locked into her secret now, condemned to it, because if she told, she'd unravel her whole life, and she was afraid of confronting her life as a ball of loose and unraveled, frightening events. She had let it go too long.

"Sorry," she said through stiff lips. "There isn't any big secret. I'm just . . . just kind of a private person, that's all."

Angie nodded, but her eyes were still sharp and speculative. "Maybe that's it, then. You hold yourself back, Kar, and I bet Rob senses that." She glanced at her watch. "Oh, boy, it's nine, and I have to call Ken, over at Scallops. He's setting up this coupon thing."

They each left a tip, and then Angie picked up the check, and Kara took it from her. They squabbled politely over it before finally splitting it down the middle. Kara felt heavy and dulled with the burden she was carrying as they left, separating into their two cars to drive to the office. Not only Jerry now, but a broken engagement.

At *Bargain Hound* she buried her feelings in a flood of work. It gave her a feeling of control to field the constant stream of telephone calls, to proofread copy and phone her accountant, dealing with daily crises of varying degrees of importance. As long as she owned *Bargain Hound* her life would never be totally in a shambles. She would always have that to cling to.

Rob telephoned at 11:00, his voice low, husky, obviously pained. "Kara. Could we meet, maybe for lunch, just to talk? We need to talk."

"Rob, what is there to talk about? We talked last night for five, six hours, we talked until we were both hoarse. We didn't settle anything. I . . . I need some more time."

"Kara, please."

She bit her lip. "I'm still so upset. I feel this is my fault," she admitted with difficulty. "I'm sorry, Rob. I wish I had answers, but I don't. We can't get married under this kind of a cloud."

"*What* kind of a cloud? What are you talking about?" he demanded. "All I can see that really happened is we had a fight about Cindy, which just kinda escalated. You have problems committing yourself, Kara, I can see that now. Maybe other problems. But it's not the end of the world. We can deal with it. We will deal with it. But you can't just close the door," he pleaded.

She was silent, hanging on to the phone, thinking what was wrong with her, what kind of fool was she, to throw away this man.

"Kara? Kara? For God's sake, don't just leave me hanging, talk to me. Say something. We have to talk. *Communicate*. If we can't talk, what do we have?"

"I . . . I don't know what to say. I can't think right now."

"Okay. I know you need time. I'll give it to you. I love you, Kara."

Tears sprang to her eyes and she mumbled something and hung up. Rob. She felt such a numbness at the center of her chest, as if her interior had somehow been injected with novocaine. What had happened to cause their love to explode like that? It *was* her fault, but somehow she could not just go running back to Rob and begin things again. Something inside stopped her. Some*one*, she corrected herself bitterly.

That was the real trouble. She had Jerry Quick in her like a cancer, and the minute she reached out for some happiness, he stopped her. He had raped more than just her body, she realized with a sinking, angry feeling.

CHAPTER 18

Jerry pulled into Detroit at noon eighteen hours later, exhausted and disoriented from the long hours behind the wheel.

His legs were cramped, and his back ached from sitting so long. He used the West Grand Boulevard exit, and found a Total station. A German Shepherd, attached to a ten-foot chain, snoozed in the shadow of the station. Its ears pricked up alertly as Jerry got out of the Ciera.

He used the can, which was greasy dirty, and changed his clothes again, putting on another of the Levi's Dockers pants owned by Ed, pale blue this time, and a short-sleeved yellow chambray shirt. Both pants and shirts were freshly pressed with sharp creases. He bought a map of Oakland County from a fat black girl who was stationed behind a cage of iron bars.

He went back to the car and got in again, sitting there with the door open so he could read the map, try to figure out just where the hell Meadowlane Drive was. Shit, why'd they make the fucking map so big? There were thousands of tiny streets forming a maze, the print so small that Jerry had to squint to read any of their names.

Yeah . . . there it was. A tiny squiggle in the center of a lot of other tiny squiggles—her street.

He slammed the car door, put the Ciera in gear and peeled out of the station, missing the dog by only a few feet.

Forty minutes later he had exited I–75 at Adams Road and was driving north on a two-lane blacktop road that ran between bluffs and woods on either side, through which suburban houses could be seen, sequestered away from the rest of the world. On the shoulder of the road, three girls in bathing suits rode bicycles, towels slung over the handlebars. Jerry swiveled his eyes toward them, noticing especially a little blonde with tiny, tight ass cheeks.

Shit, no time for that now. He had to check out Kara-lynn Cleveland's house, and he knew from experience this was the perfect time of day for it. Most people worked during the day, and odds were about a hundred to one she'd be out, and he'd have free access.

A corner was studded with fast food places, across the street from a big shopping center, Meadowbrook Mall. Jerry turned right. Consulting the map again, he drove a mile and pulled into a subdivision. His heart had begun to pound again, his pulse throbbing in his neck. Unconsciously his hand went up to his neck where his fingers splayed out, palpating the glands there.

There it was, twenty-foot-tall blue spruce trees shielding it from the neighbors on both sides, a two-story, white colonial. There were tubs of flowers on the porch, more of them hanging in baskets from hooks, so fucking nicey-nice, it looked like a picture in a magazine.

Anger flared in Jerry again, like battery acid surging up at the back of his throat.

186

She lived like this while he had been locked away at Raiford, doing hard time.

As was his usual method, he found a house two blocks away where several cars were parked in front. He parked and walked back toward Karalynn's house, assuming an easy, confident saunter, as if he were just out for a stroll. In his Ed clothes, this was convincing. He had to walk around the twirling spray of a sprinkler which splashed a few droplets on his pants. Sounds of distant lawn mowers buzzed in the air, and kids were yelling in a ball game.

When he reached Karalynn's, he reached into his pocket and pulled out a piece of paper he had put there, pretending to consult it, as if he was checking out the proper address.

He walked up the driveway like a roofer called to do an estimate, and headed around to the back yard, which he saw, to his satisfaction, was landscaped with more of the spruces, hidden from the neighbors' view. He had a small hammer and the duct tape inside his shirt, along with the knife, and he took them out now.

Three minutes later he was inside. His groin hardened at the act of entering, which was so much like another kind of invasion. The palms of his hands were sweaty, and he stopped to rub them against the pockets of his pants, wiping away the moisture.

Suddenly Karalynn was all around him, her scent faintly perfumed, like dried roses. In a little utility room there was even a pair of running shorts laid out to dry, a wisp of blue and red nylon. He picked it up and sniffed the crotch, breathing deeply. He almost came then, but held himself back. This was just a reconnoiter. He didn't know what he wanted to do yet. Maybe he would just get the feel of her, savor this for a couple hours.

He wasn't quite sure yet, something was missing. He

didn't know what. After Laurel . . . well, he had to be sure.

The house was slightly disordered, and he saw a book-shelf that had been emptied of books, as if she were packing to move. He roamed the rooms, browsing them like counters in a sex shop. He stopped in her bedroom to open her dresser drawers and paw among the fluffy bits of lingerie, all of them deliciously scented with her. Lacy bras and high-legged bikini panties, half slips, several over-sized T-shirts, and a shirt that said "WDTE Music Festival."

Small bottles of perfume were lined up on the bureau top, and he paused to unstopper one and smell deeply of its concentrated musk. Giorgio. And another one called Samba. What the hell kind of a name was that for a perfume?

On Karalynn's bedside table were two 8-by-10 photographs, one of a good-looking dark-haired man, the other picture showing the man with a little black-haired girl of about ten. The man's kid, maybe?

The child had a pouty, self-absorbed look that Jerry admired. She had just enough baby chubbiness to make her pretty; Jerry didn't like real skinny girls but wanted them to have some suggestion of meat on their bones, "something to hold," as he thought of it. He felt a stir as he gazed at the picture. Sweet, young meat.

The man, though, that concerned him. A husband? Boyfriend? He didn't get the feeling that a man lived in this house—not full time.

He stayed in the bedroom for ten or fifteen more minutes, opening closet doors, breathing in the scents of shoes and wool suits and sweaters. A couple of men's shirts, some jeans, a bathrobe, hung on a hook in the closet, but that was all. Apparently the boyfriend just did overnighters; he didn't live here.

Jerry went into the adjoining bathroom to open the medicine cabinet and vanity drawers. Bath oils, suntan lotion, hair mousse, some shaving cream probably kept for the man. There was a linen closet on one wall and he pulled it open, finding shelves of thick towels, and a plastic basket full of dirty laundry.

He fished around in the basket, pulling out a pair of blue bikini panties. He laid it out on the formica, the crotch opened to his view, while he masturbated into the sink.

Partially satiated, but still charged-up with an unreleased energy, he left her bedroom and wandered down the hallway to a small room used as an office, containing a small desk, a nineteen-inch TV set, and an electric typewriter. A small bookshelf still held a few books, its lower shelf containing a bunch of folded-up newspapers called *Bargain Hound* with the cartoon of a dog on its heading.

Shuffling through the papers on her desk, he found some letterhead with the same name at the top. *"All the sales in Rochester,"* read the subheading.

Fuck, he thought. How come she had the stationery? Did she work at the place, take ads, something like that? He poked through some papers on the desk top, finding two sheets of paper with what looked like the beginning of a letter. To someone called Rob. The boyfriend. He picked up the piece of paper and sniffed it, imagining that he could smell her on it, musky and female. He felt close to her in her house, as if he could be part of her.

The doorbell chime cut through the empty air of the house.

Jerry froze in place.

"Kara? Kar?" There was the sound of the front door deadbolt being released, then the main lock. Jerry moved on the balls of his feet to the closet, and pulled open the door which was already standing ajar. He stepped inside, pressing himself among the garment bags, old coats and suits hanging there.

"Kar?" called the man downstairs. His voice sounded upset somehow, maybe angry.

The boyfriend, Jerry thought.

He waited tensely, wondering what the bastard was going to do. Would he come upstairs? There were sounds of footsteps on the slate tiles of the foyer, then silence.

Then Jerry heard the sound of the door being closed again. The deadbolt was snapped to with a final-sounding, metal click.

In the closet, Jerry waited for the house to settle back to empty normalcy. When he judged that it had, he emerged from the closet and began to go through the desk again. But this time he wasn't just rummaging for the fun of it, this time he had a purpose.

Kara arrived home at 10 p.m., having gone to a movie alone, a lonely act that only made her feel worse. She had sat in the darkened theater, watching two movie stars make love, thinking that love in real life was far more complicated than that depicted on the screen.

Maybe there were other factors needed for a relationship, factors which she seemed conspicuously to lack.

She used the garage door opener, and waited while the door went up, thinking that it *wasn't* really because of Cindy, was it? Rob had been right. Cindy was only her excuse.

She went inside. The house smelled slightly different. Had she accidentally left food to spoil in her kitchen wastebasket? Except that the smell wasn't really like food spoiling, it was more like—sweat, maybe? But then, drawing in several more breaths, Kara no longer could smell it.

She went into the kitchen to fix herself a Diet Pepsi, and that was when she saw the shards of glass lying on the floor, many of them still covered with some kind of gray tape. They looked like odd bits of scraps discarded by workmen. A ragged, jagged circle had also been knocked out of the glass patio door, and the theft guard bar had been lifted out of its track.

Kara backed away from the broken glass, her steps small, jerky.

That smell of sweat. How stupid she'd been! That odor had come from a man's body. Someone had broken in. Maybe he was still in the house, hiding somewhere, waiting to rape or kill her.

But she didn't sense his presence now . . . she believed she would still feel him if he was here.

She kept backing up until she had reached the living room, pausing at the telephone, then fleeing past it as if it were an intruder too. Within seconds, she was out the door.

Habit made her shoot the dead-bolt as she left.

"Kara, Kar. Didn't you call the police?" Rob said. His face looked pinched, his eyes reddened as if he had been having as difficult a time as she. She had driven straight to his house, her mind entering a strange state of tight calm. She couldn't stay in her own house tonight and she needed Rob's pragmatic view, his good sense.

"No, I didn't. I—it was just a simple break-in, I'm sure. Maybe just some neighborhood kids looking for pills or liquor."

"Great neighborhood," he said dryly. "Is anything missing?"

"I don't know. I didn't look. I was afraid to."

"Oh, shit," Rob said, walking over to the wall phone in his big, ultra-modern kitchen. "Look, I'll call the police for you. You can't claim any insurance damage unless you file a police report. I'll tell them to meet us over there, and—"

"No!" she cried, running over to him and using both

191

hands to cover the numbers, stopping his fingers. "No, Rob, please! Don't call. I don't want you to call."

"But why not?" He stared at her.

She was sweating all over, her body damp with moisture. Even between her legs she had sweated, and she smelled the acridness of it on herself. The idea of the police filled her with a crawling horror.

She sought for a reason that would seem acceptable. "I don't want the police involved because it won't do any good anyway," she fabricated. "Angie had a robbery last year and they refused even to take any fingerprints. They laughed at her when she mentioned fingerprints. I don't need that."

Rob was beginning to look angry. "But the insurance, Kara. You don't even know what he took."

"I don't care what he took. It couldn't have been much because I haven't got much in the house. Maybe a couple of bottles of wine, a TV set, my electric typewriter, a bunch of boxes. Who cares?" She hugged herself, feeling goose bumps texture the flesh of her arms.

"My God, Kara, that's your stuff, your house, and you don't care?" Rob was looking at her even more strangely now. "Look, if you're afraid to go over there, I'll go for you. I'll look and see what he took. Anyway, you can't go home until someone checks to make sure he's gone."

She sank into one of the white-oak dinette chairs in Rob's breakfast nook, thinking that it had been a mistake to come over here. She should have handled this herself. She felt exhausted, her pulse rapid.

Rob opened the lid of the Japanese lacquered box where he kept his car keys. "I doubt if he'll be in the house now, but I want to make sure. Cindy's sleeping upstairs, so you stay here with her, will you?"

Rob headed upstairs, and returned with something black and compact.

"A gun?" she said, moistening her lips and feeling even

more frightened. "You have a gun, Rob? You're going over there with that? I didn't know you had a gun."

"I carry it when I have to go to Detroit. That Agnelli project last year on Lafayette. I'd like it with me, just in case. Look," he added. "Why don't you just go upstairs and crawl in bed? You can use the guest room if you don't want to sleep in my bed. I don't want you going back to that house unless I'm sure it's okay."

"I'll come with you," she said.

"No, goddammit! You stay here. I'll go."

"Rob—"

But he was already out the door.

On Rob's guest room bed, Kara lay with her eyes open, waiting for the sound of Rob's key in the front door so she could go to sleep.

She fidgeted and turned fitfully, unable to find a comfortable position, and finally she got up and raided a pile of old *Architectural Digests* Rob had stored on a table top. She sat reading about Malcolm Forbes' New Jersey estate, and someone's Connecticut home, "A Landscape Far From the Madding Crowd." It was pleasantly boring reading, the magazine's lush ads for furniture and bathroom fixtures blurring in front of her eyes. But at least the succession of designer homes kept her mind safely on a track, and away from thoughts too uncomfortable to bear.

At 1:30 a.m., she heard Rob's car in the driveway. She jumped off the bed and hurried downstairs to meet him at the garage door.

"Well, I couldn't find anything missing," he reported tiredly, coming into the house. "It looks like maybe they got scared away. Do you want me to call the police, or will you? Because one of us has to."

She put down the magazine she was still holding. "Why should I have to call them at all if nothing was taken? Rob, you know what the police are like. If nothing is gone, they won't do anything—they'll just tell me to turn on my yard lights.''

They went upstairs.

"I don't understand you," Rob said as he unloaded the .38 revolver and put it back on the upper shelf of his walk-in closet, storing the bullets in a separate box which he put in a bedside stand. "Why are you so defensive tonight? Even if nothing was taken, the police at least ought to know there's a prowler around, so they can beef up their patrols.''

"I don't want strange men poking and pawing through my house and my things," she insisted stubbornly. "I hate it. I hate the thought.''

"At least one strange man has already been there. Aren't you being a little—''

"It's my house, isn't it?" she snapped.

A beat of a second or two before Rob responded. "Most people are anxious to call the police after a break-in. Are you going to talk to me about this? About whatever thing is really eating at you?''

"I—I can't," she whispered, wetting her lips.

"Don't you trust me?''

"It's not that, Rob.''

"Isn't it? I think that's exactly what it is. You just don't want to let me in, do you? You haven't any intention of letting me in.''

"Rob," she said frantically. "I—Please understand.''

"I understand I'm not a friend to you, Kara, because friends trust each other.''

She felt sick to her stomach—sick with her own perfidy.

"Look," Rob added heavily. "I'm bushed. It's stressful going through an empty house wondering if some goddamn burglar is hiding in a closet. I'm going to bed. We'll talk in the morning, maybe we'll go out to breakfast. I promised Cindy some Belgian waffles with strawberries. Afterwards, maybe you and I can discuss this some more.''

She held her breath. The words emerged in short, painful bursts. "I'm sorry. There's nothing new to say. Rob, maybe we should admit it. I'm not right for you. I—I can't share enough. And maybe I'm selfish but I don't want to live my married life in a battle with a child. I tried to get her to love me, but she doesn't love me, and that's—"

"Stop," Rob said huskily. "You don't really mean that. I don't know what the hell is wrong, but I still love you."

Tears stung her eyes. This was far worse than she'd ever imagined it could be. She didn't know what to say. They stared at each other for a minute, their bodies leaning forward, body language connecting them.

Then Rob took her hand and pressed her fingers together, trapping them in his. His eyes were moist. "It's not over until it's over," he said.

Oh, God, she thought. How was she going to live her life without this man?

"I love you, too," she said. "But maybe there has to be more than just love. I don't think that's enough to hold things together."

She rushed out of the room, heading for the guest room.

At dawn Kara woke up and realized that she needed to go home, to be among her own things and to assess the damage. She slid out of the guest room bed and padded on bare feet to the bathroom. Rob's bedroom door was open, and she could hear his deep breathing, the sound so achingly familiar that she hurried into the bathroom and closed the door in order to blot it out.

The way he had gripped her hands last night, enclosing her in his warm strength. Had she made a terrible, irrevocable mistake? The rest of her life seemed to stretch before her, empty except for occasional fiancés whom she would jilt after a year or two, before the marriage ceremony could take place.

She dressed and left a note for Rob on the kitchen

counter by the coffee machine. *Thanks for your help,* she finally wrote after much thought, signing it *love.*

The sunrise was magnificent, puffs of fuchsia, magenta and pink clouds like dancers' tulle spread across half the sky. Since Kara seldom rose at dawn, the sight seemed especially beautiful. She gazed at it, in spite of her mood feeling uplifted. Could anything really evil happen in a world where such lavish beauty was possible?

Yes, she answered herself soberly, as she put her car in reverse and began backing out of Rob's driveway.

It could.

She drove into her own neighborhood, which was dawn-quiet except for the chatter of Rainbird sprinkler systems that had been activated on several of her neighbors' lawns. The smell of damp grass and humus permeated the air. An early morning jogger loped past her car, sweat pouring down his chest.

The exterior of her house showed no indication of the forced entry of the previous night.

Kara let herself inside, bracing herself for the strangeness that would greet her, the sense of someone having intruded into her space, invaded her privacy.

She stood breathing deeply. The slight odor of sweat she'd smelled last night was gone. She walked into the kitchen to find that Rob had cleaned up the broken glass, tossing it into the trash container. He had put a piece of cardboard in the window to prevent insects and animals from getting in. However, she would have to call Rochester Glass Service and have the patio door replaced.

The sensation of frozen calm persisted as she walked through the house, noting small, slight changes.

He had touched her things. In the laundry room her running shorts had fallen to the floor. Her sofa cushions were crooked, and upstairs in her bedroom, a drawer stood ajar, the lingerie inside bunched and untidy. He had touched that, too.

Her heartbeat began to thicken, the calmness dissipating.

In the bathroom, she saw the pair of panties spread out on the counter, crotch side visible. There were streaks of dried white across the sink and part of the formica.

A mental picture flashed into her mind, and she shuddered in revulsion. Maybe Rob hadn't noticed this, or hadn't wanted to tell her. But at least that showed what type of intruder he was . . . some man who derived sexual pleasure from women's underwear. Disgusting but probably fairly harmless.

She went into her study to get the phone number of the glass service. She'd have them come out today, she decided—as soon as possible.

She had written the name of a cleaning service in her address book, and began pulling out drawers searching for it. Damn—she usually kept it in the center drawer, but she must have moved it. She was basically a neat person, but when she worked there were pockets of clutter, and she kept finding stacks of papers, catalogs, bills and correspondence that she'd stuffed into drawers, waiting for a rainy Saturday when she could go through them. Annoyed, she kept searching, but there was no address book.

Finally she went to the phone book and looked up Mobile Maids. Dialing, she reached only an answering machine. It was Sunday, she finally realized with a dull feeling of surprise. The glass service wouldn't come out today either.

She went downstairs and collected a plastic tub full of cleaning equipment, Comet, Lysol and chlorine bleach.

On the radio of the Ciera, a rock group called Guns 'N Roses was blasting out hot, hard, tight lyrics.

Jerry drove through the center of Rochester, his nerves

edgy. The main street was lined with shops and boutiques with names like the Bear Lair, Little Green Apple, and Pier One Imports. A couple of 9-year-old boys in garishly patterned surfer shorts were chaining their bikes to a parking meter outside the Baskin Robbins ice cream store.

Jerry glared at them jealously. When he went in Raiford little boys didn't wear bright colors like that, and the bike *he* owned was cheap. Even their haircuts grated on him, combed up in wild, butch tufts.

A car with a flasher on it passed him in the outer lane, and Jerry felt his heartbeat race, but as the car passed he saw that it was only the Fire Department, not police.

He relaxed again, thinking how easy this was. Yesterday, after he left Karalynn's, he had found a small mom and pop motel on the edge of town and checked into a room. He paid in advance with some of the cash his mother had given him. He took the precaution of asking for a room on the back side, farthest from the road, and he backed the Ciera into its slot, so its stolen license plate would be hidden. Just in case any cops drove through the motel; no sense taking any chances.

"You staying long?" the woman at the desk had asked. "Because if you are, we've got rooms with kitchenettes. Refrigerators, everything you need to cook."

He took the room with the kitchenette, and a supply of cheap pots and pans, then threw himself on the double bed, falling immediately into a heavy sleep.

He ate breakfast at a place called the Kountry Kettle, and then it was back to the car again, a copy of the *Bargain Hound*, which he had stolen from Karalynn's bookshelf, on the front seat beside him, along with the address book from her desk. He drove aimlessly, knowing he had time now. Plenty of time to get matters exactly right. There would be no repeat of what happened with Laurel, which had completely repelled and disgusted him. She'd been ugly, like a witch, a death's image . . . his death. It had taken him hours to get the picture out of his head, her sagged-in, puckered scar.

Now his left hand on the steering wheel clenched, causing the prison-made tattoo to ripple under his skin. Yeah, his life had turned upside down, and it was Karalynn who was needed to change it around again, make it whole. Golden bitch Kara, so beautiful.

But still, he thought jaggedly, it was not entirely right yet. There was something still lacking. He wanted to find out what.

He drove north of the downtown area, passing a Big Boy restaurant, a Dairy Queen, a church. It only took him five minutes to find the brown, Cape Cod-style house with its wooden sign shaped like a little dog.

As Jerry drove past, he glimpsed a flash behind the plate glass window. A woman with blond hair was walking past, carrying some papers in her hand.

Was it Karalynn? Despite the photo he'd smashed, despite being in her house, it had been ten long years since he'd actually seen her. He wasn't sure he would recognize her up close. That bothered him, too. Everything was so changed, even little kids wore neon colors now; it was not the same world he'd left.

There were some boutiques up the street, all of them closed, and an ACO hardware store, which was open. On impulse, Jerry parked the Ciera in the parking lot of the hardware. He got out and walked in the direction of the *Bargain Hound*. He felt the palms of his hands go sweaty as he approached Karalynn's place of work.

He wanted to see her just once, wanted to find out if she was really as blond and haughty and beautiful as her portrait had suggested. He wanted to get in the mood again, away from the fear that Laurel had made him feel.

He sauntered toward the Cape Cod. There was only one car parked in the tiny lot, a white Mercury Cougar with lines so streamlined and glossy that Jerry averted his eyes from it. It had to be hers. Jesus, a woman driving a car like that. He hated her for the car.

He crossed the lot and stepped onto the small front walk, climbing the steps onto the porch. There were pots of geraniums, a splash of red. A bee in the flowers.

On the door a printed sign announced *Office Closed. Please Return During Normal Office Hours. We Will Be Happy To Take Your Ad.*

He lifted up his fist and knocked.

Returning with the sheaf of page proofs, Kara settled down to a long, boring read. Proofing ads was a laborious job that had to be done extremely carefully, comparing original copy with the print, so that no mistakes would be made in prices of items. Angie and Ned proofed their own copy, but she hated to print corrections, and did not want to risk losing one of her bigger advertisers.

However, with all that had happened, with the broken engagement, Rob's accusations, and the break-in, it was almost impossible to concentrate. The print for a close-spaced ad for Bordine's Better Blooms seemed to jump around in front of her eyes.

She lifted her eyes to her office window, which faced a side yard where a hedge of lilac bushes, planted by the original homeowner, had grown in forty years to tree-sized, epic proportions. In May these were an extravagance of purple blooms and heavy, sweet scent. Lilacs were a shrub of the past, she reflected. Few people planted them any more—maybe because they grew untidily, and overran their space.

She heard the creak of footsteps on the porch, and then the knock at the door. She stiffened a little. The office was closed—she was sure she'd put the *closed* sign on the door.

She got up to answer it, seeing through the pane of glass the white, Levi Docker pants, the blue striped cotton shirt of a typically suburban, well-but-casually-dressed male visitor.

The most frequent callers to *Bargain Hound* were homeowners who wanted to take advantage of her excellent garage sale ad rates. But it might also be a local business owner, wanting to take a full or half page. She decided she might as well take the ad. Every bit of revenue helped, and you never knew when an eighth-page ad might expand into a full pager, or even a twelve or fifteen ad series.

She pulled open the door, and gazed up at the angular face. Her heart gave an enormous thump.

Jerry?

Was it Jerry?

Transfixed with horror, she stared at her afternoon caller. Her mind backed away from the recognition. "Jerrys" were in every shopping mall, she'd seen one herself at the zoo. It couldn't be Jerry, it just couldn't. This was just an illusion similar to what Laurel had . . . the panicky, neurotic sightings of men who looked like Jerry but weren't.

Anyway, surely Jerry hadn't been so heavily muscular. This man had weight-lifter arms, the biceps thickly defined, their bulk distending the sleeves of his nice-looking cotton shirt. His nose was different, too, flatter, bumpy. His face was heavier, the jawline fuller.

But the eyes.

Jerry's eyes. Bright blue, gleaming with malevolence. She would never forget those eyes gloating, while Laurel cried and screamed.

"This the *Bargain Hound* paper office?" he asked in a husky, familiar voice.

She felt a sound rise in her throat, not a scream or any articulate word, just a noise. *It was him.* Instinctively she stepped back, her hand clutching the door knob.

Jerry grinned, and leaned on the door, bracing it open with his body. She saw his teeth, white, even and large.

"I saw your office," he told her. "Thought I'd stop by, see if you had any jobs. You know, distributing the papers, like that. I got a good car, I could deliver them."

If she could just get him to go away. Maybe if she pretended she hadn't recognized him . . .

"Sorry, I haven't got any jobs open right now." Her voice emerged strangely. Her pulse had suddenly gone wild, pushing and pumping at the veins in her neck. *How had he found her?*

"A circulation manager," he said. "I could be that. Don't you send your papers around to drug stores, places like that? Restaurants? People's houses?"

Her eyes darted to his face, to his hands, which were empty, and beyond him to the small parking lot which contained only one car, her own. He had walked here from somewhere. How could he be here asking her for a job like any common college kid? God—it was only an excuse to talk to her.

She'd been a fool to come here alone, an arrogant fool.

"I already have a man who takes care of deliveries for me," she said, forcing her voice into tones of distant, professional pleasantness. "If I need extra help I use college students from Oakland University. Through their student employment office."

His eyes swept down her body, and she fought to conceal her panic and revulsion, sensing that showing it would be fatal. When she saw Rob's car turn the corner by the ACO hardware, she nearly fainted with relief.

She lifted her hand and waved.

Startled, Jerry took a step backward, glancing toward Rob's car as it pulled into the lot. Kara saw his eyes take in Rob and Cindy, the pretty ten-year-old slurping a Dairy Queen Blizzard through a straw.

Joyfully, desperately Kara waved again. "Rob . . ." she called. "Hi, honey!"

CHAPTER 19

Rob pulled into one of the spaces in front of the *Bargain
Hound* office, and parked. Cindy pushed open the car door
and got out, balancing her Blizzard. Jerry had turned, and
was descending the porch steps, his route taking him past
the car. His heels scraped angrily on the cement.

Kara caught her breath. Jerry's eyes had swiveled
straight toward Cindy, hard and glittering and angry-
looking. And he wasn't looking at her face, either, but at
her hot pink shorts. At her *in* the shorts, which were a
little too small for her. Oh, God—what was the matter
with Rob? How could he have allowed her to dress like
that?

But Rob, coming around the car, apparently hadn't noticed the leer, and Kara hurried forward, putting her arm
around Rob's daughter and propelling her toward the
porch. She herself felt both hot and cold, her heartbeat
pounding.

"Kara?" Rob said. "Are you all right? You look so

white, and you're all covered with sweat." He glanced sharply toward the retreating form of Jerry, now getting into a blue car in the hardware parking lot.

"I'm fine," she managed to say. What should she do? Call the police? But how could she, without revealing everything? And Jerry had *done* nothing.

"*I* got a Blizzard," Cindy said, dawdling.

"Hurry," Kara said, pushing her a little, anxious to get her inside.

"I want to talk," Rob said. "Turn the computer on for Cindy."

Inside, Kara booted up the receptionist's computer, calling up the WordPerfect word processing program. She showed Cindy how to use the arrow keys and how to erase.

"I know all this," Cindy said importantly. "We do this at school. I can type lots of things."

Rob and Cindy went into Kara's office and closed the door.

"Who was that guy?" Rob demanded as soon as the door was shut.

"He was—he wanted a job distributing the papers," she said evasively.

"Are you sure?"

"What do you mean, am I sure? I was here, Rob. I talked to him. I—" She stopped, realizing that she was projecting too much nervousness.

"Was he coming on to you? Acting funny?"

"No, Rob, he was just asking about a job."

"Bullshit!" Rob snapped. "Dammit, do you think I'm a complete idiot? Someone dumb who doesn't have any perceptions? That guy. You were terrified of him. Your face was *white*. And it isn't the first time something like that has happened. The way you acted at the zoo—the way you're acting now—what in the hell is it? I want to know and I want to know now. I'm tired of your excuses and your evasions."

Frightened, Kara stared at him. She drew in her breath. "I'm sorry," she whispered.

"Sorry for *what*, Kara? Come on, for Christ's sake, talk to me. Communicate. Tell me what you're really thinking and feeling. Who was that man in the parking lot? He scared you, didn't he? He scared you bad. Why?"

She twirled the chair so that it faced the window and the lilacs. She felt tremors pass all through her body, like miniature hurricanes. The pressure of Rob standing behind her was like a force pushing her. He wanted something from her.

No, he demanded it. It was honesty he wanted.

How could she talk about it? If she got started it would all pour out like poison, and wouldn't Rob be shocked, horrified, repelled? He wouldn't want her. Wouldn't want a woman whose body had been a battlefield of violence.

She felt his hand on her shoulder, gently squeezing her. "Baby," he whispered. "For God's sake. You can trust me."

Could she? She hadn't been able to trust her father. But if she didn't trust Rob, what was there? Endless days without Rob. All the days of her life, and her knowledge that Jerry had taken away this, too. Was there any part of her life he had not touched and sullied?

Endless minutes seemed to inch by, punctuated by the sound of the computer keys on the other side of the door as Cindy typed. Kara battled her demons. Was she going to let the rape completely destroy her? *God damn Jerry!*

Rob sat down on the corner of her desk and waited. He didn't interrupt her, leaving all of the silence to be filled, the burden on her.

"I . . . can't," she blurted.

He said nothing. She had never experienced such a long pause before—it was nerve-wracking. He was going to wait her out, his silence said plainly. However long it took.

"I can't!"

But didn't she have to, now? Jerry was here, in Rochester. A brutal animal who had hacked off Laurel's breast, who had been implicated in other rapes before their own, maybe as many as ten. Weren't other women endangered now? Even Cindy. The way he'd looked at the ten-year-old . . .

"I'm here, babe. I won't desert you," Rob encouraged. His hand came out and covered her own. It rested on her fingers, not gripping them, but just creating a warmth of physical contact. His touch broke down something in Kara, creating a pathway. No matter how annoying Cindy had been, no matter how much she seemed to dislike her, Kara had to do what was necessary to protect her.

"Something happened when I was seventeen," she forced herself to begin in a voice so low it was barely audible. "My best friend Laurel and I had been to the beach . . ."

She poured it all out, keeping her voice low so that Cindy couldn't hear through the door.

As she talked, tears ran down her face. Only the contact of Rob's hand on hers kept her safe. His hand became a lifeline, a rope, connecting her to sanity and humanity. If she could talk about it, wasn't she partly healed? Wasn't there hope for some sort of normality?

But it seemed to her that Rob's touch changed as she continued to relate the sordidness of the police questioning, the medical exams, the defense lawyer's grilling, the long, horrifying trial. The way Jerry kept smiling in court. And then her father attacking him and nearly being jailed.

When she finally finished and looked up at Rob, instead of seeing caring, she was appalled to see Rob's brows glowered together, an expression of fury on his face. It was a very familiar expression, just like her father in one of his "castrate the rapist" modes.

"That bastard," Rob exclaimed, shaking his head from side to side. "You don't mean . . . he really cut off Laurel's breast? Mutilated her?"

Kara nodded.

"He should be shot in the head." Rob's voice rose. "And you, that scar underneath your breast, the one you said you got on a bike. And those little white scars on your hip . . . he gave you those? It wasn't a bike accident like you said?"

This was much, much worse than she had imagined. "Yes."

There was another silence, filled with Rob's shock and fury as he tried to adjust. "The viciousness . . . Why didn't you tell me? I would have cared. I would have helped you. You could have trusted me."

Trust. They were back to that again. She felt a twisting stab in the center of her chest.

"I'm sorry. It wasn't you. I couldn't tell anyone. That was why I—"

He interrupted, "Goddammit! I can't believe you would have done that. To hide such an important thing . . . we were going to be married, Kara! Were you going to hide it forever? Never tell me? Was that what you were going to do? Live a life of lies?"

Kara felt a sob well up. "See?" she cried. "See how you're acting now? I was afraid you'd act exactly as you're acting! You don't care about my rape, do you? It's all how I didn't tell you, and what you'd like to do to Jerry, isn't it? Just like my father! Just exactly!" Once she had started, she couldn't stop the furious outpouring. "Well, I *don't* want to be the object for someone else's anger at what happened to me. I want to live a normal life! It happened to *me*, not to you. *I don't want to pay the rest of my life for something that happened when I was only seventeen!*"

Rob shook his head, stunned. "Kara, Kara, that's not

even the point. I do care about the rape. Of course I care. But—''

''Then don't talk about it any more,'' she shouted, forgetting Cindy in the other room. ''Just don't mention it ever again! I *don't* want to talk about it with you!''

''God. Baby.'' He reached out and tried to take her hand again, but she snatched it away. ''Baby, I'm so sorry. I'm not your father. I'm not like him, whatever he did to you that hurt you so much. I didn't realize—'' Suddenly his apology switched gears. ''Who was the man in the parking lot? Was that Jerry Quick? Kara? *Was it him?*''

She moistened her lips, unable to speak. Her whole life had tipped off center, spinning in directions she could hardly imagine. Finally she nodded.

Rob turned white.

''That was Jerry?''

''It was him,'' she said dully.

''Jesus fucking Christ!'' he said, reaching for the phone.

''No!'' Kara cried. ''Rob, please. Don't call the police. They were—they were terrible to me. They were cruel. They made me feel so awful. I hate them. I don't want them involved. Oh, please, don't. Don't call them.''

He was already dialing.

Jerry drove back to the motel, his entire body shivering with the excitement that had thrummed into him when he had looked into Karalynn's eyes and seen the terror there. It was an incredible high, so powerful that he felt as if he'd ingested four lines of cocaine directly into his veins.

Kara *was* beautiful, far more beautiful even than her photograph, with her silky soft skin and huge, terrified blue eyes. Her mouth was wide, soft and quivering, and once her tongue had involuntarily gone out to lick her dry lips.

He was already so hard it was almost painful. He had

to shift his position in the car, in order to ease the taut sexual pressure in his crotch.

And then there was the little girl who got out of the car, the one in pink.

He'd glimpsed her tight little shorts that actually pulled up into the crease of her buttocks. Girls who dressed like that . . . they just asked for a man's attention and notice. Jerry believed it was no accident her shorts tugged up like that, showing off her femaleness.

He was so shaken he had difficulty driving for a moment, swerving close to a van in the other lane. The other driver blatted his horn. Swiftly Jerry recovered himself. This was it, he thought with growing elation. This was what had been missing, what was intended from the beginning and which he had not been able to visualize until now.

Two of them. Just as it had been before.

The police car was parked in the small lot of *Bargain Hound*, its presence attracting the interest of several passersby on their way to the Dairy Queen two blocks away. Seeing it through the front office window caused Kara's skin to crawl.

Only one officer had been dispatched to Rob's call. In his late twenties, dark-haired with a mustache, there was a wariness to him, an unwillingness to believe anything she said. A headache pounded at Kara's temples. Rob had no right to call him without even asking her first. How dared he violate her privacy in that way?

But of course he had done it because he cared about her, and was worried, and because that's what most people would do if a woman's former rapist, having jumped his parole in Florida, now appeared on her doorstep in Michigan.

"Ma'am," the officer (his name tag read Haggerty) said. "Are you sure you recognized Jerry Quick? Are you sure it's the same man? Ten years is an awful long time. Usually witnesses have a hard time identifying someone they saw two hours ago, let alone ten years.''

"I recognized him," she insisted, letting the anger in her eyes encompass Rob as well as the officer. "He was older, yes, but it was the same man. What you don't realize is that I sat in court with that person for three straight weeks. I could recognize him again even if it were twenty years from now.''

She held her hands tightly to her sides, pushing them against her thighs to stop their shaking.

"Describe him again."

"He's five-eleven, and muscular built now, with big, thick upper arms, like he'd been lifting weights. And there's a tattoo, just some numbers . . .''

"Tattoo?" The officer began to look interested. "Where? What did it look like?''

"On the left arm. I think it said 13½, something like that.''

"That can be verified with prison records. What about his car? Did you see that?''

"I told you, he came here on foot, but I think he parked in the parking lot of the hardware store. We saw him going toward a car there, I'm not sure what—''

"A blue Ciera," Rob supplied. "I didn't see the plates but they weren't Michigan.'' Cindy had returned from her temporary exile in Kara's office and was tugging at him impatiently. "What, Cindy? What?''

The child whispered something. She had one thumb close to her mouth, Kara noticed, as if only her status as a soon-to-be sixth grader kept her from sucking it.

"She needs the bathroom," Rob said, looking weary.

"Through there and down the hall to your right," Kara said, pointing. Cindy trudged past them, dragging her feet in their dusty Reeboks, her body language indicating her boredom and fear.

During this time the officer had been writing things down in a small notebook, and now he excused himself and went out to his car, saying he would be back. Rob and Kara looked at each other.

"He acts as if he doesn't quite believe anything I say," Kara said, feeling her eyes go shiny and moist. "As if he thinks I'm too incompetent to know what Jerry really looks like. I know what Jerry looks like. That was him. I know him!"

"I'm sorry, honey, but it had to be done and I had to override you."

"I wish you hadn't," she muttered.

"Dammit, Kara—"

Cindy came back from the bathroom. A little pucker on her forehead marked what in a woman of thirty would have been a worried frown. "Where's the policeman gone?" she wanted to know. She went to the front picture window and peered out. "Oh, he's still out there, he's sitting in his car."

"He's using the police radio," Rob said. "He's checking things on the computer. Calling headquarters."

"That guy," Cindy said angrily. "That guy who we saw. He had slippery eyes. He was looking at me, he was looking right at me."

That night Rob and Kara were on very cool terms with each other. Kara wanted to go home, but she was afraid to. Her "burglar" the previous night could have been Jerry. In fact probably was. She had actually smelled him in her own home. The knowledge filled her with nausea.

The police officer had told her it would be best if she stayed away for a while, until Jerry Quick was apprehended.

"But what about work?" she had asked him. "I own the business—I have to go to work!"

"Take a vacation," was officer Haggerty's advice.

212

"Vacation?" She gave an incredulous laugh. "That's not possible. I run the paper, I do all the writing, and I authorize all the paychecks, which are due this Friday. Plus I'm interviewing people and I have a ton of financial paperwork—"

The man shrugged. "Lady, if he prowled here once he could do it again."

Kara shook her head. Suddenly she felt very possessive of her life, its intricate structure she had worked so hard to build. And furious at Jerry, for upsetting it all. "My office is only a few blocks north of the center of town and on weekdays I've got a male salesman, a male delivery person in and out, and two other staff members. Also we have the public coming and going all day."

She knew her bravado was exactly that—brave words. Inside she was shaking. What *was* she going to do?

"We'll patrol it, but we're short-staffed and we can't be here twenty-four hours a day," Haggerty warned. "A vacation is the best thing."

"I'll think about it," she finally said.

Now it was evening again, and Rob had taken her and Cindy to Pizza Hut, where Cindy spent the meal peeling the cheese, mushrooms, green pepper and onions off her pizza, and eating the bare, tomato-smeared crust.

"Is that guy going to attack us?" the child asked anxiously as Rob called for the check. Her body was hunched over the table, her fingers obsessively playing with her lower lip. Her eyes looked pansy-huge and beautiful, faint dark circles smudged beneath them, the effect waif-like.

Kara felt a wave of genuine sympathy that lifted her out of her own fear. The child was scared badly—and it was her fault. "Cindy? Oh, Cindy . . . no, he isn't." She leaned over and put an arm around the girl. Cindy didn't quite resist her touch. "That's why your father called the police—so they could find him and put him back in jail."

213

"Is he a burglar?" Cindy wanted to know.

"Well," Rob began, at the same time Kara was saying, "I don't really—"

They both stopped.

Rob's face was slightly flushed as he explained, "He's a parole violator, Cindyella. That means when he got out of jail he was supposed to stay in his own town and go to his own job, but he didn't do that. He left town. So now they want to find him so they can put him back in jail."

Cindy nodded. She still looked frightened. "But what did he do? I mean, why does he have to be in jail? Did he do something really, really bad?"

Again Kara and Rob looked at each other. The waitress, a high school girl, was approaching their table with the check.

"He broke into a house," Rob finally said heavily. "That's what he did, Cindy. Now, wipe the pizza sauce off your mouth, okay? Kara's going to spend the night with us, and she's going to stay with us for a few days, maybe a week or longer."

After a bit of fussing, Cindy went to bed, regressing to childishness as she insisted on taking several of the Barbie dolls under the sheets with her. Next door, a teenaged party was heating up, the deep bass boom of rock music penetrating into the house.

"Just what we need, a party next door," Rob said to Kara. "Please, sleep in the same bed with me, babe. We need to calm down, hold each other, and make some kind of peace between us."

Kara wavered. Part of her longed to be held in Rob's arms, to experience the shelter and safety to be found there, to forget their quarrel, the broken engagement, and take comfort from Rob's strength. But another part of her couldn't allow that.

She still felt upset and distanced from him. He had

phoned the police without her permission, without even discussing it with her first. He had grilled her about Jerry, and then, just when she had let down her guard and told him things no one knew except Dr. Hay, he had gotten angry and started acting like her father.

What was it about men? As soon as they found out about a rape they went on their own macho trip. It was as if they and the woman were riding two separate trains.

"We don't have to have sex," Rob said. "I just want to hold you, okay? I want us to be together tonight."

She was sorely tempted. It would be so good to let go, to take comfort in another human body. She needed someone to hold her—so much.

"I don't think I can go to sleep yet," she told him. "I'm too restless, too edgy. Let's see what's on cable."

His eyes locked with hers, and she saw the anxiety in them, the love. "Kar . . ."

"Look. I want to but I can't. I'm confused about a lot of things. I know I love you but I keep pulling away from you and now maybe you can see why."

"No, I can't. I can't see why. I'm not going to hurt you like he did, Kara. All I want is to love you. I'll be careful with you, I'll take it slow."

It was like seeing a love scene on a daytime soap opera, all tenderness and passion, and knowing it was taking place inside the screen, far from your own touch. She turned away from him.

"Do you know where Cindy put the TV Guide? I feel like watching something on the tube, maybe a movie."

"I'll watch with you."

CHAPTER 20

A moon like a big, silver hubcap seemed to float right above Jerry's car as he cruised the boyfriend's neighborhood, using the address he had obtained from the book he had stolen from Kara's desk.

It was a fancier area than where Karalynn lived, full of big homes set back from the winding road, half-buried in the shadows of big, dark trees.

He drove slowly, staring at the occasional sight of someone silhouetted behind lit-up windows. Two little boys were in an upstairs bedroom, jumping up and down on the beds. A woman sat at a blue computer screen.

He felt his anger begin to simmer at the sight of the computer. Shit, he'd never even seen a computer close up, and a woman was running it. Unfair, intolerable, that a woman should be doing something he could not.

Rob Devers' house was on the next corner (he had already driven past it four times), and he was pleased that a party being given by some teenagers next door was making some noise. As he drove past, he could hear the heavy, thumping beat of rock music, and see them behind the windows, dancing to it. Dancing, another thing he had not done in ten years. He wondered if he still remembered how.

The world was full of things he didn't know, and hadn't done, and might not ever do, full of people who didn't even know he was there, and if they did, would turn their back on him.

This time when he drove past Devers' house, a man and a woman were standing in front of a window. Even from this distance he could see the dark gold of Kara's hair, the curved lines of her neck and shoulders.

He slowed the car almost to a crawl. His insides were twisting, knotting up inside him. Karalynn was right there, less than eighty feet away from him, and the man had to be the boyfriend. The little girl . . . the sweet little piece he'd seen, the one with the tight, crotch-hugging shorts—maybe she was in the house, too, sleeping upstairs.

His heart raced.

Of course the boyfriend would be trouble, but he could handle that. Karalynn would be begging him before he was finished with her and the girl. He was going to be the king of the universe with them.

They hadn't found anything they liked on cable, so they were watching the video of *A Fish Called Wanda*. Kara loved comedy, and especially this British one, with the non-stop sight gags and screen action, in addition to the funny dialogue. She had even managed to laugh, a feat she hadn't believed would be possible.

But all through the movie she had been thinking. Now that Jerry was in Rochester, it would surely be only a matter of hours, at most a day or so, before he was picked up by the police and returned to Florida. He'd be incarcerated again, safely put away for years more. She could go on with her life.

But it would all be different, now that Rob knew.

What should she do now? Take back Rob's engagement ring, apologize to him profusely, maybe see Dr. Hay again, try harder to make things work? Now that he did know, she would no longer have to hide anything, and maybe they could be closer, far more intimate.

Or maybe the rape would have just the opposite effect and tear them further apart, she reflected uneasily. It had been exceptionally ugly and violent—on a scale that most people couldn't deal with or accept. Men were notorious for having a hard time with things like that. Look at all the men who had left wives who had mastectomies. Why should Rob be any different, any better than the average?

But wasn't that why she loved Rob to begin with, because he wasn't average?

Kara glanced up at a car light passing slowly by the house and felt a vague feeling of apprehension. She stifled it, getting up from her chair in Rob's den, where the TV was, to pace the carpet.

"Lots of action next door from that party," she said to Rob. Through the window she watched the red tail lights disappear around the corner.

"It figures. The parents are in Spain," Rob said. "And this is just a modest party compared to the one they had last week at graduation. They had a live band that night and I think six people called the police."

The movie had ended, credits rolling across the screen. Rob got up from the couch where he had been sitting, stretching his long legs. He punched the rewind button on the VCR.

"Sorry, but I'm beat," he said, glancing at his watch. "Jeez, it's 2:30. I'm going to have to go to bed. Don't worry, I've got that gun in the house—we should be fine here. I'll protect you with my life if necessary."

Startled, Kara glanced at him. It was exactly the kind of macho thing her father used to say.

Then she castigated herself for her thought. What was wrong with her? Was she focusing her anger on Rob instead of on her rapist? Maybe she was just like her father, after all, putting anger on other people instead of where it really belonged.

"Hon?" Rob was pulling her to him. He enfolded her in his arms, and after a hesitation, she laid her head on her shoulder. "I really do love you, Kar. I don't know how to show it sometimes, but I do. So don't shut me out. Give me some time to get used to this."

She said nothing, but allowed the bones of her body to melt a little, leaning into him, breathing the fragrance of his clean shirt and spicy aftershave.

Oh, what *was* she going to do about him?

He hadn't done anything more or less than any other man would have done in the circumstances. It was she who was ultra-touchy, she who had been damaged. If the rape hadn't happened, she would have been so much different.

She felt a wild, sudden wave of longing. She wanted to be that other Kara—that strong Kara.

Rob went upstairs to bed. Kara, claiming she still felt wide-awake, had the lower part of the house to herself. She roamed through the den and living room, straightening up after Rob and Cindy, both of whom tended to leave their things around. A stray Barbie doll was seated crookedly on the leather couch, and Kara pushed to adjust its posture, thinking that even Cindy was being affected by what Jerry had done.

Finding herself in the brilliantly-lit kitchen, Kara began wiping down the formica counters, refrigerator and microwave, which was fingerprinted from Cindy's habit of warming up Elfin Loaves and other such snacks. A cry from upstairs startled her, and she dropped her damp cloth and hurried to the stairs.

It was Cindy, sobbing in the throes of a nightmare. The noise of the party next door had probably disturbed her. The ten-year-old lay tossing in her elegant twin bed with the white lace canopy, mewing and making blind, defensive motions with her hands.

"Cindy? Cindy. It's okay, you're just having a bad dream." Kara stroked the child's damp, sweaty forehead. In the half-dark, Cindy was very pretty and vulnerable, the soft, curved lines of her cheeks like a Botticelli painting. Kara felt a wave of fierce protectiveness. Little girls should never have to deal with evil.

Cindy stirred, smacked her lips, and then blearily opened her eyes. "Burglar," she mumbled.

"It's okay," Kara murmured. "It's just a dream, honey. Turn over on your side and I'll tuck you in again. You've knocked the sheet to the floor."

"I dreamed about a burglar."

"There isn't any burglar, Cindyella. I'm going to keep you safe, honey, you don't have to worry. Go back to sleep, now."

To Kara's surprise, Cindy seemed comforted as she flopped over, burrowing her face into the pillow. Instantly she was asleep again—or maybe she hadn't really awakened much at all.

Kara went back downstairs. As she reached the landing, car headlights flashed again on the street. The light glanced into the window at an angle, reflected through the railing, and created an elongated geometric pattern on the steps.

A trick of the light that tugged at memories, making Kara shiver a little.

She went to the kitchen. She had seen a package of brownie mix in the kitchen, and decided to bake a batch. It might be after two, but there was still adrenaline in her system, and unlike Cindy and Rob, she knew she wasn't going to be able to sleep much tonight.

She chopped walnuts, measured water, stirred batter, licking the spoon and then washing it in the sink.

The party next door seemed to ebb and flow. Now there were roars of car motors, engines revving, and shouts and screams in the yard. Kara listened to the noise, thinking she had never done that as a teenager. After the trial, she had gone straight north to East Lansing. Michigan State was known by her friends as a "party school," but Kara hadn't participated in that side of college life. She'd been on the quiet side, withdrawn. She'd struck up a friendship with Angie her freshman year, and Angie *had* gone to all the wild parties, but somehow that hadn't come between them.

She was just pouring the thick, gooey batter into a Pyrex baking pan, wondering whether she should have added more nuts, when she heard a noise behind her. She turned, thinking that it was Cindy, wakened by the smell of the chocolate.

A hand snaked around her throat, dragging her backward into a hammer lock.

Kara tried to scream but her cry was choked off, a hard forearm pressing against her windpipe with such terrifying strength that she thought her neck might break.

Terror spurted through her. Her hands went to her throat, trying to push the choking arm away, but it was as rigid as an iron manacle. She was being dragged backwards, off her feet, pressed into the terrifying nearness of a hard, sweat-stinking male body.

"You think you're hot, don't you, Karalynn? You think you are one red-hot mama," a voice growled in her ear as she was being dragged backwards, half-unconscious from being choked.

"No," she tried to cry, but could not get the sound out. It was Jerry. Who else could it be? She felt as if she would explode with her horror.

He suddenly dropped her, and she landed flat on her back, her head banging into the white ceramic tiles of Rob's kitchen floor. The pain caused a wave of nausea to pour through her and she gasped for air. How did he locate them? What did he want? Was it all going to start again?

The terror was a thousand times worse than before, because now she knew what could happen.

She drew breath for a scream and Jerry kicked her on the upper thigh, bringing out a knife whose blade glinted in the harsh light of the kitchen.

"Don't scream. Bitch!" Jerry hissed in a hard, knotty growl that brought back unspeakable memories. *"Bitch! Rat-cunt!"* More obscenities spewed from him, words she had seldom heard.

She was near the lower cupboard, where Rob kept a crock pot, an electric frying pan and an electric wok. She scrabbled backward, trying to get away enough to stand up and run.

But before she could spring to her feet, he had the knife at her throat, and was jerking at her with his free hand, forcing her into a kneeling position.

The position he'd made them assume before.

She whimpered as she felt duct tape go around her mouth. Its upper edge cut into the sensitive tissues of her nostrils and mashed her hair against her ears. Then her hands were jerked behind her and taped. Finally her ankles. As he worked, Jerry kept up a running stream of obscenities, words and phrases so vile that Kara's mind recoiled from them.

As he trussed her like a turkey, something shut down in her brain. It was as if her emotions became frozen in lucite, made opaque. All she could see were details. His contorted face as he wrapped the tape, his eyes almost black, their pupils huge. Jerry's mouth was opened, sweat stood on his skin. She could see every pore, every dark whisker hair.

Beyond him was a dishtowel hung from the refrigerator door handle, woven with black and white squares. A picture that Cindy had drawn, affixed to the refrigerator with magnets. A streak that she had missed when cleaning.

Unreal details, from a dream world she had once lived in.

She couldn't even feel sad; her mind had closed that down, too.

Once she was taped, Jerry hoisted an arm underneath her armpits and began dragging her out of the kitchen, toward the stairs.

When they got to the foot of the stairs, Jerry again dumped her, and Kara fell sideways, prevented by her taped hands from helping herself. But the fall shook her out of her lethargy. She began to make a scream-noise, pushing her voice and air against the hard duct tape.

The sound she made was louder than she expected it would be, and when she raised her voice to soprano level, it got louder still.

"I told you, bitch, stop screaming." Jerry hit her across the face. "Now I think I'm gonna find your boyfriend, huh? Get him out of the way so the fun can start." The steel blade was again at her throat, digging into her skin just short of drawing blood. "You like it, huh? You like the knife? You remember, Karalynn? Do you remember me?"

Did she remember him? She was almost paralyzed with her memories, her fear.

He started up the stairs. *Rob*, Kara thought, her blood running cold.

Heedless of Jerry's warning, Kara began screaming again through the tape. But her cries weren't loud. Did

Rob hear her at all? My God, why didn't he wake up? Or maybe Rob, who usually slept deeply, only thought it was party voices from next door.

She heard another murmur from Cindy's room as the girl turned over in her sleep. It sounded as if Cindy might wake up.

The thought of the child created a wild despair in Kara, a rage that burst through her like a grenade, shattering the lucite. She was crying now behind the tape, and she fought to get to her feet, to recover her balance destroyed by having her ankles pinned together and her hands behind her back.

But Jerry went past Cindy's room, heading instead toward the master bedroom. To Kara his plan seemed obvious. He would first kill or disable Rob, then he would have Kara and Cindy to himself—to do whatever hideous thing he wanted.

And she had no doubt his plans were hideous indeed. He had shown no remorse in court, had even smiled.

Grimly Kara struggled. She had to get to a phone—now.

Rob Devers was sprawled in the king-sized bed, deep in a dream of when he had played tennis on the University of Michigan team. Only in this game there were huge amounts of red paint all over the tennis court, his feet slipping and sliding in the mess. He lunged to catch a serve, and found himself falling. But just as his head was about to hit the court with a terrifyingly hard splat, he woke up.

There was something in the bedroom . . . a presence. Someone.

Struggling to wake up, he heard someone breathing, smelled sour sweat, and then, fighting to get his eyes open, he saw the flash of a knife blade in the dark.

All through his boyhood and manhood, Rob had always wondered what he would do if he were ever attacked, how he would combat it, whether he would be a coward. But this was unlike anything he'd ever imagined, or even seen on TV. There wasn't time even to draw in a breath before the man was on him, throwing him hard back onto the bed as if he were a woman. Rob let out a grunt as he landed.

He felt a sharp sensation in his side, like being thumped with something.

He gave a terrible shout, automatically thrusting forward to protect himself with his hands. More pain ripped through his right hand, so fast he had no time to protect himself.

The knife. Holy Christ, he'd been stabbed.

Kara twisted herself to a sitting position, her bound feet stretched in front of her, her hands awkwardly trussed behind her back. It was going to take effort to get to her knees, let alone to her feet. Could she hop? And how was she going to use the phone with both her hands behind her back?

Silence, dead silence from upstairs, and then a sharp, angry cry from Rob.

Groaning, she jackknifed her body, and with difficulty she folded her feet close to her chest, bringing them through the basket of her hands. If she had weighed even five more pounds she couldn't have done it. Now her hands were in front of her. Desperately she started ripping at the tape on her ankles.

That was when she heard the whup-whup whine of the siren as the police car pulled into the subdivision. Someone, after all, had grown annoyed at the party noise and called to complain.

God—thank God—

The siren was out in front of the house now, and the blue light flashed tantalizingly in through the front windows. Kara was galvanized with desperate urgency. She

225

had only seconds to react. If she didn't hurry, the car would cruise on past.

Kara pulled wildly at the tape around her mouth, feeling a sharp pain as it tore the peach fuzz off her cheeks and upper lip, then ripped the hair near her ears.

"Help! Police! Rob! Rob! Cindy!" she screamed as soon as her mouth was free.

She heard sounds behind her—Jerry taking the steps two at a time. He must have heard the siren, too.

Within seconds, he had slammed out of the patio door and she heard the clatter of his running steps on the wooden deck. Then a duller thud as he jumped to the grass and was gone, presumably into the woods, where he would exit at another yard and disappear into the night.

She and Cindy rode in the police car, huddled together in the back seat behind a wire cage, seated on scruffy, tape-repaired upholstery where hundreds of perpetrators had ridden on the way to jail. Ahead of them was the E.M.S. van, lights flashing and siren screaming. The two sets of sirens created an anxiety-producing wail. Just hearing it made Kara feel ill.

Rob's face, as they had carried him out, had been grayish, coated with so much sweat it looked as if he had just stepped out of the shower. His questions were repetitive, as he asked over and over if she was all right, if Cindy was okay.

"Kar . . . I love you," he had also said.

"I love you, too," she whispered back.

The stab wounds were in Rob's left side, near his waist, and on his right forearm and wrist—very bloody but Kara didn't know how serious. The paramedics had already phoned ahead to Crittenton Hospital and Kara had heard something about "severe lacerations" and "call in a hand man." Was Rob in shock? Would he need blood? Was he going to need surgery?

"My Dad, my Dad," Cindy kept sobbing, leaning into Kara and clutching at her. "Is my Dad going to die, Kara?"

"No, honey," Kara said, putting aside her own fright. "He was talking to us, and didn't you hear him ask whether we were okay?"

"I don't want my Daddy to die," Cindy wept. "Please, Kara, don't let my Daddy die. I want my Dad."

Kara could do nothing more than hug Cindy, and for once the little girl allowed this, burrowing her head into Kara's chest and clutching her with surprising strength. Kara found herself taking comfort from the closeness of the hot, tight little grip. She had passed through numbness to terror, to a shaky, dulled calm.

And underneath all her other feelings ran a thin vein of startled pride in herself. Amazing. She hadn't collapsed, gone stiff and frozen, as she'd done at age seventeen. Instead she'd fought back. She had screamed even with tape over her mouth, even when he told her not to. She had partially freed herself, and if she had had a gun when Jerry first attacked her in the kitchen, maybe she could have gotten to it and shot him.

She wasn't a young girl any more, she realized. She had resources undreamed of at seventeen; she possessed maturity now. She couldn't depend on the police, she added to herself grimly. They hadn't picked up Jerry, that was why this happened. He was clever and wily, and was probably miles away by now, having run through woods and back yards to his car.

As soon as they arrived at the hospital it became confusion. Rob, an IV line in his left arm, was transferred to a gurney and taken away. They barely glimpsed him before he had disappeared down the hall behind double doors.

"Kara? I have to pee," Cindy said, squirming up against Kara, her eyes huge with tears. "I really have to. I can't help it, it's a 'mergency."

227

They found a rest room. In the mirror, Kara saw her own face, looking fierce and wild, her hair in tangles, a bruise already starting to show on her left cheekbone. Cindy looked equally disheveled. The girl had dressed in a frantic hurry. Her glossy black hair stuck straight up in tufts. The child wore her pink shorts underneath a cotton pique, babydoll pajama top and had her Reeboks on the wrong feet.

While Cindy went into a stall, Kara attempted to make repairs to her own face and hair. She didn't want Rob to see her looking as if she had fallen apart. Also, she wanted to appear normal for Cindy.

When Cindy came out of the stall, she took time to comb the child's hair, too, and washed the girl's face with a damp paper towel. They switched the shoes to the proper feet and tucked in the pajama top so it looked more like a blouse.

Obediently Cindy submitted to being freshened up, all traces of the willful, petulant and jealous girl vanishing as if by magic. "Where's Dad?" she wanted to know.

"In an examining room," Kara said. She swallowed, remembering a time when she had been in such a room, her legs in stirrups for a gynecological exam by a hurried and brusque male doctor.

They walked back out to the waiting room. A TV set mounted on the wall was playing a western called *Tribute To a Bad Man*, with James Cagney. Several distraught parents had arrived because of an auto accident, which had involved teenagers, and Kara found corner chairs for herself and Cindy, as far away from the turmoil as possible. No sense upsetting Cindy any further—as it was, the child looked wan and shaken.

Two police officers came over to question them. They were clones of every other policemen she had ever talked to, young, mustached, with wary, expressionless faces.

Where was she when Jerry entered the house? How did

she think he got in? What, exactly, did he do and say? What was he wearing? Did she see a car of any kind? Exactly how tall was Jerry? How much did he weigh? Did he have any unusual scars? Did she smell alcohol on his breath? Had she noticed anyone following her today? Had the neighbors seen anything?

It went on and on, every question repeated several times. Kara struggled through the answers. Shock had already caused details to blur, and Jerry's attack began to take on a dreamlike aspect. Then Cindy was questioned. She had seen nothing, and only had been awakened when she heard the police siren.

The officers left, and, exhausted, Kara leaned back in her chair. Incredibly, it was already 3:30 a.m. Rob had been in emergency for forty minutes now.

At last a nurse came and told Kara that Rob was being taken up to surgery, but they could see him for a few minutes before he went up. They followed the woman in her squeaking rubber-soled shoes into the emergency area's warren of small rooms and curtained cubicles. Behind white curtains, a young girl moaned, causing Cindy to press herself even closer to Kara.

In an end cubicle Rob was lying flat on his back on a gurney. A plastic bag of clear fluid was being administered into his left arm by IV. His side was heavily bandaged, and there were more stained bandages on his right hand and forearm. However, his face was a healthier-looking color than it had been in the ambulance.

Cindy broke away from Kara and rushed to him first. "Dad—Dad—Dad—" She started to cry.

"What is this, Cindyella? Tears? Hey, baby, no tears, huh? I'm just going to get a little sewing done on my hand. Just a little repair job on some of the tendons and ligaments. The rest of me is okay."

Over Cindy, Rob's eyes met Kara's. He went on, "Good

229

thing I've got a little padding of fat around my middle, huh? My lucky break." Rob's voice was his normal one, and there was even a tired-looking smile that flickered at the corners of his mouth.

Kara waited, allowing Cindy her time with her father. When Cindy was finally smiling a little, she stepped forward and gave Rob a light kiss on the forehead. There were still pieces of dried blood in his hair, and smeared near his ear.

"Rob, oh, Rob, what happened?" Kara whispered, when Cindy moved away so she could approach the bed.

"Babe, I don't know. One minute I was sleeping, and the next I heard a noise and there was a guy in the bedroom. I yelled out and tried to twist away, tried to kick him in the balls, but instead he cut me." Rob grimaced. "I feel like I've been worked over by a couple of Hell's Angels. They've called in a hand man to do the repair work. But he did get me in the side. Nothing real serious, thank God. The doctor said an inch deeper and it would have been."

At the words she felt a wave of nausea, and fought it back. He looked as exhausted as she felt, but he was keeping his voice light, for Cindy's benefit.

"I'm going to go back to your house and get that gun," she whispered, leaning close. "Tomorrow."

"What?" Instantly the smile was wiped from Rob's face.

"I said I'm going to pick up that gun you showed me."

"Don't even think about it," he told her. "Jesus, once you get a gun out it escalates things. You can't say, 'hey, I didn't mean it.' A gun is for real."

"I know that." She lifted her chin. "Don't tell me I can't do it—I know how to shoot. My—My other fiancé, Chuck, used to take me to the gun range to shoot his .22 pistol. And another thing," she added, over his protest.

"I've got to take Cindy somewhere, until we can get her back to her mother."

Rob sank back on the flat hospital pillow, passing his uninjured left hand wearily over his eyes. "Okay. Yeah, good old Dee—I don't think she can get down from Mackinac until tomorrow. Any ideas?"

"I'll take her to Angie's," Kara decided. "She lives just across Livernois, we can walk to her house from here. And then I'll come back here to the hospital and—"

Rob frowned. "I don't want you here at the hospital. I want you with Cindy. I want my daughter safe, Kara."

His eyes met hers, blue-smudged and hollow-looking, and she searched them, wondering if he blamed her for this. She saw that somewhere deep inside, he did. The knowledge hit her like a hard nudge in the chest.

"Okay," she promised him, suddenly feeling so tired she wanted to lay her head down on Rob's hospital blanket and go to sleep. "I'll keep her safe. I'll do that."

"I love my little girl," Rob said, looking at her.

CHAPTER 21

It was now 4:10 a.m. Kara and Cindy exited from the door next to the hospital loading dock where Rob had been admitted. A pacing security guard gave them a bored look. At this hour the emergency parking lot was almost deserted. A gray hue of dawn had slightly tinted the sky and the air tasted moist and woodsy, like meadow grasses.

"I don't want to walk," Cindy protested, dragging her feet. "It's too dark out."

"It's a three-minute walk. It's best for us to have another place to sleep tonight, Cindy. Tomorrow morning I'll call your mother and she can come and get you."

"I don't want to go home yet. I want to see Dad tomorrow."

They walked across Livernois Road, which looked strange without its usual four lanes of traffic, then into the large Timberlea Village apartment complex where Angie lived, within the sound of ambulance sirens. All the apartment and townhouse lights were dark, and the empty street had the air of a deserted stage set.

Angie's porch light was off. They stood on her doorstep, repeatedly pressing the bell. Cindy drooped against Kara, her eyelids fluttering with weariness, too tired now to complain any further.

Pressing the button for the dozenth time, Kara felt her heart sink. She should have phoned first. She'd forgotten that Angie spent many nights with her boyfriend, Russ. If Angie wasn't home, what would they do? Go back to the hospital lobby and wait for daylight? She did not have her car, and cabs were almost nonexistent in the suburbs.

But then a light flicked on inside the townhouse, and in a few seconds Angie herself, hair mussed with sleep, was peering out of the long pane of glass set beside the door. She pulled back the chain lock, unfastened the deadbolt, and opened the door.

"*Kara*? Kara, is that *you*? And is that *Cindy*? Am I seeing things?"

"No, it's me. Us. We're refugees," Kara said as Angie opened the door. She staggered in, pulling Cindy with her.

They put Cindy to bed in the small, cluttered second bedroom where Angie kept an IBM clone computer, a TV set and VCR, and a collection of video tapes.

Kara slumped at Angie's dining room table, her head propped on her hands, trying to explain what had brought them here in the middle of the night. Now that she was here her head felt thick, and nothing she said seemed to make any sense.

Worse, Angie kept asking questions as if unable to grasp the sequence of what happened.

Kara wished Angie would stop. God—she was beyond tired, she felt like a wooden marionette whose puppeteer had gone home. Why did Angie have to persist like this? Couldn't she see that it was nearly dawn?

"This man *tied you up*?" Angie questioned in horror.

"With *duct tape*?" She was braless beneath her oversized T-shirt, and her blond hair was bed-flattened on one side of her head.

"Yes. He—he always tapes women up before he—" Kara stopped, aware that she had blurted far too much.

"Now wait a minute," Angie said, shaking her head. "How do you know what he always does? Who said he always ties up women before he tries to rape them or kill them or whatever? Did the Rochester Police tell you that? Or is it . . ." Angie's blue eyes widened. "Kara . . . you don't know this man, do you? He wasn't somebody you *know*?"

Kara looked down at the table top, scattered with a few crumbs from some earlier snack of Angie's. She said nothing.

"You did know him!" Angie cried. "Oh, God, Kara . . . who was he?"

"He was a guy who attacked me once before, back when I lived in Florida." Kara got out the sentence with difficulty.

Angie's face was horrified, and she unconsciously moved her chair a few inches farther from Kara's. "*Attacked* you? This guy attacked you? You mean, he mugged you?"

Kara shook her head no, shuddering.

"He didn't—when, Kara? When did this happen?"

"Oh, a long time ago. Ten years ago. The month I graduated from high school." Kara shook her head. "I don't want to talk about it any more. It was too horrible, I've never been able to talk about it. Now he's broken his parole and he's in Michigan."

"*Parole?*" cried Angie. "He went to prison for this? Kara . . ." Comprehension spread across her face. "Was it rape? Oh, Jesus, Kar, was it rape?"

Kara said nothing, her silence a confession.

Angie breathed out her breath in a long sigh. "I knew

it," she said. "I just knew it. I knew you had some secret you would never tell me, I've known for years that something bad happened to you, Kara. I was your best friend and you would never talk to me."

They stared at each other. Kara saw the wet shininess in Angie's eyes, the accusation.

"I *couldn't* talk," she defended herself. "Angie, Ang, you just don't understand how awful it was. It wasn't just rape. It was . . . he did things . . . he was violent! There was another girl, Laurel, she was my best friend then. He used his knife . . . He didn't kill her but he might as well have. Right in front of me."

She stopped, unable to go any further, to describe it in any more detail than that. Not even to preserve her friendship with Angie could she say more. She raised her eyes to stare at Angie through a prism of unshed tears.

But Angie hesitated only a second before reaching out to pull Kara close to her, holding her in a tight hug that contained all the warmth that had kept their friendship going before, when Kara withdrew or became distant.

"Babe, babe, you don't have to tell me any more, not now, not tonight. Not ever if you don't want to. I'm sorry. I guess I don't have to know everything about you. I already know that I love you. Hey . . . if a friendship can't withstand a few secrets, then what good is it?"

"Oh, Ang . . ." Kara felt a wave of love, and she hung on to Angie, feeling freed, as if something nailed down tight in her had finally begun to release.

"Bed," Angie finally said. "Unless you just want to stay up?"

"No, I think I can sleep a little."

"Look, I'll go upstairs and get some bedding for you, and I think I have an extra pillow."

Cindy had the day bed in the small study, so Kara bedded down on the couch in the living room. Within seconds she had fallen into a restless sleep. She was awakened a few hours later by the sound of the shower running upstairs. It seemed incredible that it could be morning so soon.

Memories crashed in on her, the strangled terror as Jerry's forearm jammed against her neck.

She twisted under the cotton blanket Angie had given her, with difficulty forcing the image away. A nagging feeling pushed at her that she was making some sort of large mistake—had made one last night. But what?

She struggled to clear her thoughts. Damn . . . she felt dopey from last night, her brain fuzzy from all the adrenaline that had been pumped through it.

Jerry . . . how had he located Rob's house?

Almost instantly the answer came to her. With the address book he'd taken from her desk.

Kara sat up so swiftly that her head spun and the blanket dropped off her legs to the floor. It had been an old book, dog-eared, scribbled with eighty or a hundred names, many dating back to her college days and repeatedly crossed out as her friends moved to new apartments or houses. But Angie's name was in that book, and the Timberlea Village address.

Just then Angie walked through the living room, looking sexy and faintly plump in a pink lace bra and a matching half-slip with lace-trimmed side slits. Her hair was shower-damp, and she carried a little makeup bag with her.

"Hey, why are you up so early? Why don't you go back to sleep? I'm going to give myself a transfusion of coffee, and then I'll be out of here."

Angie pattered past her, and went into the kitchen where she began pouring water into a Mr. Coffee and simultaneously applying her makeup.

"I have to get up," Kara said.

"You don't 'have' to do anything. Hey, I'm getting ready

236

to go to work and I'll open the office for you and I can take most of your calls, too. You can stay here for as long as you want to. Stay for a couple of weeks if you want.''

Kara rubbed her eyes, which burned from getting only three hours' sleep. Her stomach was clenched, and she could feel the spill of acid at the back of her throat. ''I can't stay here, Ang. I have to go in to work. And there's something else. I think—''

Angie interrupted, ''Don't be so compulsive. Kara, you don't have to go in. The office won't fall apart without you for a week or so. Anyway, you need some time off. Maybe you should go down to Florida, visit your father—''

''No!'' Kara cried. ''He gets on my nerves, Ang. Anyway, I can't leave town while Rob is in the hospital.''

''Well, I don't see why you won't stay with me,'' Angie said, hurt.

Kara hesitated. ''Angie . . . he stole my address book.''

''What?'' Then comprehension filled Angie's face. ''Oh, my God.''

''I'm just so damn sorry,'' Kara said, hearing her voice crack. ''I just thought of that this morning. Angie, I know it's me he wants, but maybe you ought to go and stay with Russ for a few days, just to be on the safe side. Until the police catch him and send him back to Florida.''

Kara went upstairs to take her shower and wake Cindy, and then the three of them ate a hurried breakfast of stale coffee cake Angie took out of her freezer, orange juice and coffee.

''Sorry to give you an eight-month-old breakfast, but I don't usually eat anything in the morning,'' Angie said, looking nervous.

Cindy, too, seemed subdued, and toyed with the crumbs, pushing around little piles of brown sugar and chopped walnuts. Rob's daughter was still wearing her wrinkled pink shorts and the ruffled pajama top, and somewhere last night had lost the plastic barrette she usually used to keep her hair out of her eyes.

Excusing herself, Kara made a phone call to the Troy Hilton to reserve a room for herself and Cindy. They had a room available for immediate check-in, and the pool was open. She then phoned Dee Devers at the Grand Hotel on Mackinaw Island, which was at the top of the Michigan peninsula, three hundred miles north.

She explained what had happened.

"What? Oh, my God! Is Cindy all right?" Cindy's mother could not conceal her shock and horror.

"Cindy is fine, and in a few minutes I'm taking her to the Troy Hilton." Kara gave the address and directions. "As soon as visiting hours start, we'll visit Rob at the hospital, but then we'll go back to the hotel and you can pick Cindy up there."

"How could this have happened?" Dee exclaimed. "I can't believe it. I mean, I leave for a couple of weeks' vacation, I trust Rob to take care of her, and this happens. Where was my wonderful ex-husband when all this went on? Did he just sit back and let some man break in and—"

"No, he didn't just sit back. He fought the man, he's in the hospital, Dee. As I told you, he got stabbed."

She filled Dee in on Rob's condition and completed the arrangements. As she hung up, she felt sweat forming tiny beads on her forehead. She didn't blame Dee for being upset. It must be hard to remain calm when your child had been threatened and you were three hundred miles away, enjoying yourself and thinking her safe.

"How am I going to go swimming at the hotel without a bathing suit?" Cindy inquired, her forehead puckered again with the worried frown.

Kara gazed at Rob's daughter. She didn't look the least bit interested in swimming. She was biting her fingernail, her thumb halfway in her mouth as well. Maybe she was focusing on trivialities because she couldn't think about the reality—that she had been within feet and seconds of rape, mutilation or murder.

Kara felt a wave of strong protectiveness. Whatever her flaws, Cindy was only ten. An immature ten, at that. She hadn't asked for this. What woman did? To be a woman was to be at the mercy of male sexual and violent urges.

"I don't know," Kara said, forcing a smile. "The malls aren't open yet, but maybe we can find a suit at a drug store or a Meijers store. Or who knows, they might even sell them at the hotel."

An elderly volunteer gave them visitors' passes out of a file box, along with a wrinkled smile. They trudged past the gift shop to the elevator. Cindy insisted on stopping in the gift shop to buy Rob a stuffed bear that said *I Love You Beary Much*. She was wearing the new blue playsuit Kara had bought for her on sale at Meijer's. With her face scrubbed and her hair washed and pulled back in a newly purchased blue plastic clip, the ten-year-old looked like the child star of some television sitcom.

Rob was sitting in bed reading a copy of *People* magazine with one hand.

"Hi, Kara. Hi, Cindyella." He looked up and smiled crookedly. There were shaving cuts and a bluish bruise on his jawline. His right hand was in a cast and sling.

"Daddy, Daddy, Daddy!" Cindy cried joyously, running forward to throw her arms around Rob. "You're reading!"

"A very fascinating article on M. C. Hammer. Hey, watch it, honey, don't bump me, I'm still a little sore."

While father and daughter held their reunion, and Cindy told Rob all about the Troy Hilton's pool and a little boy she had met there, Kara went to stand at the window. It overlooked the front parking lot of the hospital. Visiting hours had just begun and several cars had pulled into the lot and were cruising up and down the rows looking for spaces.

Kara watched a blue one, her eyes intent. When two elderly women in pants suits got out, she released her breath slowly. Already Rob and Cindy had been endangered, and possibly even Angie, or other people she had listed in her address book.

God . . . ten years and it hadn't ended, had it?

After a few minutes, Rob patted Cindy on the rump and asked her to go down to the lounge near the nurses' station where there was a TV set. "I have to talk to Kara, honey."

Cindy balked. "Do I have to? I don't want to watch TV there. Why do I have to go? I want to stay here and listen."

"Because Kara and I have to have some grown-up talk. Then you can come back, Cindyella, and you and I will watch something on the tiny TV. You can pick the program."

Reluctantly Cindy left the room, and Kara went to the chair she had vacated. Now that Cindy was gone, there was something still and quiet about Rob, almost accusing.

She filled the sudden silence that existed between them. "How's your hand? How'd the surgery go?"

"They think they fixed it, but I'm going to have physical therapy, and there's a chance my fine-motor movements might not come back one hundred percent. About what I expected." Rob shrugged. "Well, I can always learn to draw on computer. It's the coming thing and I've been wanting to get into it."

Guilt washed over her. "Will you be able to—"

"Let's just forget my hand for now. Dee called, and she said she'd just talked to you. She was working herself up for a good case of the hysterics. She thinks I was reprehensibly careless in allowing Cindy to be exposed to murder and mayhem. She blames you, too. She says she's not going to let her visit me again until I can convince her that Cindy is thoroughly safe. If necessary, she says she'll go to court.''

Kara expelled her breath. "I see."

This edict did not surprise Kara. Dee had taken Rob to court several times since the decree, on minor child custody disputes. It was a way of expressing her deep-seated anger at the divorce which, at the last moment, she had begged Rob to cancel.

"Kara, last night the police questioned me. I woke up this morning and all I could think about was what happened last night. That guy who stabbed me, Jerry Quick, he was someone out of your past that you never saw fit to tell me about. If I'd known there was someone like that, I could have taken some steps. I could have protected us. Dee was right, you did expose my daughter to something, and you never gave me a chance to have any say about it.''

Kara had never seen Rob so quietly angry. His voice was not raised, but each word was spoken with sharp-edged clarity, and seemed to fall into the room and break like crystal. Stunned, Kara started to speak but Rob put up his hand. "No, let me finish. I want to know right here and now. Are there any other things I should know about? Things you haven't told me that might affect our lives?''

She felt her face redden. She tensed in the uncomfortable hospital chair, her hands tightening. It was one thing to tell herself that this was her fault, but to hear Rob say it was entirely different.

Her voice shook. "You're saying this is my fault, aren't you? You're blaming me!''

"Of course not directly. But you weren't honest with me.''

Was this nightmare never going to stop? "I did conceal Jerry from you. But was it really that wrong? It happened ten years ago, Rob! He was in jail—I thought! Am I supposed to be able to predict the future, to know everything that is going to happen, every ramification of every single thing I do? I was a rape victim, Rob! I guess you can't even imagine what that's like, can you? Do you think it's easy, living with the fact that you were raped, that you were forced to stand by and watch while your best girlfriend got carved up? I did the best I could! *I coped, dammit!*"

"Hey," he said. "Jesus, Kara—"

She was on her feet, her breath coming thick in her throat. "I'm sorry about what happened, God, I am, but Cindy is okay. I'll guard her with my life, as you put it, and when Dee gets here, I'll turn her over to her mother and that will be that. And if I stay away from you and Cindy, that will keep both of you safe, won't it? I mean, why should Jerry bother with you when he has *me* to go after?"

Rob opened his mouth, but her tirade was not yet over. "We're at the Troy Hilton, Room 248, and it's a very safe hotel, Rob. They've got their own security, and there's people everywhere. I fully intend to keep the room door locked and bolted, okay? There's only a few hours to wait until Dee arrives, and then your daughter's safety won't be contaminated any more by me!"

Dee Devers arrived at the Troy Hilton at 4:30 p.m. She phoned Kara from the lobby and then took the elevator up.

Kara let her into the room, noticing that Dee's skin was sunburned, and she wore white paper-bag waist pants and a T-shirt that said *Leland, Michigan*. She was makeupless, and looked very angry at the interruption of her vacation.

"There was a huge traffic jam at the Zilwaukee Bridge. More construction. Where are Cindy's clothes?"

"I haven't got them. My friend drove me to pick up my

car, but I haven't gone inside Rob's house yet—I didn't want to do it when she was with me.''

''Oh, great,'' Dee muttered, taking the plastic shopping sack that held the damp, two-piece bathing suit Kara had bought Cindy, the pink shorts and pajama top. She bundled up Cindy as if rescuing her from a child molester.

''Mom,'' Cindy protested as her mother took her arm. ''You don't have to drag me.''

Dee snapped, ''I packed up all her good summer clothes for the visit to her father, and now she's got nothing left to wear that looks decent. What is she going to do, wear rags?''

''I'm sorry. Rob is getting out of the hospital tomorrow and he'll send everything to her,'' Kara said. ''Or he'll drive it over.''

''I can't believe you would expose my little girl to such a horrible man,'' Dee said thinly, taking Cindy by the arm and propelling her toward the door.

The child instinctively resisted, turning toward Kara. ''Come along, young lady, and don't give me any crap today,'' Dee snapped. ''I had a long drive and a ruined vacation and I'm not in the mood for this.''

The door closed behind Dee and Cindy. Poor Cindy, Kara thought. Dee hadn't even acted glad to see her, or relieved she was all right.

She stood by the window, looking down at the pool area, where a family was playing with a red beach ball in the water. There was a laughing mother and father, and two giggly little girls about six and eight. A nuclear family untouched by divorce, resentment or hate.

Kara's eyes at last filled with the tears she had been holding back. Dee and even Rob acted as if this were her fault, as if she had caused the attack by Jerry. It was not fair. She hadn't deliberately ''exposed'' Cindy to Jerry. Nor was she responsible for his being let out of prison and breaking parole.

After a few minutes, her tears were gone. She went to the long, formica dresser top, collected her purse, and made sure that she still had Rob's house key. Now that Cindy was safe, and Rob was still immobilized in the hospital, she intended to go back and get Rob's gun.

Jerry was never going to get his hands on her again.

The afternoon sun was still hot, the light taking on an orangey quality now in late afternoon. A police patrol car was exiting Rob's subdivision as she turned into it. Looking at it, Kara felt her old hostility, although now, for the first time, she began to wonder whether it was justified.

In ten years, police behavior toward rape victims had begun to change. There was more empathy—sometimes. Officers were now trained in dealing with rape victims, and even hospital personnel received special training. But it was all too late for her. Wasn't it? She felt another doubt. She had never pursued things with Dr. Hay, never stayed in therapy long enough to really work through her anger. That *was* her own fault, and was she so much better than Laurel, who had never gone to any therapist at all?

She pressed the door locks, and drove down the blacktop road that curved among the large, wooded lots, the expensive "executive" homes. Automatic sprinkler systems created wet dervishes of water droplets. A six-year-old on a bike with training wheels pedaled furiously across the street, but he was the only other person she saw.

Kara continued through the subdivision until she reached Rob's house. She turned into the driveway and parked.

The house looked exactly as it always did, a sweeping expanse of redwood and glass set back among trees and woods. In daylight, it looked like a photograph in *Architectural Digest*, almost too beautiful to be real. Even the grass was the clear green felt featured in Barefoot Lawn ads. It was almost impossible to imagine anything bad happening here.

Kara sat for a few minutes, unwilling to leave the safety of her automobile. Jerry could, she supposed, be lurking around the subdivision still. But it was broad daylight and the neighborhood was being patrolled by the police. He would be a fool to come back.

When a neighbor's poodle wandered across the lawn, snuffing at some shrubs near the drive before relieving itself, Kara pushed the "unlock" button and got out of her car. If there was a prowler, she felt, the dog would have been uneasy and barking. Anyway, she had to go in if she wanted the gun, had to take a small risk.

She let herself in the front door with the key, and stood in the foyer. She noticed that the scent of the house had changed. It now smelled of stale cigarette smoke and strangers. And was there something else, the faint, rich odor of blood?

She looked down. A smear of Rob's blood was spattered on the foyer tiles, along with the scraps of the gray duct tape she'd torn off her mouth last night.

Kara swallowed deeply, fighting back a surge of nausea so strong she wondered if she was going to have to rush to a commode. She edged past the blood stain and went upstairs, turning left down the hall into the master bedroom.

She froze in the doorway. Rob's king-sized bed was in disarray, the sheets crumpled and partly torn away from the mattress. Mattress, sheets, and the light cotton blanket Rob liked in summer, were stained with blood, and a ceramic bedside lamp lay on its side, the shade dented and stained with more dark red. It was like a scene from a crime movie, an observation that gave Kara a thick, trembling, disjointed feeling.

She forced herself to go to the bedside stand, where she took out the package of Remington cartridges Rob had put there. It felt heavy, ominous in her hand. She carried it over to the walk-in closet, where she rummaged on the top shelf until she found the unloaded .38. She fumbled through the process of loading it, feeling the dull, oily slick of the gun in her hands.

She put the revolver in her purse, amazed at the way it weighted down her light summer bag. It seemed so alien in there with her little cloth makeup bag, her billfold, her car keys, the extra pair of panty hose. She had no permit to carry it. And what if Rob was right? What if the gun drew violence toward her, rather than protecting her from it?

Another risk she would have to take.

She was shivering so hard she had to sit down in the chair where Rob usually put his clothes when he undressed at night. She set her purse on the floor, repelled at its new heaviness. Could she ever really use the gun? She'd spent some time with Chuck shooting his .22 pistol at tin cans nailed to trees, and at a target range.

Then, it had seemed exciting and fun, an adventure. She'd been proud of herself for hitting the target paper on one of the circles.

Now she remembered the loud report of the gun, and the way it had kicked back against her. And that had been only a .22. Wouldn't a .38 be harder to shoot? Louder? What if her hands shook too much? If she panicked?

Automatically she began bundling up the bloody sheets and bedding. Getting ready to leave, she lugged the entire pile of bloody laundry into Rob's garage and put it into a large lawn bag. If it were hers, she'd throw it out, but maybe he would want to send it to a commercial laundry.

Picking up her purse and feeling the weight of the gun again, she again hesitated. Did she really want this?

She heard a sudden, sharp click. Then a swishing sound outside. Kara became still, her heartbeat fibrillating so fast she could barely breathe.

Jerry? But then she relaxed, her laughter sounding thin

and nervous in the enclosed garage. It was only Rob's Rainbird sprinkler, set on its timer to begin twirling a fine, misty spray across his lawn.

She gathered the heavy purse to her and left.

CHAPTER 22

Kara stood hunched at the wall phone in the lobby of the Big Boy restaurant on Rochester Road, leaning against the wall so her words would not be heard by anyone entering the restaurant. She had decided to call the Rochester police to see what progress they had made in finding Jerry.

Food smells drifted from the restaurant, making her feel faintly nauseous. She had been put on hold twice, and now was talking to a man named Gazzarro, who apparently had been put in charge of her case.

"Where have you been?" he wanted to know. "We've been trying to reach you."

"I'm staying at the Troy Hilton," she told him. "But right now I'm at a pay phone. I didn't know I had to check in with you."

"Well, we think it would be better if we could keep an eye on you for now. Quick isn't just any ordinary burglar or prowler. We received word he's wanted in a killing in Oxford, Ohio."

"Ohio?" That was where Laurel lived. Several teen-agers in rock T-shirts had chosen this minute to enter the restaurant, laughing and poking each other in adolescent merriment. In order to hear, Kara had to press the receiver tightly to her ear. She breathed in deeply, fighting the sense of panic.

"A woman named Laurel Fearn was found dead in her home, tied up, stabbed and mutilated."

"W-what?" she stammered. *Laurel, dead.* She clutched at the metal edge of the telephone panel, her fingers going white.

"She's the woman who was involved in that rape case with you, wasn't she?"

"Yes," Kara whispered. "She was the other one."

I saw him, Laurel had blurted in that shaky, gritty voice of fear. *He hates us, Karalynn. He'd like to get us and do it again to us.* She hadn't listened, had sloughed Laurel off with anger and disbelief. She hadn't wanted to believe. And she had never made that phone call. God, was some of the blame hers?

"Mutilated," Gazzarro repeated. "You understand?"

"Oh, God," Kara whispered, wondering what unspeakable thing Jerry had done to Laurel. She hoped he would not tell her. She felt a wave of giddy faintness and then it went away. Maybe she was getting inured to shock now, hardened to it. There had been so much.

She heard his voice through a dim filter. "We're putting a patrol on your house and Mr. Devers', in the hope we can pick Quick up if he shows up there again. I'd like to do more than that, too—I'd like to put an officer in your home, Miss Cleveland. Miss Cleveland?"

She spoke with difficulty. "In my home? I wasn't planning to go back to my home except to get some clothes."

"Let the officer accompany you then." The man went on, "I know this sounds rough, but unless you plan entirely to leave the area, you will be better off with police protection. This is no man to mess with. As you know, he has a history of stalking women and there is another case in Valdosta, Georgia that he might be involved in, too. That girl is in critical condition. She's going to need plastic surgery."

She felt a surge of nausea and panic. Desperately she fought it back. She felt as if she had stepped into some horrible nightmare, beyond her comprehension. But she was going to have to deal with this somehow.

"I don't know," she said. "God, I don't know . . ." But she knew her choices were limited. She couldn't depend on Rob to guard her. Although he had been released from the hospital, his right hand was in a cast and sling, effectively immobilizing him. She certainly could not ask him to risk his life again, or Cindy's.

Besides, there was the cloud between them, more than just a broken engagement now.

Another option: She could live like a nomad at the Troy Hilton, sneak in and out of her office. But if she did that she might endanger her employees. At least if there was an officer she could go in to work. She needed work right now; it was the only stability her life had.

"Where are you right now?" he wanted to know.

"I'm at the Big Boy on Rochester Road north of downtown."

"I'm sending an officer named Randy Dorfman, he'll accompany you to your home and trade off with another officer, twelve hours each, for the next two or three days, hopefully until we've got Quick in custody. Dorfman will be in plain clothes."

She swallowed, still reluctant. The township was small and understaffed; to deploy two men meant they really wanted Jerry. Only because she lived in upscale, suburban Rochester was a police guard possible at all, she realized. If this had been Detroit, she would be on her own. And even then, the protection would only last a few days. "Do you . . . expect him to break in my home again, then?"

"Miss Cleveland, it's highly possible. We've made some phone calls to Raiford State Prison and the warden says Quick is obsessed with the fear of getting AIDS and may already have it. The other prisoners say he fantasizes repeating the whole rape setup with you again."

"But why? My God, why would they let him out? When he—"

"Miss," Gazzarro said wearily. "Don't you realize how crowded our penal system is? Nobody serves a full sentence unless they're Charles Manson."

Charles Manson. She felt a sick surge as she remembered the actress Theresa Soldana, whose assailant had openly vowed in prison to kill her. The prison system had every intention of releasing him when the time came. Maybe he would hunt down and kill Soldana and everyone would be very sorry.

She realized Gazzarro was speaking. "You stay there at the Big Boy," Gazzarro instructed, "And I'll have Dorfman meet you there."

Kara wasn't hungry—her appetite had totally vanished. But she had to wait somewhere, so she went inside the restaurant and a hostess showed her to a booth near a window.

"Just coffee," she specified to the waitress.

She sat in the booth without touching her steaming cup, thinking about Laurel and the phone calls, the "illusions" that had in the end turned out to be terrifying real. She remembered that Laurel had only been 5'2" tall, and suppressed a sob.

Ten minutes later a man slid into the booth opposite her. "Kara Cleveland?" he asked. He flipped open a billfold and showed her a badge.

"Yes." He was about twenty-six and looked cocky, a man to whom a certain kind of girl in bars would be attracted. He had a full head of brown hair cut stylishly short, and his face was clean shaven. If he was not a police officer, he might be a tool and die-maker or shop supervisor. Certainly not a man who ever attended the symphony or visited the Detroit Institute of Arts.

"Looks like I'm your guard for a couple days," he announced, grinning.

"Okay, but I can't . . . I don't want you following me around too closely. This is—I'm not used to this."

"Who is? Look, what'd you order? You don't mind, I'll get something, too. Patty melt. You ever had the patty melt here?"

"No."

"I like the patty melt," said her police guard, snapping his fingers for the waitress.

Kara spent the next three days trying to adjust to the idea of two strange men in her house, men with whom she had absolutely nothing in common. Dorfman was like a big, chatty boy, filling her in on all his interests and activities, from hot air ballooning to his aerobics instructor girlfriend. The other officer, Barry Gitlin, was older than Dorfman, and obviously bored and resentful of the duty he had drawn. He said little.

In a way, having them there was reassuring. She could go to work and feel safe, and not have to worry that she was endangering Angie and the others. She had scheduled more interviews with salesman applicants this week, and was also preparing a business loan application. For this, she was using her new Lotus spreadsheet program. It was fussy, detailed, math-oriented work that involved entering formulas into "cells," and using a pull-down menu to translate these to bar charts and projections. Excellent therapy right now because it forced her to concentrate.

She had decided to put Rob's gun, still loaded, in the linen closet in her bathroom, underneath a stack of towels where it would not attract notice. She was afraid that one of the men might see it in her purse and arrest her for carrying a concealed weapon. That was the last thing she needed—and if they confiscated the gun, then she would have no means of defense.

At the *Bargain Hound* office, she installed Dorfman at a desk in the front area, and tried to look the other way when he flirted blatantly with Lynette, her receptionist.

The younger officer was getting on her nerves. Several times he had tried to flirt with her as well. He had made references to other rape cases and murders of women, using phrases like "he did her." But he was permitting her to go on with her life, so she tried to be grateful.

As for Rob, her missing him was such a deep ache that the only way she could handle it was to refuse to take his calls. After this was over, maybe they could talk again. For now, she felt too raw, too guilty.

In the middle of one busy work day, her father phoned her from his hotel in Smyrna, Tennessee, where he was winding up his hiking trip.

"Awful pretty scenery here, baby," Ken Cleveland remarked in an expansive, slightly wheezy voice that told her he'd been tipping a few beers. "We had a little rain today so I'm kinda laying back, staying in my room. Well? Am I going to have to drive north to your wedding or not?"

Had it been that inevitable that she would break her engagement? Kara felt a rush of embarrassment and dismay. So much had happened. How could she possibly tell him about Laurel's death, or Jerry? If she did, it would throw him into a total tailspin. He wouldn't drive up to Michigan, he'd charter a small plane, and arrive with his boots on, barking out orders, questioning everyone, forcing her to go back to Florida with him, probably. He would turn her into a damaged, hurting seventeen-year-old again, frightened of his colossal wrath.

"Dad, well . . . I did break off the engagement," she finally admitted in a low voice.

"Karalynn, I knew you were going to do it way back when you called me and said you were going to marry the guy. Hey, baby, make up your mind. Am I going to get any grandchildren before I'm too old to dandle them on my knee?"

"Dad . . ."

"You got a biological clock, Karalynn, you ever stop to think about that? You're what, twenty-eight years old. That isn't young when it comes to having kids. Your mother was thirty-five when she had you, and they called her a . . ." He stammered over the words. "An elderly prima—primapara. Something like that."

She drew in her breath, hanging onto the phone and thinking how her father didn't even have to work to cut her down to size. He just did it, as natural as breathing.

"I don't think I'm ready for marriage yet," she finally told him. "I'm mixed up about it, Dad. But I have plenty of time."

"So you say. What did your fiancé say? I bet he wasn't exactly jumping up and down with excitement. Oh, well." Ken Cleveland's sigh was audible across the telephone line from Tennessee. "I guess I'll head back south to the old place in St. Pete, girlie-girl. I've hiked Mt. Sterling and Greenbriar Pinnacle, and I guess it kind of did me in."

"Dad . . ." He sounded shaky. Old. "You're all right, aren't you?"

"Oh, hell, yes. Fit as fanny, kid. I got hooked up with a P.W.P. hiking group for a couple of days, but they sort of split up and I didn't feel like doing any more climbing alone. An old fart of sixty-eight has no business tramping around in the hills by himself."

He was lonely, that was all—as she would surely be once this tension with Jerry died away and her life slid back to the routines of singlehood. Kara exchanged a few

254

more pleasantries with her father, trying to force back the feeling of anger at him that still lurked inside her, like a PCP residue.

Being a victim wasn't a one-shot deal, she reflected. Jerry had changed everything, altering her life on a new course, diminishing the feelings she had for other people and the way she reacted to them.

Two days passed and still Jerry was not picked up. His picture had been shown on the evening news. The police were canvassing all hotels and motels in the Detroit metropolitan area as far as Ann Arbor in the west, Flint in the north, Anchor Bay in the east. Several times cars had been seen cruising Rob's neighborhood, but when stopped by the policed proved to be teenagers joyriding with cans of beer in the car.

"I'm so tired of this," Kara sighed to Angie at the end of the second day. Dorfman, who had grown more and more confident and familiar, was leaning over Lynette's desk, boasting to her about a driver he knew in the Grand Prix. "Look at him. He's like some fraternity guy, only not as smart. I can't believe I have to be followed around by him. And the way he keeps bringing up rape and talking about it. It bothers me."

They went into Kara's office, where the color monitor of her Zenith PC glowed deep indigo blue. Kara poured them both mugs of coffee, accidentally slopping some down the side of Angie's cup. She wiped it away with a paper towel. God, her hands were trembly now.

"Kara, I admit he's a jerk," Angie said. "But you're reading a whole lot into what he says, things that might not even be there."

"I'm not 'reading' anything," Kara snapped. "It's there. You'd think so, too, if you heard him, Angie."

"Then complain about him. Ask for someone else."

"Maybe I will," Kara said, steadying her voice by

clearing her throat, a ploy that did not escape Angie's notice.

"Hey, kiddo. You know what a lot of stress you're living under. You've hardly eaten a decent meal since it happened—you're living on coffee. You're going to turn anorexic if you don't watch it."

Kara's smile was fleeting. "I was a few pounds overweight."

"You were not. What a crock. Kara, you really ought to consider getting away for a little while. If you don't want to visit your father, then fly out to California, maybe San Francisco. Or make yourself a reservation at Club Med. Anything. You're just torturing yourself like this . . . and another thing. Rob has called about eight times—I know because Lynette told me. Why won't you talk to him?"

Kara flushed. "I can't. We had a fight. More than just a fight. He . . . he put blame on me for not telling him about Jerry. He thinks I endangered Cindy."

"Look, I know it's none of my business, but you two need to do some serious talking, which is something I don't think you've really ever done, have you? Kar, he said some stuff in anger. But you can't blame him for that. It's tough, thinking you know a person, know all about them, thinking you're close to them, and suddenly you find out there's a whole area of their life you've been excluded from."

Kara knew Angie was talking about herself as well as Rob. "Rob has no right to blame me for Jerry."

"Rob is just a human being, Kara. Not a perfect person, just an ordinary guy, and a lot better than the average at that. Rob didn't really blame you for Jerry—he blamed you for concealing yourself from him."

Kara turned away. In her lecturing moods, Angie could strike too close to home. She said sharply, "Well, now he knows all about me, doesn't he? Nothing is concealed any more. And he reacted just as I thought he would—putting his anger on me. That's just what my father did. He changed so much, he became obsessed by rape, couldn't let it go or stop talking about it. I started to feel guilty because I was the one responsible for making him that way."

"Men aren't as strong as we are," Angie reflected after a moment. "They are threatened by rape, too. By the fact that something out of their control can threaten a woman and take her away from them."

"I don't want to talk about it any more," Kara said, sitting down at the screen and pressing the keys that would take her into the Lotus 1-2-3 program.

Jerry had moved out of the mom and pop motel and was now renting a room in Pontiac, on a dinky side street off Walton Boulevard, lined with shabby bungalows. One reason he took it, the room was over the garage, and the rent included a space there for his car.

The woman who rented him the room was white, seventy-six years old, half-blind, and an old alky who kept gin bottles all over her kitchen counter. However, she did have an old Chevy parked in the back yard, not too rusted, and Jerry told her a sad story about the Ciera having major transmission problems. He convinced her to let him drive the Chevy for an additional sixty dollars a month. He was pretty proud of himself for that idea.

Already he had seen himself four times on the old black and white TV with which his room was furnished. It was a prison picture taken with his face turned both frontways and sideways, making him look like an ugly convict, his expression scowling.

The picture bothered Jerry. It didn't seem like him. He'd looked different as a kid, twenty-five pounds skinnier with undeveloped shoulders. He was grown and muscular now. Even his neck was thicker. Watching his picture on TV, hearing the anchor man say, "Quick is wanted for a mutilation murder in Ohio," made shivers go all through Jerry's gut. They even mentioned his tattoo, the 13½.

What if someone saw him now, recognized him, called the cops on him? Shit, all it would take was one person. As a precaution, he began letting the hair on his face grow. But, hell, he could grow twenty beards, but that fucking tattoo was one thing he couldn't eliminate. He decided to wear a long sleeved shirt whenever he went out. Fortunately, good old Ed owned a couple of white shirts.

As for the old lady, he kept away from her as much as possible. He believed she passed out every night by 9:00, but he couldn't be sure she wouldn't recognize him in one of her lucid moments.

He holed up in the room, ordering pizzas and subs to be delivered, each from a different pizza place so he would not attract attention. He watched everything on TV from *Good Morning America* to *Days of Our Lives, Family Feud, Win, Lose or Draw* and *Cheers*. Old Westerns, too, those were his favorite, and all the Charles Bronson and Sylvester Stallone movies he could find.

When he started to go fuzzy from watching too much snow dancing on the old set, he went into the john and jacked off into the sink. He fantasized that he had Karalynn kneeling in front of him, naked and begging. And that other little girl, too, the one in the hot pink shorts.

He added her to the fantasy. One blond, the other brunette, just like before. Young, sweet stuff so pretty you could crawl up it and eat it with a spoon. His cure. His repeat experience, his second chance.

On the third day, it got unbearably hot. The TV said it was pushing ninety-seven. The old lady hadn't given him anything, even a fan, and all the heat rose to the top of the garage, turning it into a bake oven. By 7:00 p.m., Jerry was sweating, restless and angry. He'd had enough of being a prisoner here. He might as well be in Raiford. At least he had someone to talk to there.

He paced the room wearing only a pair of blue bermuda shorts that had belonged to asshole Ed. Perspiration trickled among the bristles of his face. His bare, muscular chest dripped with sweat, and the odor coming from his armpits was sour and funky. One thing, he hadn't brought any deodorant and he certainly smelled like it. Shit, even his toes were cracked and burning from athlete's foot, the itching driving him crazy.

He coughed, something catching in his throat. Anxiously he stroked his damp neck, feeling for the glands there, wondering if they were swollen. Some guys, the first they knew they had AIDS was when they came down with a bad sore throat that would not go away. One guy at Raiford thought he had a bad asthma attack until the prison doctor told him it was some kind of pneumonia from AIDS.

Not for the first time he wondered if Whitetop had it, if that was why they took him to the hospital four times, and why he'd lost the weight and kept saying he was too tired.

The thoughts started to get overwhelming, and Jerry discovered he was digging so deeply into his neck that it hurt. He tore his hand away. This was the bitch's fault, that he was trapped here like this, stuck with his worries. From start to finish, all Karalynn's fault.

He walked over to the opened suitcase and rooted among the clothes until he found one of the long-sleeved shirts. He put it on, flexing his shoulders, which felt too tight, restrained under all that cloth. He shoved on the pair of sunglasses, and dug his feet into a pair of Ed's fancy Reebok tennis shoes.

He clattered down the rickety, homemade staircase that had been built in the garage to give access to his room, and walked out back to the old lady's Chevy.

It started up on the third try, the mufflers blowing out a little but not too loud, he hoped. He pulled out of the spot and took off down the street, squealing his tires like a teenager on the last day of school.

Kara was working late, hunched over the computer screen with a book on Lotus opened beside her, as she tried to work through the complexities of labeling her bar chart with horizontal and vertical titles. First she selected Options from the Graph menu, then Titles, then X-Axis.

Sighing, she straightened up, rubbing at the back of her neck. Despite the air conditioning, it seemed hot, stale and close, the dampness in the air nearly preventing thought. The other employees had gone home an hour ago, including Angie, who had a date with Russ.

Now only Dorfman sat at the desk in the hall, whistling through his teeth and leafing through a copy of *Car and Driver*. The sound was irritating, and not for the first time she wondered just how much help Dorfman would really be, assuming Jerry were to break through the door.

"Hey," he called to her now, as if reading her thoughts. "Any objection, we call out for a pizza? I got the growls."

"All right."

She heard the sound of him punching the phone buttons and then ordering a pizza with extra cheese, hamburger, Italian sausage and pepperoni. All that fat sickened her.

"Please," she begged. "Just order me something vegetarian. I can't eat all that greasy sausage."

"Vegetarian?" It was as if he had never heard of such a thing, but he revised the order, getting two small pizzas. "I'll eat any of your leftovers," he informed her. "Even if it has green pepper. Green pepper tastes bitter to me, you know?"

She had phoned Gazzarro earlier in the day asking for someone to replace Dorfman, only to be greeted by a sharp exhale of breath. "Look, Miss Cleveland, I realize the officer might not be a tactful person, but he's one of our best, okay? Just cooperate with him and he'll protect you."

"He has made very unpleasant remarks about rape," she had persisted.

"Lady, rape *is* unpleasant. Look, try to hang on. Hopefully we can pick up Quick and you can—"

"I want another officer."

Gazzarro sighed. "I don't have any extra manpower. Bear with us, Miss Cleveland. As soon as we have Quick, this will all be over."

Now she saved the work she had done, exited to her main menu, and turned off the program, waiting while the screen flickered off. The work hadn't gone as quickly as she'd hoped it would; tension was causing her to make stupid mistakes.

She glanced out of the window, noticing that it was dusky outside, shadows creeping toward the building out of the lilac hedge as if to surround it. A car went by on the street, its muffler a little rattly, as if on the verge of needing repairs. Somehow the sound made her feel even more tense.

"Hey, you coming out here?" Dorfman said familiarly. "Come on out here, Kara, I got to show you a picture of a car. You want to see a real car that'll knock your panty hose off? I mean, this one's gonna excite even you."

Maybe it was the night, the dusk closing in, or the sound of the rackety muffler that reminded her of Jerry, although she could not have said why. Or just the easy, breezy, crude, male arrogance of Dorfman. But Kara felt herself bristle.

" 'Knock my panty hose off'?" she questioned him sharply, coming out of her office. "Don't you think that remark was a little sexist? Not to mention crude."

"Just a joke, lady," Dorfman said. He had leaned so far back in the desk chair it looked as if it were about to flip him backwards. His shoes, propped on the desk, were black police issue. A dried, black circle of stepped-on gum decorated the right sole.

Kara felt repelled at the sight, and averted her eyes from him. There were so many men like him, she thought. A little crude, selfish, insensitive, and always having to be "male." Men who strutted and showed off, and thought women "owed" them their favors.

"Hey, what'd you do, eat a sour lemon?" Dorfman wanted to know. "Jeez, give a guy a break. I was just trying to be funny, you know. Instead of saying knock your socks off, I said panty hose."

What was she supposed to say? This man's superior officer thought he was "one of our best." She was stuck with him and needed his good will. "Okay."

"Anyway, they should be pullin' me off this case pretty soon. If the guy don't come around tonight or tomorrow, try to prong someone, then they're gonna put me on other things."

Kara stared at her protection. 'Prong someone.' The ultimate in crudity, and it was referring to herself. Had he said it to her on purpose, to pay her back for being sharp with him? For not flirting? Was that the way men talked about it, thought about it? God, this man was really no better than Jerry, was he? The same type of man anyway.

"I need you to speak about this with some kind of consideration and dignity," she said stiffly, fixing him with a cold stare.

"Hey, what's the matter, I ain't talking good enough for you? I ain't treating you right? Hey, lady, I get paid to guard you, not treat you like a princess. Anyways, you know what I think?" He swung his feet down from the desk and lazily unfolded himself from the chair. "I think some of this rape stuff, it's over-exaggerated, know what I mean? I mean, hey, some women, they feel too guilty and uptight about sex. They just need, like, a man to overpower them a little, so they don't have to feel guilty about doing it.''

Kara walked toward the front office door, her high heels making no noise on the flat beige carpet. She slid back the dead bolt and opened the door, letting in a hot, moist burst of summer night air. She felt light and airy inside, as if freed of some heavy burden.

''Your assignment is over,'' she said crisply.

''What?''

''I said, this job is finished.''

''Hey—''

Her every word snapped. ''Leave now, and stay off this property. I don't want you or any other police officer coming back here, or to my home either. You can tell Gazzarro that too. Tell him as far as I'm concerned, 'best' is a hell of a lot more than just being able to shoot a gun.''

Dorfman insolently mimed pulling a trigger.

''Okay, okay. You don't have to get all twisted out of shape.'' He slouched toward the door, taking his time. ''I'll check in, I'll find out what's happening. They probably want me back on the job anyways.''

She waited, holding herself tall.

He reached the door, then turned. ''But hey, what are you going to do if good old boy Jerry comes through here like a dose of salts, huh? You think you're some stuff, don't you? You think you're a damn princess. Hey, it's women like you that a rapist loves to get, know what I mean?''

Kara slammed the door behind him, and then snapped all the bolts and locks, her hands shaking badly. Her triumph segued rapidly into fear. More nausea pushed up at the back of her throat and threatened to overwhelm her. She waited while Dorfman started his car, and pulled out of the parking lot. Incredible. What was it they said about police officers? That they were criminals turned inside out.

She jumped as a joist in the old house gave an unexpected crack. There was a sudden whirr as the air conditioning clicked on. Already it seemed eerie, hollow and deserted here, although Dorfman had been gone less than a minute.

God—she didn't want to be alone here tonight, no way did she want that.

Shaking, wondering if she had been an utter fool, she went back into her office and collected her purse. She went around the office, turning off the coffee pot, flicking off lights, turning the air conditioner to a higher temperature. She switched on the answering machine they used at night to collect after-hours calls. When she had finished, she activated the night light, and locked the door behind her, hurrying out to her car.

She decided to drive back home, pack a few things and then move back to the Troy Hilton.

CHAPTER 23

Amazing, the old lady's car still had functioning air conditioning.

Jerry had supplied himself with a bottle of Gilbey's gin which he'd stolen from the old bat and secreted under the front seat, wrapped up in a paper bag.

As he drove, he reached down and pulled out the bag, uncapping the bottle with easy dexterity. Shit, this was getting to be like old times, wasn't it? He tilted up the bottle and took a long swallow, feeling the heat all the way down to his stomach.

Temporarily satiated, he reached out and tweaked the car radio dial, stopping at a station that called itself "Fox Radio." An announcer had just played a song and was asking phone-in listeners to vote whether they wanted to "jam it or slam it."

Two giggling girls said they would "slam" the song, and then the announcer gave the time: 7:15 p.m.

The light seemed full of an orangey, humid haze, and

clouds to the west held a hint of gray threat. *Tornado weather*, Jerry thought. The thought excited him.

The oxford cloth shirt he'd put on was sticking to the flesh of his arms, binding under his armpits. Ed had been thinner. Jerry shrugged angrily, trying to loosen it away from his skin a little. That fucking tattoo. He was going to have to think of a way to get rid of it. Maybe he could have it shaved off sometime, by a doctor. Anybody who looked at it and knew anything about prison life would know what it was.

He took his third cruise past the *Bargain Hound* office, noting that the green Toyota that had been there before was now gone, leaving only Karalynn's white Mercury Cougar. A car as fancy and cold looking as she was.

The ACO hardware was looming up on his right again, so Jerry decided to pull in there and wait for Kara to leave, which wouldn't be too long now, he figured.

Whitetop had taught Jerry some of the fine points of following someone. People seldom paid much attention to the car behind them. The best way to do it was to pick them up somewhere on their route. You had to keep disguising your car, too—by suddenly hanging dice from the rear view mirror, or by quickly stopping to blank out one of your headlights, even having a second person in the car suddenly crouch down.

Bored, he tapped his fingers on the steering wheel, twisting the radio dial again, but then he forgot all about the radio as he saw the front door of the Bargain Hound office open. Kara Cleveland emerged.

He narrowed his eyes, feeling his pulse speed up. Her hair was dark honey streaked with gold. She wore a white linen summer suit, with a blue, low-necked blouse and some kind of white necklace. Her legs were long and she had on pale blue high heels to match the blouse, the shoes making her hips sway as she hurried across the porch, descended the steps, and went to the Cougar.

Jerry turned the Chevy's ignition key and put the car in reverse, timing himself so that he was ready to exit the ACO lot just as the white Cougar prepared to turn right, onto the traffic of Rochester Road.

It was smooth. It was silky. Jerry easily pulled out behind her. She drove south on Rochester to University, then hung a right, which told him that she was going to her own house. He didn't even have to stay behind her after that. All he did was drop three or four cars back, and proceed at his own speed to her subdivision.

Jerry's pulse reverberated in his head. This could be it— except for the little girl, the other one, the one in pink shorts. Where was she?

He wanted them both together.

It would not feel right until they were.

Barry Bennett, the GM engineer who owned the house next door, was out on his manicured lawn, prodding at the turf with his shoe, searching for weeds, bugs or thatch. He waved at Kara as she drove in her driveway, then resumed his fanatic inspection. Barry's favorite expression was, "it takes time and money to get a good lawn," and he put in both.

Kara flipped the opener, waited for the door to rise on its tracks, and pulled her car in. The stack of moving boxes reproached her.

She lowered the door and went inside. The house still smelled like Dorfman's pizzas, and was hot from having the air conditioner off. She got out a large, softsided suitcase with wheels, and went upstairs to pack. Hurriedly, she threw some clothes into it.

Separates, she decided, that could serve multiple purposes. Her jeans. Oh, yes, and a few toiletries and her hair dryer.

She closed the case, and then remembered underwear and swore to herself, zipping open the suitcase again. She tossed in piles of panties—how many would she need? Five? Ten? And, my God, there was panty hose, and she supposed, tampons, and what the hell else had she forgotten? Shoes. She needed some sandals, maybe her Reeboks—

There was a sudden roar outside her bedroom window. Kara gasped, splaying her hands against her chest.

But it was only Bennett, starting up an electric edger, engaged in his endless lawn slavery. The noise was rackety, unpleasantly filling the air.

Kara forced back the jagged, jittery feeling that had possessed her almost as soon as Officer Dorfman got into his car and drove away. Was this the way those women in gothic novels felt when they walked into the dark, forbidding old mansion? Leaping at any sound, almost sick to their stomachs with dread? This was her own house with its double door locks. But at this moment she felt no safer than if she'd barred her doors with masking tape.

Tape . . . The image brought back feelings she could not face.

She found the shoes, then turned to her dresser, pulling out a T-shirt for sleeping, several pairs of shorts, and a couple of necklaces to wear to work. Coming upon a necklace of turquoise beads that Rob had given her, she felt a wave of grief so intense that she had to stop.

She sat down on the bed and then fell backwards onto the mattress. Her fists were clenched, and her eyes leaked tears so hot she thought they would burn her clear to the center of her brain. Rob! How could she have done it, cheated herself so, by breaking her engagement to him?

Angie was right. He'd been angry because she withheld herself from him, not because of Jerry.

She'd always withheld herself.

The edger next door had set up a steady, mind-numbing racket. Kara felt a hard sob erupt, driving itself out of her like a grenade exploded underground. She couldn't stop it. She hadn't cried in so long—not like this, when her whole insides came ripping out. Her self-hatred was savage. Just as Dr. Hay said, she *had* built a wall. She hadn't let anyone go behind it—not her father, or Angie, her two other fiancés, not even Dr. Hay, and certainly not Rob. Oh, she'd guarded herself so very carefully! Everything she did and said was a lie, because it hid the terrible secret as compacted as a black diamond, buried in the center of her.

She rolled on the bed, immersed in her private agony, until the lawn edger next door abruptly shut off. The sudden silence, punctuated by a dog barking, and distant traffic on Walton, brought her to herself again.

What was she doing, lying here crying, when Jerry could be anywhere and she no longer possessed police protection?

She sat up, fumbled on her night stand for a box of tissues, and then hastily finished her packing.

She had just gone into the garage and was locking the house door behind her, when she heard the telephone ringing insistently inside the house.

Should she answer it? The sound seemed to her somehow ominous. Maybe Rob, but what if it wasn't? What if it was Jerry, calling to whisper obscenities, to mock her with what he intended to do to her? She'd bet he was fantasizing right now. Picturing her, naked and bloody.

At the third ring, the phone stopped ringing as the answering machine kicked in. From the garage, she could not hear the voice message, if any. She got in her car and clicked the door opener, waiting impatiently while the heavy door creaked backward on its track.

At her mother's house, Cindy was in the kitchen, an untidy litter of pots, pans, and cocoa mix and marshmallows spread on the counter top. She had spilled a brown trail of cocoa on the floor when she tried to carry a full pan from counter to stove, and had walked in it several times since. Now her bare toes felt sticky.

She stood by the electric stove, waiting impatiently for the mixture to boil.

A car went by on the street, muffler backfiring, and Cindy jumped nervously. She was alone in the house while her mother was out on a date with the guy called Jack. Dee said she'd be home by midnight but Cindy knew her mother sometimes stayed out until 2:30 or 3:00, if she thought Cindy was asleep and wouldn't notice.

She hated babysitting herself. When you were alone, houses made all kinds of secret noises that made her think uncomfortably about movies she'd seen, where things jumped out.

Cindy sniffed as she stirred the cocoa with a splash. Since the burglar at Dad's, she had a terrible stomachache, almost all the time. What if the car that made that strange, popping noise belonged to the same burglar, the man who had stared at her? What if he had followed them here, and knew where she lived?

Cindy had overheard Kara and her Dad talking. Kara had been all upset, talking about something horrible that happened to her. Cindy only heard a few words but they were scary ones, and the worst word of all was *rape*.

What was rape? It was something awful and terrible that men did to ladies, Cindy felt sure. Something so awful you would rather be dead. And it was what the man who had stared at her wanted to do to her. She might be only ten, but she was not dumb.

She shook her head, stirring cocoa so vehemently that liquid splashed out of the pan. She had to jump backward to keep from being burned.

The car went by on the street again, the motor louder than before. *The same car.* She could tell by the sound of the motor.

She let the cocoa spoon fall out of her fingers, into the

pan, and went, shivering, through the kitchen to the living room, where she crawled up on the couch and pulled aside the drapes just enough to peer out through the center crack.

She could just glimpse a car disappearing around the corner. It was just getting shadowy outside, a time of the early evening when trees began to seem like dark masses of leaves. She gazed out at the empty street. Across the street the halogen lights of the park had not yet come on, but would soon. Teenagers hung out at the park, Cindy knew, and sometimes the police had to come and make them go away. But that car hadn't been driven by a teenager. She could tell because there wasn't any rock music.

She flipped the curtains shut, a squeeze of fear tightening her throat. *Was* it the same car twice or was it only her imagination? Maybe being alone was making her have creepy thoughts.

She got up to start back toward the kitchen, but now the living room seemed very small and suffocating, the curtains blocking off her view of the street, so she couldn't see whether the car drove past for a third time.

Beginning to cry, Cindy returned to the curtains, found the pull cord, and opened them several feet.

Anyone could come inside their house, she suddenly realized with a twist of real fear. A house wasn't much protection, not if someone really wanted to come in. Blood . . . guns . . . knives . . . maniacal laughs . . . Scenes from videos jumbled in her mind, as clear as if she were seeing them on the VCR.

She smelled something funny coming from the kitchen, and realized that her hot cocoa was burning. Cindy rushed out to the kitchen. The cocoa pan was bubbling up huge, frothy, brown foam that splashed onto the stove top. Her mother would be furious at the mess.

Sobbing, Cindy ran toward the stove and grabbed the pot handle. As she managed to drag the boiling-over pan away from the burner, the phone on the wall caught her eye. She would call her Dad, and he would come and get her, and protect her from the burglar and she would be safe.

But before she could reach for the phone, it rang. Cindy snatched the receiver off the hook.

"Cindy, is that you?" The voice was male and unfamiliar and there were noises in the background, making it hard for her to hear him.

"Yes. . . ."

"This is Jack Biondo, your mother's friend. Well, honey, something's happened and your mother won't be home tonight. See, we were coming up to the light at 13 Mile and Woodward, and we got rear ended. We had a car accident, kid. Your Mom's in the emergency room. Why didn't you see if you can call your Dad?"

Checking in at the Troy Hilton at 7:30 p.m., Kara paid with her Visa, praying there was enough left on her credit line to carry her through.

"You have a message, Miss Cleveland," the woman at the check-in desk said.

"What? Already?" It seemed incredible that anyone could know she was coming here when she had told no one.

"Yes, it just came in five minutes ago. It was from your daughter."

Her daughter? Then Kara realized. It must be Cindy, thinking she had still retained her room here.

A bellboy obsequiously offered to help her with the suitcase but Kara refused him. On her way to the elevator, she unfolded the sheet of paper. *Call Cindy at home*, it said, and gave Dee's number in Royal Oak.

The room was hot and stale, so Kara went to turn the air conditioning on "high." She kicked off the blue pumps and stripped off the white suit, wondering whether she should take a shower now, or wait until she went to bed.

First, though, she'd better dial Cindy.

The girl picked up the phone on the first ring. "H'lo?"

"Cindy? This is Kara. Did you call me?"

"I called your house, too," Cindy said in a breathy voice that sounded close to tears. "I got your answering machine. I didn't know how to talk into it. I . . . Kara . . ." Cindy started to cry.

"Cindy? What's wrong, Cin?"

"I'm all alone here," Cindy sobbed. "My Mom went out with her boyfriend and I was babysitting myself. He called, he said they just got in a automobile accident."

"What?"

"Yes, and my Mom is at B-beaumont Hospital, and I think my Mom got a broken leg, they said, and she might got b-broken ribs . . ."

"Oh, Cindy," Kara managed over the child's weeping. "Have you called your Dad?"

Cindy was obviously struggling to keep her crying under control. "I c-can't find Dad. I called and called and called and he isn't home, Kara. I think he goes out with those people he builds buildings for, and I don't want to stay here alone, I'm scared to!"

It *was* likely Rob was out with clients but a horrid fear still clenched itself in Kara's stomach. She quieted it. Jerry had only attacked Rob because he was a barrier to herself. It was women Jerry wanted.

She moistened her lips. "Do you want me to try to locate him for you, Cindy? Hang on, and I'll call you back in a couple of minutes."

"Oh, yes, yes, but I can't stay here," Cindy gulped. "I hate staying here because—because the refrigerator makes funny noises and I burned the cocoa. An' the cars keep driving by and I don't like them. I think I saw the same car more than once. I think there could have been a burglar in it. A bad burglar."

Kara felt a wave of anger at Dee Devers' perfidy. Dee

273

had blamed Kara for endangering her little girl, then gone off and left Cindy alone in the house while she went on a date. A ten-year-old child babysitting herself! She supposed she should feel sorry for Dee, hospitalized with broken bones, but she didn't.

Even Rob had really left Cindy in the lurch. How was a ten-year-old supposed to know the names of his clients and partners? It must be frightening to have adults in your life who were absorbed in their private lives or work, when you needed them.

"I'll come over and get you," she said without thinking.

"Oh, *will* you?" The relief in the child's voice was so genuine and heartfelt that Kara's heart twisted. Cindy went on, "Oh, can we go to a movie? There's an Eddie Murphy movie at the Winchester. It's not too late. Please, please, Kara, can we go to Eddie Murphy? And get a big tub of popcorn, and you can get free refills of pop, they have it on special. They give you coupons right when you buy your ticket."

Kara dialed Rob's number, getting his machine. She started to leave a message, but stopped herself in time. What if Jerry broke in again, played the tape? Then she called his partner in the architectural firm, having a brief conversation with the man's teenaged son. "Oh, they're out to dinner somewhere, yeah, maybe Mr. Devers is with them." He didn't know which restaurant—or care much.

Kara sighed, hanging up. The Taubman project was all Rob had talked about for eight weeks. She changed to a pair of white pants, a yellow T-top, and huarache sandals, and left her room again, taking the key with her.

In the lobby a singles group had posted signs for a dance party. Dressed-up people in their forties and fifties milled through the lobby, engaged in the depressing meet and mingle cycle that Kara knew she, too, would have to rejoin eventually, if she did not marry Rob.

It was only a ten-minute drive to Dee's modest duplex in Royal Oak. She didn't even have to ring the doorbell; Cindy spotted her through the window and flung open the door.

"I was making some cocoa on the stove but it boiled over," she greeted Kara. Her cheeks were tear-stained, her lashes starry and wet. She wore the new blue playsuit, now daubed with spills of cocoa.

"Oh, Cindyella." Kara reached out and brushed back a glossy wing of black hair that had fallen out of Cindy's blue clip, the same one that Kara bought her. While the girl stood still, she adjusted the clip. She felt touched that the girl still wore her gifts. "Look, let's go and check the stove, make sure you turned all the burners off, and then we'll leave a note. No, on second thought, we won't leave a note. But I will try to call your father again."

The stove was a battle zone, covered with cocoa powder, wet chocolate, with streaks of dark burn on the electric coils. Spatters of chocolate decorated the floor as well. But Kara felt damned if she'd clean it up for Dee. She went to the phone and once more dialed Rob's answering machine.

His deep, sexy, well-enunciated voice came on the tape. *"You've reached the machine of Rob Devers, and I'm unable to come to the phone right now—"* She waited for the beep, her mind struggling with the problem of how she was to tell Rob where Cindy was, without giving any specific location.

"Dee had an automobile accident and Cindy couldn't reach you, so I have her," she finally said. "I'll call you back. I'll take care of her."

She was hanging up when suddenly, like a video tape put on "play," a picture materialized in her mind. It was Rob's .38 revolver, tucked underneath a stack of thick-piled, dusty rose, lace-bordered towels, at home in her bathroom closet. She had forgotten to bring it with her.

Kara did not dare go back to her house with Cindy in tow. Not at night. She felt it would be taking a foolish chance. She was beginning to feel very anxious and pressured. Obviously she had the responsibility of Cindy until Rob returned. She hoped it wouldn't be very long. Of all the nights for this to happen! With uncanny precision, Dee had picked the worst night of the year to have her automobile accident.

"Why aren't you going to marry my Dad?" Cindy asked as they sat with huge tubs of popcorn in the fourth row at the Winchester 8, waiting for the first preview to start.

"Cindy . . . it's awful hard to explain."

"But why? You love each other, don't you? You're love-birds all the time."

Kara hesitated, looking at the child's tense face. What did you say in a situation like this? She couldn't openly bring up Cindy's resentment—could she?

"There were a lot of things," she mumbled, avoiding the issue.

"*I* wanted to wear a pink dress to your wedding," Cindy announced. Flabbergasted, Kara stared at Rob's daughter. "Pink patent leather shoes and white tights, and I was going to carry flowers, too," Cindy went on. "Little pink roses, with this flower stuff . . . what's it called . . . lilies of the valley. . . . My Mom says those are the prettiest tiny flowers there are. Like little tiny bells."

Kara knew that her shock and amazement was written all over her face. "Cindy? You don't mean . . . you *want* us to get married? That it's okay with you?"

Cindy looked down at her lap, and began to play with the front buttons of the playsuit. Obviously she still felt ambivalent. "Sometimes," she mumbled.

They munched greasy, buttery popcorn. Kara was afraid

to comment on what Cindy had said, afraid her remarks might turn the child around again, reawaken her resentment.

"Kara?" Cindy said after a minute. "Do nightmares ever come true?"

"Nightmares are only dreams, Cin. Our mind mixing things up and making them come out wrong."

Cindy wasn't looking at her, but rather down at the huge, waxy tub of popcorn. "I know, but—bad things happen, don't they? I heard those police say . . . did something bad happen to you once, Kara? Something real, real awful?"

Kara drew in quick breath and expelled it in a soft outblowing of air. She felt a strange, woozy dizziness, as if she were walking through a doorway through which she could never go back.

"Yes," she admitted. "Something did. I was attacked by the man who broke into your father's house. But it was a long time ago, about the time you were born. I got through it. Now I'm okay."

Cindy at last looked at her, her blue eyes filled with more questions, but before she could ask them, the house lights began to go down, and the theater logo flashed on the screen.

The previews came on, and then the movie, and as they shared the tub of popcorn their hands kept brushing. Once Kara thought she actually felt the child snuggle closer to her, wriggling up to her as a cat creeps closer to warmth. Incredible. When there was a heavy-duty shooting scene, with Eddie Murphy blasting away the bad guys, she slid her arm around Cindy.

The girl's shoulder blades were small and fragile, tensed by both the movie and her other fears. Kara squeezed her a little. She whispered. "Is the movie too scary for you?"

"No . . ." Cindy said without conviction.

As soon as the movie reached a calmer scene, Murphy making love to a beautiful black woman with masses of corkscrew curls, Kara excused herself and went to the lobby to phone Rob again. As before, the machine kicked in, and this time she did not bother to listen to the tape.

After the movie was over, she would still have Cindy on her hands, maybe until midnight or later, she was thinking. What would she do with her next?

By the time the picture was over, and it was time to exit, the rest of the shopping mall was closed. Kara drove Cindy to a Ram's Horn restaurant a short distance away, specifying a table near the back where they would not easily be spotted. She paused in the lobby to use the phone, but Rob still was out. Damn him! Kara thought with angry anxiety.

She also telephoned William Beaumont Hospital, in Royal Oak, leaving a message in the emergency room area for Dee, that Cindy was with her and all right.

They ordered hot fudge sundaes dolloped with whipped cream and maraschino cherries. Cindy was in much better spirits, and chattered endlessly about the plot of the movie, and the woman star, a black singer called Vanity who oozed sex. Still, Kara thought she detected an edginess about Cindy, and there were definitely smudgy-dark circles of weariness under the child's eyes.

A man walked past them on his way to pay his check, and he had a lazy, sauntering walk like Jerry's. Kara averted her glance from him. No more false sightings of ''Jerry'' now. She'd wallowed too long in falsity and fears. Sometime she had to take charge, face it head on. Maybe that time was now. Having Rob's daughter with her was a complication she hadn't planned on, but thank God, Rob usually never stayed out much past midnight, and she would have him come and get Cindy at the hotel tonight.

They lingered as long as they could, but Cindy seemed tired, and at one point was slumped forward, her chin pillowed on her hands. Gently Kara touched the child's hand. "Hey, kiddo, don't you think it's time we went somewhere where you could take a little snooze or something? Until your Dad comes, I mean."

"I don't want to go to bed."

"I'm not talking about *bed*," Kara teased, trying to be cheerful. "I'm talking about maybe watching some TV with me in my hotel room, and if you happen to drift off to sleep, well, I won't tell anybody."

"I don't like sleeping by the TV," Cindy said. "Can I figure out the tip, Kara? My Dad always lets me figure out the tip. I can do per cents, and I know what per cent to leave. Fifteen, isn't that right?"

CHAPTER 24

It was now 11:30. The night had cooled a little. While they were in the restaurant the clouds that were massed at the horizon now had closed in, blotting out the moon and most of the stars. There was a thick, moist, vaguely unpleasant smell and taste to the air.

"It's dark out, it really is dark out now," Cindy complained as they left the Ram's Horn and headed toward Kara's car, parked at the far end of the lot. The ten-year-old shivered in her light cotton knit playsuit, crossing her arms over her chest.

Kara murmured something, occupied with glancing around the lot to make certain there were no mysteriously idling cars, or automobiles with anyone lurking in them. Amazing, how a common parking lot could take on sinister qualities. She had eaten at the Ram's Horn dozens of times, but it had never looked liked this, so frozen and harsh, the outdoor lights reflecting off windshields and car finish. In fact, eerie shadows were created, so that it looked as if some of the cars had people in them.

Her mind, tricking her.

She took Cindy's arm and hurried her a little faster. They got in the car and Kara quickly punched the automatic door locks. "Are we going back to the Troy Hilton hotel?" Cindy wanted to know, although they had already discussed this earlier in the restaurant.

"We certainly are."

"Are we going to use the pool?"

Kara couldn't help laughing nervously. Somehow the way Cindy kept glancing behind them, craning her neck to see out of the back window of the car, made her feel more uneasy than ever. "I don't think so at this hour, honey."

They turned south on Rochester Road, which would fork off into Stephenson Highway, taking them to the hotel. As if catching Kara's mood, Cindy had dropped her chattering. She sat drawing pictures with her fingertip on the moist interior of the window, slightly fogged up from the evening's humidity and cooling.

"Don't do that," Kara said automatically. "It'll make grease smears, Cindy."

Traffic was heavy, probably because several concerts at nearby Meadowbrook Music Festival and the Palace stadium had just let out. Kara moved to the outside lane to pass a slow-moving van, then back to her original lane.

"I see that man!" Cindy abruptly cried, her body going rigid. She gazed, transfixed, out of the car window as if Norman Bates occupied the car next to them.

"What?" Kara, too, was jolted unpleasantly. She felt a squeezing sensation in her esophagus, her breath catching. "Cindy—you don't see anyone. Not at night like this. It's hard to get a good view of people in other cars at night."

"He just speeded ahead, I can't see him any more,"

281

Cindy said in a muffled voice. She had edged as close to Kara on the front seat as her seat belts would permit.

"It wasn't anyone, don't scare me like that."

"It *was*. I did see that man. I did. The one that came to the Bargain Hound, I saw him. The bad burglar. The very, very bad one."

"Cindy, you *couldn't* have seen him, you're just letting your imagination go. It was just someone who looked like him, that's all. Anyway we were passing him, so he couldn't have been following us. He's—you're just tired, that's all."

Cindy thrust her jaw out, but after a minute or two, she gave up, and slumped against the car door, cradling her cheek on her folded hands.

By the time they got to the Troy Hilton, Cindy was asleep. Kara drove around the huge parking lot, noting with annoyance that it was jammed with cars from the many banquets, weddings and singles parties that the hotel hosted. Caribbean steel-band sounds floated over the hotel building; there must be a band outdoors by the pool.

Damn, she thought, circling the lot for the third time, automatically bypassing valet parking. But at least the big influx of people guaranteed their safety, which was why she had chosen the Hilton in the first place.

An older couple had just left the hotel, the woman in a long, white beaded chiffon dress. Kara slowed up, following them to a Lincoln Town Car parked at the far end of the lot. She would grab that slot, take Cindy inside, park her in front of the TV, and call Rob again.

Upstairs, her room had now been chilled down by the air conditioning to refrigeration level. Cindy stood in the middle of the room with a blank, exhausted face, staring around her as if she barely recognized where she was.

"In bed with you, Cindyella," Kara said, pointing to one of the queen-sized beds. She adjusted the room temperature at the thermostat. "I'll warm this place up a little."

"I have to pee."

"Go, then, and wash your face, too, Cindy. You have hot fudge sauce on your chin."

Like a little puppet, Cindy did as she was told, and within minutes had crawled beneath the Hilton bedspread, her small body barely raising a mound.

Kara went to the phone and dialed Rob.

This time he picked up on the second ring. When she told him where she and Cindy were, filling him on what had happened with Dee, he sounded stunned.

"Oh, Jesus, Kara, you don't mean you've been trying to get me all night? I was at one of those damned meetings with the Taubman people. They're really putting us through the wringer."

"Cindy tried to call you," she said. "She was alone in the house and scared, and when she called to me and appealed to me—well, what was I supposed to do?"

"I'm coming over," he said.

It took Rob only fifteen minutes. By the time he arrived, Kara had unpacked her clothes and put them in a drawer, and was sitting in a chair leafing through the magazines and city guides provided by the hotel.

Rob stepped into the room and re-bolted the door. He took a quick, sharp look around the room, making sure that Cindy was in the other bed, before turning to Kara and pulling her into his arms. The cast on his right hand made their embrace awkward.

"Damn, I can't believe this mess," he said into her hair. He smelled like shaving lotion, cigarette smoke and bourbon. "Thanks for going to get her. I can't believe Dee would just leave her alone like that. I didn't know she was leaving her alone when she went out."

They sat down on the other bed, facing each other. Kara felt an unexpected surge of electricity as she looked at her former fiancé. Rob was still wearing the lightweight, tailored suit he had worn for the dinner meeting, its impeccable cut looking even better on his rangy body. The bruises on his face had faded, and only the white sling reminded of the attack at his house.

"I'm learning to shave as a leftie," he said, grinning as he saw her inspection of him. "See? Only two cuts today. That's down from four yesterday."

Suddenly he looked irretrievably dear to her; the good, firm skin, the laugh creases at the corners of his eyes, the lines at his mouth that were so ready to break into an easy smile.

She almost reached out to touch him, to throw herself into his arms and beg him to give her back her ring, to let them start over. But a shyness held her back, a doubt. She tucked her hands beneath her as if to keep them safe from doing what she wanted them to do.

"Rob, I stopped the police escort," she said in a low voice.

"What? Oh, Christ!" he exclaimed. "I thought—you mean the police aren't watching you any more?"

"I couldn't stand it. That Dorfman was so sexist," she blurted, feeling for the first time the full weight of her stupidity.

"Sexist!" Rob looked incredulous. "You're thinking about *sexist*, Kara, when you have a goddamned maniac on your trail? When you have my daughter with you?"

She heard her own voice, tight like crystal. "He was a slime ball, Rob, and I don't apologize for getting rid of him. I didn't know Cindy was going to be joining me when I did that. You know," she added, leaning forward, "There's something I'm hearing in what you say to me, and I think we need to get it out in the open."

"What's that?" Rob looked wary.

"You seem to have this idea that I can see into the future, that I can make decisions based on what *might* happen. Well, I can't do that! I haven't got control over everything. As the old saying goes, 'shit happens.' And now here we are, and we've got Cindy with us, and I think—'' Her words wavered. ''I mean, Cindy said she thought she saw someone when we were driving here.''

''What?''

''Now, I'm just about sure it was nothing. This was a car we'd overtaken, so he couldn't have been following us, and besides, how easy is it to recognize someone at night on the road when you're driving at forty-five, fifty miles an hour?''

''Oh, Christ,'' Rob sighed, glancing over at the other bed where Cindy was a small, dead weight. ''I don't know what to do. I can't drag her out of bed and take her home at this hour—I don't want her in that house. Maybe we'll stay here tonight. If you wouldn't mind.''

She glanced at the two beds, one of which was already occupied by Cindy. ''No, I won't mind. But, Rob . . .'' Her voice was small, barely audible. ''I've thought of something else. My address book . . . Dee is in there. Dee's phone. Maybe you'd better not take Cindy back there, either, until this is over.''

He stared, obviously too startled to speak.

Her nervous giggle born of stress turned into sudden, shaky tears. ''God, Rob, I'm so sorry . . . I can't believe this. Jerry has turned us all into damned refugees. I hate him, Rob. I hate him so much. I . . . I can't tell you how much I hate him.''

''The fucker,'' Rob growled, reaching across the bed to take her into his arms.

Rob got on the phone, rousing up the mother of Cindy's friend, Jennifer (''*She's* not in your damned book, is she?''). He made arrangements to leave Cindy there for a few days. The family was planning to drive to Holland, near Lake Michigan, for a five-day stay. They promised to take Cindy with them, which caused an expression of profound relief to cross Rob's face. He arranged to drop his daughter off there in the morning.

"Thank God," he said as he hung up. "That's one big worry off my chest. This couldn't have come at a poorer time. I've got meetings with the Taubman people all day tomorrow again, and I can't possibly get out of it. This is a big, big project, Kara, and we need it."

They undressed. Kara felt Rob's eyes on her as she changed into the extra-large T-shirt she had brought to sleep in.

"Babe," he whispered. "You still look so beautiful to me."

She turned, the shirt half over her head, knowing this pose highlighted the full, high curves of her breasts with their pinkish nipples. She was showing herself off for him, something she seldom had done, but tonight it didn't feel wrong.

"Get under the covers," he murmured, glancing toward the empty bed.

"Rob, Cindy . . . I can't . . ."

"My daughter sleeps like Rip Van Winkle, I'm happy to report," he said, reaching out to switch off the bedside light. "But just to keep the proprieties, I'll only hold you. God, I thought I might never get to hold you again. I do love you," he added, cradling her face in his hands in the air conditioned dark. "Do you believe that, Karalynn? Do you believe that I love you?"

"I believe it."

"Then what has come between us? Can it really be Cindy, Kara? Is she really the cause for you throwing your ring back at me?"

Kara moved close to the long, warm male body that seemed to exude such sexiness, electricity and strength. They moved and murmured and made accommodations for the plaster cast.

"No," she whispered after five long minutes had gone by. "It's because I'm afraid, Rob."

"I know that. I've always known that. Kar . . . I don't want to be part of your fear. I want to be the good part of your life, what makes you happy. Can I be that? Cindy and me? Cindy can learn to love you. In time, I know she can. You're very lovable."

There was another long silence, while Kara remembered how Cindy had still been wearing the playsuit she gave her, and the pink hair clip. How Cindy had talked to her, and even leaned toward her in the movies, snuggling briefly. But most of all, how Cindy had wanted to wear a pink dress to their wedding.

She said, sighing, "Cindy won't ever love me as a mother."

"Maybe you shouldn't expect her to."

"But—"

"Kara, when I was a boy I had an uncle, he was only nineteen years old, but I looked up to him as if he were Mickey Mantle. I loved him, I'll never forget him. He was killed in a car accident when I was fourteen. I was heartbroken. Kar, don't you see there are so many kinds of love in the world, so many different kinds?" Rob held her very tightly. "You and Cindy, well, maybe you'll just have to find your own way to love."

Kara didn't say anything again for a very long time, and Rob didn't ask her for it; he just held her, his breathing gradually slowing and deepening as he moved toward sleep. Finally Kara said into his neck, "Okay."

They fell asleep in each other's arms and Kara had the best night of sleep she'd enjoyed since she was seventeen, since Jerry.

In the morning, while Cindy showered and Kara blow-dried her hair, Rob telephoned Mac Deacon, his partner. He hung up with an annoyed frown.

"Damn it to hell, Kara, they've called a surprise meeting on me in Southfield for breakfast and I've got to get down there. Like, right away."

"But, Cindy?"

"Could you drop her at Jennifer's? I'm sorry to do it to you, but I have no choice, and I'm already late now—" Rob was already dressed in his suit, and he went over to rap on the bathroom door, from which clouds of steam were emerging. "Cindyella? Cindy? I have to go now. Kara is going to drop you off at Jennifer's house and you're going with them to Lake Michigan, would you like that? Kara will call your mother and tell her where you are."

Cindy emerged from the bathroom, her hair hanging in wet strands, a towel wrapped around her narrow torso in exact imitation of the way her mother probably did it. "Dad . . . I want to be with you and Kara."

"You will be, babe, next week, maybe sooner. Honey," Rob added as Cindy's face looked tearfully mutinous. "Hon, you can understand, can't you, that we have a problem? Your mother can't take care of you, and I've got business and I can't be with you during the day, and Kara has to work."

Cindy's forehead puckered as she absorbed this news, but she finally nodded. She turned to Kara. "Where's my blue hair clip? My very best one I got at Meijer's? The one with the flowers on it?"

After Rob left, they turned the room inside out, and looked among the bedcovers, but did not find the hair clip. Kara loaned Cindy a yellow silk scarf that she found in her luggage, and the child allowed her to tie its bright folds around her hair.

Cindy preened in front of the mirror, inspecting herself from all angles. "This is too big," she pronounced. "I still want my clip. Are we going to have breakfast in the hotel?"

"If you'd like."

"Can we have pancakes? And sausages? And orange juice?"

"Anything you want."

Breakfast was decorous and leisurely, and Kara found herself regarding Cindy a little differently, more inclined to be patient when the girl chattered endlessly, or demanded an extra jug of syrup for her pancakes, then spilled the jug when it arrived. Maybe she'd been expecting too much, both of herself and of Cindy. Not letting the girl find her own way, and not waiting for her own emotions naturally to grow.

Rob hadn't said anything about giving her back his ring—yet—but Kara expected he would. She still felt anxiety about accepting it. Now that Rob knew about her rape, it wasn't an automatic assurance that all would be well between them, that they'd suddenly be able to communicate. Life was never that simple, was it?

She'd been hiding herself so long.

Could she really change? She wanted to, but . . .

They finished breakfast, went up to the room to get Kara's suitcase, and took the elevator back down to the lobby. In daylight, the hotel looked prosaic. A few travelers were gathered at the desk to check out.

When Kara and Cindy stepped outside under the portico, the same ordinariness prevailed. It was another hot June day. Wind picked up scraps of paper and swirled them over the walk, off toward the valet parking area. Cars whizzed past on Stephenson Highway, a light industrial area of plants and offices.

"I don't have any clothes to wear to Jennifer's," Cindy was saying as they reached Kara's Cougar.

"Can't Jennifer loan you some? She's just about your size."

"A bathing suit?"

"Sure. Jennifer strikes me as a girl who'd have more than one bathing suit." Kara pulled open the car door, clicked the automatic lock so Cindy could get in on the other side, and slid in herself. The car smelled stale and sour. "Anyway, she can loan you that, too. I'll give Jennifer's mother a check in case she needs to buy you anything, Cindy."

"Okay," the girl agreed, obediently reaching for her safety belt. Kara fastened hers, too, and started the car, putting it in gear.

She felt a bump from behind, something touching the back of her seat. Before she could react, a white shirt sleeve flashed in front of her, as swift as a karate chop. From it protruded a wiry hand, from which extended a long, evilly glinting knife blade.

"Hey, bitch, I've got you now, don't I? The both of you, huh? I stole your extra car keys. Shit, it took you long enough to get out here." Jerry's grated whisper was full of hate.

CHAPTER 25

It was like one of those nightmares in which you struggled against something so horrific that you woke yourself with your own choked scream.

Jerry was leaned forward so that his face protruded in the space between the two front seats; he was almost up in the front with them.

The smell of him was sickeningly acrid; it had been there in the car when she got in. God! Why had she ignored it?

"Drive!" he ordered her, jamming his forearm around her neck and choking off Kara's breathing. "Start the fucking car and drive, damn you! Or I'll slit you right here in the parking lot—and the kid, too. Make the choice, babe, because *I don't care*."

She believed him.

The horror geysered in her, almost stopping her brain from functioning. She felt dampness between her legs—had she wet her panties?

It was happening again—all of it.

She would never escape it. Only this time, he would cut her as he had done Laurel, before stabbing her to death.

Beside her, Cindy had begun to sob, tearing at her seat belts, in her shock unable to find the release button. Something in the sight of those small, pudgy, scrabbling fingers released Kara from her floating state of terror.

Her voice creaked out of her throat, an unrecognizable, animal cry. "Get out of the car, Cindy! Run!"

"NO!" Jerry's arm snaked out and caught the frightened girl, slamming her against the seat back so hard her head bounced. "Honey? You want to stay alive? You want to stay nice and pretty and sweet? Then you do what Jerry says. *Just what Jerry says.* Hear me? You hear me?"

Cindy shook and sobbed, writhing up against the car door.

"You hear me, girlie?" The knife movement happened so swiftly it almost eluded the eye. One minute Cindy's slim, rounded forearm was clean and porcelain white; the next, there was red running down it.

The little girl cried out and clutched at herself, more blood running through her fingers. "Kara!" she screamed.

"DRIVE, BITCH, AND I MEAN IT. PUT THE FUCKING CAR IN GEAR AND GET OUT OF THIS FUCKING PARKING LOT OR I'LL CARVE HER UP, AND THEN YOU. GET IT?"

Could this be real, a reality that was happening to her in her semi-new car with the upholstery she carefully kept clean and now was being dripped over with blood?

Kara gasped for air, struggling to find a way to think rationally. Wildly she glanced around the large parking lot, now nearly deserted. They were at the back of the large lot. There were no people around to help, and the valet parking was at the front of the hotel, near the portico. Anyway, on a hot day the valets lounged inside the lobby entrance.

Her mind skipped and slid, like water droplets in a hot frying pan. She felt her thoughts disintegrate, her breath loud in her ears, her heartbeat seeming to knock her backward with each ferocious pound.

"Kara," Cindy sobbed. "I'm bleeding!"

The cry pulled Kara back from the edge of wherever she had been.

"Where? Where shall I drive?" she managed to say. A fury filled her of such potency that it was like a shot of cyanide. "And, please . . . don't cut her again. Please. I'll do whatever you ask."

They were trapped in the car, which was filled with the nauseating stench of Jerry's reeking, foul-smelling sweat. Cindy still wept wildly, the sight of her own blood apparently having frightened her far more than Jerry.

"If she doesn't stop bawling I'll kill her," Jerry hissed.

"Cindy." The words seemed to come out independent of herself, urgent. "Cin, you're going to have to stop crying. Take the yellow scarf off your pony tail and fold it up, put it on your arm to stop the blood."

"I . . . I can't . . ."

"Do it, baby," she told Cindy. "You have to. Fold the cloth up. Use it like a big bandage."

Jerry told her to turn north, toward the village of Rochester. With a deep, arctic chill, Kara realized his destination—her own house, That was where he would . . . do it.

Her frozen mind would not say the word, or call up the images.

To exit, she had to turn right on Stephenson, then use a U-turn lane to loop left again. Driving past the long hotel portico, she saw a bellboy pushing a cart loaded with several suitcases. She opened her mouth to scream but Jerry jabbed the knife in her side with such force that the point penetrated her skin.

"I told you, cunt, no screaming!"

"Kara," Cindy wailed, terrified.

Kara barely felt the pain. The world seemed to segue in and out of a strange reality. It had all been like this before. Yes, now she remembered the high-pitched, strident, harrying voice, the obscenities. Jerry seemed sexually excited, explosive.

"Okay," he ordered her, releasing a spew of expletives so vile he must have learned them in prison. "Now, drive up until we're on Rochester Road and then keep on going through Rochester; I want to go to your house. And if I see you even look out the car window, or wave to anyone, or do *anything* funny, I mean *anything* . . . I'll do you. Know what I mean?"

God, help us she thought.

"KNOW WHAT I MEAN?" Jerry screamed.

"Yes," she whispered. "Yes, I know what you mean."

"Then drive!"

She drove. Managed to make the left turn, turning behind a big truck that said Dobbs Furniture.

"Drive!" Jerry screamed at her. "Drive, dammit! Get in the slow lane, don't attract attention, Karalynn." With his right hand he reached out and swiped at the weeping Cindy with the knife. But this time Cindy threw herself away from it, and the tip only grazed her.

Kara could do nothing more about Cindy right now. She forced herself to concentrate on driving. It was only a fifteen-minute trip to her house, she knew, so that was exactly how long they had. What would happen after they arrived? If the past was any indication, Jerry had a roll of tape with him, and would use it to tie them up, to—

Laurel, her mouth open in hideous, repeated screams that shrieked on and on, hurting the ears with their awful terror as she tried to twist away from the knife blade that inserted itself in the center of her nipple and then pulled downward, blood spraying, to carve a crude red circle.

The screams, and Kara's own sobs, and the knife digging and jabbing, cutting a living, human girl as if she were butcher shop meat . . .

The memory collapsed, imploding on itself.

A spurt of sour stomach bile forced itself into Kara's mouth. Desperately she swallowed it back.

Was this going to be like before? Repeated? Only with Cindy and herself as the ones on whom Jerry would carve? Kara's mind ran up and down horrible corridors, seeing nothing but red, bloody ends.

And then two words spoke in her head.

The gun.

The picture of it slid into her mind like a computer graphic, in black and white, lying inert exactly where she had left it, at the bottom of the pile of towels in her upstairs bathroom closet. For the first time a little thrill of hope entered her brain. She had left Rob's .38 revolver at the house and it was still there, and if she could only figure how to get it, she could shoot Jerry dead.

And she could shoot him.

Her hate was strong enough. She didn't have any doubt about that at all.

Jerry was in a state of euphoria as he leaned forward into the front seat area of the Cougar, keeping the two women in the front of his thrall, paralyzed by their terror.

God—there was nothing like this feeling, nothing in the whole fucking world.

He felt powerful! In control! Almost godlike!

It was a sexual feeling, too, growing more intense every time the little girl cried. Cindy was huddled against the car door as far away from him as she could get. It made Jerry feel like a powerful animal, a bull, maybe, with the cows at his mercy, to whom he could do anything at all he wanted.

He loved the feeling. Ten years in Raiford and he'd

295

dreamed about this every night, the glory of it. Oh, he hadn't forgotten. Not for one fucking minute. This was better than ten orgasms, or even twenty, a whole lifetime of single, separate climaxes. The bitch Karalynn didn't live that far away and it would only be a few minutes before he had them spread open to his command.

"Please," the little girl began to beg. "P-please, I—I have to pee . . . I can't hold it . . ."

"Hold it," Jerry commanded, loving the way she flinched, her face so white he could see the veins in her cheeks. He was already iron hard, his erection larger than it had ever been, a huge club straining at the zipper of his pants.

They had forked onto Rochester Road now, passing under a freeway bridge, then some strip shopping malls and fast food places. They went past a road called Big Beaver. Jerry laughed harshly to himself thinking of a road named Big Beaver. Why'd they call it that anyway?

God—his cock was throbbing between his legs with such intensity he knew he wasn't going to be able to hold back much longer.

"Stay behind that truck," he ordered Kara, thinking that a truck driver would be able to see downward, into the front of the car.

Obediently she did as he ordered. He loved it, the way she shuddered all through her body and then did exactly as he said.

Wattles Road, Long Lake Road, Square Lake Road, South Boulevard, Auburn Road. Each one brought them closer to the unspeakable. They passed on their right the car dealership, Crissman Lincoln Mercury, where Kara had bought her Cougar.

She'd been fool enough to leave her extra set of keys carelessly in her desk drawer—that was how he had caught them.

She felt a wave of hatred for her own stupidity. Despite her preoccupation with locks, it had never occurred to her anyone would really break in, or that if they did, they would take anything other than her TV set. She had done everything wrong, hadn't she? And now she and Cindy were going to pay for that.

Unless she could get to Rob's gun.

She would have to maneuver it so he let her go upstairs . . . Her mind squeezed down, choking off any further plans as Jerry forced her to turn left at Avon Road, in order to avoid the downtown area. Kara's blood chilled as she realized how well Jerry already knew Rochester; he must have been driving around for days, or maybe he had gleaned this knowledge by following her. His craftiness was frightening.

They were now headed for the next north-south road, Livernois, the same street on which Angie lived, near the hospital. Kara felt a wild wave of longing for the safety and love of her friend. Then loss, so strong it washed through her like a flood.

Would she ever see Angie again? Or Rob?

He had killed Laurel, and mutilated that girl in Georgia. He would kill them, too, when he was done with them. What else was there for him? That was all part of it—their bloody deaths.

"There, there, turn there," he ordered her as they reached the corner, by the Hamlin River, where a banquet hall called the Rivercrest shared a parking lot with a complex of doctors' offices. Kara had even been to the Rivercrest for a dance, once, before she met Rob. She felt as if she was dying already. Her life flashed before her, snippets of memories. Dancing in someone's arms. Meeting Rob that day at Scallops, her blind date fixed up by her former editor at the *Eccentric*. She had taken one look at him and her heart had constricted in her chest. She'd thought, *oh, my God.*

Now this. Ending it.

"Drive, drive north, hit the right lane and stay there," Jerry ordered when they passed the first light, and Livernois widened into four lanes.

Within seconds, it seemed, they had reached Walton Boulevard, and were turning into Kara's own subdivision. Some time back Cindy had stopped crying. She was hunched against the car door, her right hand clenching the bloodsoaked ball of silk against her injured arm. Her eyes were huge and frightened.

Thank God—Cindy didn't know yet just what Jerry was. Kara would have to find a way to save her. If there was a way. If she could not reach the .38, then there would be no way.

She turned into her subdivision, took a right on Fieldstone, another right on Meadowlane. Even the street names bespoke the tranquility of the area, and she seemed to see it all with new, fresh eyes. The Colonials and brick ranches set back on the green, manicured lawns, each as pretty as a photo in *Better Homes and Gardens.* Children playing with Smurf balls in front of one of the houses, a pregnant woman in shorts watching them while she gardened. A sight so beautifully ordinary that it tore at Kara's heart.

They were now within only four houses of her own. Already Kara could see, up ahead, the outlines of the huge blue spruces that decorated her property, and of which she had been so proud. Their branches were fat and piney, and each year they seemed to grow several feet in circumference.

"I have to *pee*," Cindy cried again, and Kara realized she had been saying this for the past block, only she'd been too locked into her own head to hear. Now her mind eagerly seized on the idea. Yes . . . that was it, she'd get

Jerry to let them go upstairs, use the bathroom. Or she'd promise Jerry unimaginable delights, if only he'd let her—

"Slow the fuck up!" he snapped at her as they reached her driveway. "You got a garage door opener? Use it, man. Do everything just like normal. Go in the garage and shut the door behind us."

What other choice was there? In the adjoining yard Barry Bennett was out on his back deck, doing something with an electric hedge trimmer, the sound racheting through the air. Kara was furious at him. The compulsive bastard ran his motors every night and half the weekend—and there was no way she could call to him with that damn noise.

She reached toward the space on her dashboard where she kept the plastic opener device, her hand shaking so hard that she dropped it on the floor of the car and had to reach down and pick it up.

"Sorry," she heard herself mutter.

"No funny stuff!" Jerry snapped.

They sat in the driveway while she pushed the lever and the door skittered up on its tracks, the motor badly in need of oiling. To Kara it seemed like the sound of doom. Once they were inside the garage with the door shut they would be closed off from the world. He could do anything he wanted—right then. They wouldn't even have to go in the house.

The door was now open. The two-car garage loomed ahead, full of junk, the detritus of Kara's life.

She pulled the Cougar in and shut off the motor, giving Cindy a sharp, hard look and a jut of her chin, trying to signal the child to jump out of the car and start running.

But before Cindy could react, Jerry leaned forward, aiming the knife spear-like at Cindy's stomach.

"Oh!" Cindy cried involuntarily. Tears spilled from the ten-year-old's eyes as she crammed herself against the car door, quailing away from the blade.

"Don't try nothing!" Jerry snapped.

"Kara," Cindy wept, gagging. There was the sudden, sharp stench of urine in the car, as her strained bladder finally released itself. "Don't let him cut me! I don't want to be cut! Please!"

To Kara the sound of the child pleading was horrific. She thought if Rob could hear it, he would go berserk. But he was not here, and she knew the responsibility was all hers. Cindy apparently wasn't going to try to run. She was going to be like Laurel, too frozen to move or flee. As she herself had been, before . . .

"Shit, she wet herself," Jerry exclaimed angrily. Then, incongruously, he laughed, the sound chillingly boisterous.

He moved, changing positions, and Kara remembered that hers was a two door car, and there was no back door from which Jerry could quickly exit. He would have to wait until one of them got out.

Did they have a chance after all? What if she were to spring out of the car and run, before he could climb out of the back seat to grab her?

But there was Cindy. She was flattened against the car door, frozen. Kara could run by herself, but Cindy wouldn't run, and what then?

But she didn't have to make that particular decision. Jerry began to climb up over the center console into the front seat area, thrusting his bulk between them.

He grabbed Cindy's arm, yanking her toward him.

"Okay, little pussy . . . I got you now, I got both of you, but I won't hurt you, eh? I won't hurt you if you do just a couple things for me. If you do everything I tell you I'm going to let you live through this. Jerry promises. But if you don't, bitches, hey, you get a knife right across the throat. Know what I mean? Filthy fuckin' ratshit bitches!"

The words, the obscenities, seemed to have an eerie, played-back echo. With a jolt of terror, Kara realized why.

They were the exact same words he had said to her and Laurel.

The hedge trimmer next door was still roaring, filling the air with mindless noise.

Jerry held Cindy hostage, the knife blade at her throat, dragging her behind him while he forced Kara out of the car, kicking her in the back of the knees so that she fell to the garage floor.

The pain of hitting the cement with full force of her palms and kneecaps sent pain screaming through Kara's body. She crouched there, sobbing with anger. She could feel the reckless, dangerous fury well up in her, the hatred of ten years, and she tensed her thighs, preparing to spring up and attack him.

She didn't get a chance. There was an agonizing whip of pain down her side. She realized he had cut her with the knife tip, slashing away the side seam of the yellow tee-top she wore. Her wound was not severe, she didn't think. But blood immediately gushed out of her, to soak the knit fabric which now hung around her like a bum's tatters, revealing most of her T-strap bra.

She struggled to her feet. In Jerry's eyes she read sexual pleasure heightened to almost an excruciating degree. Yes, she discovered, looking at his pants. He had an erection so huge that it distended the front of his trousers, making him look bulgy and fat.

He was now taking something out of his shirt.

A roll of duct tape.

The familiar sight hit Kara like a grenade. He always used duct tape, a big, gray, greasy-looking roll just like this one. This was real. It wasn't any TV show, and it would not end at the half-hour, or the commercial. She had to get them in the house and up the stairs, so she could get Rob's gun.

Self-hatred debilitated her. Why hadn't she done something in the driveway? She could have banged on her horn, or switched on her emergency flasher, she could have rolled down her window and shrieked bloody murder. But of course she hadn't done those things because of Cindy, and because she had to get in the house, because that's where the gun was . . .

"In!" Jerry commanded, pushing Cindy ahead of him so viciously that she fell against the door that led to the house. "Goddamn it, Karalynn, get out your fucking key. Or I'll break in the goddamn door."

They were in the lower hallway, by the stairs, near the little wicker table that Kara had painted herself, and arranged with knick-knacks and pots of peach-colored silk tulips from the Silk Garden. Sunlight streamed in through the living room windows, illuminating the tiny, mysterious motes of dust that always seemed to float in the air.

It was her house in all its peace and calmness, filled with objects she loved. Pictures she had chosen, a pillow her mother had needlepointed, a figurine from the Ann Arbor Art Fair Rob once gave her.

"Take your clothes off," Jerry ordered, waving the knife at Kara. "You and her too. Both of you."

Appalled, Kara stared at him, realizing that all the horror they'd experienced up until now was nothing, was no horror at all, compared to what was going to come—within just a few minutes now.

It was almost on them. Just as before, in all the hideous memories she'd blocked out that were now flashing back to her, agony upon agony.

Blood on the floor and splattering on the bed, and running down her midsection to soak her stomach and mat her pubic hair . . .

"OFF!" Jerry screamed, and Kara realized he had already done so several times. "OFF, GODDAMMIT, GET 'EM OFF AND DO IT NOW."

Cindy collapsed into frightened sobs, exactly as Laurel once had done, paralyzed by the evil she had no means of combatting.

Jerry thrust out a hand and began yanking at the girl's blue playsuit, rattling the girl, shaking her like a terrier, as he stripped her.

"No!" Kara screamed, losing all control. She ran forward and pulled the child from his hands, dragging Cindy away.

The bloody T-shirt hanging off her shoulders, her knees still burning with pain, Kara clutched Rob's daughter to her. Gripping Cindy's arm, she backed toward the staircase and began pulling the girl up the risers, one step at a time. Like a little puppet, Cindy cooperated.

Jerry looked surprised.

"Oh, so you want to do it in the bedroom, do you?" he gloated, his smile wolfish. "Yeah, you want it, don't you? Yeah, yeah, you want Jerry, you want the King of the Universe, don't you, honey?"

His pants were stained in front, but the orgasm had not calmed him any: if anything, he seemed more frenetic than ever, more tightly wired. It had been that way before, too, Kara remembered in that eerie unfolding of memory heretofore blocked. And she remembered something else, too.

"Mirrors," she blurted. "I have bathroom mirrors . . . a big vanity mirror . . . you like mirrors?"

"I don't know," he said suspiciously. He feinted the knife blade in front of them, forcing them to climb higher. He already had the roll of tape out and was pulling a long strip off it, preparatory to binding them with it. Obviously he thought he had them under his control now, and could do as he wished.

"Mirror," she said desperately. She ripped at her top, pulling its shredded and bloody sections off her. Anything to grab his attention a little longer, to lure him into the bathroom.

"What the fuck?" Jerry muttered and a scowl knit across his narrow, blade-shaped features.

She was entering the fantasy with him, and he wasn't sure how to take it, it was shaking him up a little, she realized. She felt a pure curdle of fear. Was she pushing this too far? Would she only make him even more savage, more vicious and depraved?

Now she was three-quarters of the way up the stairs, Cindy scrabbling with her, wild-eyed with terror. Only a few more steps and they'd be at the top—and then only a few more paces and there was the bathroom and the gun.

She could do it, Kara told herself. She had to. No matter how horrible it got, she could not let anything stop her.

The racket from next door suddenly paused, creating a huge, echoing silence. But before Kara could draw breath to scream, the noise started up again.

"Fuckhead," Jerry said. "Fuckers and their fancy lawns."

He took the step that separated them, a strip of tape readied. Within seconds he would have it around her hands, her ankles, she would be helpless, at his mercy, just as before. Kara uttered a little scream and jumped up the remaining step, desperately dragging Cindy with her.

"In the bedroom," Jerry commanded, a slick of spittle moistening his lips.

Kara felt a cut of disappointment so sharp it was almost like being stabbed. *No, no,* she thought desperately.

"Now, Karalynn—you got mirrors in your bedroom, don't you? Dresser mirrors? Those're the kind I like. I want you in front of the mirror. I want you looking at me, eating me with your eyes, begging me. Yeah, begging. You know how to beg, Karalynn? That's what I want, what I need. You begging. Yeah."

CHAPTER 26

In the hall, Kara posed for Jerry as she had done for Rob, amazed at the sinuousness she was able to project, born of desperation. She thrust out her chest, pushing out her breasts in parody of a *Penthouse* model. Beside her, Cindy watched, horrified.

Anything, she thought. She had to make him trust her a little. Was he so crazed he would really believe she wanted him? She'd better pray he was.

"The bedroom," Jerry repeated, pointing with the knife tip.

Kara's darting mind realized that he knew which direction her bedroom was. Which meant something . . . yes. She remembered he had been here before, and had probably searched the house carefully. He hadn't found a gun then, because there hadn't been one.

He might not suspect there could be one now. That might save them. She didn't dare glance down the hall, where the bathroom door stood ajar, a section of mauve-

305

and-blue Country French wallpaper and matching mauve towels exposed to view. She was afraid if she did, she'd betray her intentions.

"Okay," she said. "But you'll have to promise me that you won't hurt us, that you'll—"

She suddenly doubled over, gagging and retching. The sounds she made were quite genuine; she did feel perilously close to vomiting. She knew her face must look sweaty and white; all the better. How ridiculous, that she should be engaged in this huge struggle to get into a bathroom.

"What the hell?" Jerry said.

"I have to—" she gasped, clutching her stomach. Then, waiting for the knife blade to descend, she turned and fled toward the bathroom.

She only got a few feet. Jerry's hand gripped her by the elbow, jerking her around with such violence that pain shot up her entire arm to the shoulder. Her eyes watered from the pain. He wasn't going to let her. She sagged in his grip, defeated.

Their last chance—and she had blown it.

"Where you going?" he demanded.

"A call of nature!" she cried defiantly.

Jerry's scowl twisted his whole face and made him look malevolent, explosive. "Fuck that," he said. "There, in your room, you've got the big dresser mirror. Go in there, and take your clothes off like I said. If you want to live, rat-cunt."

Rat-cunt. It was what he had called her before. The word was like a jolt from a cattle prod, pushing her out of her despair.

"I *have* to use the toilet," she snapped, glaring at him. "I *have* to go." She didn't care any more; he was going to murder her anyway, what did she have to lose? Let him kill her now if he didn't like it.

Without waiting for his permission, she marched ahead

306

of him into the bathroom with its double sink vanity. She pushed Cindy ahead of her, because what else could she do with her?

Whimpering, Cindy allowed herself to be propelled. Once in the bathroom, Kara gave Cindy a shove that forced her nearly into the bathtub. The girl huddled near the ruffled shower curtain, her eyes huge.

"You take a squat. I'll watch," Jerry said.

Kara gave a loud and angry laugh. Her hatred for him was an endless river now, a spring flood flowing down from the mountains to choke a river bed. It was all the anger she'd ever felt, all the fury and grief and shame, so strong it almost lifted her up off the floor. She floated on it, flowed on it, free.

"Oh, yes," she snapped. "You love watching, don't you? But tell me, Jerry. Can you make love to a woman when you haven't got her tied up with a knife at her throat? Answer me that."

He stared at her, his eyes opaque. She could see his erection, a crooked lump that seemed to move inside his pants, alive.

"Use the fucking toilet," he grated.

"Violence," Kara cried recklessly. "That's it for you, isn't it, Jerry? You can't get off without it, can you?" She moved to the commode, across from which was the linen closet door, standing an inch or two ajar. But as if sensing her plan, Jerry came to stand in front of it, blocking it as effectively as if it were padlocked.

Damn, she thought, despair pressing against her.

"Go ahead," he said, cutting off a couple more strips of tape with the knife. "Pee. I'm going to do little Miss Muffet here."

Over Cindy's cries and her struggles, he trussed the ten-year-old, wrapping her ankles tightly with the duct tape, and then taping her hands behind her, as he had done with Kara several days ago, and with her and Laurel a lifetime ago. As he handled her, Cindy's eyes rolled wildly, and her mouth clamped shut on a scream.

Laurel. Laurel had looked like that, too. So desperate and despairing, and beginning to realize the horribleness of what he was about to do . . .

But he had moved away from the closet door.

"Tampon," Kara said desperately. "I need a tampon."

Quickly, she pulled open the closet door. Inside were shelves neatly piled with bedsheets, extra blankets, pillows, and stacks of towels she had bought at white sales at Hudson's and the Linen Center.

Her hand seemed to move like a slow-motion movie shot. In one swift movement she thrust her hand under the stack of towels and closed her fingers on the revolver.

It happened fast. She whirled out from the closet with the .38 in both her hands, remembering to cock the hammer, bracing herself against the loud report and kick-back.

Jerry uttered a loud, roaring cry and lunged toward her with the knife.

There wasn't time to aim; she could barely get the gun lifted in time.

She pulled the trigger.

There was a deafening explosion, twenty times louder than any target shooting she had ever done wearing ear protectors.

Jerry staggered backward against the vanity, blood soaking out from a hole she had made in his right chest. At the same time Cindy was screaming a high, pure, little-girl shriek, and Kara realized she was screaming, too.

But Jerry did not fall down as bad guys did in movies when Eddie Murphy shot them.

"FUCK!" he screamed, as if unaware there was a hole in his chest. He seemed to spring his muscles together. Howling, he raised the knife and came at her again.

Kara was past rational thinking. Instinctively she raised

her right foot and kicked at him, trying to hit the knife, or at least put something between her and the blade. Her kick touched the knife but did not knock it away.

With a savage, baseball-batter swing, Jerry swiped the gun out of Kara's hands.

The gun fell on the bathroom tile and skidded off next to the toilet where Kara could not bend down to get it without exposing herself to his attack. However, Jerry's balance, upset by the swing, seemed to waver. For an instant he staggered like a drunk.

The blood on Jerry's white shirt front had thickened and was coming out of him in red spurts. She jumped back from it. Impossible that he should be alive. But he was.

He swayed, holding the knife, his face purplish, lips drawn back from his teeth. He slashed the air with the blade like street fighters Kara had seen in the movies—only the movement wasn't graceful. It was as staggery as he was. He was dying. He had to be.

But he was still clenching the blade and she knew he could still kill her, even as he fell. She grabbed a pile of towels from the closet and hurled them at him. Towels fell all over the floor. She was pressed against the wall, trapped, unable to get past him.

"AAAAH," he screamed, mucous thickening in his throat as he staggered toward Kara, raising the knife high. It was like stories Kara had heard of Viet Cong still attacking despite ten or twelve bullets in them. He was slowed down, but he would still kill her.

"*Kara, Kara!*" Cindy screamed.

A little vanity stool stood near the closet. Kara snatched it up and pointed the legs toward Jerry, using it as a shield. He screamed thickly, and tried to hit the chair away from her. Even dying, he was strong and she knew in a few minutes he would tear it from her.

And then she saw Cindy. The girl had managed to half-roll, half-hop forward, and was positioned behind Jerry. Bending low, she butted him with her head, hitting him in the back of his knees.

It was a surprise blow in one of the body's most vulnerable spots, and it would have toppled even a healthy man. Jerry seemed to collapse in segments. First the wobbly bend of the knees, then a deeper bend, the knee caps hitting the tiles, and the almost graceful slump of the spine as Jerry's body collapsed on itself.

Kara rushed forward and snatched up the gun off the floor. She stood over Jerry with the revolver, pointing it straight down at his face.

His cheeks were streaked with tears now, his mouth rubbery. The knife lay on the tile where it had fallen, a few feet from Jerry's hand. Still aiming the gun, Kara kicked it away. She didn't want to touch either him or his blood.

"Why? Why?" Jerry asked, like a piteous child.

Kara stared down at him, gripping the gun with both hands. His face had gone ashen blue and his eyes already seemed glazed over, their sheen drying. She could kill him right now, she thought.

This was the man who had raped her so hideously—who had mutilated Laurel and would have done the same to herself if her father had not stopped him. Who had smiled during the trial, a cold, hard, cruel smile that was indelibly engraved on her mind to this day.

She felt her hands shake as she clenched the gun. It was her fantasy of being enclosed in a room with Jerry at her mercy. One squeeze of the trigger and that smile would be nothing but splattered red.

No one would blame her if she shot him.

Many would applaud.

"Shoot," Jerry whispered, his voice thready. His face was turning a terrible shade of purple-gray. Red bubbled up through the hole of his shirt, and there was a foul stink as Jerry lost control of his bowels and bladder.

Kara stared at him, transfixed.

"Shoot," he told her, his lips getting bluer by the second. "Shoot . . . me . . . rat . . . cunt."

She felt something happening in her, something dissolving like salt in water. It was an eerie feeling. All that hate . . . melting. It left a space behind it.

"I can't," she said, pulling away from him, making sure she had the gun in case Jerry somehow managed to get up again. She grabbed Cindy and pulled her with her, and they both backed out of the bathroom and into the hall.

Upstairs there was only silence.

Downstairs, Kara ripped the duct tape off Cindy's ankles and wrists, and grabbed a couple of old T-shirts from a laundry room basket for each of them to wear.

"Put this on, Cin," she said, lowering one of the shirts over the girl's head. It covered Cindy from neck to mid-thigh. Cindy was no longer crying, but she trembled violently, her eyes saucer huge.

"We have to call the police now, Cin. But don't worry because I'm here with you. I won't let them separate us. We won't be afraid of them."

"Kara. Kara." Cindy flung herself at Kara, burrowing toward her, hands clutching her. Kara gripped the ten-year-old, enfolding her fiercely. She felt such a rough surge of love she was almost overwhelmed by it. She had saved Cindy, hadn't she? So that made her hers, too.

Her child.

At the hall phone, she dialed Gazzarro and told him what happened. Then she called Rob at the hotel in Novi. Within minutes there was the sound of sirens. Kara stood at the foot of the staircase holding the .38 pointed upward. Just in case. Triumph filled her, the sweetness of strength.

She hadn't folded—not this time. No one, no Jerry, would ever hurt her or her loved ones again.

"My Dad," Cindy whispered, holding on to her.

"He's coming, honey, he'll be here any minute." Kara hugged Cindy back. There was time for them to love now, to learn about each other's ways and feelings and needs.

And there was Rob. His arms, his love, was the ultimate safety.